Cat in a
Crimson Haze

By Carole Nelson Douglas from Tom Doherty Associates

MYSTERY

HISTORICAL ROMANCE

SCIENCE FICTION

FANTASY

*also mystery

Cat in a Crimson Haze

A MIDNIGHT LOUIE MYSTERY

Carole Nelson Douglas

A Tom Doherty Associates Book
New York

CAT IN A CRIMSON HAZE

Copyright © 1995 by Carole Nelson Douglas

This book is printed on acid-free paper.

A Forge Book
Published by Tom Doherty Associates, Inc.
175 Fifth Avenue
New York, N.Y. 10010

Forge® is a registered trademark of Tom Doherty Associates, Inc.

Library of Congress Cataloging-in-Publication Data

Douglas, Carole Nelson.
    Cat in a crimson haze / Carole Nelson Douglas.
        p.   cm.
    "A Tom Doherty Associates book."
    ISBN 0-312-85901-5
    1. Midnight Louie (Fictitious character—Fiction. 2. Barr,
Temple (Fictitious character)—Fiction. 3. Women detectives—
Nevada—Las Vegas—Fiction. 4. Cats—Nevada—Las Vegas—Fiction.
I. Title
PS3554.O8237C25   1995
813'.54—dc20   95-2066
                                                        CIP

First edition: May 1995

Printed in the United States of America

0 9 8 7 6 5 4 3 2 1

For Ed Gorman,
the Sage of Cedar Rapids,
godfather of the mystery scene,
and a benefactor of writers and readers
of all genres and genders

Contents

Lionized Louie

I want one thing on the record, straight off.

Millions have seen a television commercial with a giant, metal-gilded, Art Deco lion-dude striding across the sand-choked Las Vegas scenery. When he stretches out, he hunkers down to become a high-tech Sphinx of sorts. In a touch of computer-graphics magic, the new MGM Grand Hotel and Theme Park fans out from his hind-quarters like a green-glass peacock's tail.

Put down this: I am not impressed.

There is only one major pussycat in this town, and the name is Midnight Louie.

Even now I can glimpse the kitchen bulletin board, where my PR–conscious roommate has posted my latest newspaper likeness.

This one is nothing to phone home about: I look like something the dog dragged in. Ears flattened and eyes at half-mast, I am being menaced by what looks like a UFO, but is actually a clear plastic breathing apparatus. This photograph commemorates the moment when I was supposedly rescued from the clutches of the cat crucifier of my last adventure. The fireman flourishing the plastic mask is allegedly administering life-saving oxygen to my air-starved puss after I was given a chloroform muffler and tied into a burlap bag.

In this instance, a picture is not worth a thousand words; it is not even worth a three-day gig at the bottom of a finch cage.

Suffice it to say that I engineered my own escape from the burlap bag. I was even ready to direct an all-feline uprising to save Miss Temple Barr from a premature toasting, when the clumsy firemen interfered. I no more needed oxygen than a fish needs an air hose, but the redundant firemen had to do something to look good in the media. I am not a victim of anything in that snapshot except an ill-conceived photo opportunity.

At present, however, even a prime-time pussums believes in observing the signs of the times. I can read the hieroglyphics on the wall: this televised muscle-bound feline escapee from Virtual Reality City is indeed a poster boy for the Times They Are A-Changing.

Not only has the MGM Grand Hotel resurrected itself far from the ashes of its former location on the Strip (now Bally's), but it has roared back with 5005 rooms, the most in all the world. Sharing the MGM's hot new scenery are the new Luxor and Treasure Island hotels. Guess what? Las Vegas—the capital of crass . . . the headquarters of chutzpah . . . the nerve center of the salacious—has sold out.

The name of the game in this toddling town nowadays is two words that would stop a stripper cold in mid-grind. It might even chill a bookie's soul right where he carries it, in his back pocket with the rest of the cash.

The catch phrase of the day is Family Values.

Call me cynical, but it is my observation that Family Values never come into play with so much enthusiasm as when the bottom line is at stake. And the bottom line in Vegas these days is no longer the thin, white tan-streak left by a thong bikini.

The bottom line is that gambling has become a national sport. Las Vegas is no longer the champion Sin City that it used to be. Nowadays you have your Atlantic City, you have your state lotteries. You also have your Native American version of surround-the-cavalry and take-your-revenge-in-chips, previously known as Reservation Bingo. All these legalized forms of gambling now affect more states than once spangled on the Confederate flag. My home town, the Mecca of the Mojave, must now hustle more than its bustle to draw the same crowds of yore; it must appeal to a whole new wholesome clientele.

What can I say? Las Vegas—the shining star of the glitz parade—has gone Brady Bunch. It is enough to make a home-grown dude sniffle into his Snapple juice.

Luckily, I touch almost nothing but water these days, or else I would not believe my eyes.

There is much to decry in this town, and I usually have not wasted my breath doing it. An invasion of decency hardly seems worth the bother. I have my own troubles. One floor above me abides a jet-black babe who goes by the name of "Caviar." Her street name is Midnight Louise, and only I know what *that* means.

Luckily, she has not yet figured out my own moniker, or I would be lunch meat. I must confess that I fear this feisty, featherweight lady more than any three-story lion-dude outfitted in skin-tight gold lamé.

Yet another floor above this Caviar doll lurks the golden-haired Karma, a creature of reclusive habits who also enjoys baiting Midnight Louie. Was ever a dude so beset?

To add offense to injury, my resident little doll, Miss Temple Barr, has been absent from home of late, tending to public relations business.

Does no one care that this town is going to heaven in a handbasket? Does no one care that Midnight Louie has personal problems of a perplexing nature? Does no one care that the eighties economy of fun, frivolity and foolishness has crashed in the Sober Nineties? That changing times are ringing in hype, tripe and gripe?

The answer, of course, is a resounding *nyet*.

In the silence of one lone whisker waving, I lay my kisser upon my folded mitts and snooze.

Chapter 1

Bless the Beasts and Children

"How old is—?" Temple stared at the bald, bouncing, burbling infant, desperately seeking a safe synonym for "it."

And failing.

She would have to commit.

Suicide.

"He/she?" she uttered in a rush.

"Cinnamon is five months." Van von Rhine, the no-nonsense manager of the Crystal Phoenix Hotel and Casino, spoke with maternal fondness.

"Cinnamon," Temple repeated, dazed. "You can call her . . . Cinny for short."

Temple winced at her own small talk, but hoped that she at least had the gender right. These days, given naming trends for both sexes, one could not be certain. Such uncertainty was no way to impress the boss. The potential boss.

Luckily, fond maternal doting was deaf as well as—apparently—blind.

"Isn't she adorable, if I do say so myself?" Van, a petite pastel-blonde who was nevertheless the terror of hotel staff everywhere, and at the Crystal Phoenix in particular, hefted Cinnamon to her shoulder for a back-pat and a burp. "Nicky wanted to call her 'Nicole,' but I convinced him that French names are too trendy nowadays. Men are so vain."

While Van von Rhine frowned at her husband's natural inclination to give his first child a name that echoed his, Temple recalled a rumor that "Van" was short for "Vanilla." That would make little Cinnamon a chip off the maternal spice rack. Men weren't the only blindly vain ones.

"How's Louie?" Van asked in the tone of one giving equal time to a guest's nearest and dearest.

"Huh?" Temple was seldom flummoxed by sudden subject changes, but pretending to admire babies turned her usually astute brains to, er, pablum. A PR person loathed nothing more than something she knew *nada* about.

"Oh, would you like to hold her?" Van von Rhine's tone now indicated that she had been seriously and socially derelict.

"Ah, no thanks. Louie? Oh, you mean the cat!"

"Yes." Van's madonnalike smile matched her bland blond serenity. Princess Grace was not dead but resurrected in time for the evening news. "But Louie would not like being referred to as 'the cat.' There is nothing generic about Midnight Louie."

Yessir, that's my baby, Temple's brain insisted on drumming. "Louie's . . . fine. I'm sorry he wandered away from the Crystal Phoenix—"

Van nodded to a lurking teenaged nanny who quickly removed Cinnamon before Baby burped Gerber's split-pea soup on Mother's immaculate champagne-pale Versace suit shoulder. Talk about *Exorcist V*.

"We miss him," she said simply.

"I do, too, now and then," Temple chimed in before catching herself. "I mean, he does come and go as he pleases."

Van von Rhine nodded. "Louie is his own fur person. Nicky finally convinced me that there was no point in trying to keep a rolling stone. I'm amazed that Louie deigns to reside with you on a semi-permanent basis."

"Free-to-be-Feline," Temple confided.

"I beg your pardon?" Van von Rhine's pale eyebrows elevated like polite ghostly caterpillars.

"Louie would never leave his Free-to-be-Feline," Temple explained with laudable confidence, "especially now that I dish shrimp creole over it. Lots of shrimp. Cans of it. It's good for him; the Free-to-be-Feline, not necessarily the shrimp."

"I see." With Cinnamon whisked away, Van's voice indicated boredom with feeding formulas. She sighed. "As for your presence today, Nicky insists it is high time for a hotel makeover. I suppose he's right, given the appallingly short attention-span of the American public. In Europe, hotels pride themselves on their immutability, not on an annual facelift."

Temple remembered the lightly tanned Italian Romeo who had accompanied his wife to the convention center office to reclaim Louie weeks before, luckily to no good effect. Louie, borne away in a silver Corvette, had returned alone and on foot, and that was the end of his unofficial residence at the Crystal Phoenix. Temple wondered why, then sniffed a lingering scent of infant on the air—part Johnson & Johnson's powder, part Pampers, part pea. Perhaps Louie was even more allergic to something besides unadulterated Free-to-be-Feline.

"Wasn't the Crystal Phoenix completely redesigned only a couple years ago?" Temple asked.

"Exactly my point." Van von Rhine, baby and beast dispensed with, resumed her executive manner by folding pale, manicured hands on her sleek, glass-topped desk. "Las Vegas is changing before our eyes, Miss Barr. When Nicky and I introduced the remodeled Crystal Phoenix, 'class,' *élan*, what-you-will was a novelty in Las Vegas. Now . . . well, I can't say the town has grown sophisticated, but the marketing emphasis has changed. One must keep up with modern times. The Crystal Phoenix is not about to desert the 'classy' image that has set it apart, but we also must bow to modern economic pressures. We must offer a Family Plan."

Temple nodded seriously. She had never fallen in love with Las Vegas, although she had always rather admired its unpretentiously wacky instincts. But the feisty, money-grubbing town that Bugsy Siegel had imagined in the forties, that had exploded in the fifties, expanded in the sixties, frolicked in the seventies and splurged in the eighties had foundered in the nineties.

Las Vegas needed more than a face-lift to compete with Disney World and dial-a-lottery. It had to showcase more than babes, betting and blinking lights; more even than computerized slot machines and the occasional dose of class. It had to dispense family entertainment.

"Gentleman Johnny Diamond, our ballad singer," Van went on, "was always behind—and therefore has come out ahead—of his time. The hotel decor, which I supervised, is refined to the max."

Temple winced at the last word of the last expression, for personal reasons.

"Our floor show," Van said with prim satisfaction, "was always more reminiscent of the Lido in Paris than the Lace 'n' Lust downtown. But I admit that the Crystal Phoenix lacks the proletarian approach. We must reposition ourselves to attract the full-value, family customers that Las Vegas seeks nowadays. Can you devise a program for us, Miss Barr, that converts 'class' into 'family class?' "

"What a challenge," Temple responded to buy time. "Perhaps I should inspect the operation first."

"Excellent idea." Van von Rhine's trim fingernail, buffed to a rosy sheen, pressed a call button on her desk.

Instantly, a young man knocked on the door and entered the office. "You rang? Your slave is absent and I was passing by, so I thought I'd answer and see what was shakin'."

"Ralph," Van said, looking none too pleased, "Miss Barr needs a tour of the hotel. Is Nicky around?"

"Nicky is always around."

Ralph's lazy grin struck Temple as familiar, not only for its easy intimacy, but for its current shape and form.

Ralph was not an apt name for a suavely swarthy guy in his late twenties wearing a Nino Cerutti ice-cream suit guaranteed to melt female hearts at fifty paces. Temple would have taken him for the lounge singer, Johnny Diamond, had Van von Rhine not called him "Ralph."

"In other words," Van said, frowning, "Nicky's nowhere to be found when he's needed. I'm afraid that you'll have to escort Miss Barr yourself."

Ralph shrugged exquisitely padded shoulders. "No problem." His introductory glance was flattering to Temple, who had recently passed the landmark of thirty, and was therefore likely an "older woman" to him.

"One of Nicky's brothers," Van von Rhine added dryly. "I think you'll be safe."

"Really?" Temple's voice lilted with interest.

The Fontana brothers were infamous in Las Vegas for their obscene number (nine or ten, Temple recalled), their spiffy tailoring, and their latent mob tendencies. Nicky, of course, was the impeccably respectable businessman of the bunch with his purchase and restoration of the Crystal Phoenix and his marriage to Van, the daughter of a German hotel manager. The other Fontana boys were unwed, and apparently unemployed in any recognized legal occupation. Temple had never met a Fontana brother in the flesh, besides Nicky, and found the species attractive but too overwhelming to take seriously.

Ralph managed to beat her to the office door without looking as if he had moved, and flourished it open. Normally, Temple hated gallant gestures, especially when performed in Cinemascope, but a Fontana brother was too much of a living legend to rebuke.

She sailed through on her conservatively tailored Evan Picone pumps, hoping that she sounded as brisk and businesslike as Van von Rhine at her most Teutonic. Landing a Strip hotel account was big-time, almost more than Temple liked to handle for a reasonably relaxed lifestyle.

Still, if she had to pick her favorite Vegas hostelry, it was the Crystal Phoenix. This was not simply for sentimental reasons: that it was, for instance, Midnight Louie's former headquarters, or that Max Kinsella had wined and dined her at the rooftop Fontana Lounge when announcing their joint purchase of the Circle Ritz condominium.

Temple frowned. Best not to let past disappointments shadow the present.

"Are you familiar with the hotel, Miss Barr?" Ralph inquired with a smile that was almost shy. Perhaps the bachelor Fontana brothers were used to running in a pack.

"I know the public areas," Temple said, "but not the quirky little aspects every hotel has."

"Quirk is my specialty," Ralph promised, extending his hand like a tour guide, the better to display the gold oval of a Roman ring. A real Roman ring.

Where did the Fontana boys get their money? Not from their notorious uncle, Macho Mario Fontana, at least not publicly. Temple began to chafe at the notion of getting mixed up with shady company. The Crystal Phoenix, and Nicky and Van, had impeccable reputations, but the brothers did not. Of course, Temple's own record on shady associates wasn't triple A, thanks to Max (Mr. Interpol Pinup) Kinsella.

Ralph proved to be a decent guide. While he did not neglect such highlights as the water-garden lobby, the Ultrasuede-covered gaming surfaces and the palm-dotted outdoor pool area, he did point out the quirky.

"The Midnight Louie memorial pond," he said solemnly with crossed hands and bowed dark head near a stand of calla lilies.

Temple gazed into the shade-dappled pool, in which large, richly scaled fish schooled like angry piranha.

"Gorgeous goldfish!" Temple admitted.

"Chef Song's private stock. And don't let him catch you calling them goldfish. Or carp. My brother Armando called them carp in his hearing once, and almost lost his ears to a meat cleaver. The word is 'koi.' K-o-i, but you pronounce it like it had a 'w' in it. K-w-o-i."

"Kwoi," Temple repeated, amused by Ralph's careful explanation. She already knew the term, but decided not to tell him. "Why is it Louie's memorial garden? He isn't dead yet."

"Not for any lack of Chef Song's meat cleaver. That old black cat is too fast for him, despite his looks, and he takes a lot of look-sees at the koi in this pool, believe me."

Temple did, and followed Ralph indoors again to meet Chef Song, and his staff and meat cleaver, in the hotel's pristine stainless-steel-equipped kitchen.

She also toured the cavernous basement from chorus girl dressing rooms, an area of apparently avid interest for Ralph, to the huge below-stage elevators that wafted sets and scenery up to the waiting audience above.

"This reminds me of my days at the Guthrie Theatre in Minneapolis," she remarked in the echoing silence of the stage's under-belly. "What's topside like?"

Ralph escorted her into a service elevator in a deserted area of the basement. Their first stop was the theater level, where Temple wandered onto the deserted stage under the cold, dead spotlights to eye the empty seats.

Ralph, apparently having no dramatic instincts, remained by the backstage light switch.

Temple hadn't been on a stage in . . . oh, years now. The theater's eternal, invisible magic lurked in the darkness, like the Mystifying Max about to launch an illusion at an unsuspecting audience. The wooden stage floor echoed the crisp snap of her high heels, throwing shards of the sound all the way to the back row.

Temple found a deserted theater both romantic and creepy, a beast of sleepy silence on the brink of breaking into screams and howls. In any theater, a sensitive ear could detect memory echoes of all the lines, action, drama that had ever taken place on its abandoned stage, and ever would. But this was a Las Vegas hotel stage; the action fated for it was as gaudy, gleeful and hokey as the more unrehearsed dramas playing nightly in the hotel gaming and bar areas.

Ralph blinked the backstage light off and on to signal his eagerness to move on, so Temple rejoined him without indulging the urge to recite Portia's "quality of mercy" speech, which she still knew by heart from the high school play.

"Johnny Diamond has been the headliner here as long as I've been in Vegas," Temple said, "but I've never seen his act."

Ralph rolled his eyes in grudging envy. "That guy. What a voice. Always packs 'em in, Wednesday through Sunday nights."

"You're dark two nights then, Monday and Tuesday?"

"Yeah. Except when some special group comes in for a one-night stand, like the Gridiron in a few weeks. Must be some sports thing."

"The Gridiron? That's going to be held here this year, really?" At Ralph's mystified nod, she couldn't help bragging a little. "The Gridiron's the local journalists' annual satirical review. I usually write skits for it, and take a role now and then, when dragooned into it. Lordy, is Gridiron time here again already? Funny, I haven't heard a call for scripts."

"You mean this Gridiron is just a bunch of local newspaper types writing stuff?" Ralph sounded deeply disappointed. "Why'd they rip off a sports name then? To fool people?"

"The Gridiron show satirizes politicians at the local and national level: movers and shakers and newsmakers. It's called a 'Gridiron' because its wit is supposed to skewer the local public personalities, put them on a gridiron until they feel the heat. All in good fun, of course."

"Like a roast of some movie star?"

"Roasted and toasted."

"All right! Speaking of hot times on stage, you should see this place when Johnny cracks out the vocal chords . . . women throwing themselves at him, along with their room numbers and other little personal items, what we would call—"

"Niceties?" Temple supplied diplomatically.

Ralph frowned at the obviously unfamiliar word. "No nighties, more like naughties. Johnny's as married as Queen Elizabeth, but they don't care. He's got his hair long like Michael Bolton now, and that really wows 'em. I been considering a ponytail myself. What do you think?"

Ralph turned to display a neat nape of patent-leather black hair.

"Um, it might interrupt your collar line."

"Yeah. And I don't know how you girls comb all that stuff back there, either." He glanced at Temple's halo of rambunctious red curls and frowned again. "Maybe an earring."

She reached automatically to her naked lobe. Was she missing something?

"Not you. Me. Whatta you think?"

"I think the ring is enough."

He fanned his hand to regard his Roman beauty of a ring as well as display a manicure as subtle as Van von Rhine's. Temple edged her snagged forefinger nail behind her back. The only thing subtle about her home-made manicure was today's pink color: Ravished Rosebud.

"Yeah." Ralph was still meditating on his grooming. "This knuckle knick-knack is the genuine artifact, dug up along the Appian Way—not the phony Appian Way at Caesars Palace across the Strip, but the real thing. In Rome. It's a street, but like real old."

"Well. When in Rome, Mr. Fontana, we ought to take a tour."

"Right. The roof's next."

"I can hardly wait," she murmured, following him back to the service elevator.

The roof, fourteen floors up, featured the aforementioned Fontana Lounge, looking shabby. By daylight, its lavish neon was a grid of dead, gray tubes you might see in a forties black-and-white mad scientist movie.

Ralph conducted Temple around the rooftop obstructions, holding her hand so she could navigate on the wobbly gravel.

"What's the big attraction up here?" she wondered.

Ralph's grin was wide. "Nicky and Van's penthouse."

"I don't think we should intrude—"

"Why not? They ain't here. See, this is the hot tub area. Spiffy, huh?"

"Very nice." Temple corrected herself internally. Very, very nice. She eyed the molded whirlpool bath surrounded by decking, chairs, carelessly tossed towels and shrubbery. What a great place to view the stars—or even more of a light show, the neon of nighttime Las Vegas.

Ralph had wandered over to a long wall of glass, pressing his face against it all the better to see inside.

Temple was feeling distinctly nervous. "I don't think we should violate the Fontanas' privacy by slinking around here."

"What's to violate?" Ralph sounded indignant. "They're not here, I told you. Besides, I'm a relative. You should see the bedroom. Ritzy. Even has a moonroof."

"A . . . moonroof, like in a car?"

"Right. Only bigger, and right over the bed. Slides back so you can see all the way to Serious, or whatever star is out there."

"Really, Mr. Fontana, I'd rather see the hotel's more public areas—"

Ralph Fontana suddenly lifted his hands and pushed his ears forward, like an elephant's. He stuck out his tongue and made rude noises.

Temple, speechless, decided that the Fontana family ran to insanity at great heights.

Ralph laughed as he turned away from the window, smoothing the hair at his temples. "Kid was crying. I fixed that. Surprised the pea-soup out of it. Say, that little oh-pear girl is some nice .piece of fruit, isn't she? Van got her from England. Classy, just like the Crystal Phoenix."

Feeling like a peeping tomcat, Temple tiptoed to the window. Luckily, the au pair girl had her back to them, but the fussing infant propped over her shoulder was now grinning like a pumpkin.

"Let's skedaddle before we're arrested," Temple muttered, treading over the littered rooftop without a backward look.

Ralph Fontana soon caught up with her, but the tour was mostly over, except for a detour to the seventh floor. There Ralph escorted her with pride and fanfare to a door bearing the number 713.

"This is just a regular room," Temple noted.

"Hey, it's not regular at all. It's a suite," Ralph reported.

"So it's a suite. Lots of hotels have them."

"Not like this." Ralph flourished an old-fashioned pass key from his breast pocket.

Obviously, this was the tour's big moment. He unlocked the door and pushed it open, at the same time drawing Temple behind him as if to protect her from the contents.

What was this? An unauthorized drug raid on an unsuspecting guest?

Ralph edged into the inner dimness, then vanished.

In the hall, Temple wondered whose privacy he was violating now. She sincerely hoped it wasn't that of an ex-mob hitman who'd been residing here quietly under the federal witness protection program and who still considered an Uzi an appropriate retirement companion.

A crash came from inside the room. Ralph cursed so colorfully that Temple couldn't translate it. A light—but not much—clicked on.

"Come in," Ralph urged, still muttering under his breath.

Temple crossed the threshold and found her sharp heels sinking into rose-floral carpeting. She was aware of too much green, clunky yet prissy furniture, and satin draperies teased into fantastic shapes.

"The Ghost Suite," Ralph announced with pride of possession. "They haven't changed a doily in here since the forties."

Temple wrinkled her nose.

"All the original stuff. Funky, huh?" Ralph opened another door deeper into the dark. "Here's the bedroom. Imagine. Jersey Joe Jackson slept here." His voice had sunk to reverential depth. "Was he an operator! Right up there with Bugsy Siegel and Howard Hughes. Died broke, though, but not really."

"I've heard about Jersey Joe Jackson," Temple said. "One of the local legends. But I didn't know he kept a suite in this hotel."

"This place was the Joshua Tree then. Man, that dude was into everything—real estate, gambling. Made a pile. Nobody could figure why he died so poor—until Johnny Diamond and the little lady he's now married to did some of their courting on these premises. Guess what they found in the inner spring of the mattress?"

"Inner peace?" Temple hazarded. She was getting really fed up with peeking into other people's bedrooms, probably because no one would want to peek in hers now that Midnight Louie was its sole masculine visitor.

"Nah." Ralph did not miss a beat. "Silver dollars. The big round kind that would make a Kennedy half-dollar look like a BB. Big as . . . yo-yos," he bragged. "They actually made money like that in the old days, and these were old coins, too, hijacked by the Glory Hole Gang in the forties and hidden away until Johnny and Jill jounced 'em loose a couple years ago."

"Not exactly a story fit for family consumption," Temple suggested.

"Huh? It's good enough for my family. Look, I got one of the coins as a lucky piece. We all got one."

Ralph pulled something from a slack pocket and sent it spinning toward the ceiling.

Temple watched the thin silver disc wobble its way down to Ralph's waiting hand like a UFO on a leash and wondered why she kept getting such flaky clients.

Ralph slapped the coin to the top of his free hand and sneaked a peek. "Heads. My lucky day. Wanta bet?"

"I only bet on Kennedy half-dollars," Temple said with apt untruth. Those were about as rare nowadays as the Mystifying Max and a sane client.

Ralph gave another of his affable shrugs and showed her out the door.

"Whatta you think?" he asked in the dead-quiet tunnel of hallway leading back to the elevators. "Can you cook up a campaign to turn the Crystal Phoenix into a place that would appeal to kiddies?"

"Without adding a theme park that costs several million dollars? I don't know, but I'll think about it," she promised.

Ralph nodded sagely, insisted that she enter the elevator first, then faced forward into his sleek stainless steel reflection. He ignored her as they descended seven floors.

"Maybe I'll stick with the ring thing," he said at last.

"Good idea."

"In my nose."

Brother!

Chapter 2

More Blessed Beasts and Children

Even though it was Saturday morning, the playground thronged with milling, laughing, squealing children.

Temple also studied an awesomely interwoven melange of scampering, barking, quacking, braying, howling animals.

Obviously, animals were an attraction kids adored, but she couldn't picture this melee on the elegantly landscaped grounds of the Crystal Phoenix. She didn't even know what she was doing here, except that the whole thing was her idea.

"Lemonade?" Sister St. Rose of Lima chirped beside her, holding up a Big-Gulp-size paper cup.

While Temple hesitated, the diminutive nun quickly added, "It's on the household."

"I think you mean 'on the house,' Sister," Temple said, taking the beverage.

"Whatever." Sister St. Rose's elderly eyes softened behind the magnifying lenses of her plastic-framed spectacles. "Oh, how nice to see the parish presenting such a fine face to the world after that awful business with poor Miss Tyler."

"This mob scene certainly does resemble a casting call for Noah's Ark," Temple admitted, surveying the panorama she had stage-managed down to the last detail, including the refreshments. About to sip her lemonade, she regarded Sister St. Rose of Lima sharply. "Oh . . . you haven't been doctoring the beverages again—?"

"Goodness, no! This is not an emergency. Besides, the bishop's brandy is almost all gone from the last time."

"I don't doubt it." Temple's nostalgic smile vanished with a sip of tart lemonade.

"Anyway, at fifty cents a glass, we couldn't afford it," Sister St. Rose added a trifle sadly.

"How's business at the lemonade stand?" Temple glanced at the long white tablecloth that hid a trio of pushed-together card tables.

Stainless-steel urns with spigots alternated with signs reading *Lemon-Aid Our Lady of Guadalupe.* A ragged line of people crowded the tables, eager for cool liquid refreshment.

Temple blew a breath upwards to lift her bangs from her forehead. She sometimes thought the whole town was a mirage glimpsed through a shimmering force field of heat. Even in late September, Las Vegas simmered with desert heat, which accounted for the indelicate bouquet of animal stew hanging over the playground.

"Rose!" The nun's twin came bustling up, wearing the same serviceable pastel cotton blouse and skirt, except on second glance Sister Seraphina O'Donnell was taller, wider, slightly younger and much spryer. "Would you take over my spot at the lemonade table? Channel Twelve has come to film a feature," she added rapturously enough to be announcing a sighting of Tom Cruise—or, in her own hierarchy of heavenly treats, the angel Gabriel. Temple didn't detect much difference between the two mythical beings.

"That's wonderful, Sister," Temple said, proud of how quickly she'd mastered the native form of address around Our Lady of Guadalupe. Not bad for a fallen-away Unitarian who hadn't been inside a church of any denomination in years.

"And it's your doing, dear."

Temple let only two people in the world call her "dear." One was her energetically outgoing landlady, Electra Lark; the other was Sister Seraphina. Both were over sixty and both were candidates for

She-Who-Must-Be-Obeyed t-shirts, though neither would ever don such a homely item, for quite different reasons.

Sister Seraphina turned to survey the bustling playground, pushing her slipping trifocals against the bridge of her nose. "Combining an animal blessing ceremony with a giveaway of Miss Tyler's cats was so ingenious. But I'm glad you talked the Humane Society into handling the placement of the cats."

Temple glanced at another rank of cloth-covered card tables, this one staffed by volunteers from the local animal welfare group.

"That's a cardinal rule of public relations, Sister. Kill two birds with one stone whenever you can."

"I doubt the Humane Society people would approve that expression in this instance, or any other, but it is apt. We not only publicize the parish fund drive, but find homes for the late Miss Tyler's excess of cats."

"We hope," Temple answered cautiously. "Finding homes for dozens of cats is no sure thing."

She panned the scene again, as critical as any old-time director. Leaping lizards! But bless you, she thought at second glance from a safe distance, approving the Technicolor-bright two-foot-long iguana perched on a pre-teen boy's shoulder. Her publicity-conscious eye also dwelled fondly on the picture-perfect, pig-tailed seven-year-old girl with a pet goat, and an ancient Hispanic woman carrying a truly magnificent rooster with a splash of black-taffeta tail feathers worthy of a chorus girl at Bally's.

All creatures great and small, feathered and scaled, furred and coated—and their fond owners old and young—made first-class grist for the ever-grinding mill of the media cameras. Who could resist animals and kids—at least from a distance?

And then the drama. . . . Temple studied Father Rafael Hernandez in his long black cassock with the shorter lacy white overthing. (Temple knew there was a name for this garment; she would have to ask Sister Seraphina what it was.)

Two adorable eleven-year-old altar boys, similarly smocked, clung to his side as he moved from group to group, a silver-haired shepherd blessing the helpless beasts to ward off illness and mischance.

"What a mob. I supposed you're responsible," a voice announced above Temple's right shoulder. "You have a parade permit for this?"

Temple snapped her head around and found what she expected: Lieutenant C.R. Molina of the Las Vegas Metropolitan Police Department, loitering with intent.

"Are you serious?" Temple demanded.

Molina shrugged. "Unfortunately not. Can't you tell I'm off duty?"

Temple took in an oversized denim shirt studded with the occasional rhinestone, jeans and—my turquoise tootsies!—beaded moccasins on Molina's size-nine feet. How lucky that Temple herself had paired her quiet khaki culottes with a red-and-white top and her Plexiglas-heeled, red grosgrain-ribbon-trimmed Stuart Weitzman heels. If Molina was putting on the dog, she didn't want to be caught looking like one.

"Supporting the parish fund drive?" Temple asked, knowing Lieutenant Molina lived in the neighborhood.

Molina nodded over her semi-sparkling shoulder at the long table without the lemonade. "Supporting the Humane Society. I'm getting a couple of Miss Tyler's cats."

"You like cats?"

"I don't have much choice," Molina said wryly.

Temple couldn't imagine the towering homicide officer doing anything against her will, so she squinted toward the animal adoption table. A pair of half-grown tiger stripes meowed in a wire cage while an attendant filled out forms. She spotted a young girl in blue jeans and L.A. Gear sneakers fidgeting before the cage just as Molina called, "Mariah! Got a minute?"

Mariah. Temple straightened as this genuine mythical beast—hard-nosed Lieutenant Molina's pre-teen daughter—ambled over with a docility sure to vanish utterly in a couple of years when the hormones kicked in.

Meeting a mini-Molina did nothing to make Temple feel adult and superior. At ten or eleven, Mariah matched Temple's height (five-feet-flat) and outweighed her by a good twenty pounds.

Temple faced a chubby youngster with grave dark eyes nothing like Lieutenant Molina's spooky electric-blue ones. And braces were in the cards, Temple remembered. She winced for this awkward almost-adolescent whose mother was a local cop and who faced at least four years and a likely attack of ego-erasing acne before any signs of a silk purse would emerge from beneath the rough-cut, lumpy denim. Given the kid's plain-clothes mother's femininity quotient, Mariah didn't have much of a role model for turning from cabbage moth into Monarch.

But Mariah Molina wasn't Temple's problem, thank God.

"You're the cat-lover?" she asked the girl.

Mariah nodded shyly. No smile. Probably hiding the braces-doomed teeth.

"And a fan of gerbils and hamsters, which she already has too many of," Molina added with patience that was either maternal or paternal. With Molina, it was hard to tell when the authoritarian cop was speaking or when the woman was, if ever.

Father Hernandez and his entourage were edging toward the trio just in time to break an uneasy silence.

"I'd better get the cats ready for their official baptizing," Molina murmured, moving toward the completed paperwork and the cage.

"You can't baptize cats," Mariah remarked with a dubious giggle, her widening eyes half-tempted to take her mother literally even as she watched Temple for agreement.

Temple would have liked to have bent down to reassure the child, but there wasn't a height difference, dang it.

She did lower her voice, at least. "Don't mention 'baptizing' the cats when Father Hernandez is within earshot. He got into quite a fight with their last, and late, owner over that very issue."

"Miss Tyler was crazy." Mariah dismissed her benefactress with pre-teen disdain for such as yet personally unexperienced states as insanity.

Wait'll she hit thirteen! Temple thought. "Miss Tyler was cat-crazy, that's all."

"And that's okay?"

"That's fine, as long as you don't have too many."

"Do you have any?"

"That's debatable." Temple glanced at a pair of cat carriers parked under the shade of a towering oleander bush pruned into a tree shape. "One cat seems to have me. His name is Midnight Louie."

"Did you bring him here to be blessed?"

"Yes." Temple sighed. "He's not too happy about it, to tell the truth."

"Isn't he a Catholic cat?"

"He isn't even a domesticated cat. But I figured since this was my idea, I should participate."

"Why are there two carriers if you only have one cat?" Mariah asked. All kids under twelve love to demonstrate that they can count.

"The other cat isn't mine. Say, are those the L.A. Gear sneakers with the red lights in the heels that blink every time you step? Let me see! Cool."

Mariah had turned to display her footwear, her midnight-brown eyes warming at Temple's interest. "How'd you know about that?"

Before Temple could answer that no pair of unusual shoes debuted without her knowledge and probable panting after them, Molina as well as Father Hernandez and his altar boys had converged on them for the ceremonials.

Father Hernandez's ascetic and slightly careworn face smoothed into a smile as warm as the day. "Carmen. Mariah. You've taken *two* of Miss Tyler's cats? What a fine act of charity. I must admit that cats are not my favorite beasts."

Temple tried to keep from sinking right through the playground asphalt. Lieutenant C.R. Molina's first name was *Carmen*? As in Miranda? Or, in Molina's case, as in Miranda rights? Ay, yi yi yi. . . .

Molina, sensing the direction of Temple's thoughts, flashed her what could only be interpreted as a dirty look. "You can call it an act of charity, Father," she told the priest, "but I call it an act of self-defense."

She smiled as she gently yanked the long, black braid threading down Mariah's back. The girl smiled up at her mother, sudden sunshine, then bent to remove the first tiger-stripe kitten from the cage. It squirmed in her arms, rolling perfectly round yellow eyes.

While the solemn altar boys—Hispanic angels with honey-colored skin and India-ink eyes—stood at attention, Father Hernandez intoned some soft Latin syllables. His upraised hand, oddly held in the edgewise position of a karate chop (Temple noticed now that she was acquainted with that art), pantomimed a sign of the cross on the hot, arid air.

Tiger kitty kept still, and retired gracefully when returned to the cage. The sibling was extracted, held, and—no doubt cowed by the crowd—kept reverent silence while it underwent its own blessing.

"And you, Miss Barr." Father Hernandez turned to Temple with a sly smile. "You've been doing so much for Our Lady of Guadalupe lately that I will have to make you an honorary parishioner . . . what can I do for you?"

"Uh, nothing! That is, you can do my cat. I mean, bless him. I guess."

Stunned into stammering by the threat of conversation, Temple hustled over to the tan-colored carrier, bent to pinch the metal latch to the open position, and hauled out a very reluctant Louie.

"Come on, big guy. You know you hate being penned up. I'm the cavalry here. Don't fight me."

"My, he is massive," Father Hernandez commented.

"That's right, Father." Sister Seraphina had come over, a trailing television cameraman behind her. "You didn't see him the night of the fire alarm. This poor cat almost met the same fate as poor Peter."

"No!" Father Hernandez was shocked, as anyone would be when reminded of how the convent cat had been nailed to Miss Tyler's back door. Peter had survived nicely, but Temple doubted that the clergy at Our Lady of Guadalupe would ever get over such perverse violence. "Then he must have a special blessing."

Father Hernandez's hand reached for Louie's forehead, while the big tomcat wriggled in Temple's arms.

He was slipping through her grasp, all nearly-twenty pounds of him, his shiny black fur licorice-slick. Temple bent her knees to prop Louie's weight on her thighs, feeling his hind claws curl into the folds of her crinkle-cotton skirt for purchase. In a minute she was going to look as if she'd been tattooed by a staplegun.

"I'll take him."

Matt Devine's voice came out of the blue like a miracle. Although he had driven here with Temple, he had vanished after their arrival, she had assumed to confer with Father Hernandez.

But Matt was here now, almost as magically as the Mystifying Max had always managed on stage, cradling Midnight Louie like a fussing four-footed baby, and holding him out to Father Hernandez.

Mariah Molina stared up at Matt, who was a stranger to her, not because he was movie-star-handsome, or as blond as she was dark. Mariah wasn't quite old enough to fixate on either attribute. What she did notice—Temple knew with sudden sympathy—was that Matt might be old enough to be her father. Her apparently absent-without-leave father.

Temple was a bit miffed to observe that mother was as transfixed by Matt as daughter, and Lieutenant *Carmen* Molina was darn well old enough to know better.

Father Hernandez murmured and waved his right hand. Louie struggled fruitlessly in the grasp of a martial arts expert, scowling with flattened ears as if he were being cursed instead of blessed.

If beasts could talk . . .

But not even Midnight Louie could do that. Matt returned him to the carrier with no more incident than a parting yowl. Then Matt opened a smaller, powder-blue carrier and brought out a small shadow of Louie.

"Midnight Junior?" Father Hernandez joked.

"Midnight *Louise*," Temple put in. She was always fast on her feet with a quip.

Everyone gave this one the obligatory lip-quirk it deserved.

"The Humane Society people called her Caviar." Matt stroked the little cat's fine, fluffy fur.

"Welcome, Caviar," Father Hernandez intoned in high-priest solemnity, before returning to the Latin litany he was bestowing on all the animals.

Sister Seraphina leaned near to Temple. "He should do it in English, or he could do it in Spanish, but he's old-fashioned. He says the ancient Latin soothes the animals."

It soothed Temple, who liked the long, Latin names of healing herbs and drugs. Father Hernandez's Latin blessings had hummed around the gathering all afternoon, like the drone of lazy, overeducated bees. Behind him, the camera's Cyclops eye focused on cat and company.

Then the vignette dissolved. Matt turned away to whisk Caviar back to her carrier. Father Hernandez and bracketing boys moved on to the old lady with her rooster. The television camera clung close behind, its lens leering over his white-garbed shoulder.

"We'd better get our booty home, Mariah," Molina was saying

briskly, hefting the heavy cage back to the Humane Society table and handing one young cat to her daughter while cradling the other.

Tiger stripes. Wouldn't you know, Temple thought, that Molina would go for a critter that wore prison garb?

"Awkward age," Seraphina murmured at Temple's elbow. "When I see these kids, I get such an itch to teach again. But . . . I'm too old."

"You're not too old," Temple said automatically, watching Matt Devine approach Molina and child. He patted the two cats, smiled at Mariah and began talking seriously to Molina. What about?

"Besides," Temple absently reminded the nun beside her, "think of what stalks even grade school kids nowadays. Gangs. Drugs. Weapons."

Sister Seraphina glanced at the trio that Temple studied, her benign face puckered with uneasy memory. "Our grade schools were haunted in the old days; we were just too innocent to know it."

"What do you mean?" Sister Seraphina's self-accusing tone brought Temple's attention back to the conversation at hand.

Seraphina's expression grew both more guarded and more thoughtful. "Some youngsters have always grown old before their time. It's not the street, or the playground, that damages them, but what they grow up with at home. At least nowadays we admit it."

"You mean . . . drugs, even then?"

Sister Seraphina's head with its clumsy curlicue of permanent waves shook a definite "No." "Cigarettes and alcohol then, mostly harmless stuff to be sampled in secret and forgotten afterward, after the dare was done. No, in the old days the poison was the secrets themselves, only then the Family was sacred, untouchable. You didn't dare suspect, and you certainly did not dare interfere."

"You're talking about child abuse," Temple said.

"I often wonder," Seraphina said, staring at the charming tableau of children and animals with priest and altar boys moving methodically among them, "how much damage we did by being so innocent. We made ourselves into hypocrites before all those children who knew what life was really like, or what their lives were really like. We prattled of saints and suffering and mortal sins. Sometimes innocence is a greater sin to atone for than guilt."

"Have you ever questioned being a—?"

"Being a nun? My vocation?" Sister Seraphina's wry, amused eyes pierced Temple's confusion, then melted into the ineffable content Temple had always sensed in her. "Never." Her mouth hardened. "But I do question innocence when it is a shield for the evil-doer. And there are evil-doers among us, Miss Temple; all around us."

The nun's darker tone carried more weight than Father Hernandez's lulling Latin murmurs. Temple glanced around the sunny playground, feeling an internal shiver. Here, too? That kind of evil? But Peter Burns was in jail. It was over, wasn't it?

She saw that Molina and daughter had left. Now Matt was standing sentinel by the two cat carriers, under the green and fuchsia dapple of the oleander, watching Father Hernandez with an expression Temple couldn't name: part vigilance, part anger, part bleak hunger.

Matt had worn robes like that once, had blessed, if not in Latin, at least in English, and perhaps not animals, but people. Temple herself had seen him bless Miss Tyler when she lay ill. The Anointing of the Sick, which used to be called by the more dire name, Extreme Unction. What did it feel like to wield such invisible power, to assume a position of arbitrating between God and man or woman? Or had Matt always seen himself as a mere intermediary? Now there was a long Latin word for you.

She watched him with concern, remembering how unwilling he, the ex-priest, had been to judge Father Hernandez's odd behavior during the uncertainty of Miss Tyler's death. She remembered even more strongly how uncertain Matt Devine was about being judged by Father Hernandez, who was not an ex-priest.

"It's never easy, dear," Sister Seraphina was saying encouragingly. "Judging situations. Judging people. I've made my mistakes," she added, a bittersweet twist to her lips as if she had just sipped sour lemonade.

Temple glanced at Matt again. He had made his mistakes, too. Was he still making them?

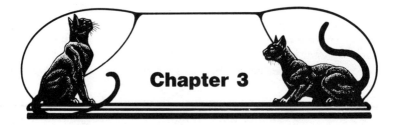

Chapter 3

Grim Pilgrimage

Matt was accustomed to institutional decor—plain, functional and eternally dingy no matter how well scrubbed.

The Las Vegas county jail had one additional attribute: an enigmatic air of sordid doings just beyond reach.

Matt signed in and submitted to a brown-uniformed woman jailer who clipped a plastic visitor's badge to the collar of his knit sports shirt. She was short and stocky, with buzz-cut bleached blond hair. Despite the gun holster riding her amply padded hip, she looked no more dangerous than a veteran hairdresser armed with a black blow dryer.

Appearances, Matt reminded himself, were deceiving. His own were a prime case in point.

"Lieutenant Molina okayed this," the woman noted by way of verbal confirmation. "The prisoner has no lawyer yet to do the honors."

"I understand he's representing himself."

She looked up, interested. "You know the old saying—"

"Anyone who represents himself in court has a fool for a client."

She nodded. "You a lawyer?"

Matt spread his arms to display casual sports shirt and khaki slacks. "Do I dress like one?"

Her lips approximated a smile, as much expression as she could muster in her stern, bureaucratic job. She nodded him past.

Everyone beyond the small entry area was either armed or wearing a visitor's badge like his. Matt was finally escorted to the naked and neutral space he expected from years of seeing television shows. He had hoped for the high-tech glass barrier and the twin phone receivers, simply because the novelty of the arrangement would take his mind off the difficult task ahead. He talked to hundreds of people on the phone, but never saw their faces.

Indeed, it was the quintessential scene of cliche: facing hard chairs, intervening wire-reinforced glass barrier. The setting reminded him of a bombed-out confessional, where the bare bones of furniture remained standing, oddly isolated, after the sheltering walls of true confidentiality had been blasted away.

The word that came to mind again was "naked." A bored but watchful uniformed officer on guard did nothing to allay that impression.

Matt sat where indicated, and waited.

In a couple of minutes, a door beyond the barrier opened. His quarry appeared, wearing a loose jailhouse jumpsuit colored a garish orange.

A small man, he looked almost boyish in the outfit, but there was nothing juvenile about his expression when he saw Matt: distaste screwed tight into contempt. And Matt didn't even know the man.

Contempt always made Matt nervous, as if he had done something wrong he had forgotten about. Conditioning. Right now he was trying desperately to do something right, only he didn't quite know how to go about it. Who was lying? Embittered blackmailer in jail, or honest parish priest? During his campaign to harrass the Our Lady of Guadalupe congregation, Burns had threatened to expose Father Hernandez as a child molester. Was this charge a baseless taunt, or the simple truth spoken by an unlikely source? Matt was the only one on earth, besides the two men involved, to know of the blackmail. Hernandez denied the allegation, of course, but denial was a way of life to those addicted to unholy pursuits. Either way, whether Matt reported the facts to the diocese or did nothing, he might be abetting a monster. He had to know the truth for the sake of his own conscience. Success would depend on correctly handling this volatile man. Matt was good with people, but he was used to dealing with well-intentioned people.

Peter Burns was about as ill-intentioned as anyone could be. He was an aggressively unrepentant murderer.

"Well." Burns had planted himself in the chair opposite Matt and snatched up his receiver. "So much for the holier-than-thous. No one from Our Lady of Guadalupe has visited me but you."

"I'm not from Our Lady of Guadalupe."

"You could have fooled me. You sure were hanging around the old parish lately. Just what *was* your angle?"

"Sister Seraphina at the convent asked me to help with the obscene phone calls."

"What are you, a lineman for the county?"

Matt resisted his cynicism. "I'm a telephone hotline counselor."

"That's a nun for you. Runs into an obscene phone caller so she calls on a telephone counselor for help."

Matt didn't bother explaining that there was a lot more to it than that. "Did you enjoy making those calls?" he asked.

"Me? I haven't enjoyed anything since I was about four years old. The church saw to that."

"What about abusing the cat?"

"Frankly—" Burns leaned back in the chair.

Matt, hearing his feet knock the barrier between them, almost jumped. The only barriers he trusted to hold here were psychological ones.

Burns watched him with a dawning smile, an open-mouthed opportunist's almost-smirk. Taunting. "Frankly," he went on, "I enjoyed all of the stuff I did—the cats, the old nuns, the old bat in her cathouse. It was like a license to commit Halloween, you know? Very liberating."

"Not . . . completely." Matt eyed the bland surroundings.

Burns shrugged. "What's your name?"

"Matt Devine."

"Whew!" Burns's stalled smile made a daring loop-de-loop into a high-pitched laugh. "Perfect. Devine as in 'devotional duty,' and Matthew after one of the four gurus of the Gospel. I bet you were born to be teacher's pet at St. Mary's of the Holy Cross-eyed

Hallelujah Chorus. Old Sister Mary Malaria calls, and you come running like a good boy to dust the blackboard erasers and find the nasty kid who's making naughty phone calls. What do you want here? Plan to shake some chalk dust in my face? Don't bother. I'm proud of what I did. No holier-than-thou is gonna make me feel otherwise. So what brought you here, Mr. Matthew Dee-vine?''

Matt didn't bother correcting the guy on the fine points of his first name. "It isn't the calls, and it isn't the cats.''

Burns shifted again in his hard chair, restless as a twelve-year-old kid. "Yeah. It's the Big One. Murder. What do you want to know?''

"You'd tell me?''

"Sure. We're not in court. And, anyway, I'm demented, didn't you know? Why else would an upstanding pillar of the Church and the Court kill a nice old lady, his own great-auntie, no less? Anything I say can't be held against me, because I'll say something else in two seconds.''

"I'm not here about Blandina Tyler's death.''

Burns's lips puckered in a mock-pout of disappointment. "What would it be, then?''

"You didn't just call the convent.''

"Oh, yeah . . . my little anonymous notes to the rectory.'' Burns leaned forward, avid. "Father Raf-a-el Hernandez send you? Bet he's still sweating silver bullets. Hit the Coors, did he, the good Father, after my letters got to him?''

"No one sent me.''

"You're a real busy-body, Matthew. None of this is your business.''

"It's all of our business. I grew up Catholic, too.''

"Aw, poor baby. Bet you were an altar boy, right?''

Matt's nod felt stiff even to him.

"Hey, that's okay, Matthew. Somebody's got to get the gold stars on their school papers. Somebody's got to wear those little gilded halos.''

Matt set his teeth. He hated his full name enough in the correct form. Having a more common form constantly hurled at him was like being whipped with a dead snake. Maybe Burns wasn't so crazy to represent himself; he would be terrific in the courtroom.

"You're creating an extreme to rebel against.'' Matt suddenly unleashed his own weapon, psychobabble. "Some people demonize the people and institutions in their past. You've sanctified them. I'm not this paragon you need to create just to tear down.''

"You're here, aren't you? Doing your good deed of the day for someone else? You have nothing to do with this, Devine. Why bother?''

Matt decided to try candor. "Look. I was reared Catholic. Like you, I didn't have a perfect life, or perfect parents. I've had my own problems with the past. I just want to know the truth about your accusations.''

Burns was watching him with brittle, clever eyes. "You heard my whole sad story in that lady lieutenant's office.''

"I can sympathize," Matt said. "You had a rough upbringing: born out of wedlock, handed to a foster family who never stopped reminding you of your 'unworthy' origins. I'm not saying it was right. We're both products of a less enlightened time.''

"Listen to yourself! 'Products.' 'Less enlightened.' You're intellectualizing, Mr. Phone Shrink. You're dodging the bullet I caught in my teeth and spit back at the world. I bet you envy me.''

Matt barely stopped himself from pushing away his chair as if avoiding a spitball. "You know what you hate," he conceded.

Burns nodded, pleased. "Most people, they get so confused by the idiocy they're taught when they're kids they don't even know that. I even looked like what they said I was: a bastard. I never grew much; maybe I wanted to stay small so no one would notice me and call me names. And it was worse when they *didn't* call me names. 'You! Come here,' my foster-grandwitch would yell, pointing her cane like the damning finger of God. And, God, it hurt when she poked me with it, hit me with it. Hit me with religion, over and over, with bad words. Yeah, it made me ugly." He looked up, eyes as corrosive as dry ice. "Nobody made you feel ugly.''

"Don't be so sure.''

"You sound like you mean that.''

Matt said nothing.

"You still go to mass?''

"Not . . . often.''

"Fallen away but unable to cut the apron strings to Mother Church, eh? Then why do you care if my charges against Father Hernandez are true or not?''

"If they're true, they should be pursued."

"Truth is the last thing anyone ever pursues, especially about themselves." Burns pouted his lips again. His forefinger traced an invisible pattern on the drab Formica tabletop. "Why wouldn't they be true? Why *not?*"

"You were harassing the entire parish structure. You weren't a genuine obscene caller, you just mimicked one to upset the nuns. A lot of your tricks were diversions, so no one would guess your real target was Blandina Tyler. So, yeah, your blackmail of Father Hernandez could have been another smokescreen. It had the proper effect; it kept him away from the Tyler house."

"He didn't run to the diocese with it, though, did he? Makes you wonder. Makes *you* in particular wonder, Matthew."

Matt shrugged. "If it's true, and if you're as bitter toward Our Lady of Guadalupe and the church as you say, I wonder why you haven't produced any evidence yet."

"I got a few other things on my mind."

"Or, you were just play-acting again, playing the blackmailer as you enacted an obscene phone caller, and as you aped a Satanist when you crucified the cat."

"You think I was just play-acting that, huh?"

"You tell me."

"I don't have to, Matthew. I'm free. You're not my prosecutor, or my parole officer or my shrink or my confessor. I don't have to even give you a hint. Besides, what would you do if you had any evidence?"

"I'd make sure it was investigated."

"By whom? The church? You know how they kicked everything under the cassock all those years. Years and years of innocent kids being abused, and all they did was send Father to some monastery to mumble penance."

"They're cleaning house now."

"Because they have to! It's prime-time news. Hard copy. A current affair that happens to have a very long history. I know why you're here, not to uncover anything, but to hush it up. You make me sick. Whether it's an inconvenient kid on the way or an inconvenient kiddie diddler, you all conspire to sweep it under the rug. You hypocritical goodie two-shoes can't keep your noses out of telling everybody else what to do, but you never wake up and smell the shit you forgot to bury in your own back yards. And the women are the worst.''

"Maybe that's because women have no power but the aura of superiority the church confers on them.''

"An aura's the same as a halo, isn't it? Blessed Virgin Mary-Blue-Gown with her eyes cast down, as blind as Old Lady Justice. The Law is just as crooked, and wouldn't you know it hides behind some woman's skirts for its symbol of integrity. Yeah. The church is a man's game, and the church knows power, but the church is over a barrel now, just like you are, not knowing what nasty scandal in their precious priesthood is gonna hit next. So watch and wait, Devine.''

His sneering paraphrase of Christ's instructions to his disciples in the Garden of Gethsemane—like Eden, another garden of betrayal—made Matt wince. Burns smiled and executed a lawyerly lunge for the verbal kill.

"As for Father Raf-a-el Hernandez and whether my threats of exposure have any basis in evidence or act . . . guess!'' he finished triumphantly.

"You're bitter, and have reason to be.''

"Don't turn the other cheek. When I tried that I got my cheeks pounded. That's what they all did, used religion as a club, a cane. Baby Jesus this and the Advent windows opening every week before Christmas and endless stories of the Blessed Birth from the point of view of the Magi and the shepherds and even the damn donkey. Who was the child who was born on the outskirts of everything? I was the Baby Jesus, and there was no room in the inn.''

Matt once might have shuddered at such angry blasphemy. Now he had to admit that Burns had a point.

"You loyalists with your plaster saint patience,'' the prisoner muttered, calming somewhat.

"Don't underestimate me. I'm a product of Catholic schools, I've been . . . involved with the church all of my life.''

"Tell me about it, only I never fit in; I was always a walking, talking sign of sin. Hypocrisy is the hallmark of the church. Look at these aberrant priests, saying mass and seducing altar boys on the same Sunday morning.''

"That's just it; they are aberrant. You must remember many good priests and dedicated nuns from your school days."

Burns snorted. "Is nothing bad enough to turn your stomach and vomit up the past? What does it take to make you angry, golden boy?"

Matt answered without hesitation. "You don't want to find out."

Burns looked into his eyes and finally shut up.

But Peter Burns had made Matt angry. The interview had been like spending a long, dark night of the soul, not alone, but in dialogue with his own dark side.

Once, young and impressionable, Matt the child had dreaded the church's bogeyman: he wondered if he could hear the Devil taunting him in his mind to do the wrong thing. Peter Burns had resurrected that primitive fear, for he was everything Matt had tried not to be: bitter, unforgiving, vengeful, exuding the pus of murderous rage until he threatened to infect everyone around him.

Within half an hour of that jailhouse encounter, Matt was in his favorite place for psychic rest and recuperation, for meditation, if not prayer. He wasn't sure that he prayed any more, but at least he thought in peace.

Around him sandy desert paths wound through a wilderness of cactus. The land was gently rolling, giving the illusion of mini-hills and valleys. Though groups of people wandered the sere landscape with him, at times he was alone. At other times, their chatter and their presence, as benign as that of squirrels, would confront him with the existence of the everyday.

He did not quite have to eat locusts, but he was as far removed from reality here as anywhere in Las Vegas. And, like the others who enjoyed this private garden of thorns, he gained admittance for nothing.

The Ethel M. Chocolate Factory was located on 2 Cactus Garden Drive south of Tropicana. Filing through the front doors for a tour of the pristine premises brought an instant release from the frenetic pressure to have expensive fun on the Strip. The people here were engaged in the benign business of making life sweet. If you wanted to buy their sweetness, gift-wrapped by the pound, they would oblige. They would give you one taste-bud-smothering sample for nothing.

An extra attraction was the extensive cactus and botanical gardens out back, a low-pressure invitation to gawk at nature in an unnatural consolidation of its wonders.

Tours of the gardens were "self-directed." That meant you could get lost here, and no one would notice.

Matt wandered the familiar paths, marveling at nature's stubborn survivability. Most cactus blooms lasted only a day, but hundreds sprouted. Cacti were the camels of the plant world, able to hoard water in the burning summer. They could survive the winter night's chill temperature plunge. These plain, often ugly growths' dead-green color seemed more a matter of camouflage than beauty, yet they could flash those spectacular, one-day-wonder blossoms. They wore their own crown of thorns, stabbing anything that blundered into their midst to the quick with inches-long quills.

Today, each plant reminded Matt of Peter Burns. The cactus was twisted and thorny, yet superbly adapted to its hard-scrabble environment for those very reasons, just like Burns. Matt could see how, encountering a diatribe like the one Peter Burns had unleashed on him, priests in the old days would attempt to exorcize such perverse blasphemy. Nowadays, they more often needed to exorcise themselves.

Seeing Burns had reminded Matt of the past, of a deeper and older injustice he needed to pursue. There was another man he needed to confront, for his own sake, the man who was his sole reason for relocating to Las Vegas in the first place. Matt knew why the business of earning his daily bread, of finding shelter had postponed his mission. Meeting Temple and getting drawn into her dangerous quandaries was another, unanticipated detour. Temple herself, and her attractions, had become a formidable distraction. . . . Maybe he had welcomed diversion from his real, ugly and difficult goal. Maybe vengeance was the Lord's alone. And maybe the long-gone man he sought was a mirage like so many other things in this city, this dry, hot indifferent desert.

Matt sighed. With his fair coloring, he shouldn't linger in such unfiltered sunlight. But he liked the heat, the searing sun. It was cleansing and uncompromising. It would bleach the freshest bones as pale as the fangs of T.S. Eliot's three white leopards. It would, in the end, atone for everything.

His mind, prickled by the thorny past, returned to the immediate problem. Burns would be no help with Hernandez, as Matt had expected, but he had needed to try. He would have to find other avenues. Molina was out; she was too closely connected to Our Lady of Guadalupe and would instantly suspect more than he wanted her to. So were other law enforcement representatives; they had their own rules to follow, as religious orders did, and did not discern any fine line between crime and punishment. Temple was out as well; she was too curious. But she had mentioned somebody once. . . .

Matt waited until a nearby clot of tourists—men, women and children in wrinkled cotton bermuda shorts and t-shirts advertising an array of Strip attractions—passed through the small shop on their way out.

Then he followed.

No one was in the cool, narrow white room with the glass case displaying a bevy of chocolates like a toothsome Sleeping Beauty of Sweetness.

The ladies behind the counter, their hair shrouded by white plastic caps, reminded Matt of certain nursing orders of nuns. Order: that is what one found at Ethel M's, and a pristine environment that did not feel prissy.

Food for the soul. Matt bought two boxes while the women stole glances at him, giggling, as if he were a movie star that they did not quite recognize.

He did not quite recognize himself either.

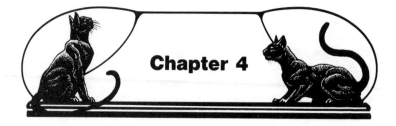

Chapter 4

Midnight Louie Saves His Soul

The moment my ears hear the name "Crystal Phoenix" they stand to attention.

The fact of the matter is, I am none too enamored with the Circle Ritz crowd at the moment—not that I have any quarrel with my delightful roommate, Miss Temple Barr, other than the nightly battle for prime snoozing space.

I have mentioned other, less amenable tenants now among the roster of Circle Ritz occupants. I suspect that one is bombarding me with the feline equivalent of "good vibes." Often when snoozing I sense a purring not purely on this plane. The perpetrator of this psychic static, I suspect, is that high-falutin' feline priestess on the penthouse level, the ever-omniscient (at least in her own mind, which has apparently been handed down for generations through a process she calls reincarnation) Karma. No wonder she is so reclusive: I would not advertise my presence either if my little gray cells were mostly cast-offs from defunct users.

As for the vexing matter of the young lady only one floor above me, Caviar, originally known as Midnight Louise, I suspect that between the do-gooder vibes from above and my own conscience, I am in danger of making an unnecessary confession that could be hazardous to my health. So far I have managed to keep the shell-pink interiors of her dainty little ears free from any whisper of my moniker, Midnight Louie.

It seems that I have paternal tendencies, at least genetically.

However, this little doll that Miss Temple rescued from a Humane Society cage in a weak moment sports a savage temper that is particularly directed to the absconding bounder that fathered her. Given her snazzy ebony color scheme and comparative youth, the odds are likely that I indeed did have some brush or other with her mother. In fact, I may remember mama—an ebony lady long-hair down on her luck who crossed my path an even unluckier year or so ago. So I could be slapped with a paternity suit—and a lot more, like four slashing shivs attached to an agile paw—were Miss Caviar to discover my real name.

Therefore, I live in fear of being found out, a position I am used to inflicting on others, particularly evil-doers. The claw pinches when it is on the other paw.

Also, I have a lingering dissatisfaction with my role in certain recent religious ceremonies. True, I have spent some time of late around and about Our Lady of Guadalupe church and convent. This was purely in the performance of my usual duties—tracking down wrongdoers and murderers, protecting my naive roommate and saving the skins of cats everywhere. It was not in the nature of a religious conversion.

So suddenly there I am, thrust once again into the portable cell and imported against my will into an environment that is not to my taste: a convocation of all creatures great and small, including far too many immature humans for my taste. Amid the parrot and goat droppings, the bray of the occasional donkey and the barking and yapping of an overpopulation of dogs, I am confined and subjected to unrelenting cacophony.

I have not seen anything yet. Soon I am summarily hauled from my cage, by Miss Temple Barr yet, who owes me a good deal, if not several first-class meals for professional and personal services, and held up to public ridicule.

While the sun bakes down on my unprotected head, I am the target of uninvited invocations in a tongue more suitable for ancient dudes who favor miniskirts. I suspect that I am being subjected to a "bless-ing," but it depends upon your point of view whether this is a good or a bad thing.

For one thing, I am not Catholic. If I am any kind of Christian at all, it is a confirmed Copt. That term has nothing to do with law enforce-ment, despite my history. A Copt is a modern Christian version of a follower of ancient Egyptian rites. In fact, I do not even qualify as a Copt, since the only Deity I recognize is an obscure Egyptian god-dess and head benefactress of the long-gone city of Bast, which bears her name. Speaking of this little goddess-doll's head, I believe it was exceptionally handsome as well as possessed of a supremely wise expression. You can see its likeness in every creature of my ilk that you come across. I do not know if Bast also had the impressive set of whiskers that I have, but these high-up Egyptian babes were often control freaks who would don false whiskers to lend authority to their appearance. At least they knew what counts.

I do not know what Bast (may her whiskers increase!) would think to see one of her loyal adherents doused with drops of holy water in the hot sun, and muttered over in a strange tongue.

I may have to make a pilgrimage to the banks of the Nile to erase this enforced baptism of sorts. It does not appear to have done me any permanent harm, but I am tired of spending so much time at Our Lady of Guadalupe when I am not a parishioner. Frankly, the churchy ambiance leaves me cold. I prefer scenes of a seamier nature, where I can put my nose to the groundstone and sniff out larceny, greed, lust and murder. Also carp.

So when I overhear Miss Temple on the telephone scheduling a meeting at the Crystal Phoenix the next day, I figure it is time to investigate a new turf—in this case, a former venue.

True, I left my previous and cushy situation at the Crystal Phoenix because of an interloper there—a crawling, squalling, bawling bun-dle of babydom spawned by two people of whom I am too fond to criticize for the quality of their offspring, Mr. Nicky Fontana and his wife, Miss Van von Rhine. (Being a career woman, Miss Van von Rhine does not answer to the epithet of "Mrs.")

However, human offspring do not sport any claws worth worrying about, and their teeth are decidedly tardy in coming, not to mention dull in the extreme.

It strikes me that a return to the Crystal Phoenix might save Midnight Louie from domestic dissonance.

Besides, I always had a fondness for birds, legendary or not, as well as fish.

Chapter 5

A Temple Too Many

"This is so much more than we bargained for, Miss Barr," Van von Rhine was saying in a flabbergasted tone.

"Temple," Temple replied with a smile that could sell broccoli to George Bush and maybe even green beans to Hillary Rodham Clinton. "Yes, I know you were just looking for a market repositioning, but—with all the high-powered competition on the Strip—I concluded that you need something concrete to sell."

Nicky leaned over his wife's pale-suited shoulder, bracing a hand on the desk to read Temple's proposal.

"Not concrete, glass," he noted. "You went for glass. 'Phoenix Under Glass.' I like it." He flashed Temple a smile whose wattage matched her own.

"But . . . the construction. The cost." Van von Rhine frowned at her husband and Temple as if suspecting a conspiracy of spendthrifts. "We put a fortune into restoring the Crystal Phoenix just a few years ago. And where—?"

"Out behind the pool," Temple said quickly. "It's a perfect site, not too close to the hotel. Listen, this is just a raw concept, but I doubt it would cost the moon. It would be worth hundreds of thousands in publicity value alone."

"And cost millions," Van added. "All right, describe this . . . terrarium again, with more detail."

Temple smiled again. "I don't do detail. I just come up with grand schemes. Anyway, I visualize a huge glass dome over an exotic cactus garden, with lots of neon. At night little fairy lights on the cactus light up and the place becomes an exotic setting for dinner—call it 'Al Fresco's.' "

Nicky winced.

"Something wrong?" Temple asked.

Van shook her head. "The name veers a little too close to Nicky's shadowy antecedents, that's all."

"But what's the draw for kids?" Nicky asked.

"That *is* the whole point of this campaign," Van reminded Temple, her blue eyes cool under arched pastel eyebrows.

Temple grinned. "First, the kids can tour the cactus garden in the daytime; it's educational. Second, the dome also houses a petting zoo. Kids love that."

"Petting zoo?" The disbelief in Van's voice was almost comical. "What kind of petting zoo?"

"A classy one, with attendants to educate kids and care for the animals. And all of the animals will be indigenous."

"They usually are," Nicky muttered, wrinkling his nose.

"Indigenous is not a dirty word, Mr. Fontana; it just means native to Nevada. Critters who get a bad rap, like lizards and spiders and snakes—"

This time Van von Rhine made a face.

"Little boys love them," Temple said with the blithe authority of the childless. "We'll also have furry creatures like jackrabbits, fox and coyote, maybe even a mule. Oh, and you know what would be *great?* A camel. The government tried camels as military mounts out here in the nineteenth century. You could give the kids rides."

"We know," Nicky and Van said in pained concert with an exchange of glances, "about the camels."

"Well, then, you can see how logical it all is. A few animals can't be too expensive to maintain."

"What about the keepers?" Van asked.

"Volunteers from local schools, supervised by a couple of experts. This is the nineties. Ecology is in. Nobody can say that the exhibit isn't classy. I don't know what it would cost, of course, but it's worth looking into."

Nicky's dark head was nodding. "What about it?" he asked his wife.

She shrugged elegant, Armani-clad shoulders. "An intriguing idea. I realize that the hot new hotels have raised the stakes on the Strip." She glanced at Temple. "My only problem is that I don't know how to pay you, Miss Barr. Coming up with a concept for a major attraction is more than I expected of you."

"Look into the idea. If it works out, you can worry about rewarding me later. Meanwhile, I'm still on a PR retainer. And my name is Temple."

This time Van's smile was like hot caramel melting the almond icing of her demeanor. "Temple. Except for the spelling, just like Temple Bar landing on Lake Mead; have you ever considered opening a theme park there in your honor?"

"Really? There's a place on Lake Mead called 'Temple Bar?' "

"Only one 'r' in the 'Barr,' alas," Van answered.

"I never knew that, although I did know about the one in England."

"Wait a minute." Nicky's dark Italian glance was playing ping-pong between the two women. "What are these places and why have I never heard of them?"

"The site on Lake Mead," Van said, "is off-the-beaten-path, a landing for boats. Boating is not one of your vices, Nicky dear, thank God."

"And the one in England," Temple added, "was a gateway closing the entrance to the City of London from the Strand, near the Temple where British barristers have practiced law at the Inns of Court for centuries. That one I looked up, and it doesn't have a double 'r' in it, either."

"Why do you suppose your parents named you that?" Van asked a bit pensively. "A sense of humor?"

"Because," Temple answered wryly, "they were just like Nicky; they didn't know a thing about the other Temple Bars. Ignorance, not wit." When Nicky winced, she added, "Neither do most people, which is fine with me. But I never knew there was a Temple Bar around here—"

"I can hear her PR wheels turning," Nicky told his wife with a laugh. "You shouldn't have mentioned it."

"Speaking of things I shouldn't mention," Van said, "did I see Midnight Louie loitering by the doors to the grounds today?"

Temple grimaced. "Oh, that Louie. He just strolls out to the car with me and waits by the door. It seems mean to leave him behind. I hope it's all right if he looks over his old stomping grounds."

"Maybe," Nicky suggested, "he can start excavating for Phoenix Under Glass."

"He's big," Temple admitted, "and strong. But not that big."

She gathered her papers and thrust them into the tote bag of the day, a bronze metallic quilted number that matched her Via Spiga pumps.

"I've got a business lunch up top at the Fontana," she said nodding to its namesake as she stood up.

Nicky unleashed his smile again. "More empire-building?"

"No, just a little unofficial snooping."

"Another murder?" Van asked with interest.

"No, only intent to commit."

"Who's the committer? Anybody we know?"

"Me," Temple said with a grim smile, making her exit and leaving them, if not laughing, at least as curious as hell.

Sunny Cadeaux was tall, thin, blond and waiting at a window table when Temple reached the 14th floor circular restaurant that was Nicky Fontana's namesake.

Trust Sunny to charm a desirable table out of the head waiter in Hades.

Temple waved off the maitre d' and joined Sunny, navigating the tables and chairs by guiding her bulky tote bag around them. When she arrived at the table, Sunny lifted her purse—a wafer-thin fold of cobalt leather that could hold one letter and several very thin dimes—from the empty chair.

Temple collapsed into the seat, slinging her tote into the well between herself and the window.

"We missed you at the last WICA meeting," Sunny said.

WICA had nothing to do with witchcraft, but stood for Women In Communications, Associated, an organization that included PR and media women. Sunny was a television reporter with a local channel, a woman so unflappable that she was sometimes suspected of being an attractive corpse. Temple knew her impassive air wasn't impartiality, but rather an attempt to keep wrinkles from her pale, porcelain skin.

"I've been a tad busy," Temple admitted.

"We've read about it. Isn't your job to get news of your clients in the paper, not yourself? Or your cat's puss in print?"

"Can I help it that Midnight Louie is so darn photogenic? And I wish they had cropped me out of that fire rescue photo. I looked like Little Orphan Annie fresh from a spin-dry."

"You looked adorably rumpled. I wish I could look adorably rumpled."

Temple eyed Sunny's blond chin-length hair, smooth as satin except for the pert flick at the ends. "Believe me, rumpled is not your style, even in life-threatening situations."

"You've been prone to those lately," Sunny noted, leaning back to make room for a padded vinyl menu cover large enough to play checkers on.

Temple cracked hers open, then peered over its top. "This is as hefty as the Ten Commandments and it's just the luncheon menu. What do they offer at dinner—an encyclopedia?"

"The waiters probably wear sandwich boards." Sunny snapped the impressive volume shut. "I'll have the usual. Why did you want to see me?"

As the waiter approached, Temple desperately eyed the menu. She was having her usual identity crisis about what to order from a strange bill of fare. The banana, papaya and kiwi fajitas sounded truly intriguing, but then so did the swordfish quiche.

She caved in and ordered what Sunny always did: salad, but a fruit version instead of the house greens.

"Are you doing anything for the Gridiron this year?" Temple asked.

Sunny's pale blue eyes grayed with wariness. "Maybe. Usually I play a bit part in the show."

Sunny's bit parts always involved wearing filmy lingerie, if the male skit writers had anything to do with it.

"I meant, are you writing anything?" Temple said.

"No. I seldom do."

"Well, I always do, and I just realized I never got an announcement requesting skits for the show. I've been a little stressed out lately," Temple added modestly, referring to her moment of disheveled glory on page fourteen of the *Las Vegas Sun.*

"Really?" Sunny unfolded her napkin and sipped from her goblet of spring water, in which floated the obligatory lemon slice.

"Really. Sunny, you're always on the fringes of the Gridiron group. What's going on?"

Sunny's long, pale fingernails nudged the silverware this way and that while her eyes considered the panorama beyond the window, the familiar flock of Las Vegas hotels grazing along the Strip like a colorful exhibit of architectural dinosaurs.

"Sunny!"

Temple was at last rewarded with a direct glance, one that quickly dodged again to neutral territory. "I didn't know you hadn't heard anything, Temple. Honest. But, if you didn't, it *might* have something to do with this year's chairman."

"I've always participated in the Vegas Gridiron Show, just as I used to in the Twin Cities." Temple's tone of voice wavered between puzzlement and a grumble. "My song satires are usually chosen for the opening and closing production numbers, for heaven's sake. Why would they forget to tell me about it? They need my stuff. What chairman?"

Temple was forced to interrupt her tirade in order to make way for a platter of leafy greens topped with such exotically sliced and contorted fruit that they appeared to have come fresh from the hands and meat cleaver of Chef de Sade himself.

"We should have split one," Sunny said ruefully, gazing on her own humongous house salad.

"Sunny! *What* chairman?"

Sunny did what she seldom did, so Temple knew the situation was really serious. She sacrificed her deadpan composure and her rice-paper complexion to make a face.

"Well, who is it?" Temple demanded.

"Crawford Buchanan."

"What? Who would make *him* show chairman? He doesn't even write for a real newspaper—"

"Neither do I; I broadcast. And you're not in media anymore."

"Still, I'm a Gridiron veteran, and nobody ever had any problem with my participation before. So Crawford has blackballed me?"

"Maybe it's not personal. Nobody who usually writes for the show has been notified of a skit deadline."

"Nobody? When's the show this year?"

"October eighteenth."

"That's less than a month away! Rehearsals will begin any day now. What can Awful Crawford be thinking of? Even he isn't crazy enough to . . . oh, no!"

Sunny nodded as she nibbled a leaf of undressed romaine. "Um hmm. The word is he's going to write the show himself. Solo."

"So *low!*" Temple corrected her with feeling. "That egotistical . . . worm. He's written a skit or two before, but what makes him think he can come up with ninety minutes of topical satire—funny topical satire—all by himself?"

"Male ego?" Sunny suggested.

"That answer insults males everywhere. Crawford has the ego for a stunt like this, but his qualifications in the other department are very iffy."

"Temple, I know you don't care for him, but maybe he'll do all right."

She shook her head, rejecting the possibility that Crawford Buchanan could come up smelling like anything other than an onion. "How did he get named to the job? Why doesn't the Society of Journalists' committee ever name a woman show chairman? Don't answer: apparently women aren't as overbearing as Crawford Buchanan."

"I heard he made a pitch to the board about how he could do it better than anybody. Cited his experience covering the Vegas entertainment scene."

"Crawford doesn't 'cover' it, he oozes all over it."

"Why do you hate him so much?"

"It's not him, Sunny, it's the principle of the thing. Although, when Crawford Buchanan's involved, principles usually have zilch to do with it." Temple sat back to view her truly awesome salad from a distance. She picked up a convoluted curl of kiwi. "Buchanan is incompetent, self-important, sexist, greedy and utterly thoughtless, hardly a candidate for Man of the Year."

"You've got no argument from me about the creep, but don't let him get to you."

"I can't help it. He offends my sense of justice. Maybe it's what a friend suggested: I secretly envy him for getting away with being so useless. God knows what the subjects of this year's skits will be, much less the quality."

Sunny smiled. "Especially without your socko openers and clos-ers. You're a whiz at that."

"Thanks."

"I suppose you won't do your annual stint on stage either this year?"

"You mean if I even get asked? Will any of us WICAns be asked? Knowing Crawford, he'll recruit the night shift from the Lace 'n' Lust. I wouldn't appear in 'Crawford's Follies' for anything. I do hate to see a good tradition sink under the overweight ego of a featherweight like Buchanan."

Temple pushed away her untouched plate, kiwi curl and all. "Anyway, I have bigger salmon to sauté. I just presented the owners of this hotel with a hot new scheme to pump up their popularity with the family traveler."

"Really? A whole concept? That's a big commission, Temple."

Television reporters seldom sounded impressed, even off the job, but Sunny did now.

Temple decided to let Crawford Buchanan crawl away into the back of her mind where he belonged, like a scorpion in the sun on a faraway wall where it couldn't hurt anyone.

"Yeah." She managed a smile now that she had digested the shocking Gridiron news, if nothing else. "I'll have my own show to stage-manage, if Nicky and Van go for it."

"That's the spirit!" Sunny's smile lived up to her name, then softened to a certain slyness as she leaned across the table and lowered her voice. "I told you what you wanted to know, however unpleasant. Now you tell me about that great-looking blond guy I saw you having dinner with a couple of weeks ago."

Temple ordinarily believed in a free exchange of information, but this subject was highly privileged.

"That," she said firmly, "is a story-in-progress and strictly confi-dential. Shall we ask for doggie bags?"

"Whatever will your heroic cat say about that?"

"Nothing complimentary." Temple eyed her exotic plate as she snapped her credit card to the tabletop. "Besides, Louie wouldn't deign to scrape kitty litter on this lettuce extravaganza if he were starving. And I doubt he is, because he was last seen today in the vicinity of the hotel koi pond.''

Sunny broke tradition twice in one day and grimaced again. ''Please. Not after lunch. I hate blood sports.''

Chapter 6

Past Imperfect

"How'd you hear about me?" the old guy asked.

"A semi-satisfied client." Matt knew the smile that accompanied his statement would mystify the man, but Eightball O'Rourke was supposed to be a detective, wasn't he?

Let him figure it out.

"All clients are 'semi-satisfied,' " the guy riposted without pause. "They think private dicks are fairy godmothers in a trenchcoat, that we wave a wand—or a gat—and whatever we dig up will stop or start a divorce, help them duck a gambling debt or a child support payment. Most people don't really want to know what I find out. You don't act too sure about wanting to find this 'missing person' yourself—"

O'Rourke glanced at the spiral-bound notebook on his pool-table-sized desk. The lined pages crinkled at the corners as if the pad had been forgotten in a drawer for thirty years. Maybe it had.

"This person is missing only to me," Matt admitted.

Eightball drew a box around the name on the note pad. "All you've got on him is a history of coming to Vegas to gamble. Must be sixteen million guys who fit that profile over the past thirty years. You don't even know whether he uses his right name here. If he's ever welshed on a gambling debt, you can bet he doesn't."

"Regulars get known around town."

"Maybe, but the casino personnel changes from year to year, sometimes from season to season. You know his hangout of choice?"

"No," Matt said.

"Any friends he might have here?"

"No."

"Hell, given the hot new gambling spots opening all over the whole U.S. of A. these days, he could have bid Vegas a fond farewell years ago."

"Anything is possible."

O'Rourke's ballpoint pen was drawing rings around the box that surrounded Cliff Effinger's name. "Parents sure liked 'f's,' didn't they? He have a nickname?"

Matt shrugged. "Not that I know of."

"You don't 'know of' much, buddy. So all I got is a guy past sixty, lifelong gambler, from Chicago."

"That's all I have."

Eightball shook his head, which didn't disturb his haircut, because what little hair he had left was white and close-cropped. He looked more like a frankly bald cue ball than the black number-eight billiard ball of his nickname.

He was a stringy little guy sparring with seventy-something whose face was sandblasted by time and—Matt knew—a lifetime in the desert. That meant he had been isolated from the Strip during his fugitive years, so he'd be starting from scratch. That was all right with Matt. He wanted somebody low-profile for this job, and you couldn't get anybody more low-profile than Eightball O'Rourke.

"One thing," Matt said.

Eightball raised whitened eyebrows as extravagantly bushy as his hair was scant. Mother Nature grew whimsical with old men.

"I don't want Temple Barr to know about this."

"Listen, my cases are confidential."

"Sure, but if you didn't know my terms, you might let something slip."

Eightball grinned. "That little gal is damn good about getting folks to let something they want kept private slip, isn't she?"

"Amen," said Matt.

"She reminds me of my granddaughter Jill. When that much will comes in a small package, it's the bottom line. You know about me and Jilly?" His nonchalant manner begged Matt to say no so that Eightball could fill him in.

"Some," Matt said.

"Well, do you know about me and the Glory Hole Gang and our cache of silver dollars?"

"Stolen silver dollars, weren't they?"

"Aw, we were young then, the boys and me. It was a lark. Spent our lives hiding in the desert when we didn't really have to. This house's the one my wife finally managed to buy for herself and our daughter."

He glanced around the plain room and up to its high, horizontal fifties windows with a nostalgia unrelated to its attractions, which were few.

"When the wife died, our daughter was already gone, so the house went to Jilly, me being out of circulation. Jill gave me the place after the silver dollar thing was all cleared up. She didn't need it, not when she was married to Johnny Diamond—you know, the soupy-song singer at the Crystal Phoenix, but he makes lots of money at it." Eightball shook his head. "I don't know why grown men nowadays have to go around looking like Samson. Anyway, all the other Glory Hole boys live out at our ghost town attraction on Highway Ninety-five, except me. So my place is old, and the neighborhood is just this side of a trash dump, but it's the only house my family ever had. I like living here. I like being in a city with lots of people. I like having a job after all those hard-scrabble years hiding in the desert. I even like finding people, Mr. Devine, but I kind of like to know why."

"Maybe I don't know," Matt said carefully. "Just see what you come up with, and we can go from there."

Eightball lifted the plain blue check on the desk in front of him. "It's your money."

"And . . ." Matt began.

Eightball screwed up his face as if he saw a spitball en route. This was it, his expression said, the hidden clause.

"I'm looking into something myself. Something . . . someone . . . even more confidential. Maybe you could advise me in a general way from time to time."

"Sure. Another missing person?"

"No, not missing, but maybe a part of his past is."

"There's books in the library, Mr. Devine. You know, *How to Hide Anything,* and *How to Find Out Anything About Anybody.*"

"No," Matt said, sitting up straighter. "I didn't know. What section?"

"Ask a librarian. I don't go by the self-help books. I write my own."

Matt nodded, but he planned to check the library. He had to start somewhere.

"This guy you're looking for." Eightball lived up to his unlucky name; he liked a hopeless case, for all of his grousing.

"Yes?"

"He's a mite younger than me, ten years or so. That could give me an edge in figuring out where he was and where he might be now. Vegas veterans have their patterns."

"That's what I figured." Matt stood and held out his hand.

Eightball O'Rourke wrung it until the skin burned. "Good luck at the library, sonny."

Matt didn't go to the library next. He went to the convent.

What a route. Jailhouse. Poorhouse. Motherhouse. What a cast of characters. Murderer. Gumshoe. Nun.

He'd had quite a day, Matt thought. A good thing his day job meant working nights.

He stood before the front door of the rambling Spanish-style house, a box of Ethel M candy held in the shade so it wouldn't melt.

Las Vegas was slouching toward the cool of autumn and winter, but the sun was still warm enough to melt caramel through a cardboard box.

"Yes?"

Matt unconsciously bent down to the wizened face peering around the door frame like an ancient child's. Sister Mary Monica was ninety and quite deaf.

"I'm here to see Sister Seraphina O'Donnell," he enunciated carefully into the beige plastic appliance in her visible ear.

Before the old nun could indicate whether she'd heard him, a voice bore down on her fast from behind.

"Sister," it rebuked fondly. "You shouldn't answer the door. It might be someone we don't want to—" The door whooshed wide, revealing Seraphina herself ready to glower at a possible gang-banger trying to extort protection money. "Oh, Matt!" Her about-face in tone from challenging to charming would have flattered him if he'd been in the mood. "Come in."

He stepped onto the quarry-tile entry hall floor, feeling the cool shade of the house settling on him like a cloak.

Sister Seraphina swiftly shut and locked the door behind him, a silent commentary on the safety of Our Lady of Guadalupe's venerable neighborhood in these days of youthful crime.

She shooed Sister Mary Monica back into the front parlor, where a television set blared out a soap opera, of all things. Ninety-year-old nuns were not what they had used to be.

Farther down the hall, the visitors' parlor was the same tidy retreat of pale stucco walls, burnt-umber tile floor and Hispanic-black wooden furniture embellished with formal carving.

Once ushered within, Matt noticed one of the convent cats, Peter or Paul, ensconced in a slice of sunlight on the windowsill.

"Peter," Sister Seraphina said behind him, her voice content, all the industrious bustle gone. "He's done beautifully. Doesn't even walk with a limp. Perhaps cats have nine lives, after all."

"I doubt that's sound theology, Sister," he returned, surprised to hear the tease in his voice, to realize how quickly he fell into old ways.

"Peter's theology consists of a firm belief in the power of the multiplied loaves and fishes, with an emphasis on the fishes." She sat on one over-formal chair and gestured him to another.

Today the heavy wooden cross that was her daily decoration had been complimented by a pair of wooden button earrings. It still disconcerted him to see nuns in permanent waves and costume jewelry, with a touch of lip gloss or blush. He knew he was reacting in a more old-fashioned mode than his relatively young age required, but archaic symbols die hard and nuns were the everyday anchor of the Catholic faith.

Matt remembered the oblong box wrapped in white paper and handed it to Seraphina like an apple to a favorite teacher. She had been that, as well as a sometimes feared one.

"Oh, Matthias, you shouldn't have, but how nice. My, Ethel M. Sister St. Rose of Lima's favorite. You always were the most thoughtful young man. . . ." She pulled off the white paper and deposited it on a tabletop, then lofted the box cover with theatrical relish. "Lovely. Would you—? Well, I'll share them later with everyone."

Their mutual smiles grew uneasy. The years and their present roles rose like a flood tide between them, a moat no number of chocolates could bridge.

"How is everything here now?" he asked.

"Back to normal. The cat's recovery is splendid, as you can see. Sister Mary Monica has forgotten all about the obscene phone caller—that's a beatitude for the aged: blessed are the forgetful. Rose and I no longer worry about Father Hernandez. He's been rock-steady since Peter Burns was unveiled as the worm eating away at the heart of our parish."

"No drinking," Matt said, hating to be explicit.

"I realize that you're worried, Matt. I realize that you felt a tremendous responsibility about knowing that Father was . . . not himself, but no, Matt, he touches nothing but sacramental wine these days. Amazing. I've never known someone to recover so swiftly from that kind of addiction."

"It was fairly recent."

Her permed white head shook briskly. "Still, once the bottle sings its siren song . . . look at Sister Rose and the bishop's tea! I didn't dream what we were drinking until afterwards."

"We'd all had a shock. Even Lieutenant Molina didn't spill the beans."

"Yes, most unlike her."

"And Sister Rose meant well. She must have heard of restorative brandy."

"But in tea! She hadn't heard enough about it. Ah, Matt, there'll never be another generation of nuns like us, true innocents."

He kept silent, thinking that there might never be another generation of nuns, period.

They were a dying breed, as priests were a wounded breed nowadays. His mind flashed back to the seminary. He saw the eager, scrubbed young women who had made up ten percent of the student body even in his day. They ached to become priests because the role was forbidden them.

Now that the priesthood itself was tainted, perhaps these earnest, feminist, budding theologians, could redeem it—if the church could overcome centuries of male centrism to admit women as fully functioning clergy. The women's motives were purer, of course, because they were would-be pioneers; that didn't mean they wouldn't fall into the same old traps. He wondered if anyone had the amazing grace it took to embrace a religious vocation anymore.

"Matt? You're not still worrying about Father Hernandez? He's right as rain, I promise."

Only it doesn't rain much in Las Vegas, Sister, Matt thought wryly. *And you don't know the whole story behind the good Father's recent bout with the bottle.*

So here he was, Matt Devine, needing to know something much more sensitive from Sister Seraphina O'Donnell than Father Hernandez's relationship with alcohol, and needing to disguise his purpose.

He had become like Molina, he realized, prying information from an unsuspecting witness. An ex-priest was used to keeping confidences, not extracting them. But Temple could do it, Eightball O'Rourke was right about that. And so could Matt, especially here and now, because Sister Seraphina trusted him. She thought they spoke the same language, she assumed they had the same objectives.

And they did. Salvation. Their own souls. And the salvation of other souls.

"You know something about alcoholism, Sister."

"Are you surprised, Matthias? After all those years of teaching? Oh, we nuns were supposed to be utter innocents, but we saw more than everyone thought. We knew why certain fathers never came to parent-teacher meetings, why some mothers wore this sad, cringing, broken look, and their kids too." She shook her head, her mouth curled as if tasting spoiled milk. "Especially their kids."

Matt digested this confession. "Sure, the kids themselves knew what went on at home, but the rest of us kids never thought about those things either," he said carefully. "We would just get quiet when certain parents were mentioned, as if they were unspoken bogeymen, but we never wondered why. 'Mr. Johnson' was just 'like that.' Maybe mean, or maybe erratic and surely to be gingerly avoided. We never thought in terms of alcoholism, or abuse. We just thought that was the way life was. It was normal.''

"That's the trouble!" The flat of Seraphina's hand slapped her chair's ornate wooden arm. "There's nothing normal about alcoholism and abuse, no matter how common it might be, or might have become. Kids accept the unacceptable because they know nothing different. All those children. All those years. If we—we all ... I!—had been better informed, had been more honest with others and ourselves, had been educated in the terrible cost of all addictions, we could have intervened.''

Matt knew real regret when he heard it. He had heard enough formal confessions, despite the sacrament's fading practice. The large, welcome space had suddenly shrunk to the claustrophobic dimensions of an old-fashioned confessional. The room seemed to darken with deep self-examination. Seraphina's worry perfumed the air like a censer dispensing the odor of penance. She blamed herself for something, perhaps for years of somethings. Now, she could do nothing about it but rue the golden old days.

He felt needlessly cruel. He didn't want to stir up the demons of ancient guilts; he knew their many guises too well in his own sleepless nights. "Holy innocents." That was what he and Seraphina had been encouraged to be, each in his or her own way, both in their own generations. Holy innocents had a way of discovering years later that they had been neither.

"They say the family's disintegrating now," she was saying. "Nonsense. These hidden flaws were always there. We just denied and ignored them.''

"Like the problems of priests," he put in.

Her voice grew sharp, even fearful. "What problems did you have with the priesthood, Matthias?"

"None," he said with a relieved laugh. "I had problems with myself, with my reasons for hiding within the priesthood. I admit that I was literally swaddled in that 'holy innocence' you mentioned. I craved it, I sometimes think. I was even worse off than you; I never saw the seeds of trouble sown in the seminary. The church was so rapt with the ideal of the priesthood that no one thought to wonder that some young men who would choose a sexless life in the modern secular age might have a natural barrier to an ordinary, lay life of marriage and children."

"I've never talked with a former priest. That shows you how sheltered I am, so don't apologize, Matt. And don't blame me for being . . . curious. What was so . . . rotten about the church's pattern of screening for the priesthood that all these awful cases are hitting the newspapers now?"

"Unholy innocence. In seminary, the emphasis was on suppressing the sex urge, on desexualizing, and even demonizing women. No one was sophisticated—or honest—enough to admit the existence of other sexual preferences, other ways of being sexual. In a way, pederast priests, or gay priests who were not celibate, could almost convince themselves that they were worthier than heterosexual priests who were not celibate."

"Didn't you wonder about gay seminarians, at least?"

"No. We were all so young, so feverishly dedicated to the vision of a religious vocation, so determinedly neuter. I've read the memoirs of other ex-priests. Some express a fear of being gay, but I never even noticed that. We may have made crude celibacy jokes among each other, but we only discussed the real nitty-gritty of our sexuality with our spiritual director. What about nuns?"

Sister Seraphina reared back at the very thought. "No one has ever asked me that. We *are* almost all elderly now, I fear, and the aged achieve a neuter state so naturally, at least we nuns did. And women molest children far less than men, perhaps only because we are reared to be more law-abiding than from any moral superiority. I do think the role of motherhood is more intense and therefore less likely to be abused in such perverse ways. But what do I know about that? Or you? Perhaps I fool myself with the veil of innocence again. Still, I think I would know. Nuns live communally; we may be more docile by upbringing. We have not the priest's temptation to move alone through the church, to make solitary decisions."

"Oh, pastors may look like they lord it over their flock, but, believe me, priests are not the free agents you suspect they are. Nor bishops. Not even the Pope."

"Have you lost your faith, Matt?"

The question was timidly put, coming from Sister Superfine, but it was the most serious issue yet. He paused before answering.

"I don't think so. I recognize that I had a true religious vocation.

I understand that finding it once was my salvation. I will never lose respect for the many dedicated religious I knew, no matter what the headlines read. I will never judge a brother, or a sister." He could feel his lips trying to smile. "I am impatient with bureaucracy, with hypocrisy, with lack of tolerance, and sometimes the aisles of Mother Church seem jam-packed with all three. I recognize all the modern conflicts: the church is patriarchal; its institutionalized sexphobia has caused endless crisis in the lives of laity and celibate clergy. I'm not decided on every shade of these issues. My conscience may ultimately decree a position that puts me outside the doors if those inside them can't accept what I must be. I don't know yet."

Seraphina shuddered. "Such . . . questions you raise. I'm glad I'm retired, waiting as usefully as I can until I'm called to the place where there are only answers. I still don't understand why you left."

"To do that, you'd have to understand why I entered the priesthood."

"And—?" Her ungoverned eyebrows lifted quizzically, like an ancient, anxious terrier's.

Matt had never seen Sister Seraphina at such a genuine loss. It made her look very old.

He answered in a rush, like a seven-year-old kid making his first confession. He was surprised by how practiced it all sounded.

"I entered the priesthood to become perfect as my heavenly Father is perfect. I entered the priesthood to become the perfect Father. I entered to avoid sex and marriage and children because I was terrified of all three. Don't worry, I have never broken a priestly vow, but not because of my faith or strength. How could I be tempted by what terrified me? I am named for the apostle who replaced Judas after the betrayal and death of Christ, yet I found myself finally walking away from the shoes of the fisherman at the age of His death—thirty-three."

"But why, Matt? You were a model student, and devout even as a boy, the perfect altar boy, in fact. Was it perfection . . . was it—?" Sudden suspicion enlarged the pupils of her eyes to matte black. Her voice became a whisper. "Matt, as an altar boy, you weren't . . . abused. By Father—?"

He shook his head. "That would have been almost easier to overcome."

"Easier. Dear Lord, Matt, what? My ignorance paralyzes me. I was your teacher. I was so proud when I learned you'd entered the priesthood, and now you tell me that decision was an escape that had begun to form when I knew you as a little boy. What had I failed to see?"

"Don't blame yourself. Catholics always blame themselves too much. I told you that none of us even saw our own situations then. Remember Mary Lou Zyskowski?"

"Oh, that impossible red-headed girl! Always in trouble and so sullen and stubborn about learning."

"I ran into her again—at a therapy group. She was sexually abused by her older male cousins all through grade school."

Sister Seraphina was too numb to wince. She just shook her head.

"None of us noticed, student or teacher," Matt assured her. "She didn't even understand then what was wrong herself."

"We never dreamed families could go so wrong back then. And the Family, the Father, was sacred. You didn't . . . meddle."

"Too many people still feel that way. She remembers you kindly, by the way."

"Me? How did I come up in a therapy session?"

"You nagged her into going to the convent for summer reading lessons after sixth grade, remember? She screamed and kicked all the way, but says now that if she hadn't gotten good enough at reading to survive in high school, she would have never made it."

"Well, we tried. Sometimes we gave extra attention to kids from large families who were ignored, or railed at. And I suppose even we suspected some unbearably ugly truth beneath the facade. Some children were accident prone, always bruised, always bruising themselves. One did wonder and try to be as kind as possible."

"What about the kids who never showed anything," Matt went on, "whose parents were too cagey to paste them in the mouths? The kids who feel impelled to protect their parents from the physical evidence that these mothers and fathers don't know how to love? Then, when the kids finally recognize and admit the abuse, they are disbelieved. They have become their own worst witnesses."

"Kids can live amazingly bitter lives and say nothing, can seem to be paragons of behavior," Seraphina said, nodding her head.

"Who would think that Mary Lou Zyskowski appreciated those lessons she came to with dragging feet and sour temper? And the child can go in an opposite direction, pretend to a perfect life. In fact, one would almost think—"

She looked at Matt, really looked at him.

He had come here to learn something from Sister Seraphina that she didn't know. Instead, she had discovered something she had always known, and never acknowledged. Her hands covered her mouth even as she spoke, as if hoping to deny the words, the understanding, so long in coming.

"Oh, dear God—now I see what I never could bear to face then. Dear God."

No doubt about it, Matt thought with the kind of wry relief honesty between friends always brings. He had the makings of a good priest, but a lousy detective.

Chapter 7

Koi Sera, Sera

There are those who claim that they never forget a face.

In my business, faces come and go. I never forget a place.

So I am strolling again through the ersatz tropical gardens of the Crystal Phoenix Hotel, surrounded by such an aura of nostalgia that you could bottle it and sell it to passenger pigeons. (If there were still any passenger pigeons around; I understand that these unusually useful birds are now extinct. I—I am happy to say—had nothing to do with it, and the carp population seems firmly prolific.)

Ah, carp. It is a homely little word of one syllable, but sweet to me. Whether one says "carp" or uses the fancy Oriental term of "koi," they are both goldfish to my mind, and splendid eating.

I circle the pond where I was once wont to wander and wonder, as lonely as a clod. My Walden. My wellspring. My floating buffet.

No one can accuse me of picking on the helpless. Some of these colorful fish are the size of pit-bull pups. When they are nudging fins at the waterline while jousting for gobbets of Tender Vittle-like treats you can see how muscular these fish are.

For Midnight Louie to land such a beauty is similar to a millionaire snagging a blue marlin off Florida. And I always *eat* my tasty prey, rather than tastelessly exhibiting it on my walls. I picture Miss Temple Barr's reaction were I to return home with a glittering trophy skin of my fishing prowess. She would shudder at the least, and accuse me of depraved appetites, but then, it is not the first time that I have stood so charged and it will not be the last, if I have anything to say about it. Depraved appetites are the last to go, being the most fun.

A soft desert breeze riffles the big, shiny leaves on the calla lilies that surround the pond. I am reminded of harem fans swishing gently to and fro, not that I have ever been in a harem, but a dude can have aspirations.

At my feet, a large blue-and-white carp executes a swishy turn and flays my toes with a lash of water drops. Uppity fish, these imperial koi.

I settle quietly under the shade of calla lily leaves. Let them cavort like the orca act at Marine World. I have heard the merfish singing, and it is for my supper, not their own.

But supper is a long way off and I can afford to wait. I drowse to the accompaniment of a circling bomber-bee high above. Even the shrieks of gamboling children in the distant pool do not disturb my contemplative frame of mind. My nose imbibes the odor of recently sprinkled dirt and the slight fishy bouquet of the carp next door.

Then a shadow crosses my face. My eyes flash open as round and wide as a green traffic light. Go!

The shadow is still there, moving languidly between me and my carp pond. All serenity shatters as I draw my lounging form into an irritated huddle that any sensible being would know better than to irritate.

But the interloper is no sensible being. It is the girl upstairs known as Caviar.

"What are you doing here?" I hiss.

"The same thing that you are," she answers calmly, brazen enough to come nose-sniffing close. "Enjoying the view." She arches her neat little head to gaze into the trembling waters.

"Overripe," she sniffs. "These fish are all flash and no flavor. The best carp should be no longer than a bobcat tail."

"Since when are you the expert?"

She shrugs, a gesture that emphasizes her well-honed shoulder blades. This kid could use a decent meal, but if she is too hoity-toity for well-fed fish, it is her problem.

"What are you doing here?" I ask, showing my teeth.

"I could ask you the same thing. As it happens, I heard that my so-called father used to hang around this place."

I gulp. "Why are you looking for him?"

"Oh . . ." She stretches lazily, arching her lithe belly to the flagstones and hoisting her pert hindquarters in the air.

This display would be a lot more enticing did I not immediately notice a certain absence of scent in the petite Caviar. You might say that she has an "altered" air about her. Since we last met, she has been transported to the House of Dr. Death for a neutering operation.

I sigh in tribute to things not to be. I tell you, in this day and age it is getting downright difficult to encounter members of the opposite sex who have retained any gender at all. I am all for preventing unwanted kits, but it does look like the simple act of reproduction is getting a lot more difficult to indulge nowadays.

"He looks a lot like you."

Her considering tone flashes past me like the performing cleaver of a Japanese chef and my blood runs as cold as it can when the temperature is eighty degrees in the shade.

"So do a lot of dudes," I growl.

She blinks bored carp-gold eyes. "Oh, do not worry, Gramps. You are too old and out-of-shape to be my rotten, kit-deserting father. My mother was still sweet on the bounder and described him to all us kits *ad nauseam:* black coat shiny as tar on a long, muscular frame; white whiskers and eyebrows, not from age but birth; grass-green eyes; sharp, clean white teeth. A Hunk of the Month, apparently. I am sure that this smooth operator did not have to descend to removing aged fish too slow to flash a fin from hotel ponds."

I do not know whether to be relieved at her error, or furious at her reasoning. Going by Caviar's youth, my assignation with her mother had transpired only a year ago. A dude does not deteriorate to such an extent in a mere year. Obviously, Caviar's opinion of yours truly differs greatly from that of her older, wiser mother.

"Where is your mother these days?" I inquire. Perhaps I should look the old girl up.

Caviar snicks out her shivs and dabbles them in the fish-filled water. I swear I can see her smile as they flounder away, slapping fins and making waves.

"I heard she got picked up by the animal control patrol, so she is either dead, or domesticated."

I shake my head. Either fate is ugly. If she is domesticated, she is also "fixed." What do they mean about practicing "safe sex" (not that I need any practice whatsoever in this department) when "no sex" is rapidly becoming the order of the day for dudes of my disposition? I hate to contemplate how long it has been since I have had an assignation of an amorous nature. In fact, I even remember my last partner, but that is because this encounter was more than mere kiss-and-skedaddle. A mental image of the Divine Yvette pussyfoots through my memory. Now there is a lady as loving as she is lovely. Next to her, Caviar is . . . dog meat. Not that I would suffer one of my next-of-kins to meet such a fate. Still, the girl needs to learn to respect her elders.

"I will find him," she says, the gold coinage of her eyes narrowing to edgewise slits of metallic hardness.

"I do not doubt it," I say hastily, since she already has. "What will you do then?"

"I will tell him what I think of him."

"That sounds most therapeutic, according to what I hear on my favorite daytime television shows, Phil and Oprah and Sally Jesse. Geraldo was a great dude, but they banished him to the evening hours because of adult subject matter, when Miss Temple is watching the TV, so I never see him anymore. Miss Temple Barr has many good points, but she is utterly uninterested in educational TV. She will not even tune in 'Inside Edition' unless I get my mitts on the remote. Then she thinks my preferences are 'cute' and changes the channel on me."

"I am not interested in your relationship with your keeper," Caviar snaps.

(I mean it; she really snaps, flashing her choppers at a carp so bold to stick its kisser out of the water looking for food. This Caviar has possibilities, if she would forget her obsession with finding her birth father. I have no such hangup.)

"Miss Temple Barr is not my keeper, but my roommate," I correct her calmly. Age has its advantages. "And what of your new situation with Mr. Matt Devine?"

"Oh, he is quite undemanding, except for talking to me now and then and the occasional condescending head pat. At least I have managed to arrange for the same bathroom-window privileges that you enjoy."

I nod. Caviar is a street-kit, like her old man, may she never discover his identity. She can probably worm her way out of any hole as wide as her cheekbones and worm her way into any human heart around, if it takes her fancy. Mr. Matt Devine, when it comes to females of any stripe whatsoever, and even of solid color, does not stand a chance.

"So what are you doing here?" she asks me.

"Taking the sun," I say. "Miss Temple Barr is conferring with the hotel owners inside. She is up for a big job here."

"At least she cracked me out of that crummy cage," Caviar says. "It is too bad you were already in residence. I am sure that I could wind your roommate around my whiskers."

"Perhaps. But everyone tends to underestimate Miss Temple Barr, from Lieutenant Molina to one or two murderers now incarcerated."

I fan the fingernails on my right mitt to admire the faint crimson glint of blood through their pearly length. I cannot understand why Miss Temple Barr paints her personal shivs with opaque lacquers that hide the quick. And lately she has been using an anemic rosy-pink tint that does nothing for me, unlike the blood-red that so becomes her and underlines her bright red coat, scant as it is.

Caviar yawns. "Well, if you hear anything of a good-looking black dude that has been seen hereabouts in the last year, let me know. I will be on my way. I have work to do."

The last jibe is not lost on me and I watch her turn tail and undulate away. What a waste! Not only the veterinary procedure, but a close relative to boot!

Neither is it lost upon me that little Miss Caviar thinks I am not good-looking enough to be her father. Kits these days! They have a lot to learn. I just hope that one of the things she learns in her explorations is not our kinship.

As for me, my father never hung around to see me get my first nose-scratch, but I bear him no disdain. Dudes of our ilk do not take to domestic responsibilities. We are better off leaving the scene of the crime before we are forced to do the time in the nursery.

So I remain in my special spot, my enjoyment of thrashing carp strangely muted after my encounter with my own flesh-and-blood. Despite my impressive size, I am not easily noticed when I sit still, and especially when I concentrate on blending with my background.

From my vantage point, I watch Chef Song, meat cleaver in hand and apron dotted with substances of a ruddy nature that encourage much speculation on my part, make his daily afternoon head count of the carp. This ritual owes itself to my frequent presence, I am proud to say. I am not so proud to say that today he gives a steely-eyed nod of satisfaction and vanishes back into the hotel.

Caviar's presence and disturbing mission has done the unthinkable: affected my appetite.

I remain indisposed, sourly watching carp cavort unchallenged, until the shadows begin to fall and I should think of heading home. Miss Temple may be worried, and I do not like to unsettle a meal ticket.

It is then that I notice two tall dudes of a nefarious nature tiptoeing through the calla lilies.

"Maybe we should behead all the carp," one suggests.

I stiffen, taking instant umbrage. I need no assistance in my hunting technique.

"That would unhinge the lady manager, I bet," the other says.

"Not to mention the early-morning guests coming out to wet their tootsies in the pool tomorrow. Hey, we could put the bodies in the whirlpool!"

"Dead fish is dead fish," the other sneers. "We do not need to mess with such dirty work yet. We are professionals. Let us case the rest of the joint and come up with something real ugly."

"If anybody can, you can, Vito."

From my unseen post, I agree. Vito's mother came up with something really ugly a long time ago.

I want to growl to myself, but know better than to tip these bozos off to my presence.

It never fails. Apparently Miss Temple Barr has once again placed herself dead center in a scene of forthcoming skullduggery. Luckily, Midnight Louie has come home to the Crystal Phoenix just in time to save the day. Again.

It is a pity that Miss Caviar is so oblivious to my possibilities, but then so are these thugs. I will just have to earn my kit's respect by showing her what a crimefighting kingpin her old man is.

Chapter 8

Phoning Home Phony

Matt stared at his bedroom phone, the cheapest model Centel offered. The huge push-buttons and numbers made it an almost perversely ugly object. Like the cheapest casket in a funeral home showroom, this phone was designed to repel rather than attract. It was made to be rejected, to force the customer to up the ante. Everything in Las Vegas was intended to sever the sucker from his money.

The homely phone suited him. Matt's background had made him invulnerable to consumerism. So far. That background also made him invulnerable to much that was taken for granted in late-twentieth-century lifestyles.

No matter their looks or lack of them, phones were his friends . . . almost an extension of his senses now, an artificial limb he was used to donning. No headphones here at home, though, just the naked ear against the cold, bare receiver, that beige plastic fist that reminded him of Sister Mary Monica's hearing aids.

No wonder his palms sweated. He wasn't waiting for a call to come in now, he was waiting to make one. He was working up the nerve to lie, not easy for one of his inclination and training.

Worse, he was going to have to call the diocesan office to imple-ment his lie. Lies. One lie always begat another, like Biblical pa-triarchs founding lines of limitless offspring.

Matt straightened the fresh stenographer's notebook on his tiny nightstand. He appreciated the blank page, its paper tinted green to ease eye strain, its thin blue lines designed to keep his jottings on the straight and narrow, unlike his intent.

He picked up the felt-tip pen, chosen because it would flow more smoothly over the paper than a ballpoint. He would have to pinch the cumbersome receiver between head and shoulder while he took notes and steadied the notebook with his left hand. Maybe he should get a home headset. Yes, Devine, you do plan to lie on that scale, don't you? Again and again.

Matt leaned over to stare at the massive Las Vegas phone book on the bare floor, splayed open to the white pages. He squinted and dialed simultaneously, his eyes darting back and forth from the phone book's minuscule numbers to the reassuringly large buttons.

"Diocese of Reno-Las Vegas," a crisp female voice announced.

"Hello," Matt said, sounding remarkably calm. The black pen lay diagonally across the notebook, like a miniature fencing foil waiting to be picked up for a practice session. Matt's right hand curled into the rough fabric of his pants leg. "I wonder if you can direct me to the proper person. I'm, uh, a parishioner at Our Lady of Guadalupe—"

"Oh, yes." The voice had softened, like hot apple crisp, now that he had identified himself as one of the faithful.

"We're getting together to honor Father Hernandez—" Matt's hesitancy at the falsehood sounded like mere shyness in the face of officialdom.

"I see. On the successful conclusion of the recent fund drive, you mean? How nice."

"Right." How nice. How nice and easy it was to deceive, how eager people were to think the best. "I'm in charge of the entertain-ment. We're doing a 'This Is Your Life' program to surprise Father Her—"

"What a wonderful idea! How can I help?"

"We want to produce some surprise guests he hasn't seen in years, from his previous parishes."

"Oh, he will love it! And you need to know his previous assignments? How far back do you want to go?"

"To the seminary, I guess. Or . . . it'd be great to have someone from grade school too. His whole life."

A pause. Nothing holds its breath better than a dead phone line when you know somebody is on it. Had he gone too far? Should he backtrack and say that just Father Hernandez's former parishes would do?

"That might require some checking," the voice said, slow enough to sound doubtful.

"We'd really appreciate anything you can do," Matt said in a rush he instantly regretted.

"Oh, I can get all the information, but can you afford to import guests from too far away? I don't know Father Hernandez's record offhand, but I think the bulk of his service may have been way across the country."

So much the more suspicious, Matt thought. "Some of us have set up a special fund to fly in the special p-people from his past," he said with a slight stammer of enthusiasm, or anxiety. "We're going all out on this." Was he ever!

"How sweet. Sure, I can look that up. Or even mail a copy of his postings to you—"

"No! No mail. We don't want to alert Father Hernandez to the surprise. It's all hush-hush."

"Then I'll call you back when I look up the record, Mr. . . . ?"

"Peters," Matt said with a swift ironic twist of his mouth.

Why hadn't he invented a more believable phony name before dialing? Next time. He recognized the fandango his subconscious was performing: Peters as in Peter Burns, the parish betrayer, Peters as in Simon Peter, the first apostle and the first to deny Christ in the Garden of Gethsemane. Peter as in turncoat. Turncollar.

"No, don't call here. I'm at the office," he added in a softer, apologetic tone. "I'm not supposed to make personal calls. But I could call you back."

"Certainly. Give me fifteen minutes."

"And I should ask for . . . ?"

"Oh, I always answer the phone here, Mr. Peters. Madeleine McCafferty."

"Thanks, Miss McCafferty." She did not demur at the form of address, so he had hit it right on the head: a maiden lady dedicated to the church. "And I'd, ah, appreciate it if you didn't mention this to anyone. You know how word leaks back to the parish level."

"Of course I do, and of course I'll keep . . . mum. I wouldn't want to do anything to ruin Father Hernandez's day of glory. He is such a dear man."

Matt let the phrase replay in his mind as he hung up: "such a dear man." Not the way he would describe the touchy and proud pastor of Our Lady of Guadalupe, but devout Catholics tended to crown their clergy with premature halos. No wonder they so seldom noticed any tarnish.

Romancing the Drone

Phones didn't ring anymore. They yodeled.

Temple hated waking up to that piercing mechanical warble. She glanced at her beside clock—close enough, with red LED numbers big enough, to read without glasses.

Eight-thirty on a Saturday morning? What did the caller think? That she had no social life, no big Friday night out? As it happened, that assumption was humiliatingly correct, but unknown callers didn't have to rub it in.

Probably a wrong number anyway.

Should she bother stretching for the phone when all she was likely to get was the droning snub of a dial tone?

But those who live by the phone must always answer the phone. She was sure that motto was written in some profound but trendy tome, like the collected works of Kahlil Gibran.

Temple reached for the red plastic high-heeled shoe at her bedside, clamped the heel to her ear and chirped "Hello?" into its sleek toe. Too bad Agent 99 couldn't have used this up-to-date model on the old "Get Smart" spy shoe. Er, show.

"Temple?"

The basso male voice made the phone line sound defective. Who did she know with a bedroom voice besides Max Kinsella? The hair on Temple's forearms lifted with an unseasonable—and worse, unreasonable—chill as she sat up in bed.

"Yes?"

"I need your help."

"Who is this?" She hated to ask in case she got a shocking answer.

Both hands clutched the slippery shoe-phone now and her sweaty palms were developing static cling. Just like Max to show up in her life again as a disembodied voice on the phone. At least that would prove he was alive. Or . . . would it?

"Don't you know?" the man asked.

That was the problem, she didn't know and being reminded of this irritated her.

"Don't get coy, or I hang up," Temple threatened. "I've had enough of anonymous phone callers lately."

"Really?"

The deep voice sounded interested, even titillated. By now Temple knew it wasn't Max. He was never coy. Instead of being disappointed, or relieved, she was angry.

"I mean it about hanging up—"

"No, wait! God, T.B., I need a favor."

Oh. Crawford Buchanan and his matinee-idol basso. She should have known. Why on earth was he calling *her*?

"Try going to a party, C.B., if one will have you. Sometimes they dispense favors."

"Just hear me out. I'm in a pickle."

"You are in a crock, Crawford, as usual."

"I need you to write some stuff for the Gridiron."

"The Gridiron? I thought *you* were the whole show this year."

"The deadline's in two days, and I can't come up with enough skits. You churn out this lightweight fluff like it was pulling cotton candy."

"You were planning on mounting something heavy like Eugene O'Neill for the Gridiron?" she suggested tartly.

"You know what I mean. I need a cute, satirical touch."

"By when?"

"Rehearsals start Monday night."

"Galloping Gridiron, Buchanan, that's damn short notice. If you hadn't have tried to hog the whole thing, you wouldn't be in a pickle in addition to your regular crock. I should let you stew in your own vinegar."

"I know, I know! I thought I could do it and then . . . my heart's been acting up."

"Putting on shows is a high-pressure gig. You should know that too."

"At least I know who to call when I'm in a jam," he put in with sly flattery and his deepest baritone.

"Who else have you put the squeeze on at the crack of dawn on Saturday morning?"

"No one," he admitted sheepishly. "Just you. I need a big closing number for the whole cast. Something that says it all for Las Vegas this year. Danny Dove, the so-called director, says the show is cooked if we don't get the right closer."

How sweet it is, Temple thought, idly uncoiling her long red telephone cord with her long, freshly lacquered crimson fingernails. Should she leave Crawford twisting slowly in the wind—she wound a length of cord around her forefinger, tight—or bail the dastard out?

"All right, but it's only for the good of the Gridiron. I could not care less if they opened and closed the show with a literal roast of you. I'll work up something this weekend and fax it to you Monday."

"No, no. You need to come down to my office at the *Scoop* to write it so we can . . . consult, if necessary. No one's in today, so there are plenty of available computers. I'll be here all day, and tomorrow too."

"You really think that I have nothing better to do than hang out with you all weekend?"

"We really need that number," he said.

"All right," she grumbled, hanging up without saying "goodbye." Unfortunately, she would be saying "hello" to Crawford all too soon.

The *Las Vegas Scoop* office was about as reassuring as a floating crap game site.

Temple had driven past it often enough, never failing to wrinkle her nose when she thought of Crawford Buchanan toiling here night after night like some pale-bellied black spider with soft furry legs—no, that comparison was unfair to spiders.

Temple considered herself open-minded, but she hated his daily "Buchanan's Broadside" column, and its leering tours of the lowest nightlife in Vegas. She hated the *Las Vegas Scoop*, a finger-smudging tabloid, dirty in more ways than one with its tawdry, full-page photos of "escort" boys and girls, including private dancers of every sexual persuasion from vichyssoise to Brazil nuts.

Temple parked her freshly washed Storm in front of a sidewalk littered with dead sporting events stubs and the aforesaid escorts' faces wearing the imprint of size twelve shoes. Standing before the *Las Vegas Scoop*'s narrow, almost clandestine doorway, she hated to touch the scratched doorknob. The place reminded her of a porno movie theater; you always wondered who had been here, fingering what with what.

"I must be insane," she muttered.

But she did write a heck of a production number, and how nice to have Crawford come crawling to her for rescue, not that crawling was such an alien occupation for him!

The grimy front door was locked. Oh, great.

Temple jammed on her red-framed sunglasses again and glanced back at her car. She hated working away from her home office anyway, although she prided herself on versatility. Mostly, she hated collaborating. She who writes best, writes alone. Having Crawford close enough to collaborate with was not a happy thought.

The door opened and there he was, not wearing the usual pale, prissily tailored suit, which gave the Fontana brothers' signature look a bad name.

Crawford Buchanan wearing a pineapple-yellow knit shirt and—ugh!—white Bermuda shorts was a sight to make even sunglass-shaded eyes sore. Apparently equating him with a furry-legged spider had been eerily on target, Temple observed with a quick, distasteful downward glance.

"You look . . . perky today, T.B.," was Buchanan's smarmy opener.

"Show me to the computers," Temple growled, brushing past

him without brushing anything else obnoxious, such as a finger-print-smudged doorjamb. One never knew when the police might require physical evidence.

The place was deserted, as advertised. For a moment Temple wondered if Crawford was going to try anything funny, anything funny being an unwanted pass, either verbal or physical. He fancied himself a ladies' man, and no number of acid put-downs could disabuse his bottomless ego of the notion.

"We can work in my office," he said, turning to wend through a room crowded with desks, computer terminals, dismembered *Las Vegas Scoops*, overflowing aluminum ashtrays, and empty styrofoam coffee cups that looked as if they had all suffered the runs. The only thing missing was a disheveled dead body.

Temple inhaled stale cigarette smoke—and the super-sweet reek of more than one cheap cigar—deeply regretting the moment she had answered her kicky red phone to begin this descent into journalistic hell.

"You have an office?" she asked hopefully. Crawford himself was at least clean to the point of fussiness. It had to be better there.

"Sure," his deep, disc-jockey voice said cockily. "I'm a key columnist for the *Scoop*."

The office even had a door on it, apparently another perk for a *Scoop* employee.

Temple edged inside, making sure her swollen tote bag never brushed the door frame. The furnishings were old, but dusted. Everything was organized, down to the two computers sitting back to back on the desk.

Temple raised a fire-engine-red eyebrow.

Crawford's shrug only demonstrated how much nature had shorted him on shoulders. "I moved another computer in here so we could consult. And I figured you could do without inhaling the cigarette halitosis of the city room."

"Thank you," Temple said, eyeing a neat pile of bond paper. "Are those the scripts for the show?"

Crawford nodded.

"Are they any good?"

"I wrote them all," he answered with irritation.

"That's why I asked."

Temple swung her tote bag onto a vacant folding chair. Let

Buchanan try anything and he'd learn what self-defense tactics Matt Devine had taught her in the past few weeks. Plus, she was in group therapy. She was no pushover, despite looking no larger than a Munchkin.

"I don't know why I have to work here," she complained, pushing the power-on button and watching the computer screen perform its usual opening routine, while she fretted about the forthcoming task.

Come up with an instant closing number for the Gridiron . . . what topics were worth shish-kebabbing this year in particular? Las Vegas's usual hyperactive civic bloat offered a surfeit of suitably large targets.

"Just work away and don't mind me," Crawford suggested with a simper from his perch on the desk edge. "Nice shoes, T.B."

Temple glanced up. He was eyeing her legs, not her shoes. Make that drooling. Surely her conservative beige Van Elis, the businesswoman's basic dress heel, wouldn't merit much notice. Crawford begged to differ.

"I do like those hooker shoes."

"These are not hooker shoes! Hooker shoes have heels four inches tall and are trashy. And cheap. These designer pumps will pump three inches of iron spike into your shin if you don't sit down and stick to business, whatever it is the sole author of the Gridiron does when he's short of scripts and begs for help."

He followed her suggestion with irritating slowness. "Don't mind me. I'm here to answer any questions, that's all. Pretend I'm a piece of furniture."

Temple stared at the cursor and typed "wp" for WordPerfect. The familiar program flashed up in amber characters. Imagining what piece of furniture Crawford Buchanan could be was distracting, but she settled on Victorian model of water closet named after its inventor, a certain infamous Mr. Crapper, and smiled.

For a while she was only aware of the sharp clack of her long fingernails on plastic and the speedy chuckle of the computer keyboard under her fingertips. And the occasional turn of a tabloid page beyond the computer screen.

By the time Temple had a screenful of idea fragments to consider, half an hour had passed surprisingly painlessly. Why was Crawford being so good? She eyed him over the computer screen. Of course he wasn't doing anything, except skimming the rag he worked for and watching her work; it was probably all he did all day anyway.

"How about," she asked at last, "a production number on all the big new hotels and theme parks."

"We did skits on those projects as they came up in past years."

"Yeah, but this would be the Mother of all Modern Redevelopment skits: a Theme Park from Hell bigger than anything that has hit the Strip yet."

"It's hard to top reality in Las Vegas, T.B."

"That's why you brought me in on this, C.B."

"Try whatever you think. I'm final arbiter, though."

"Oh, great. You beg me to contribute something, then you're going to play judge and jury, plus impresario?"

"That's the show chairman's job. Life is full of uncertainty. I'm sure you'll rise to the occasion."

He leaned around her computer to leer in the direction of her legs again.

"You are disgusting, or hasn't anyone told you?"

Crawford smiled. "They tell me all the time, but flattery doesn't cut any ice with me."

"Nor does good taste," Temple said with a snarl, returning to the job that brought her here: creating a clever, fresh, workable script out of thin air while being ogled by the city's worst black sheep in Tom Wolfe clothing.

Chapter 10

Present Tense

Three o'clock in the morning wasn't really a bad time—if it was the end of your working day, so to speak. The Las Vegas air was cool, maybe sixty-five degrees. Street lights and stars sprinkled the black desert sky.

Matt liked the middle of the night. That was one of the things he had discovered while working for ConTact. Maybe he was a monastic throwback to a time and a tempo of life when monks heeded the canonical hours devoted to prayer around the clock.

Now would be lauds.

Las Vegas marked fleeting moments of meditation in its own inimitable way.

Hearing a hoarse roar in the distance, Matt let his fancy roam farther afield. Had the MGM lion lived up to its own TV commercial and opened its gilded maw? Or maybe the Luxor's Sphinx had broken centuries of smug silence to unhinge its stony jaws for a good, noisy yawn. Or was it just Midnight Louie, taking a lauds stroll through the nearby shrubbery with his sizable stomach growling?

Matt knew what force really hurled the faint, howling challenge to the night: theme-hotel indigestion. The Mirage's volcano was preparing to belch its clockwork stream of ready-made fire.

Still, anything could happen in Las Vegas. Including crimes against a person who walked alone at night.

Matt always studied his surroundings on these long walks home. He wasn't particularly afraid, just cautious. Everyone knew the usual tourist pitfalls of the Strip—private dancers who performed the ever-popular routine called the Customer Shakedown, and that's all . . . prostitutes who rolled high-rollers for high-dollar Rolex watches . . . creeps who sold dangerous designer drugs. The biggest danger in the city's neighborhoods was the same phenomenon that dogged all other large cities. Gangs. If you were unlucky enough to get caught in the sudden lethal spray of a gang shoot-out, it wouldn't matter whether you were walking or riding, or whether it was day or night.

So Matt felt a warning tingle at the back of his neck. A car was following him. A lone walker, a driver who perhaps was not alone. Businesses that opened at ten A.M. and closed at six—or ten P.M., tops—lined the street. ConTact kept the latest hours in this area. Its women employees were always escorted to their cars, a duty Matt often performed.

All the employees had cars, except Matt, though nobody at ConTact had noticed. He arrived on time, left on time, and always came back the next night. A man wasn't stalker-bait as women were. Nobody worried about him, including Matt. He knew he was always armed by the formidable depth of his unhealed rage.

Still, a car was following him, creeping down the street about a hundred feet behind at an idling speed unnatural to anything made in Detroit.

Matt managed to kick a discarded Dr Pepper can, stumble, then turn as he regained his balance. He glimpsed a barge as broad as a boat, a late seventies Monte Carlo. Gang-bangers liked all that macho metal from Old Detroit, liked to keep their rustbuckets in surprisingly good running order.

Yet this car did not broadcast the low, throaty growl of a souped-up street bomb. It crawled along with a discreet cough, fatigued tires hissing as the elderly rubber peeled over the asphalt.

Matt wasn't surprised that somebody was following him. He'd

been tossing out so many lines of inquiry that one could have snagged anyone: a concerned but truculent supporter of Father Hernandez; Molina or one of her minions, annoyed that he had imitated Temple by playing amateur investigator; an aggravated associate who had heard Matt was looking for a man who wanted to stay missing.

Or it could be the man himself.

That thought stopped Matt's breath for a moment. Rage surged so strong that it felt, for a moment, like fear. Neither emotion was useful now. Matt calmed himself, tried to think.

If he had stirred up this kind of interest, he was on to something, in either area he was investigating. He could learn from his stalker. He could teach his stalker that a man walking alone at night is not always a target. Sometimes he is a mobile trap.

Ahead of Matt and the car a semaphore was blinking its timed changes: red, amber, then green. Matt paced himself to arrive at the intersection when the light was red. He would be forced to stop. So would the car.

This bare, deserted corner offered no place to hide. Matt scanned ranks of locked shops with eerily ill-lit display windows. There stood a cheap furniture store, its window infested with scabrous lamp shades. Here was a mailing center flaunting empty cardboard boxes. Next door a low-rent liquor store's windows were papered with hand-written specials on unrecognizable brands.

Matt buried his hands in his pockets and pretended to watch only the red light, waiting for it to change.

What changed was the discreet trailing behavior of the car and its unknown driver. With a squeal of protesting tires, the vehicle made a huge sloppy circle-turn in the empty intersection. The big old car zipped up to the curb by Matt, its showroom sheen as much of a memory as its original olive-green color faded now to pale chartreuse.

The windows were tinted up-to-no-good, double-dark charcoal, but the driver leaned across the wide seat to roll one down.

Matt waited, ready to bolt, drop to the street, or dive in, whichever was called for.

"Need a ride, counselor?"

The light across the street turned green. Matt grasped the pitted chrome handle and yanked the massive door open. A sodium iodide streetlamp bled soft pink light onto an expanse of cracked vinyl upholstery. It also cast shadows into the lines that seamed the driver's face.

Matt got in and stretched out to swing the wide, heavy-metal door shut. "How did you know I'd be walking this way?"

"I'm a detective, ain't I?" Eightball O'Rourke grinned into the rearview mirror. "Guess no one from the LVMPD saw that illegal turn. You always that easy to tail, and that relaxed about it?" He glanced curiously at Matt.

"I wasn't relaxed," Matt said tightly.

Eightball nodded. "Good. It's not always bad to look easy, as long as *you* know better."

"Why didn't you contact me at a normal hour?"

"This is a normal hour in my line of work. And yours too, I reckon. Besides, I wanted to avoid calling at the Circle Ritz. I wasn't sure you'd relish Miss Temple Barr knowing your business."

"You're right. I should have given you my phone number at ConTact."

"No way. Ain't no way I'm gonna call one of those weepy lines. Might get mistaken for a wimp or something. Might get some soupy free advice."

"ConTact isn't like that."

"Sure. Maybe I'm not being modern about all this breast-beating and twelve-step stuff, but I'm from a generation that helps themselves."

"Helps themselves to a lot of things," Matt said with amusement.

"Will you forget those blasted silver dollars! That was what you call a youthful peccadillo."

"What do you call this crate?"

"A car, which is more than you have, Mr. Devine. Cars are important out here. I know Miss Temple lets you drive her cute little Storm hither and yon, but why don't you have your own wheels?"

"Because all my money is going to windy private investigators."

"Well, at least you get your money's worth." Eightball rotated the giant steering wheel in a slow arc, wallowing the car around a corner.

In minutes the scenery grew familiar. A block away, a stark

canister of black marble hunkered like a World War II bunker in the dark, or a cemetery monument. The Circle Ritz.

Eightball pulled the car to the empty curb and shifted into park, turning off the engine.

Suddenly, the night was silent.

"You . . . found him?" When Matt finally asked that question, his voice was steady.

Eightball nodded, his face just visible in the pink puddle of another streetlight. The car's immense hood looked the color of cat vomit, an unappetizing combination of puke pink and pea green.

"Where?" Matt wanted to know.

"Around. He doesn't settle anywhere much. Keeps moving, like a man on the run. A man up to something. He's a bad sack of potatoes, but I 'spose you knew that."

"You mean . . . professionally."

"Professionally! Hah. This guy is about as professional as a wounded rattlesnake. Uses the name you gave me sometimes. Sometimes not. He's been seeing the wrong company, some out of town mob lookin' for an inside track on Vegas. Mean but not necessarily smart. He owed them money; now he owes them more. Half the time he's duckin' them; half the time he's huddling with 'em when they catch up with him."

"How . . . is he?"

"What do you mean? I just told you."

"What sort of . . . health is he in? How does he look?"

"Looks like a man who's been pushing his luck for forty years ought to look. Wrinkled skin, wrinkled suits. Slack but beefy. Got a whiskey nose that W.C. Fields would envy. He looks the wrong side of sixty from the wrong side of the tracks. Women all over this town have sworn out assault complaints, then they usually drop 'em, and it isn't because he's been sending them posies, except to the chops. He's been in jail, but he's never done anything bad enough to keep too long. One thing's certain: he never keeps that prize-winning whiskey nose clean when he gets out again. He's trouble, Mr. Devine. If I were you, I'd forget about finding him. Losers are sometimes best off staying lost."

"I have to find him."

"Sure." Eightball leaned back in the bench seat and pulled a slip of paper from his pants' pocket. "That's where he's staying now. Araby Motel. I don't recommend it for your visiting Aunt Sarabeth. I don't recommend it to a nice, clean-cut young fellow like you. I don't babysit, neither, so what you do with that address is up to you."

Matt nodded. He couldn't quite read Eightball's scrawl in the streetlamp, but he knew the information would be accurate.

"What do I owe you?"

"Enough to keep you from getting a car for a while. I make it about eight hundred dollars, give or take a few minutes between friends. Come see me after you visit the Araby Motel and we'll tote it up."

"Aren't you afraid that I might not make it?"

"I don't believe in bilking the dead, Mr. Devine, but I don't believe you're ready for that yet. Jest don't act too easy. This guy is a hard case to crack."

"I know," said Matt, getting out of the car. "Thanks for your . . . discretion."

"Discretion is my middle name."

Matt slammed the door shut—today's cars sure didn't sound like that. He remembered his stepfather bragging about the solid slam of his car door, a dirty bronze-green '69 Olds Cutlass F85 that Matt would never forget for its smoky, sour smell, for the constant presence of rancid burger wrappers and stale newsprint, for the sounds of yelling, arguing, slapping. . . .

Eightball O'Rourke's car gargled off. Matt pushed the hand holding the slip of paper into his pocket, as if afraid that someone would see it—at three o'clock in the morning?

As if afraid that he would see it.

He had his quarry in the palm of his hand now. What would he do? Eightball must be wondering that, too. That's why he had postponed payment. He wanted to hear the end of the story. He wanted to know who would be left standing. He was a born detective. He wanted answers more than he wanted solvency.

Matt smiled as he finished his short stroll toward the Crystal Phoenix. He was looking forward to Caviar's inquisitive greeting, her warm, winding presence and wide, unblinking golden eyes. She welcomed him without asking any unwelcome questions.

He was looking forward to the peace and quiet of his half-furnished rooms. Soon it would be four A.M. Time for lauds. Time for a prayer of thanksgiving. He who was lost, is found.

Too bad that Matt was no longer a shepherd, and that the man he sought had never been a sheep, but a wolf.

Nobody much mourns lost wolves.

Chapter 11

A Thrush in
the Bush . . .

"I'm sorry," Matt said. "I know I've left you dangling lately; at least
I feel like I have."

"Is that what the Ethel M candy and this is all about?" Temple
glanced around the restaurant, a dimly lit place as cozy as the small
brass lamps that warmed every table, even their intimate, for-two
model. "An apology?"

Matt's smile was softer than the incandescent light filtered
through their lamp's pleated, mauve chiffon shade. "And I might
need some help," was his sheepish answer.

"That's what friends are for," Temple said briskly, unrolling a
forest green linen napkin that covered her meager lap like a lawn.

Despite her delight at Matt's sudden invitation to "a nice dinner," despite this slightly hokey, undeniably romantic atmosphere,
she wasn't going to make the classic *Casablanca* mistake of expecting too much. A kiss is just a kiss, after all. Especially one committed at a high school prom held on the high desert more than fifteen
years too late.

Matt moved his knife and spoon into more perfect union with

the fork opposite, so they bracketed the empty, white linen space like spit-polished pewter soldiers on parade.

The "Blue Dahlia" was truly a find beyond the normal reach of a social novice like Matt, Temple thought. How on earth had Max Kinsella—master discoverer of the underestimated asset—missed this gem? Maybe the restaurant was too new; Max was definitely old news now. Matt, on the other hand, was a front-page item, at least to her. Tonight he wore a lightweight ivory blazer she had never seen before over an open necked pale yellow shirt. She was glad she had broken out her green silk Hanae Mori dress; tonight might be an occasion, after all.

"After all you . . . did for me," he was saying, "I feel that I've been derelict—"

"You're the world's worst delinquent all right, Devine," she interrupted. "Listen: you didn't have to wine and dine me in retaliation for my makeshift prom night on the Big Sandy. That was just an experiment; me being a bit madcap . . . wild, impulsive creature that I am."

Her nonsense didn't break the ice, for there was none, but it broke through the thin skin of self-justification that was draping Matt like a cocoon. Temple hated apologies, especially when they were unnecessary.

Maybe her tactic worked, for Matt decided to quit tiptoeing around the reason for this evening out like a wild duck waddling around the dangerous puzzle of an ice-fishing hole. He inched his spoon a trifle closer to the knife—now was that a Freudian slip or what? Temple speculated—took a visible breath and began.

"I didn't end up in Las Vegas by accident, Temple."

She refrained from saying, too bad, and adding that she had always figured him to be a member of Gamblers Anonymous on the run from a cabal of mob accountants in New Jersey.

"I'm . . . looking for someone," he said.

She refrained from saying that almost everybody is.

"I'm . . . looking for a man."

Oh, no! Was this true confession time? Had Matt discovered that he was gay, after all? Well, hell, a thoroughly modern woman could use a good gay friend or two, of either sex, but it helped a lot if she didn't find them physically attractive. Temple sipped from her water goblet, trying to keep the ice cubes from clicking against her teeth. They were sexy, crystal-clear ice cubes, too, probably made with distilled water. Oh, well. The Blue Dahlia made an ideal romantic rendezvous, but there was no point in being flattered now.

"I've never been here before." Matt had noticed her looking around. "I hope it's all right."

"Terrific." Temple resisted the urge to let a cold cube slide into her mouth so she could crack her teeth down on it and see if her fillings held.

"He's my father."

"Huh?" Temple was startled enough to scan the room again.

"The man I'm looking for," Matt said patiently.

Temple prided herself on not letting any relief show, although underneath the table her toes uncurled against the satin-smooth purple leather lining her best Kelly-green high heels. "Why the big secret, then?"

Matt wasn't quite listening, at least to her. "He's my stepfather, actually."

She nodded. This was going to be a complex night, given how Matt was leaking vital information at 33 1/3 speed. Laser disc, lightning-fast he was not.

That meant this information was important to him, that and the shamed way the word "stepfather" sidled out of his mouth like a mud-spattered dog peeking from under the best couch. It also told Temple that this was not to be the romantic evening out that she might be inclined to hope for.

She wriggled her tootsies free of the confining toes of her shoes. Thanks to an old-fashioned floor-length tablecloth, no one could see her informality. No one could see her play footsie with Matt, either, because it wasn't going to happen, at least not tonight.

One thing that *was* going to happen tonight had her second-most-primitive urge polishing its pistons, though: curiosity. Matt was finally going to squeeze out some details about his family.

Temple slid her knife to line up with the tines of Matt's meticulously placed fork opposite her. "Is he a good stepfather or a bad stepfather?" she asked carefully.

Matt sighed again, a short, frustrated huff of air. "Maybe okay by some people's lights. Bad by mine."

She nodded, not surprised.

Having gone this far, Matt must have decided to plunge in with both feet. His eyes and fingers fussed at the arrangement of the tableware while his voice and mouth rattled off a messy cornucopia of facts.

"My real father—odd expression, isn't it?—left my mother while I was still an infant. I don't know why, and she would never say. I knew her as a single mother, working all day and worrying all night. I guess finding a man to take care of her answered half of that unhappy equation. They got married, of course. I wish they hadn't; then he wouldn't have been real, my fake father. But they did. No big ceremony, but a church wedding. Marriage was it for women in St. Stanislaus parish, even as recently as the liberating sixties; that, the single life, or living in sin, which was as good as the streets for a Catholic woman. So she married him, and then we were all stuck. For eternity."

"You got away," Temple observed.

"Escaped, you mean. You're probably right. Into the neighborhood when I could, later into school. Finally into the seminary."

"What was wrong with him?"

"He drank. Just beer, Mom said at first, but 'just beer' can drown even a dry alcoholic, and he was a career beer-drinker. That's what men did in poor, working-class neighborhoods in Chicago. They drank. They still do. Only with him, the hard stuff came later."

"Did you have brothers or sisters?"

Matt's head shake was a gesture so abrupt and tight it resembled a tiny shudder. No, thank God, it seemed to say.

"After my real father left, there were no others. I think—"

Temple waited, beginning to understand what it must have been like for Catholic priests in the old days, behind their dark wooden confessional doors, listening and waiting and wondering when to speak, when not to speak.

Matt looked up, his expression both guarded and searing. "I think when my mother found out what my stepfather was really like, she made sure there were no more children." His eyes shut. "It would have been a sin, of course. A mortal sin. She didn't go to confession much after he came along."

"Is your mother . . . still alive?"

"Sure." He seemed surprised by her question, which was natural, since everything he spoke of seemed steeped in the bitter dregs of days-gone-by. "She still lives in the parish. Retired. Goes to confession now. He left, years ago, but after I did. She was a . . . beautiful woman."

"How many years ago did he leave? How old—"

"Was I?" Matt's mouth stretched clothesline tight before he spoke again. "When he left? Sixteen. It was before I went into the seminary. I never would have left her alone with him."

"So . . . why do you want to find him now?"

Matt shook his head. "I was just a kid then. Maybe I'm still just a kid in a lot of ways. I don't . . . understand. I need to understand *that* before I can understand"—his pale hands spread in the lamplight, over the empty place setting, as if offering an unconscious blessing on . . . nothingness—"this."

"Where you are today, you mean?" she prompted.

This time his smile was ironic, and personal, and quite charming. "Where I was *before* today. But why I'm looking for him isn't the reason I asked you here. It's how. I've been trying in my own clumsy way to make inquiries, and nothing seems promising. I thought you might have an idea or two. You know how to get things done."

"Certain things." Temple sighed in her turn. How touching that Matt found her the Quintessential Organizer, the Fixer, the Solver. "Why do you think he's here in Las Vegas?"

Matt shrugged. "That was the only thing he cared about, cutting out on Mom and me and spending a few days—and half her paycheck—in Las Vegas. I came to regard the city as a kind of personal savior, after a while. For all its Sodom and Gomorrah reputation, it got him out of our house and our hair."

"But, Matt, that was—" Temple was not adept at mental math, so there was a telling pause while she calculated and he hung on her every grimace.

"Seventeen years ago," he finally furnished for her.

"Seventeen years. So much has changed in Las Vegas since then, so many new places to gamble elsewhere in the country have cropped up since then. Your stepfather might have moved on to Atlantic City, or the new riverboat establishments near Chicago. He might be—"

"Dead," Matt finished for her, his tone as grim and final as this ultimate in four-letter words.

She nodded. "Maybe you'd be better off if he was."

"I'd be better off *knowing*, that's for sure."

"Can I ask one . . . personal question?"

"You will anyway."

"Why not look for your . . . real father?"

Matt looked dumbfounded. "He's not real to me. He's not the one who—"

Temple hung on every word, recognizing the importance of this answer, above all the others.

Matt must have recognized it, too. He suddenly grew silent, leaving her to twist slowly in the weightless vacuum of his unfinished phrase. *"The one who . . ."* Who what? Hung the moon? Killed the goose that laid the golden egg? Made a priest out of young Matt Devine?

"Was your stepfather's last name Devine?" she asked.

"No. That was my birth father's name. Mom went back to it after he left. I had never taken *his* name."

"Then your mother must account for the Polish in you."

"Yeah. Kaczkowski. I swear to God," he added, smiling. "Devine is Gaelic."

Gaelic? Like Kinsella? Oh, no! "Hey," Temple said, recovering, "at least your real father left you a pronounceable last name; that's something."

He nodded, lost again in his quandary.

"As for your stepfather, from what I've seen of Las Vegas regulars, they stay pretty faithful to the old town. What are you doing, checking the casinos and hotels for his name?"

"Yeah." He hesitated. Temple suspected that he was coming to the issue that really troubled him, and that more was troubling him than his family history. "And lying a lot."

"Why?"

"Can you get information from unsuspecting people without lying a lot?"

While Temple considered that question, a cocktail waitress in a gathered skirt about a centimeter longer than the control-top line on her off-black pantyhose sauntered by to offer them menus and take drink orders.

Matt kept his nose in the eyebrow-tall menu and his eyes on the entrees, though Temple noticed that the waitress's skirt was just the right height to scratch his nose, were it or she so inclined.

Temple always wondered why the taller the woman, the shorter the skirt; on her this ebony ruffle would be nearly knee-length. Glancing around, she saw that the serving staff were all dressed in sophisticated black-and-white. Maybe Central Casting had sent them over from the nightclub set in a forties movie. The men wore tuxes and pencil-thin mustaches. The women wore lots of abbreviated black with pencil-thin white-lace ruffles in all the right places, from bustier to bustle, including the black satin pillbox hats tilted over their right eyebrows like vintage bellboy caps. *Caaall for Phill-llip Moooor-ris the Cat,* perhaps? *Hot-cha-cha.* Where is Jimmy Durante when you really need him?

Matt emerged from his menu only when the waitress had sashayed away. He leaned across the snowy linen to Temple. He spoke *sotto voce,* despite the growing buzz of other diners.

"This place was supposed to be quiet and have some nice atmosphere." Matt frowned. "I didn't know about the, er, ambiance."

"I suppose all this black-and-white is a rather perverse reminder of your past," Temple couldn't resist commenting.

Matt remained unruffled, despite the environment and despite suffering from the recent embarrassment of revealing a past. "Most of the religious I knew were post-habit days," he said to quash her sense of mischief. "I was referring to the noise level."

Temple noticed only then that a trio had appeared in a dim corner lanced by needles of spotlight. A tenor saxophone was running up and down its liquid metal trills, while a snare drum in the background emulated a soft, rhythmic rattlesnake. A piano's bluesy, throaty tinkle underlay it all like a smoker's cough.

"Isn't it odd," she said, "that they're making all these nun movies—like *Sister Act* and *Nunsense*—only now that nuns wear civilian dress?"

"Now it's safe. Less chance of offending a habit-wearing hard-liner these days."

"I guess people have always been fascinated by priests and nuns," Temple mused. "First there's the distinctive uniform; then there's the celibacy mystique."

"I've never heard celibacy called a 'mystique' before," Matt said dryly, leaning back to make room for the waitress and her lethal ruffled hem. She deposited a lowball glass and a long-stemmed, slow sip of leg before him at one and the same instant.

"What's that?" Temple stared at the dark, murky drink in front of Matt, not having noticed his order.

"A Black Russian. What's yours?" He nodded at her long-stemmed glass.

"A White Lady. I felt like something . . . elegant. At least we're in tune with the color scheme."

They laughed and lifted their glasses. Then they sipped their drinks and began to talk of more important things, like themselves.

Matt had another confession to make. "I'm glad that you like the place, and that you could come tonight. I was worried that you might think I was avoiding you."

"I know you've got commitments, Matt. Besides, I've been busy too."

"So I noticed. With what?"

"Oh, it's fabulous." Temple's natural optimism loved an audience to bubble over on. "The Crystal Phoenix has hired me to reposition the hotel for the new family market. That's like playing Tinkertoy with a whole, real little world, a magic kingdom without Disney's capital letters, or capital investment. And then I was roped into working on a Gridiron skit—you know; the annual political satire show like in Washington. Awful Crawford is show chairman this year and got writer's block on a production number, so I've invented the most outrageous, unbelievable Theme-Hotel-from-Hell. Trying to out-Vegas is a real challenge."

"I bet, but why bail out Buchanan? Isn't he your *bête noir?*"

" 'Black beast' is too good a phrase for the lowlife! Bargain-basement bastard is more like it." Temple settled down, not wanting to ruin a lovely evening. "But my skit is lots of fun. Maybe you, uh, might want to go to the Gridiron. With me. To see it performed, I mean."

"Sounds great. If . . . my exploits as an amateur P.I. don't require me to be elsewhere."

Temple nodded her understanding, already planning what she would wear to the Big Event. She'd never had a date for a Gridiron before. Not in Minneapolis, and not even here. Last year, Max had a conflicting show at the other end of the Strip; even a professional magician couldn't be in two places at once. Temple winced to recall that less than a year ago, she and Max had still been together.

In the background, a torch singer was tuning up the vocal chords.

Temple let a few seductive riffs of sound coil around her blue mood like the cigarette smoke nicely absent from the restaurant. In seconds, she was back in the present, and pleased to be there. Umm, this place was a genuine find. So romantic. Matt was looking soulful, thanking her again for being understanding.

"I'm so lucky that you live at the Circle Ritz, too," he was saying. "It's like I was . . . guided . . . there. Mrs. Lark, Electra, has been so supportive, and you, you're my 'open sesame'—"

Temple's tootsies curled again, sans shoes but with pleasure, as if they were the turned-up toes on an Arabian Nights slipper.

"It's amazing," Matt went on, "how many doors you've opened for me. To the past, and to the future."

The music had assumed a familiar rhythm. You must remember this, Temple told herself. A kiss is just a kiss. A new day is just another sunrise. Don't blow it. Don't fixate on old news.

A woman's deep, dusky voice had joined the sax's soulful whine. Burgundy dark and deep, it moved from times gone by to singing of the man that got away. Then came the drums' relentless, coital beat, like the rain and the rocking chair and the train pumping its iron-hearted way out of town.

And after that, the beat/beat/beat of the tom-toms, night and day. And the man that got away. And the frail that wails near the jail. House. Jailhouse rock. No, wrong song. Wrong era. Wrong time. A kiss is just a kiss, and fundamental rules apply. Always. No matter how many kisses, how many near-misses. As time goes by. As time goes bye-bye.

"Temple." Matt leaned nearer, looking concerned.

She saw him through a musical mirage of stained glass, as if through a rain-rippled train window and he was leaving town, or she was, and nobody could run fast enough to reach the fleeing coach, to hear the rhythm, catch the beat, listen to the song.

Two and woo, love and you, missing and kissing and such a familiar song, a familiar voice . . .

Matt's hand covered Temple's on the table. He still looked concerned. Concerned is nice, but . . . dammit!

Temple twisted away from Matt, leaving her hand in his custody, like a living creature coiled in the safety of its shell. She turned to the murky stage, to the sleet of bright, piercing spotlights and the melody so familiar, in reprise.

The singer sat sharp as a silhouette in a pinspot, a brunette butterfly pinned on white damask . . . her skin tapioca satin, the flower in her hair a dark, velvet growth. Her figure was as murky as an El Greco portrait, her features carved from backlit salt.

She sang.

The old, slow-train blues classics.

In a deep, true alto that made Temple's bones vibrate like the strings of an abandoned cello in a warehouse.

She made everything moot. The past. The present. The man in black. The man in blond. She was . . . so familiar, like the song and the ache.

"Matt—!" Temple managed to warn him with the last, surprised breath that was in her.

At last he turned away from her toward the shadowed, tiny stage that had caught Temple like a light-jeweled net in a silver sea.

The announcer, wherever he was, took this opportunity to add a slick, baritone coda to the night's first set.

"And now, ladies and gentlemen, an appreciative round of applause for our own 'Blue Dahlia'—our mistress of moody blue mystification, the incomparable Carmen."

"Of course. Carmen," Temple breathed, not surprised so much by the name, but by its presence here. "Makes you wonder what the bloody hell the 'R.' stands for!"

"Carmen?" Matt repeated with maddening confusion. "Isn't that—is it possible? Lieutenant Molina?"

Chapter 12

. . . Equals Molina in Hand

"I didn't want to interrupt."

Lieutenant C.R. Molina gazed down at them from an artificially abetted height. "I spotted you two the moment I came on stage, but you seemed so . . . self-absorbed."

Temple looked down, to Molina's feet. High-heeled platform shoes.

Molina had the actual nerve—at her already intimidating height—to wear platform shoes! Black suede. With straps over the toes and anchoring the heel. Clunky forties shoes, like the Andrews Sisters used to wear. Where were Molina's sisters? Wasn't this a sister act? No, Molina was apparently here solo, a spotlight hog!

"You're really wonderful," Matt was saying, his confusion instantly converted to effusion. "We could have been listening to the radio, or a record. CD," he corrected himself quickly. Not many CDs in the seminary, Temple would bet.

Molina allowed herself a modest smile. Gollee, Temple thought, she sure looked silly with that blue-velvet orchid perched behind her left ear. At her height, someone might mistake her for a jaca-randa tree.

"You mind if I join you? I'm on a ten-minute break."

"Of course." Matt leapt up to snag a chair from a neighboring table.

Molina sat between them, smiling from one to the other with the serenity of an unwanted maiden aunt who is quite sure that her presence is both unexpected and annoying to all parties.

Temple sourly studied the woman's outfit now that her shoes were hidden under the table—a midnight-blue silk-velvet draped frock from the forties, like all clothes of that era both no-nonsense and as subtly slinky as a snake.

"That time you came to the Convention Center," Temple said with dawning suspicion, "when the ABA killer was after me and the entire fire department showed up. You were wearing some vintage getup, too—black crepe with copper beading!" she accused.

"What a memory. You've caught me red-handed." Molina spread the hands in question to show her supposed defenselessness. "I can't commit to a regular performance schedule here, but I come in and do a gig when I get some time off. Every cop should have a hobby."

"Hobby," Matt repeated, his tone contradicting her. "You sing like a pro."

"Maybe." Molina's smile was the slow, slight one that's not for show, but for one's self. "Not much commercial demand for my kind of music. I'm lucky to find a place willing to put up with my hours. You really didn't notice me, did you?"

"Well . . ." Matt glanced at Temple.

"We didn't even expect live music," she said quickly, irked at being so unobservant. Matt was definitely a bad influence. She hated that Lieutenant Molina might come to the same conclusion, and she would. "We've never been here before."

"You'll probably never come here again," Molina suggested silk-ily.

Of course they both protested, in tandem and too much. The idea of conferring about private matters against the background crooning of a homicide lieutenant was pretty offputting.

"Only the manager knows what I do for a living," Molina went on, her long fingers turning the heavy class ring she always wore.

Her nails were cut almost straight across, Temple noticed, her own crimson claws drumming the padded white tablecloth, and didn't give off even a glint of clear polish.

The street-length dress had a bouquet of velvet flowers at opposing hip and shoulder; Molina wore no jewelry beyond the class ring, not even a wedding band. With her physical presence and blue eyes, even earrings would have been too much. Her only apparent makeup was a vintage shade of Bloody Murder Red lipstick so dark it looked black in the lamplight. Now those lips thinned into a Dracula's Daughter smile.

"Serenading cops are not marketable," Molina noted, "except on St. Patrick's Day. I'd appreciate your keeping my real occupation to yourselves."

They swore that they would, in breathless unison and much too intensely.

Molina frowned, looking exactly like an undercover cop in drag. "You two aren't up to something in the amateur crime detection department again, are you?"

"Who . . . us?" Temple provided the indignant chirp. She was so good at it. "Absolutely not. Counselors and publicists need to get away from the job, too."

"Well—" Molina stood slowly, as only a woman as long as she was could. She smiled down on them in the dramatically dim light. In this environment, in that getup, her leonine air seemed as feminine as it was languidly dangerous. "Enjoy yourselves."

The sax man huffed and puffed a bluesy intro on his gleaming instrument. Molina threaded through the tables to the small stage, moving like a leopard thinking about an appetizer.

Temple glanced anxiously at Matt. He still looked stunned. And a bit guilty. "She really is first-class." He glanced at Temple to find her frowning. "I mean, at singing. Who would have thought it?"

"I don't know. Everybody has their surprises to spring," Temple noted with intent to point fingers.

He smiled disarmingly. "What's yours?"

"I haven't decided yet. But don't expect me to break into 'Melancholy Baby.' I couldn't carry a tune in a violin case." She remembered Matt's expert organ-playing at Electra's wedding ceremony. "Can you?"

"Only in church choirs," he said, too lightly.

If Temple could have kicked herself with one of her doffed shoes she would have. She had attended a Catholic mass only once in her life, for a cousin's wedding. The priest had intoned—sang—several parts of it. Of course Matt sang; it once was a career requirement.

Now Lieutenant Molina—or her surprising alter ego, Carmen—was singing again.

And now that they knew exactly who was providing the restaurant background music, Temple and Matt found themselves glued to their chairs like good little kids: hands folded, heads attentively tilted, unable to look away from the stage or say a single discouraging word to each other.

Their food finally arrived, providing a distraction they dove into with knife and fork as if the harmless stainless steel utensils were hammer and tong.

In fact, Molina's sardonic "Enjoy yourselves" had created the reverse effect.

"It's blue murder," Temple muttered after dismembering her fried catfish fillet, "to discover you know the performer you're ignoring. And even harder to ignore her once you know who she is."

"It's especially hard when you know she's a homicide lieutenant," Matt added, attacking a pair of pork chops as if they were renegade wild pigs.

By eating only half their servings and foregoing dessert, they were ready to leave in twenty minutes flat.

By then a lot of diners were paying attention to Molina and her music. She perched on a stool at center spotlight, where the overbright light faded her skin into a luminous mask. Only her Joan Crawford eyebrows and maroon mouth stood out: dark, well-defined, like the empty features in a mask of tragedy.

Carmen Molina had launched into the lengthy Cole Porter masterpiece, "Begin the Beguine," so they were stuck for another ten minutes.

When Matt whispered to the waitress for the check, Temple piped up, "A doggy bag, please. For the cat."

She was soon delicately flicking fish flakes and pork into a hinged styrofoam box in time to Molina's tempestuous tango beat while the lieutenant moaned about nights of "tropical splendor" and a lost love "evergreen."

"It used to be one of my favorite songs," Temple hissed to Matt. He looked sympathetic. "And this—Molina—has ruined it for you?"

"Her and somebody else." Temple watched Matt lay two twenty dollar bills on the tray bearing the bill. No credit card. Yet. Why hadn't she seen all these signs sooner? Lord, he could have been an escaped convict and she'd have never noticed.

When his change came, Temple insisted on leaving the tip. Then they left, bumbling in the way that aims at being super-quiet but makes a spectacle of itself instead. As they exited the restaurant, surrounding diners clapped enthusiastically. Molina's dark head bowed repeatedly in the spotlight, so it looked like the damn silk orchid over her ear was blowin' in the wind. Another ex-favorite song after tonight, Temple thought sourly.

Outside, the sun had blown town and the dark felt like a cool chiffon curtain. The Strip was far enough away that they could look up and see the big desert stars without any neon competition. Temple couldn't even hear the roar of the Mirage volcano.

Autumn was coming, and nights toyed with growing chill. She rubbed her hands up and down her bare forearms, feeling goose bumps. The night felt fresh. Senses sharpened now that the heat was withdrawing from the pavement beneath their feet like fever from a healing patient. Out in the desert, night life of another sort than the Strip's frenetic pace would be stirring, scuttling. Here, on the fringes, the city of Las Vegas was quiet for a change, keeping decent hours. Only nine P.M.

They walked around the free-standing building, smiling at its neon frills, to the side parking area. It wasn't easy to find Temple's low-profile Storm among a lot crammed with alien cars that had arrived since they came.

"Popular place," she commented.

Matt looked thoughtful. "Maybe—"

"I know. Maybe Molina's the drawing card. But you heard her: nobody knows when she's going to show up."

"That's a terrific trait in a police officer. Maybe in a singer, too."

Temple shook her head and pulled the loose-woven shawl she carried over her shoulders. "When you know what she does for a living, it colors the show. I thought I'd die when she launched into 'Someone to Watch Over Me.' "

Matt laughed. "Me, too. I mean, here I am asking you how to get information out of unwilling witnesses. And, not twenty feet away, there's the city's top homicide cop in eavesdropping distance—only she's singing her lungs out."

"Well, she's 'a' homicide cop. I don't know if she's 'the top' homicide cop."

"The top homicide cop we know. And then when she sang 'The Man that Got Away'—"

Temple started laughing and couldn't stop. She laughed so hard that she nearly dropped her doggie carton. "Holy Guacamole! Louie would kill me if this stuff went 'splat.' 'The Man that Got Away,' please! Oh, God, do you suppose she . . . she . . . dedicated it to Max?"

Matt was laughing harder than she was now, leaning against the car's aqua side, his elbows on its now-cool roof. "Max?"

Temple lurched against the car's fender, crushing her straw handbag between herself and hard metal, barely able to talk. She nodded, controlled her laughter for a few instants before it came bubbling out again with her words. "Max. Molina—" A whole glissando of guffaws. "—wants to, to interrogate him—" Temple almost slid along the fender to the asphalt, she was laughing so intensely "—in the worst way! Oh, my side . . . I think I—"

"Stop it!" Matt commanded between his own sputters of hilarity. "We could . . . could hurt ourselves laughing like this after a big dinner."

"What big dinner?" Temple squeezed out, doubled over. Tears showered her face. "We were so shook up we could hardly eat a . . . a bite."

"Yeah, Molina really put the collar on our . . . appetites."

They both went off again, laughing uncontrollably. "Maybe," Temple sputtered. "Maybe she could sing at Weight Watchers meetings!"

Everything they said, everything they thought, seemed hysterically funny. They laughed until it hurt, and until they couldn't stop even though it hurt. They still laughed when they had run out of words. Just an assessing glance, to see if the other had sobered up, so to speak, sent the assessor off to Ha-Ha Land again.

Temple finally shook her head, wiping away tears with her bare hands. Matt pulled himself upright, away from the car, like a man trying to shake off a drunk. He offered her a plain white linen handkerchief. Who carried handkerchiefs nowadays, she wondered—except maybe funeral directors? And priests.

"Nothing we said was really that funny," Matt pointed out.

Temple nodded agreement, wiping her face with the harsh linen, clutching her shawl, her purse, her carton. The occasional trill of laughter still broke free without warning, like a hiccup.

"I guess you had to have been there," she said, "and unfortunately—we were!"

They laughed again, an exhausted emotional eddy of self-circling sounds that faded into breathy coughing, some disciplinary lip-biting and finally rueful smiles.

Matt shook his head. "It's not my night."

"Nor mine. Listen, Matt." Temple tried real hard to get serious, because what she had to say *was* serious. "What you were asking me in there is important. I hate to preach at you, but if you take on the task of finding out something other people don't know, of pumping people who may not want to tell you something, or who don't know what you're really after, you've got to have a . . . an ethic."

He nodded. Ethics he understood instantly.

"I may seem simply nosy to you, but I used to work as a TV news reporter. Maybe this isn't news to you, but all our institutions—governmental bureaucracy, corporate leaders, the church—" she added pointedly "—they all operate on a 'need-to-know' basis, just like the spy guys at the CIA, or something. They figure that we—the citizen, the consumer, the client, the public—don't need to know the inside scoop, the motive, opportunity and the real reasons. They want to keep us ignorant 'for our own good.' "

"A major failing of the church, as the hierarchy is finding out now to its eternal regret."

"Regret?" Temple asked sharply. "Or chagrin that it can't keep washing its own dirty laundry in private?"

Matt shrugged, waiting for her point.

"So. There you are. Or I am. We think we are pretty decent human beings with pretty decent motives, and we think that knowing the truth is better than not. We have what journalists call 'a right to know.' That's in direct opposition to the 'need to know' everybody running things wants us to have. So we have to be clever instead of confrontational. We have to ask the right questions of the right people, pull back all the wrong curtains and peek. And guess what?"

"If we pay attention to the man behind the curtain—"

Temple nodded. "Sometimes we find out he's got his hand in the till, or in the wrong underwear or in messing up the future of the country."

"Sometimes we find out it's a her," Matt put in.

Temple nodded again. "And sometimes, we find out . . . he's only pissing."

That set him laughing again.

"That may be vulgar, but I couldn't resist," she said.

Matt sobered faster than she did. "Truth usually is vulgar," he said. "That's your message. You can't clean a window to see through it without smearing some of the dirt around first. Isn't it hard now, to be on the other side?"

"You mean doing public relations?" Temple leaned against the fender again, setting her purse and carton on the hood, pulling her shawl closer. "That's the beauty of freelance. I work for myself, not Them." She sighed. "That's how I got involved in the murders; I couldn't just let the victims be swept under the rug, especially those poor strippers' lives, which were so rotten already anyway. I guess my only rough time in PR was at the Guthrie, when I collected a salary to protect an Institution."

"Sounds like a vocation."

She grimaced. "Even an organization as benign as an arts group can harbor its secrets: an actor who's temperamental, or drunk and disorderly on the set, or a druggie; money shenanigans. Not that Guthrie confronted me with anything like that, but the world-renowned children's theater had a ghastly PR problem years back, if you can call it such a trivial thing. The founder and director was a pederast." She glanced at Matt. "When it all came out, they discovered he'd had one youthful molestation arrest, and he'd been in the seminary briefly—"

"Shit!" Matt said, shocking her. "Sorry. I don't usually . . . it's like having been in a war, and then finding out half your comrades have been fighting for the enemy."

"Some poor woman was PR director for the children's theater when that broke." Temple shuddered, though the night was not that cool. "I'm glad I've never had to smother that kind of fire. I'm glad I don't work for anyone anymore that I can't walk away from at any time. I'm even glad that Max Kinsella pried me loose from my 'position,' then left me high and dry and a freelancer in Las Vegas." Her smile grew crooked. "Sometimes I think the ethics curve is higher here, believe it or not. They've had enough decades of honest greed, lust and fun to be forthright about it."

"What about the mob influence?"

"Virtually dead, from what everybody says."

"So you believe everybody?"

"Never. But in this case I believe the mob's been bought out by the corporate mafia of international consortiums. Listen to us: ethics and the mob and rogue theater directors. So you have to lie a little—play dumb—to learn what you need to know. What's it about?"

Matt took Louie's carton from her, and smiled. "I'm still working on my right to find out. Let's say I'm just looking for the man behind the curtain. And I haven't the foggiest idea what he's doing yet. Shall I drive, or you?"

"Me." Temple fished out her keys and jingled them like spurs for a mechanical steed. "I like to know where I'm going."

Veni, Vidi, Vito

I am generally suspicious of ugly customers, and this Vito character I first spot by the carp pond is one of the ugliest I have ever seen.

But one should not judge on external appearances. These Siamese fighting fish, for instance, would give Godzilla a good name in the beauty department, yet they are highly regarded and expensive. Not to mention tasty.

Still, I am most suspicious of ugly customers when they spend all their time in a gambling casino and are not paying clients. At this odd occupation, this Vito-person is a master.

I spend many hours tracking him around the Crystal Phoenix, which keeps me well out of the baleful purview of the captivating Caviar. Vito displays an admirable tendency for dim corners, out-of-the-way places and a profile so low he is as invisible as an earthworm to those engaged in the hustle and bustle of a gambling establishment.

Luckily, Vito is so busy looking over the Crystal Phoenix that he completely overlooks my presence. If he does spot me, his sneaky gaze rakes right past me, as if I were a piece of furniture. I like to maintain a well-upholstered condition, but jet-black mohair I am not. Vito is most fond of the basement, and there I cannot fault him.

While all of the Phoenix is kept frigid to prevent customers from feeling the heat or letting the dealers see them sweat, the basement is not only as cool as a sea cucumber, but it is blessedly quiet during the days. I myself like to ramble among the empty dressing rooms, watching the showgirls' ostrich-feather headdresses tremble seductively on their high shelves in the icy stream of an air-conditioning vent. The slight shimmying motion of hot-pink curling plumes is a sensory delight second only to the silver hairs of the Divine Yvette shivering with the faint pulse of her throaty purr.

Vito also seems most interested in these dainty feathered artifacts, for he climbs up on a chair to peer over and around them until strings of his greasy black hair steal across his pock-marked, sweaty face like Michael Jackson tendrils that are slumming in a *Bad* neighborhood.

In fact, I begin to suspect that Vito is something of a pervert, for I also find him poking among the racks of costumes set along the hallway walls. He will even go down upon his knees to burrow into the foaming masses of sequined silks and garish feathers.

Disgusting! I am quite attracted by feathers myself, but this is a natural affinity, as is my passion for the smell and taste of leather. You could hardly call it a fetish, any more than you could label Miss Temple Barr's innocent fondness for high-fashion high heels a fixation. There is high-camp taste and then there is outright kink.

With a creature like Vito, however, any tastes are likely to be debased to their lowest common denominator, and I say that with confidence even though I have no head for numbers at all.

Neither does the unfortunate Vito, apparently.

When he is not delving below in the lonely dustbins and among the leftover sweat-stained costumes, he lurks around the Phoenix casino areas. I watch Vito watch the blackjack and craps tables. I see him prowl the slot machine aisles, staring with hungry eyes the size of midget currants at the happily oblivious gamblers and house employees. Yet never once does he commit so much as a nickel to a slot machine, or slide a ten-spot across the cashier's hard marble sill or place a chip on a taut, cushioned surface of Ultrasuede.

What a cheapskate! Obviously, Vito is Up To No Good, but what kind of No Good is he up to?

This I cannot figure, and it is driving me catnip-crazy.

So is the smell of old bananas and cigars about his person. Perhaps he smokes old banana skins *as* a cigar. I would not put it past him.

After a few days of surveillance I am so intrigued that one morning when I see him waddling out of the Crystal Phoenix at three A.M. when all the action is just getting going, I decide to tail him.

Luckily, he walks wherever he is going. I do not think that Vito is the kind of a dude that would care to be linked to a specific license plate at this time and place.

Anywhere Vito can walk without scaring the horses, I can. I am a stalking shadow that blends into night whenever I wish to. And I do wish to, for Vito stops and turns to scan for suspicious sorts every so often.

I am as suspicious as they come, but he never sees me. Even if he did spot me, he would dismiss me as some mute, homeless dude of no danger to him. That is the beauty of my cover: everybody underestimates me. And I am known for keeping my mouth shut.

Anyway, we stroll the cooling streets toward the south side of town where the rents get lower and the clientele descends to their level. Soon we have hit bottom: the parking lot of the Araby Motel.

What can I say about the Araby Motel? Forty years ago, it was a chi-chi little motor lodge, the latest thing in Western accommodations for the travelers wishing to see the U.S.A. in their Chevrolets.

Today it is someplace only Bette Davis could love. What a dump. Even the stray dogs in this town avoid the Dumpster behind the Araby Motel, for fear of finding an unappetizing dead body or two. Sometimes they are even human.

Not many cars litter the asphalt, but those present are missing mufflers, paint, various windows, brake lights, door handles and other accoutrements of safe motoring. Many are also missing valid Nevada license plates.

The Araby Motel is laid out like an exclamation point: a long, low one-story string of rooms stretching out from a registration office that sits under a tower of tired neon. Earthworm-pink cursives spell out "Araby Motel" above a sputtering green minaret. These are "Miami Vice" colors with an emphasis on the "vice."

My quarry does not stop at the so-called office to collect a key, but heads for the littered sidewalk in front of the string of rooms. Each room has a door and a big rectangular window that is more or less covered by a sagging drape in varying patterns of Filth, Dust or Disease.

At number four, our feather-sniffer stops to knock.

It opens enough to showcase another appetizing sort, a tall, blowzy man whose face and form seem to have sunk into a permanent state of walking decay. The two talk for a moment. The tone does not seem particularly friendly from my vantage point under a permanently parked seventies-something Opal with an oil leak that would do credit to the *Exxon Valdez*. I wheeze, trying to breathe over the chemical fumes, and miss the dialogue.

Then Vito is reluctantly admitted to the other man's castle. Through the sagging arras at the window-slit I can glimpse a homely glow of candelabra and no doubt hear the pluckings of the village troubadour upon a lute if I perk my ears in the proper direction. Certainly my imaginary view of the room's interior is more pleasing than the likely landscape, which I have no desire to see in person, or imagine in reality.

I belly-crawl past a flattened tire, avoiding the oily mess, when I spot another stalker in the shadow of a Woodstock-vintage psychedelic-painted Volkswagen van.

On soft-soled feet I pussyfoot closer for a look.

I am not reassured to recognize the dude who is unknowingly sharing stakeout duty with yours truly. I know what has brought me to this unlikely site: the suspicious behavior of the unlovely Vito, who likely has mob connections.

But what even more unlikely circumstance has brought the darling of Our Lady of Guadalupe and the ladies of the Circle Ritz to this debased joint in the surreptitious flesh at half-past three A.M.?

Mr. Matt Devine is not about to answer my humble question, and the situation promises to remain an impasse, so I slink away.

Chapter 14

Game for Murder

Temple was beginning to know the Crystal Phoenix almost as well as she had known the Guthrie Theatre in Minneapolis, from front to back and top to bottom.

She loved being house-mouse familiar with the ins and outs of a major public building possessed of a certain aloof glamour. Everybody likes to be an insider, but nobody demands the inner circle view more than a reporter turned public relations specialist.

Despite the Crystal Phoenix's low-brow, high-profile image compared to an understated arts institution like the Guthrie, theater and hotel weren't that unlike beneath their dramatically different skins: each had lobby, bar, stage and a paying audience.

And the belly of each beast was a fascinating below-stage labyrinth of storage and dressing rooms, props and costumes, and elevators that whisked the initiated to the performance areas above.

These vast, semi-deserted spaces seemed mysterious, especially in daylight hours. They whispered and rustled with the ghosts of a full house of impending noise and activity after dark.

Temple's high heels challenged the echoing silence as she trudged alone through the area, her tote bag swinging against her hip like a metronome keeping time to an unheard rhythm. She peered into empty dressing rooms; how could anyone ever resist the drama of such places between shows? Maybe she was superstitious enough to wonder if some of the whispering ghosts might be the shades of Kitty or Glenda. Or did she expect to encounter one of their legion of sad, still-living sisters? They all were glamorous but victimized women that men liked to look at . . . and often used and abused 'til death did them part. Stripper or showgirl, they all claimed they made a good living off the men in the darkened houses, no matter how many of them came to a bad dying.

No one was down here now, Temple told herself: not at the Crystal Phoenix, where not even the ghost of Max Kinsella prowled. Not some creepy stalker, and not some unsuspecting victim, *especially* not her. Now.

Then she heard voices, echoing and arguing. Her pace quickened. There *was* a creep down here, after all, but not an unexpected one. Unfortunately, she had an appointment with him.

The ajar doors to the unused set-construction area were tall enough to admit King Kong. Temple scuttled through, following the trail of the voices around an impromptu screen of vertically stored flats. About fifteen people milled near some empty metal folding chairs strewn across the paint-splotched concrete floor.

On its Jackson Pollack surface, masking tape outlined a rough quadrangle shape that duplicated the dimensions of the hotel's secondary stage upstairs. An upright piano, once painted shiny white but aged to crack-checkered ivory, sat solo where the orchestra would be.

A small man in a tangerine knit shirt leaned an elbow on the music rest, picking out loud, familiar notes with one lollygagging hand.

O-kla-hom-a, the syllables rang in Temple's head, only she had recently rewritten them: *Oh, Las Ve-gas . . .*

Crawford Buchanan hadn't lied, then. This wasn't some sleazy ruse to get her alone in the hotel basement, but a legitimate Gridiron rehearsal of her skit.

Temple, suspicions lulled, finally allowed herself to feel pleased. Writers for the Gridiron were traditionally forbidden any role in rehearsals. They would see their work onstage only for the one-time performance, like the rest of the paying customers. They wouldn't even know which—if any—of their submissions had been accepted.

In fact, twenty-five years before, Temple had heard, women writers couldn't even attend Gridiron shows. They had been forced to write their skits blind, ignorant of audience and ambiance, which was just as well. She had also heard about earlier Gridirons: raunchy, foul-mouthed, sexist, racist exercises that committed an almost as bad crime against humanity by not being remotely funny. No wonder so few women wrote for them in the bad old days, or had wanted to.

That was then. Now Gridirons across the country had died of disinterest, hopefully due to low-grade content. The Mother of all Gridirons in Washington had always been a bigger, tonier affair. Las Vegas also mounted a major show each year. After all, the city was choking with performing spaces and talent that included top acts from Hollywood and Nashville.

One of them was walking toward Temple right now.

She'd only seen Gentleman Johnny Diamond in bigger-than-life photos on hotel placards; in the flesh he was almost as imposing as the Colossus of Rhodes figure straddling the entrance to the Goliath Hotel. He was big, broad without being burly, and blond in a robust way reminiscent of frontiersmen. The shoulder-length hair he swept back into a trendy ponytail furthered the Old West impression, as did his no-holds-barred handshake with Temple.

She liked that. Nothing made her feel worse than being treated like a porcelain princess.

Johnny Diamond's voice was as big as his body. "You're the PR whiz who's going to turn Nicky and Van's magic kingdom here into the family farm," he boomed into the giant echo chamber of the hotel basement. "You also sling a mean satirical line. I'm gonna have fun doin' this gig. Nice to meet you."

Since Gridiron roles were unpaid, Temple practically did a somersault to hear that her suggestion for the lead singer of "Las Vegas Medley of 1994" had gotten past Crawford. Having its headline singer in the show's big production number wouldn't hurt the host hotel—Temple's current client—either.

She actually turned to an advancing Buchanan with a leftover smile on her face, which faded quickly. He had traded his around-town suit for his idea of informal rehearsal attire: blue jeans about six shades too new (even for Beaver Cleaver) and a golf shirt in an obnoxious shade of lime. (Were there any other shades of lime clothing? she wondered. She would have to look into that later.)

"How's it going?" she forced herself to ask.

"Fine." Crawford seemed distracted. He barely glanced at his guest star, as hard as Johnny Diamond was to miss. "The director's over here. He wants to see you."

The director was a guest star too: the Phoenix house choreographer named (honest-to-plain-Pete), Danny Dove. His crimped dark-blond hair was as woolly as an English barrister's wig and framed a genial, slightly homely face. Temple was surprised that Dove was so slight-looking; most male dancers had to be strongmen to partner and sling about the females of the Terpsichorean species, who were often tall. Temple pictured Danny Dove piloting Carmen Molina through Swan Lake and fought back giggles.

"Cute skit shtick," Dove pronounced after Crawford had introduced Temple, pushing up the sleeves of his black, Gene Kelly turtleneck to his bony elbows.

Danny Dove's jeans were black, too, and so well-used that they looked chalk-dusted in places, though they fit tighter than the skin of your chinny-chin-chin after a ten-thousand-dollar facelift. They sported a completely sincere frayed horizontal slit in one knee, also bony.

Danny Dove was a spare man whose gestures were bigger than he was. They had to be to control dozens of dancers, including giraffe-tall showgirls.

"I'll do a total takeoff of the 'Broadway Melody' shows of the thirties," he said, separating his hands into the frame of a proscenium stage. "The backdrop will be wallpapered with chorus girls kicking their little asses into next week against a Big White Set. You know, kaleidoscopic knees and such. That's what you intended, right? The overdone approach. Do you dance?"

Danny Dove's dark eyes zeroed in on Temple's legs in such a professionally assessing way that she could not take offense, though Crawford Buchanan's monkey-see scan was distinctly unwelcome.

"Yes," she said. "I mean, I don't dance, but I did envision an over-the-top production."

"One thing." Danny Dove scratched an angry pimple on his five-o'clock shadow. "We might be smart to lay off on a few things."

"Oh?" Temple's voice had moved into cool neutral. She wouldn't tell Danny Dove how to block a ballet; she hoped he wasn't about to tell her how to write a revue.

"This mob stuff, isn't that rather old?"

"That's the idea. It leads into the 'Luck, Be a Lady' part of the number."

"Frankly, my dear, I don't give a damn what it leads into, it's such a hokey concept. The mob. I've been in Vegas for over fifteen years and the only mobster who's set tacky wing-tip in this town since then is the figurehead from Little Caesar's pizza chain."

"The skit satirizes all of the legendary forces that shaped and tried to control Las Vegas," Temple said patiently. "Crime syndicates were no laughing matter in the early days. Sure, musical comedy gangsters don't run this town, anymore than a secret government alien-intelligence installation sits under the new Luxor's pyramid. Let's just have some fun and pretend all the clichés are true."

Danny Dove shrugged. "It's your show, but I hate to put my dancers into those tacky brown zoot suits with white ties." His blasé face brightened. "I could have the ladies wear just the jackets and skip the baggy pants, though, and do a bluesy Kelly nightclub number." He came as close to a smile as a choreographer who was a combination of Tinker Bell and General Patton ever could. "Yeah. It would play."

Danny Dove retired nodding and happy. Too bad Crawford Buchanan had suffered no such mood change.

"Maybe he's right." Crawford's deep voice burst in the air right next to Temple's left ear like a bad-news bomb.

She tried not to jump, and tried even harder not to jump into a defensive position. That would be sure to cement Crawford's irritating objections.

"I think so too," she said sweetly. "His notion for the Gangster *Guys and Dolls* bit sounds terrific."

"Yeah, a lot of leg is always good, but maybe we should soft peddle the mob angle."

"Why? Everybody agrees they don't exist, right?"

"Sure, but—" Crawford leaned uncomfortably close. "Maybe we shouldn't aggravate 'em, just in case."

"This is a satirical show." Temple's voice was rising to match her aroused temper. "It's supposed to aggravate *every*body! Maybe I should write out the alien enclave; that might make E.T. phone home with a complaint about stereotypical misrepresentation."

Crawford visibly thought about it, nodding solemnly. "The UFO people do take this stuff pretty seriously. And the Luxor might be annoyed. Not to mention the government."

"The Luxor should be delighted with the publicity. The UFO people will feel vindicated to be even mentioned! The government can't do anything about conspiracy theories because they're everywhere in real life. This is only a stage show, Crawford. For Helen Hayes's sake, don't take it so seriously."

"Easy for you to say. I'm in charge of this show. You're just a hired hand."

"Thank you for explaining the facts of life. May I stay a while and watch?"

He looked around as if searching for government toadies to okay her request. "I guess so, but you gotta promise not to meddle."

Temple folded her arms over her chest, which Crawford had been concentrating on rather too much. "I won't if you won't," she promised.

And on that unpromising note, the rehearsal began.

An hour later, Temple took the back stairs up to the hotel's main floor, just to hear the angry clatter of her high heels on hard cement.

The rehearsal was so preliminary that they barely got through two phrases of her script at a time. She had expected that.

She had not expected Crawford to sit beside her, whining with worry over every phrase. How on earth do you put on a satirical revue if you're afraid of offending someone? she fussed to herself. And why was Crawford so worried about offending people at this late date? The notion had never troubled his tiny little mind before.

Temple was huffing and puffing by the time she emerged in the service hall, another reality that ruffled the temper that went with her red hair. She wasn't used to climbing stairs.

Then who should be awaiting her but a brace of Fontana brothers?

Temple blew damp bangs off her slightly clammy forehead. And Crawford said the mob was dead in this town. Who did he think these boys were, the sales reps for 31 Flavors?

"Miss Barr," the first Fontana brother said with a friendly smile.

"Ralph?" she asked.

As he shook his dark head, she saw the golden glint of an earring. This must be the reason why Ralph considered a bloodletting for his earlobe. Big Brother had already done it.

"Emilio. Not to worry. We get mistaken for each other, don't we, Rico?"

He eyed his swarthy clone in a pale suit, who nodded. No earring. In response to Temple's inquiring look, Brother Number Two jabbed the Southwest-colored silk tie making like Monet's water lilies on his chest. "Rico. Van said to see if you needed any help."

"What kind of help would I need?"

Brother eyed brother. "I do not know," Emilio finally confessed to her, "but we are here to provide it, whatever it is."

Temple sighed. These Doberman dandies would not be called off until they had performed what they saw to be their duty.

"Actually, I haven't seen much of the gaming area. I'm relatively new to Las Vegas; all these craps and baccarat rules confuse me. Maybe I could use a crash course."

"Say no more." Rico held up a palm with the aplomb and authority of a grade-school crossing guard who was dressed by Nino Cerutti. "Emilio and I are experts at games of chance."

"We are also tops at escorting babes in Toyland," Emilio added.

"I believe you mean 'babes in the woods,' " Temple said.

"Whatever." Rico shrugged. "Babes is babes."

"I am not that kind of a babe," she said firmly. "I am a self-supporting professional."

The boys' eyes widened like windows. Temple realized that they had taken her too literally, or not literally enough. Either way, she was getting a headache.

"Show me everything from the slot machines to the craps table. I need to start at square one."

"Hey," Rico admonished her, adjusting the knot on his tie. "There is nothing in the least square about you, Miss Barr."

It was a square knot, of course.

* *

Temple had to say one thing for the Fontana brothers. They were generous to a fault, spending deeply of their own pockets to demonstrate the hazards of slot machines, video poker, blackjack, craps and other forms of gambling.

Temple had never paid much attention to the inferno of noise and humanity that eddied in the casino areas. Sure, she had shoved a few nickels into the odd slot. That was about all she ever got out of it: a few nickels and a slot where the odds were never even.

She was pleased to see Fontana, Inc., strike out at the slots as rapidly as she had.

"Sucker City," Emilio confided. "If you're gonna play the chrome-armed bandit, at least do the quarter and dollar slots. They pay off better."

She watched Rico lose two hundred and forty dollars at blackjack in two minutes. She could have bought a really radical pair of Weitzmans for that money. She watched Emilio do something at the craps table—lots of somethings—but he didn't win there, either. And these guys were experts.

The brothers reluctantly drew away from the action to explain the arcana to her.

"The lead player actually plays," she said, "and the other people bet for or against him?"

"Right."

"So they put their chips on certain places and sometimes they win, sometimes they don't . . . but there's no pattern to it, no sense. Everybody's excited, but I can't tell for the life of me why or for what—"

The brothers looked properly sympathetic, and were about to explain the whole tedious set of inexplicable rules one more time.

Then the crowd around the craps table oohed and aahed as the dice rolled and they all leaped back screaming at the sound of a thud so strong it seemed to rock the immediate area.

Maybe the dice were hot, but even the ceiling was giving off puffs like smoke. A woman began a shrill screaming that just kept going and going up and down the scale of distress.

Temple could see why: the craps table was an utter mess. You couldn't tell whose chips were on what, Temple couldn't begin to figure out who had won or lost, because of the man's body lying there, covering everything, limbs splayed to the table's four corners.

People were backing away, even as her intrepid Mario Brothers—uh, Fontana brothers—were pushing close to the table, along with a couple of armed guards in burgundy uniforms who had materialized from nowhere.

Someone was calling her "folks," and telling her to clear the floor. There had been an accident and they needed room.

The people behind Temple drew back lawfully, but the immoveable object before her was just a private security man, after all, and she was small enough to duck under his arm. She was a legitimate hotel employee, a public relations person, and she had a pressing need to know. . . . She pressed forward when everyone else ebbed back.

The brothers weren't at all surprised when she burrowed between them for a good look at the craps table.

"It's pretty hard to see the action right now," Rico apologized, "with this stiff lying all over it."

Temple consulted the brothers' intent, suave young faces. "Doberman" wasn't half wrong.

"Are you sure he's . . . dead?" she asked.

Emilio nodded mournfully. "We'll never know how the dice landed now."

The man who fell from the ceiling lay there, mum, not moving, not giving away a thing, not even the action.

Temple concluded that craps was not her game.

Chapter 15

Oddball Witness

"You witnessed the victim's plunge onto the table, too, Ma'am?"

Temple looked up at the homicide lieutenant, dazed.

Not Molina. He was not Molina. She couldn't believe her luck. Too bad she didn't care for gambling. Today would be her lucky one.

Lieutenant Hector Ferraro not only was *not* as tall as Molina, he was also balding—definitely not Molina's personal grooming problem. Ferraro's coloring was as dark as hers, however, and his attitude as unforthcoming. Must be something in the water coolers at Las Vegas Metropolitan Police Department headquarters, Temple thought.

"Yes, Lieutenant," she made herself answer, after realizing she had been thinking too much and saying too little. "We all saw him fall."

"You and the . . . um, brothers Fontana?" The officer's stubby pencil tip jerked toward an urbane clot of custom tailoring a few feet away. The Fontana Brothers smiled as smoothly as a juggling act. Emilio even waved.

"That's right."

"They say you're a freelance public relations person." Lieutenant Ferraro sounded as if he didn't quite believe that, but not believing people and things was part of his job. "What were you doing with the brothers?" The way he posed the question, he could have been asking Temple why she had been caught cold in the company of a cadre of cockroaches.

"They were instructing me on the fine points of craps."

"Learn anything?" he quirked out of the side of his mouth.

"Zilch. That poor man came crashing down before I could figure odds from evens. How did he . . . die?"

"Not from the fall, that's for sure. You know what's up there?"

"Eye in the Sky," Temple replied promptly, eager to show her mastery of some Las Vegas facts of life, if not of gambling. Realizing she sounded like her former TV newswoman incarnation, she modified her statement. "Not a traffic helicopter, but the surveillance equipment every casino stashes above its gaming areas." She leaned around the lieutenant's awesome stomach paunch—as taut as a wind-filled sail in its pristine white broadcloth—to eye the evidence. "Isn't that a . . . hole in the victim's temple?"

"No doubt you're an expert on temples," he responded deadpan.

Glancing up, she decided that he was kidding her, maybe even flirting.

"Sure. I've seen a dead body before. A murdered dead body."

"Where and when?"

"As a TV news reporter in Minnesota a few years ago. And . . . I was doing PR for the stripper's competition a few weeks back."

"Oh, *you're* the one." Lieutenant Ferraro spoke with unnerving emphasis.

"I can't help being observant."

"Neither can I, or I get canned. Now. Give me your address and phone number, and I can get on with being observant myself."

Temple hesitated just long enough for his pathetic pencil to lift from the notebook page and point at her. "It's required information, Ma'am."

She provided her vital statistics, still trying to glimpse the crime scene crew as it fussed around the craps table.

A ring of eyewitnesses was forced to watch the police go about their business, but the area was otherwise private.

That was because the floor pit boss and the Fontana boys had moved like red-hot lava—deliberate but inexorably effective—to stop the action, calm and corral witnesses, then banish any curiosity-seekers.

By then, Temple had thought to suggest that they ring the area with portable curtains from the exhibition area. It had been accomplished before the police even arrived, thanks to the security personnel's quick work.

Beyond the burgundy linen circle, Van von Rhine and her husband Nicky waited impatiently for news, Temple knew. Figuring—hoping—that she had been dismissed, Temple slipped through a slit in the curtains. She was back amid the noisy bustle she had heard even within the charmed circle of death and detection-in-progress. Back with the quick and the curious.

"What's happening?" Nicky asked staccato-fast.

Van shot him a warning look. "Temple might like to sit down for a moment and rest. It must have been a terrible shock."

"I'm fine," Temple insisted, veteran of sudden death that she had become. Funny that her knees knocked a bit. "The police are awfully interested in your brothers," she told Nicky.

"The police are always interested in my brothers. They can handle it. So. Is the dead guy some sort of delusional diver, or did someone push him?"

"I think someone centered a bullet on his left temple, unless he was born with a large and unsightly mole he never had removed. The police didn't allow me near enough to check it out."

"Really," Van said. "You two talk as if murder is a daily event in Las Vegas. At least these curtains are in place. I'd never have thought the police would be so sensible."

"They weren't," Temple said. "I asked for the curtains, and the staff set them up in triple time."

Van nodded, pleased. "The sooner this . . . mess . . . is cleared away, the better. Death is always an unwanted guest at a hotel, particularly violent death." She winced. "That poor man. A Cliff Effinger. He's not registered at the hotel. That's the first thing the police asked. But who would have shot him in the ceiling? It must be suicide.''

"There's plenty of room up there," Nicky said. "Not over the entire area, but there's the command post, and various service accesses to the cameras. Nobody messes with them that often. The guy could have been shot a week ago, and not be detected until next Easter. We're lucky the ceiling panels gave way."

"Please." Van was beginning to look in need of a seat herself. "My expertise is hotel management, not such sleazy matters as spying on our customers and employees. I do hope that man hasn't been dead for as long as Nicky thinks."

"No way," said Temple, not mentioning the slight, sweet-and-sour odor she had detected. Death was a fast mover, but the man's ghoulish pallor indicated an earlier date with death than the moment of his fall. "And why would the ceiling give way?" she wondered aloud. "A man doesn't weigh any more dead than alive. Maybe someone pushed him, all right, but *after* he was dead."

"Why?" Nicky was skeptical. "That means risk of exposure. The pusher would have to get out of there fast."

"Everyone was too distracted by his spectacular descent to react quickly enough to catch anyone. Security sent some guys, but they didn't find anybody. You can bet the police won't."

"They may find how the ceiling was rigged to fall," Van von Rhine put in. Her china-blue eyes narrowed. "I supervised every stage of this hotel's renovation. I can testify to the impossibility of a ceiling giving way like that, particularly one in the security area."

Temple's thoughtful scowl matched Van's frown. "You know, this kind of death is not without precedent in Las Vegas."

"What do you mean?" Nicky asked.

Temple shrugged. "A man was found dead some months ago in the security area over the Goliath Hotel casino."

" 'In?' " Nicky questioned.

Temple nodded soberly. "He didn't fall on any gaming tables, but he was just as mysteriously dead as this guy. Murdered."

"Anybody know why?" Van sounded aghast.

"The case is still open, as far as I know," Temple said. And, she added to herself, Max Kinsella is still a prime suspect.

Even as she worried at the knots of her particular past, the curtains behind them parted to a stream of exiting police technicians, Lieutenant Ferraro, uniformed officers and, finally, the dark plastic length of a body bag.

"This way." Van intercepted Lieutenant Ferraro to conduct the mob to the shortest, if not the sweetest way out, Nicky close behind her.

Even then the procession had to pass before quite a crowd. Gape-mouthed gamesters focused bleary eyes on the pre-funeral cortege before turning back to their diversion of choice.

After a hesitation in the spinning, chiming and clatter of the slot machines, the hubbub resumed its tempo and traditional volume.

Temple, forgotten but not gone, shook her head and retreated down an aisle of nickel slot machines. She could see the hotel's security staff dismantling the curtains that surrounded the fatal craps table.

While she watched, an unholy cataract of coins slammed into a stainless steel sill behind her. As seldom as Temple gambled, she couldn't resist the sound of paydirt being struck.

She turned to the still-clucking slot machine to see a sheepish figure hunched on the stool before it. He held his hat, a Frank-Sinatra-style straw fedora, under the blizzard of coins as they overflowed the till and streamed onto the floor.

Temple squatted quickly to scrape up the overflow before someone else did. She rose to drop two fistfuls into the hat.

"Looks like you hit it rich, Eightball."

The old guy rubbed his mostly hairless head with one hand and wrinkled his nose at the loot. "I ducked down this aisle so the cops wouldn't spot me. Then I threw a few nickels in the slot for cover, and now I'm the center of attention."

Temple studied the wide-eyed players gathered around to watch Eightball stuffing nickels into stacks of paper cups.

"Jeez," he complained. "If my pals hear I hit a big payoff on the nickel slots my name'll be mudslide in this town. Nickel slots are for tourists and cheapskates."

"Then why'd you put a nickel in?" Temple asked, her mind adding the rest of the old lyric, *in the nick-le-lod-e-on; all I want is you, and mu-sic, mu-sic, mu-sic.*

Eightball's answer surprised her.

"I needed to duck the cops."

"Why? You're an honest private investigator, aren't you?"

"Reasonably so," he said sourly. His money transferred to a formation of paper cups, he clapped his trademark straw fedora back on his head. "That dead guy there?" He jerked his head toward the fatal craps table.

"Yeah?"

"I think he's someone I been looking for."

"Who?"

"Just a guy someone wanted to find."

"What someone?"

"You know better than to ask that. A client."

"I'm glad to see that you abide by client confidentiality rules."

Eightball's crooked smile showed crooked teeth. "Yup, little lady, sometimes I abide by the rules, even when I'm itching not to."

He stood up. "Better cash out before anyone who knows me sees me with all these damn nickels."

"I'll help you carry them to the cashier," Temple volunteered.

"You're a real lady," Eightball said with a half-courtly bow.

"Whoo-ee," came a gleeful cackle from the slot machines opposite.

A white-haired woman wearing a mint-green knit pantsuit over a wildly overgrown blouse of violets turned to grin at them, her finger never leaving the button that rotated a greengrocer's rogues' gallery of renegade fruits. "Just imagine. Eightball O'Rourke busted down to playing the nickel slots. Wait'll I tell the Glory Hole Gang."

"Hester Polyester," he retorted with gusto, "if you squeeze out a peep about my activities today, I'll get a knitting needle and sew your lips shut so tight that you'll never shout 'Bingo!' again."

The woman recycled some dead nickels from her till back into the machine's pitiless maw, never losing her rhythm: feed/feed/feed . . . push . . . scrape/scrape/scrape . . . push.

"So you claim you're too hoity-toity for the nickel slots, are you? Guess you got a secret vice, O'Rourke. As for sewing up anybody's lips, you're so crooked you couldn't stitch a straight seam up a highway center line."

Hester Polyester was still cackling and cranking away as Temple and Eightball elbowed through the crowds to dump their booty of nickels at the marble-silled cashier's booth. Its brass grillwork made it look like a cross between a downtown bank's teller station and St.

Peter's toll booth at the Pearly Gates. In a couple of minutes, Eightball was pocketing forty-three dollars in crisp bills.

They turned as one back to the casino floor. The craps table that had been the center of attention was indiscernible from the other tables in play, unless you knew exactly which one it was. And you could only tell that by looking up at the ceiling where a piece of bland cardboard filled in a jagged hole.

The Crystal Phoenix had little to worry about. Most gamblers never looked up, not even the ones who knew—or cared—about the Eye in the Sky.

Eightball shrugged without saying anything.

"I wish I knew who your client was," Temple said with a sigh. "I bet the police would love to know too."

"A client," Eightball said, with a particularly piercing look, as if toothpicks in his eyeballs wouldn't get any more details out of him. "A client who's gonna be mighty disappointed to know his search has hit a dead end."

"He?"

"You're fast, Missy, but so are chuckwalla lizards. I don't tell them the time of day, neither."

His horny fingertips touched his fedora brim before he left, both a poorer and a richer man.

"Cliff Effinger." Temple breathed out the syllables with which Van had labelled the dead man, lost in a fog of speculation.

It was a nondescript name, which matched the unimposing corpse she had glimpsed. She reviewed her mental picture of the man: a loser in a short-sleeved shirt and corny polyester tie; middle-aged, slack-stomached, thin-haired. A time-tuckered face loosened by booze and late hours, maybe even by a recent fist fight. Some petty crook, Temple guessed. Possibly a small-time loser who had lost too much. Who at the Circle Ritz was hunting such a man?

She was suddenly intensely curious about the identity of the man found dead above the Goliath casino floor. No one had ever breathed a name or an occupation to her. Drat. She almost wished Molina had this case so she could ask her, although Molina probably wouldn't reveal anything. Not until Temple had fed Molina some tidbit about Max, and Temple was running on empty when it came to Max.

Temple stared at the craps table. People, mostly men, again

leaned low over its depressed surface. They pleaded and cajoled the dice that rolled over the navy ultrasuede cryptically marked in red. They begged for naturals and cursed "snake eyes."

Temple had viewed another kind of "snake eye" on that soft, seductive gaming surface. A bullet hole. She wondered if it had exited the other side, or lay imbedded in the dead tissue of a formerly live human brain.

Maybe the tacky man had possessed a good heart. Maybe he had a mother who had adored his every baby step; a toddler who had once called him "Daddy;" or just a dog who had come when called. Maybe he had once been a dapper, upright member of society who had lost it all long ago in Las Vegas.

Maybe.

Maybe Cliff Effinger was somebody someone would miss.

Maybe even Eightball's client.

Temple recalled her instant image of the man, and rather seriously doubted it. Fairy tales don't come true, and—if they do—they don't happen to you. Or to men who look like that.

Chapter 16

Homewrecker

Temple was working her way through an Ethel M vanilla cream, sucking the thick chocolate shell to the sweet dissolution of sugary memory, then letting the smooth filling melt on her tongue.

Yum. She seldom indulged her sweet tooth, poor deprived thing. The only time it got something other than complex carbohydrates, fruits, vegetables and nonfat yogurt was when she watched "Mystery" on PBS.

Tonight's installment featured Inspector Morse, a series that met her high dramatic standards, but mystified her in one way the script writers had never intended. She'd never seen a man so chronically attracted to women and so chronically incapable of doing anything productive about it. One would think that a sharp sleuth like Morse would know better by now than to bother.

Temple reached for the remote control peeking out from under Midnight Louie's front paw. He liked to lounge atop the television schedule and hog the remote control, his claws moving in and out with contentment and possession.

Temple lifted the paw, avoided the claws and retrieved the device. Three presses of the proper button lifted the sound level to barely understandable. Why did Brit films always sound like they were recorded in a rain barrel during a thunderstorm? And the actors mumbled as if they were all chewing pinto-bean cuds. . . .

A noise elsewhere in the building obscured one of Morse's dour observations. Drat. Morse's dour observations were generally important clues. Temple returned a second Ethel M morsel to the box and leaned forward. She aimed the device at the television screen two-handed, as if holding a firearm, and shot the sound up two more rounds.

Still garbled. "Dic-tion," she sternly ordered the TV screen. "You British screen actors are too bloody porridge-mouthed—!"

Another loud thump erupted above. What was somebody doing? Moving furniture? Hopefully, just moving out.

She frowned in concentration, but . . . oh, no! Morse and Lewis were doing a scene in Morse's bloody red Rolls Royce. Now the overamplified auto noise was drowning out the dialogue.

Crash.

Not on the screen. Above. Honestly. Temple stood up and aimed her remote control one last time, zapping Morse, Lewis and the vintage roadhog to Airwave Heaven.

"This is just too much," she told Louie, who blinked in solemn agreement. "On a Thursday night, too. What are they doing up there? Working out on a punching bag? Skipping rope? Bowling? I'm going to express my displeasure in clear, articulate Guthrie Theatre diction, and in person."

She glared once more at the now dead-gray television screen, nodded to Louie, snatched her key ring from her tote bag and headed for the door.

Righteous indignation is an excellent propellant. It pushed Temple to the stairwell and up one floor, still seething. It compelled her halfway down the circular hall—if there is any halfway point to an eternal ring-around-the-rosy. Her indignation fizzled only when she realized that she had no way to tell which unit was the noise polluter.

She stood alone in the dim-lit hall, infuriated, struggling to take a logical approach to her illogical business.

"It sounded like the Second Coming right over my head," she muttered. Oops. Maybe what sounded like godawful chaos to her was just good fun to the offenders. How embarrassing to storm up to someone's door and discover that she had interrupted a romantic moment in a rumpus room! Still, there was no need to do anything with such gusto that it upset the other occupants.

Or maybe instead of making love, the offending tenants had been making war. With these thick old walls, it was often hard to tell the difference. Someone could have clobbered someone else. And she had heard it. Another murder? Right overhead?

Now she was afraid to pound on a door, any door. Her life was full up with dead bodies at the moment.

Maybe a TV had been turned on too loud . . . and it was tuned to a retrospective on the L.A. earthquake, sure.

While she dithered, she moved down the carpeted hall. Her cooling ire still fanned a few bright embers of indignation. She was beginning to believe that it was her civic duty to find out what had happened.

She faced the short cul-de-sac leading to a door exactly like hers. All was quieter than Sunday morning at the moment. Too quiet. If whatever had produced the noise was a normal activity, it wouldn't have just . . . shut off like this. Would it?

She tiptoed down the narrow hall. The faint lamp beside the coffered wood door illuminated a number: eleven.

The heel of Temple's hand smacked her forehead. Now she knew where she was! Eleven was directly over her place. And it was Matt Devine's unlucky number, at the moment.

Oh, boy, she was going to look nosy, but what if something had happened to him? She glanced at her wristwatch, then thought. Use your brain, she told herself. Thursday night. "Mystery" comes on at 10 P.M. Matt *couldn't* be at home. He would have been working at ConTact since seven. Temple bit her lip. Okay. So, what if something had happened to his apartment while he was gone? Had happened *in* his apartment?

She had a duty to investigate. How? She didn't have a key. She supposed she should. . . .

Temple eyed the doorbell, then shrank from setting those mellow, old-fashioned chimes ringing. That seemed silly in an empty apartment, and Matt's place appeared empty even when he was there, so meager were its furnishings. So how was all that noise possible?

Temple's lifted fist rapped briskly on the door.

Ow! Forty-year-old mahogany was hard and thick. She had to rough up her knuckles to make a decent knock.

No sound. No answer. But then, she had expected none.

Rap again, longer and louder. Temple shook her stinging knuckles, waiting for the answer that she knew wouldn't come.

"Hello?" she tried. "Is anybody there?"

Should she call Electra? What if she was wrong? What if the sound had been caused by something perfectly normal—like Caviar bouncing off the furniture in a game of feline ping-pong (petite little Caviar?), or garbage collectors emptying the Dumpster out back. On Thursday night at ten P.M.? Still, she hated looking like a nosy neighbor, particularly with Matt's place. Maybe she'd just forget it.

Temple edged a few steps back down the hall.

And if something were really wrong? She hated being indecisive worse than she hated being nosy.

While she stood there, ambivalent, she realized that she hadn't tried the obvious. The door itself.

Refusing to let any objections enter her head, she marched back to the door, grabbed the big brass knob, turned it and . . . walked into the unlocked apartment.

Dumb move. Fatally dumb move. If it wasn't locked . . .

No light was on, but a faint streetlamp glow shone through the glass panes of the naked French doors. The lurid, orange-pink aura reflected like spilled mercurochrome from the few things present in the room, outlining the figure standing directly in front of her.

A man's silhouette stood statue-still a few feet farther into the room, as if he had walked in, stopped and frozen into a monochromatic image of himself.

Scared to death, Temple reached for the hall light switch—at the exact location as in her place. She pressed it, hoping that it would work.

It functioned so well that she blinked at the sudden brightness, which half blinded her just when she might need to turn and run.

Her eyes adjusted to an impression of Chaos Central. Matt Devine was standing in front of her, only his back visible, surveying the shattered ruins of his orange-crate bookshelves. His books had been scattered to the living room's oddly angled corners as if hurled by a demon censor.

"Matt. Why aren't you at work?"

He turned at her voice, but looked right through her . . . and she wasn't the one acting like a mute ghost of herself.

He shook his head, his eyes squinting in the brightness as he turned again to survey the damage. "Let go," he finally said, without glancing back to Temple. "Not fired." At least he had anticipated her surprise. "They didn't need me tonight."

"So you came home early to find . . . this?"

He just shook his head. Temple edged farther into the room. He was okay, she was okay. Whatever had happened made a mess, but she was an expert at cleaning up other people's messes.

"Doesn't look like any substantial damage to the apartment itself." Little Miss Optimist. "No windows or doors seem broken. And you didn't have a lot of fancy Memphis modern for anyone to trash."

She checked his face as she came alongside, but her smart remark hadn't thawed the frozen expression that deadened his eyes. Shock. Temple considered what it would be like to return home to find her place ruined, and winced. Violation. That was the only way to describe the sensation, no matter the motive.

"If they were looking for anything to steal, they were out of luck here," she said. "Maybe that's why they got mad and turned to vandalism. Have you checked the bedroom yet?"

Matt shook his head again, his face still expressionless.

She clattered across the bare wood floors, then paused on the threshold to what was her bedroom a floor below. "This it?"

He nodded as she reached for the light switch. Dumb again, Temple lectured herself. What if an intruder had retreated at their entrance, but not left? Who would help her? At the moment, Matt looked about as useful as the statue of David at Caesars Palace.

Her finger had already flicked the switch upward. The room's central ceiling fixture spread wan light on a landscape as bare as the living room, but in apple-pie order.

Nodding satisfaction, Temple turned off the light and clicked back into the outer room, feeling like an interior decorator on a mercy mission.

"Okay in there. Where's Caviar?"

"She, ah, hasn't been around. Much. Lately."

He was still talking in jerky phrases, like someone whose brain was only partly plugged in. He frowned, struggling to recall a trying detail.

"She was here, though. But I think she must have . . . left. Again."

Temple decided to focus on the future.

"Look, Matt, this could be a blessing in disguise. We can get you some new stuff. I know a great unpainted furniture place and about six dozen thrift shops filled with kicky little furniture items at a low price—vintage Fifties Yuck, you name it. We'll redecorate."

He finally moved. Bent to pick a book from the floor, unbend its pages, shut it.

"I'm sorry," Temple said, sinking under a sudden helpless feeling. Sometimes a stiff upper lip was not enough; sometimes it was an insult.

He sat on the arm of his overturned sofa. The cushions lay on the floor like giant playing cards.

"Who would have done this?" Temple's ever-ready indignation was rising again, this time in a serious cause. "Kids looking for electronic equipment to sell for drugs? Frustrated punks can be destructive, just for the hell of it. And how did they get in? Did you check the French door locks? We *are* three stories high here."

His troubled expression was a barrier, putting him beyond her reach. Temple began to panic like a swimmer suddenly out of her depth. Maybe she should call his hotline compadres; maybe he needed some emergency counseling.

She sighed, not knowing what to say for once. Then she bent to gather the splayed books, shutting splintered spines, smoothing crumpled pages. Unfamiliar names and titles slid under her fingertips. C. S. Lewis. G. K. Chesterton. *The Seven Story Mountain*. Ah. *The Little Prince* in the original French. Some philosophy books by a man named Rollo May. Novels by Romaine Rolland, Iris Murdoch and Susan Howatch.

Matt sat on his pie-wacky sofa and stared at the floor, at her moving among the ruins of the room.

Temple stacked some books knee-high. Without anywhere to put them, it seemed pointless. "You have so little, why would anyone—? Unless. . . ." Matt was barely watching her. She turned to him suddenly, as they say in the old plays, galvanized.

"Unless . . . Matt! My apartment is just below this one."

He looked up with lusterless brown eyes.

"Don't you see? *This* could have been a mistake. Someone might have been looking for *my* place. For *me*. Maybe those men who assaulted me are back. Of course. *That* makes sense. No one's been after you, no one would be. It's me. They're still looking for Max. Maybe they got mad when they thought I wasn't home. Maybe they just wanted to warn me. Oh, God, I was sitting downstairs with Louie, just watching 'Mystery'—!"

She cupped a hand over her mouth to stop it from saying any more scary things.

Matt straightened, responding to something she had said for the first time. He shook his head yet again. "No."

His voice was hoarse, as if someone had tried to strangle him. For a wild moment, she wondered if he *had* interrupted the intruders, and had been hurt.

She watched him intently, alarmed. "Matt. Are you all right?"

"No." His voice was stronger now, and even hoarser.

Temple blinked. " 'No,' that whoever broke in was after me, or 'No,' you're not all right?"

He stood. "No, nobody was trying to get to you, Temple. I can't let you think that. No, it isn't you at all." His hands spread to encompass the mess. "It's me. Only me. Just me. Me. Me, me, *me-a culpa, mea maxima culpa.*"

She swallowed at the sudden violence of this confession, feeling dazed and half-frozen herself. What had she said wrong?

Matt's hands spread wider. She noticed then that the knuckles were scraped raw, as if he'd been knock, knock, knocking at Heaven's door, and it was a lot harder mahogany than the Circle Ritz's. "You don't have to look high and low for the culprit. He's here. I did it."

"You?" She gawked again at the destruction. "What happened?"

He stared at her face, her incomprehension, maybe her disappointment. Then he sat again, his fingers intertwined between his knees, his eyes on the book-strewn floor.

"Somebody died today," he said.

Oh. Death wasn't always a puzzle that happened to someone distant, Temple thought, like an unknown murder victim. Sometimes death singled out someone so close that it seared the lives around that person like heat lightning. His mother? But why such rage?

"I'm sorry, Matt."

"Don't be. It wasn't anyone . . . close."

"But . . ."

He glanced up and laughed. "You look like a little fox terrier I had for a while when I was a kid. Itchy. When that dog wasn't scratching, he was tilting his head and looking so puzzled. God knows he had a lot of reason."

"I'm trying to understand."

"It isn't anything you can understand. I don't." Matt gazed up at the ceiling light fixture as if trying to stare into the sun. "Irony isn't the kind of accident that offers easy answers."

"Can you tell me who died?"

He still stared at the shallow white frosted glass fixture as if examining a UFO glued to the ceiling. "A man. My stepfather."

Oh. "So you did find him, in a way."

"But not alive. He had just died, Temple. Now. Today. Just as I was about to find him." Matt's right hand made a fist and kept it.

"So you'll never be able to confront him."

"I did once, long ago."

"And—"

"He left, and I stayed."

"So you won."

He shook his head. "He won. He always won by being what he was, and now he's won again. He's escaped."

"Escaped what?"

"Me," Matt said again.

Me, me, me echoed in Temple's mind. "You know now why you wanted to, needed to, find him?"

He nodded. "Now that it's too late."

"And why did you?"

Matt eyed the leveled living room. "To beat the hell out of him. If I could, I'd pull him out of his coffin and beat the hell out of him as soon as he's buried."

Such violence from easy-going Matt Devine was as shocking as a fist in the stomach, and Temple had recent reason to know what that felt like.

"Why?" she whispered, feeling dumb as a dog, after all. Feeling mute and stupid and blind as a bat on top of everything. "Why are you so angry?"

"I didn't know I was. I hid under a bushel, under the sanctimonious secrecy of endless confessions and penances, even under the pious platitudes of psychotherapy. I had reached such a rational plateau that I couldn't see the mountain of buried rage crumbling under my feet. Until he was dead."

"Why? Why any of it, all of it?"

Matt licked his lips, rubbed his nose, like a punch-drunk fighter getting up to take more. "He hit us, when we couldn't fight back. I thought I wanted to understand why, to hear his story, but I really just wanted to the write the end of my own. I wanted to beat the hell out of him, and he escaped. He cheated. He ran to death first."

Temple sat on the floor like a kid at a particularly grim storytime. All she could do was ask her simplistic questions, and hope that his answers might answer something lost within himself. How did you understand another person? You listened and you tried not to judge. Temple suspected that Matt's stepfather was not capable of understanding anybody else, and therefore would never be understood. But now Matt had lost even the chance to fail.

"Us?" she asked quietly.

"My mother, myself. It was the liquor, she said, but it was more. It was meanness, it was raw inarticulate envy. It was a lot of ugly, unnamed things. I knocked him down finally, one day. And he left. If he couldn't beat on us, he had to find someone he could. Once was not enough. I thought it was, I talked myself into thinking it was. I told myself that I wanted to know the past, not tear it into little tiny pieces. But then he played his last, mean trick on me. He died, and showed me just how shallow my motives were. I wanted to find him and kill him, Temple. Somebody else got there first."

"He was . . . killed? Today?"

He nodded. "Yeah. I didn't find him dead, but the day after I learned where he was, he was dead. Just killed. I never even had a chance to be noble and *not* kill him, so he's won again—forever."

"Matt." Temple felt an awful sense of foreboding leavened by poetic justice of a particularly ironic sort. "What was your stepfather's name?"

"I hate even saying it. At least I'll see it inscribed on a marker soon. Effinger. Cliff Effinger."

"We never did find the hoods you fingered in the mug book. We don't even know if you identified the right ones."

"I thought the mob was dead in this town."

"That doesn't stop wannabes and cheap imitations. The death of Elvis didn't."

Temple had no snappy retort for that grisly comparison, except that the hoods who attacked her certainly hadn't looked as if they could sing.

She didn't want to remind Molina of where they had last met, and of who had accompanied Temple. She had to keep Matt out of this as long as possible while he repaired his shocked psyche. Listen to her! she admonished herself. Now she was protecting Matt. Who would protect her? Not Molina.

"You still haven't heard from your ex?" the lieutenant was asking, eyes narrow to trap any obvious lies.

Temple shook her head. "About the Goliath. Other than the fact that Max had been appearing there, and vanished just as the body in the ceiling was found, what indicates that he had anything to do with it? The only criminal record you can find on him is that ancient IRA thing from Interpol. Even you admit it was for suspected association, and not proven. So why would Max be murdering men in Las Vegas fifteen years later?"

"Las Vegas is always a target for ambitious and clever thieves, and the IRA always needs money."

"I'd be willing to bet that Max's IRA involvement was a youthful extreme. He just wasn't that political when I knew him, nor willing to be that ruthless. If he ever was, he outgrew it."

"Maybe he never outgrew the high of doing something illegal, of tricking the system, whatever it is. A magician is perfectly placed to do a lot of damage of that sort. He travels everywhere. He's uniquely skilled in the right areas. He knows how to divert attention and how to vanish."

"Max wasn't that money-hungry. He made plenty the old-fashioned way."

"But he was that attention-hungry, wasn't he?"

Temple couldn't answer that as fast as she would have liked. Molina had touched on an aspect of Max that had always troubled her: his constant need to mystify, to astound, to manipulate. If magic had become too routine. . . .

"Maybe," Temple said finally, "but he liked to hang around and take the bow afterwards."

"That's why I'm still looking, and watching."

"Watching me?"

"How could I avoid it? You turn up like the plague. I suppose I can expect to see you underfoot around here for some time."

"Don't worry, Lieutenant. I'm not leaving town until I can take my bow for the Gridiron."

Molina nodded her dark head and looked satisfied. She moved on without a farewell word. Temple watched her head bob above the milling crowds in the casino until it vanished.

Hard to imagine the same woman drawing out smoky syllables in the spotlight of an intimate nightclub. Carmen. She had to hate that name as much as Matt hated the longer version of his own. Matt's loathing was understandable. His name had been a warning and a weapon in the arsenal of his vicious stepfather, until he came to hate the sound of it almost as much as the man who used and abused it.

The name "Carmen" had been a verbal weapon for peers, Temple guessed, with its echoes of grand opera and sultry cigarette girls, of Hispanic songstresses with fruit-basket heads. That would all hit too close to home to a tall, awkward, maybe chubby teenager, and Temple suspected that Mariah Molina was a pretty accurate duplicate of her mother at that age.

So had Molina finally lived up to her given name and become a saloon singer? Or was she living down her past by creating an alter ego who was quite successfully Carmen in the arena made for her, on stage?

Temple eyed the gorgeous but mythical Lalique bird one last time, then plunged into the ever-moving mob herself. Living in Las Vegas accustomed a person to crowds and a certain restless energy that became addictive.

The background chime of slot machines produced its own heavy metal music. Temple welcomed seeing characters about town, like the Leopard Lady, who only wore clothes in that pattern, or Eightball's friend, Hester Polyester, or Nostradamus. They all recalled bit players in some elderly Broadway musical comedy. Even the occasional murder seemed a dramatic touch designed to bring down the first-act curtain. That is, it all seemed slightly unreal until you knew the victim, whether that was a stripper acquaintance or your neighbor's never-met stepfather.

Temple wondered, given the second casino killing, if she might not unknowingly know another, as-yet-undiscovered victim: Max Kinsella. Molina would be sorry about pursuing Max so heatedly if he were actually dead. . . . No, Molina would not be sorry, but Temple would.

"Wait'll you see the set."

Danny Dove sat cross-legged on the floor like an elderly but double-jointed elf as he rustled through a pile of sheets the size of house plans.

"Your skit inspired it," he added impishly.

Temple cast dignity aside to join Danny on the cold concrete floor of the rehearsal room. Crawford had been such a stick-in-the-crud about her skit that Danny's enthusiasm was exciting.

Dove brandished a crackling paper covered with scrawls. "Here's the backdrop for the whole show—a velvet painting with all these lurid outlines of existing Las Vegas landmarks mixed in with your fictional ones. Tiny colored fairy lights will twinkle like toe-dancers all over the skyline and sky. Isn't it too, too divinely tacky? And for the finale at the end of your skit, the sky explodes with stars— forming a constellation of a Technicolor Elvis down to his blue suede shoes!"

"Dazzling," Temple agreed.

"For the final medley, I use the stage trap door to bring up the entire cast, like miners from below the earth, the government secret agents, the Cosa Nostradamus muscle, the concealed aliens *and* their spaceship, which will fly into orbit around Elvis's enormous paunch, which has toy *cars* racing around it. . . ."

"Gross," Temple said with admiration.

Danny looked over the tops of his clear plastic half-glasses. "It's not easy to outdo Vegas Garish at its own game, but I believe I have created the backdrop for a truly tasteless Tinseltown east."

"Everything looks fabulous," Temple said. "I suppose Crawford is in clover."

"Crawford," Danny Dove enunciated in tones of deep disdain, "would be *pushing up* clover, if I had anything to do with it. What an ugly little man. However did the show committee decide to let that cross between Pee Wee Herman and General Sherman run things?"

"I think Crawford marched through a committee meeting in a sharkskin suit. He's awfully overbearing to direct a cooperative effort."

"Listen, young lady. Nobody directs anything on this Gridiron but yours truly." Danny Dove leapt to his threadbare-tennis-shod feet in a single, gravity-defying spring.

Temple struggled upright, trying not to twist a tall J. Renee heel.

"We start rehearsals tomorrow at two P.M. Do drop by. You might offer some little suggestion that would be amusing. You are such a clever girl."

"Thanks, but won't it irritate Crawford if a mere writer shows up to consult?"

Danny crossed his hands on his chest and tilted his head like a good child. "Yeth," he mock-lisped with an angelic grin. "It will annoy our little man no end. So don't be late."

Even Temple heard the happy spring in her step as she left the empty rehearsal area.

Her fictional remake of Las Vegas was getting a first-class production, despite Crawford Buchanan's sneering acceptance of what he treated like a second-class script. Her actual and ambitious remake of the Crystal Phoenix's image was being embraced by the hotel's enlightened managers. That was putting pence into Temple's pocketbook as well as elevating her ego.

She tripped up the stairs to the hotel's main floor, her hand on the wooden railing as light as her heart . . . and then she just tripped.

The railing had become a long, bouncing baton as it pulled off the wall and caromed toward her legs like a log.

She lost her footing and her ankles took two terrific bangs. The high heels collapsed like a tower of poker chips. Temple was falling down the long flight of stairs, their sharp concrete lips digging into her tumbling body. The railing clattered down ahead of her like a giant's berserk drumstick.

Everything happened too fast for her to scream, and there was nothing to catch onto. She tried to roll with the fall, martial arts style, even while trying to grasp with her hands and her mind at something that would stop her before she got—ow!—seriously hurt.

The noise echoed down the long, empty basement spaces. Immobile at last, she lay sprawled over several steps. Her tote bag sagged open three risers down, its contents trailing in forlorn clumps all the way to the bottom step.

An oncoming slap of running footsteps mimicked the pace of her runaway heart. She clasped her arms over her hollow stomach, happy to find it in the proper position.

"Oh, Miss Temple—!"

Danny Dove vaulted the railing lying askew on the bottom steps and deftly avoided her strewn belongings to race up to her two steps at a time.

While he asked her if she were all right, he expertly tested the mobility of her joints: her neck, her wrists, her . . . ow! . . . ankles.

"What happened?" he demanded.

"The railing just pulled off the wall. Then it knocked my feet out from under me like a bowling ball—or like a bowling baseball bat." Down the frighteningly long ripple of step rims she could have rolled over, she spied her empty shoes, both standing perfectly upright on their sleek heels.

"I don't remember my shoes coming off—"

"Of course not," Danny said, "a bad fall is like being in the funnel of a tornado, dear girl. Well, nothing about Our Little Dorothy seems particularly damaged but That Ankle." He frowned at the offending joint. "You must sit right here and collect your crumpets whilst I rush below for some cold water. The minute you get home you must elevate and ice-pack it. Now, don't move!"

Off he went, leaping airily down the treacherous steps.

Why would she move? Temple felt several dozen numb tinglings that were trying to be bruises, and worse, she was breathless and shaky. But she didn't feel like bawling, a distinct improvement over her behavior after her last physical disaster. Perhaps Matt's martial arts training was making her into a big, brave girl.

From above her came slow, ponderous steps. A security guard was lumbering down toward her, angling over to the wall she huddled against to take hold of the remaining section of safety rail.

While she watched, he clasped it, stepped down, grabbed on, and gazed in horror when it came away in his hand. Temple, looking up, saw another runaway log *en route* toward her stranded body at a bouncing, unpredictable clip.

She curled into a ball protecting her head, expecting imminent collision.

Instead she was showered with a dash of cold water and surfaced sputtering.

The runaway railing was bouncing to the bottom, knocking over her upright shoes on the way down.

The guard, still vertical, made his huffing way down to her and her baptizer, Danny Dove. Danny shrugged at her damp condition and lifted a half empty pail.

"Sorry, kiddo. It was either a bath or another beating."

"I never seen the like." The elderly guard sat on the steps above Temple to collect his breath and himself. "That there railing would have whomped you good, but this fellow just hoppity-skipped up the stairs like lightning and clipped the thing in mid-air so it bounced off the other wall. You do Kung Fu or something, mister?"

"Ballet," Danny Dove answered promptly, kneeling to plunge Temple's right ankle into the icy water. " 'Swan Lake' could train pole vaulters."

The guard twisted to regard the bare walls. Empty wrought-iron railing brackets clung to them like large, predatory flies. "What's going on here?"

"Criminal negligence," Danny Dove snapped. "Obviously the screws were loose, not only on the railing brackets, but in the head of whoever is responsible for maintaining the basement area. If this had happened a few hours later, when those stairs are used by dozens of dancers, it could have been a mass tragedy."

Temple squeaked politely. Danny looked down at her water-logged ankle again.

"Sorry, dear thing. Am I winding this too tightly? It's only some sheeting strips left over from a set-flat dutchman job, but the best bandage available.

"If you," he told the guard severely, surveying the man's Elvis-paunch middle, "can manage to crawl up and get the maintenance staff, and Miss von Rhine, we can clean up this mess and get Miss Temple on her way to some real treatment."

The burly guard nodded and worked his way upward, grabbing

the occasional bracket like a mountain climber clinging to pitons.

"There, there," Danny Dove crooned as he lifted Temple's sopping foot from the bucket. "You'll be dancing the marimba again in a day or two."

"That's funny," she said, "I sure couldn't dance it before."

When he laughed at her apt paraphrase of the ancient surgeon/violin joke, she added, "I don't think I could even *cook* it."

Chapter 18

Devine Revelations

When Nicky Fontana's silver Corvette convertible pulled up in front of the Circle Ritz, Electra and Matt were waiting by the curb that the 'Vette's tires came close enough to kiss.

Their identical expressions of concern took a comical turn toward other emotions as they eyed Temple's mode of transportation. Dark, dashing Nicky Fontana did not make a low-profile chauffeur, either. Electra's gray eyes glimmered with speculation; Matt's looked wary.

Had Matt's troubles not been so much more serious than hers, Temple might have enjoyed his shock.

Nicky vaulted over the driver's side door without opening it—apparently he was as light on his feet as Danny Dove—and came around to release Temple via the passenger door.

Electra was poised on the curb, tsking constantly in manic Mother Hen style, to take Temple's tote bag. Nicky helped Temple exit the low-slung car, but Matt was quick to support her once she was on her stocking feet.

Being the centerpiece of such intense concern might comfort

some; it might even flatter some women, since two of the solacing trio were attractive men.

To Temple it was sheer hell. She wished she could shake off their quite literal support, but her shoes were in her tote bag and her aching ankle was too quirky to rely on.

Had her current state resulted from an outright assault, it might hold a certain tawdry glamour, as it had the last time. But, no. This time she was just someone who had creamed herself while walking up the stairs—badly. A clumsy klutz. The self-description particularly stung: trotting about on her trademark three-inch-high heels had been Temple's personal declaration of independence since she was fifteen.

"Really, I'm fine," Temple insisted gamely through the throb, as she had been doing since succored by the amazingly adept Danny Dove.

As everyone had been doing since her fall, they turned a deaf ear.

She glanced at the nearest unheeding orifice, Nicky Fontana's, as it happened. Temple decided that the social necessities would remove the focus from her unreliable foot. Introductions were in order.

"This is my landlady, Electra Lark," she said with a wave of her only free hand. "Matt Devine is a neighbor and . . . my martial arts instructor."

"And I know *that* ole boy from way back." Nicky nodded toward the Circle Ritz entrance. A black cat sat in the shade.

"Louie!" Temple was touched. Even the cat, watching them, looked almost solicitous.

"How do you know Temple's cat?" Matt asked.

She hastened to finish the introductions before Matt reached erroneous conclusions of his own. "Nicky Fontana owns the Crystal Phoenix, where I had my . . . mishap. That's where Midnight Louie used to hang his collar, if he ever had one. Then one day he moseyed up to the Convention Center and found a dead body and caught my eye. He's been with me ever since. Now I'm working at the Phoenix, when I'm not falling flat on my face, and Nicky was kind enough to insist on driving me home."

Nicky nodded at Temple's friends, unintimidated by Electra's punkish hairdo or Matt's martial arts expertise. He was also unaffected by Temple's tendency to pooh-pooh her injury.

"You didn't fall on your face; you fell on your foot. A bad ankle sprain," he announced in the tone of a doctor transferring a patient's care to a new team. "Our choreographer, Danny Dove, has seen dozens of dance injuries. He prescribed elevation and ice packs. And"—Nicky smiled at Temple with stern charm—"it was no trouble bringing Temple home. She's doing a lot for the Phoenix. Plus, I don't want any personal injury suits."

"I'd never—"

Nicky's smile had faded into a frown. "Van would have my head on a shish-kebab stick for saying this, but I doubt that your 'accident' was one. Those screws were deliberately loosened."

"How would anyone know when I would walk up those particular stairs—or that I'd take them instead of the elevator?"

"They wouldn't. I don't mean that someone meant to injure you, only that you happened into a trap planned to injure a cast of thousands . . . well, dozens anyway—and the Crystal Phoenix Hotel and Casino itself."

"What exactly do you mean?" Matt asked.

Nicky nonchalantly twirled his key chain around his forefinger. "People have tried to put the Crystal Phoenix out of business even before we reopened. They attempted this sort of sabotage before they came right out in the open and tried to trash Van's remodeling." He glanced at Temple. "If you weren't so busy feeling foolish about something that wasn't your fault, you'd realize that those rail brackets were loosened with intent to cause bodily harm. Your body was moot."

"But why?" Temple wondered. "Why then, and why now?"

"I don't know. We never pinned the last round on anybody specific. But this time the stakes have escalated: we ended up with a dead body on the premises." He pointed at Temple, keys jangling. "So get plenty of rest before you come back, and be ready for more fires to put out. Obviously, just the whisper of trouble at the Phoenix is enough to eat into our operation. In the meantime, I'll have my brothers look into it."

Temple must have looked less than impressed. Nicky abruptly ran a hand through his dark hair, then cleared his throat. "And . . . I, uh, might lean on my Uncle Mario for some backup too. So not to worry."

"Don't you worry, either," Matt said pointedly to Nicky, sounding flatteringly possessive. "We've got her now."

Nicky's seasoned glance dropped from Matt's face to his arm at Temple's waist, holding her weight off her feet.

"So you have," Nicky agreed. He nodded at Electra. "My big brother would kill for that earring. Really radical."

Then he was again vaulting into the low car without benefit of door. The engine thrummed as if uttering a challenge to the bridled Hesketh Vampire motorcycle shut up in its storage shed. The next instant the Corvette was a smooth silver streak peeling around the corner without so much as a squeal.

"What a *nice* young man," Electra observed in tones that were hardly maternal, her forefinger giving the Harley Hog earring in her right ear a swing.

"He's married," Temple said, as much for Matt's benefit as Electra's. "Ouch."

Apparently that was Matt's cue to scoop up Temple and head for the bunkerlike bulk of the Circle Ritz. She was always getting into these post-bridal positions with Matt, Temple reflected, at least as far as crossing thresholds went, without benefit of any engagement, not to mention foreplay.

In the sleekly bare lobby, Electra deposited the tote bag on Temple's elevated lap with an apologetic smile. Louie twined himself among the legs still touching the floor, which did not include Temple's.

"I've got a wedding at three—two soap opera stars," Electra said with zest. "Guess who? Lorelei from 'Heaven's Heights' and Brando, the hunk from 'All My Sins,' are getting married! I mean, the actors who play them, whoever *they* are, are getting married, not the characters. I don't want to start any irresponsible rumors. I'm going to surround the bridal arch with 'champagne bubbles' of clear balloons. It will be soooo cute. I'll check on you later, dear." She glanced at Matt. "Much later, of course."

Temple shook her head as she watched Electra glide away in the usual eye-dazzling muumuu. "Aren't you playing the organ for the ceremony?" she asked Matt.

His answer came disconcertingly close to her ear, which was unblessed by any radical earrings.

"Soap opera isn't in my musical repertoire." He paused by the elevators while Temple did her part and pressed the call button. " 'I'm Forever Blowing Bubbles' doesn't lend itself to a wedding march, not even on an instrument as ponderous as an organ. I suppose I could play 'Whispering Hope.' "

" 'Whispering Hope,' " Temple repeated nostalgically. "I didn't know people even remembered those old songs, like 'Silver Threads Among the Gold' and 'Jeannie with the Light Brown Hair.' They were rather obsessive about hair color then, weren't they?"

"There wasn't much of a music selection in seminary," Matt said dryly, stepping into the elevator with Temple, tote bag and all.

Not until she had produced her keys and was borne to her living-room sofa did Temple feel like someone who could stand on her own two feet again, even though she sat.

Something had changed in the weeks since she was attacked by thugs desperately seeking information about Max. Maybe the change had come since she had arranged her ersatz prom night with Matt. The remote hope of intimacy between them had become less remote and less of a hope than a . . . threat. They had a fledgling relationship now: anything that pushed it into a new configuration could be as much loss as gain.

She felt clumsy again, and awkward, and as if even that were her fault.

"Guilt," Matt said, taking the word out of her mind if not her mouth.

"What?"

"Guilt makes people apologize for something negative happening to them. It's a bad habit."

He vanished into the kitchen. Temple heard him wrestling ice cubes from the dang plastic twist-trays that she could do nothing with . . . except break fingernails on them. She winced at the wrenching squeak when the cold little devils popped from their plastic condominiums into the warm, cruel world where they would shortly melt into oblivion.

Matt had no such problems overempathizing with ice cubes. Her ankle was soon collared in a damp towel lumpy with ice.

Matt moved a pile of newspapers on the oversized ottoman and sat in the vacancy.

"How are you feeling, really?" he asked.

Temple's head wagged from side to side in the gesture that meant "so-so." She suspected that her congealing bruises were beyond counting, but she had sustained no major hurt. Her ankle's aching and burning had eased already. Her pride was still in a touchy, tender state, though.

"Electra will spend the evening with you," Matt said. "This is my shift. What can I do?"

"Nothing for a while. I just want to sit and think about it."

"The accident?"

"The maybe-accident. Nicky seemed pretty serious."

"Who's his Uncle Mario?"

"I was afraid you'd ask. I'm afraid that I know: 'Macho Mario' Fontana. Once upon a time, when the mob still ran this town, Macho Mario was a big wheel over all the little crime cogs in this town."

"And you work for his nephew?"

"Nicky's the white sheep of the family, honest. With the Gaming Commission eyeing every transaction, nobody in Las Vegas could get away with crime connections now."

"I see. So elves murdered my stepfather."

"I'm talking about organized crime, not the usual freelance round of lust, larceny and murder. Las Vegas's dicey reputation gave it a kind of hard-edged glamour in the old days. Poking fun at it is like teasing a paper tiger nowadays. Heck, even my Gridiron skit plays on all the paranoid conspiracy theories that grew up around this town. I created a secret stash of mob money under the new Scarab theme hotel, affectionately known as 'the Scab,' only the underground area is also a clandestine government nuclear testing site, where they've hidden all the aliens that landed at Nellis Air Force Base, and there are thousands of those. It's a sendup of the excessive, spooky stuff that gets said about this city."

"Sounds weird enough to dazzle even Las Vegans."

"You should see the set they're gonna do! Danny Dove was showing me the plans just before I made like Jill-up-a-hill. So spectacularly garish—that isn't easy to achieve in this town."

"And here you were worried because your arch-rival Crawford Buchanan was show chairman. Sounds like it turned out okay."

"Okay . . . as long as I don't see much of Crawford. And as long as he doesn't mess with my production number. Oh, and they persuaded Johnny Diamond to sing my Las Vegas Follies medley; he is such a powerhouse! Listen, can you go to the Gridiron? I mean, with me?''

"My investigations have reached a dead end, so I suppose I can get the night off if I ask in advance." Matt paused to pick up a section of the *Las Vegas Sun*. "Sure. Will Lieutenant Molina be doing a solo too?''

Temple's good mood plummeted. "Only around the Crystal Phoenix crime scene.''

She leaned forward to adjust the towel on her ankle. Matt leaped up to help, ruining her attempt to buy time while she decided whether or not to tell him something personal.

Before Temple could lean back, he had stuffed a couple of supporting pillows behind her. Solicitation made her nervous. Anything that made her feel helpless did.

"One thing my tumble taught me," she began.

He waited, unaware that this was not what she was going to say originally.

"I think I'm less afraid of being hurt. Not that I'm getting masochistic, but since I've been attempting martial arts, I see myself as less fragile. I know I can get hurt and that I'll heal.''

"That's good. If you feel durable, you'll act that way. When it shows, people are less liable to mess with you. And if they do, you're more resilient. That's the trouble with our sexist society: women are so afraid of getting hurt that they let their lives be scribed by that fear.''

"Men don't?''

"Maybe men don't let on. That's what we're supposed to learn in team sports: how to get hurt . . . and go on . . . and not let on. Men fear getting hurt in other, less tangible ways.''

Temple nodded. "So do women. Your stepfather's murder—''

Matt kept still, even when Midnight Louie leaped atop the newspapers covering half of the huge ottoman. After some comfy pawing and paper-crackling, his big black paws tucked into each other. Temple was reminded of a mandarin innocently slipping his long-nailed hands inside his robe sleeves for warmth and security. Now Midnight Louie was listening, too. Temple hated broaching a mutual sore spot in public, but she had to do it.

"Molina's on the case now.''

"I thought you said it was some other homicide lieutenant."

"It was. It is. But Molina's got an open file that ties into the Effinger death. That file just happens to involve Max's disappearance."

Matt's listening posture stiffened. In a way, Temple was glad that mention of Max Kinsella made him as nervous as talk of his late and definitely unlamented stepfather. Maybe it substantiated his innocence.

Temple finally plunged in where Molina would never fear to tread.

"A man was found dead above the Goliath Hotel gaming area the same night that Max disappeared. The corpse, which was never identified, was wedged into a cubby-hole fashioned from the air-conditioning duct. Molina figures an ace magician would be a natural to set up that spy-hole."

"Why?"

"Who knows? Not me. Not Molina. But, coupling the man's sudden death with Max going AWOL that night, Molina is convinced that something was rotten at the Goliath . . . besides the body odor in the air-conditioning duct."

"Do you think Max is capable of shady dealing . . . even of murder?"

"No. But I didn't know then what I know now."

"What?" His eyes met hers for the first time since she'd brought up his stepfather's death.

Temple squirmed on the sofa. At least Matt stayed put now, instead of jumping up at her every move.

She bit her lip. "Molina found an old record on Max. Nothing much, an Interpol file. Max was still a teenager then, but he was suspected of IRA involvement."

"Figures," Matt said promptly. "Kinsella's an Irish name. Tons of Roman Catholics are Irish, and more than a few succumb to backing the IRA."

"Don't you think I'd know if I were living with an international terrorist?"

"Don't get agitated; you'll hurt your foot."

"Forget my foot! Just figure the likelihood that Max was some sort of undercover agent."

"Didn't he travel a lot?"

"Magicians do. They have to go places to perform."

"Out of the country?"

"What are you? Junior detective?" The ache was no longer just in Temple's ankle. "Sure, out of the country, and all over it."

"I can see Molina's point." Matt looked annoying calm. "He traveled, and I assume he was clever at deceiving people?" Temple nodded glumly. "Physically fit?" She nodded again. "Molina is not incompetent, however much you'd wish her assumptions were wrong."

"You're right. See! I *don't* wish everybody to be wrong. The point is, with your stepfather dead, killed in that place and particular way, I don't know what to think about the first death anymore. I even wonder if this second killing means that Max is . . . back. But then that makes him a murderer, and I won't believe that I lived with a murderer."

Matt kept silent, pleating a corner of the newspaper he'd held since the conversation had taken this turn.

"You don't believe that you *loved* a murderer," he finally corrected her in a subdued voice. "We can love terrible people, Temple, even people who behave terribly to us."

"Your stepfather?" she suggested quickly.

He shook his head. "He was too cruel, too alien. And he hurt my mother, too. But she . . . put up with it. She saw no other answer. Her family, the church, the way society thought about abusive men then certainly encouraged her to play the martyr, even to relish the role. His violence became her secret crown of thorns. She would win honor in heaven by forgiving it, and him, by enduring it, and him, by being the perfect doormat. She became his silent partner. I knew, even when I was still pretty young that she had sold us out, but I loved her anyway, though I didn't understand."

"You're saying that if you ever at any time had a decent relationship with someone, you have a big stake in believing that they didn't use you, didn't abuse you. You become a little blind."

He nodded, then tossed the mangled newspaper aside.

"Why should you listen to me? Why should anyone listen to me? I've figured out my own case down to the finest point. I've sat with counselors and shrinks and worried my own past to shreds, until I thought I had turned into cerebral stone. 'The Thinker' as boat anchor. I've learned exactly why I became what I became, am what I am now. I just don't know how to change it."

"Maybe it's too soon," Temple pointed out. "Does your underlying motive mean you fear relationships because they were so painful to you? Are you afraid to be disappointed, to be hurt?"

Matt shook his head. "That would be simpler. I suppose there's an element of that; there always is. But my monster wears its hide inside out. I'm not really afraid of *being* hurt; I'm afraid of hurting."

Temple sat up, away from the comforting pillows. She looked at Matt as if she had never seen him before. She had never felt the need to look at Max Kinsella that way. Perhaps she should have.

"You think . . . you would have killed Cliff Effinger, if you had found him before someone else did?"

Matt regarded the floor. Louie, moved by some mysterious feline impulse, merowed impatiently and twitched his tail, as if urging Matt to 'fess up.

Matt looked up with dead-serious eyes. "I would have hurt him, Temple, if I could have. I don't know if I could have stopped myself."

"What if he was still bigger, and meaner? He could have hurt you, killed you, had you entangled again."

Matt shook his head. "Not now. He's not . . . wasn't . . . dangerous to me anymore. Knowledge is power, and power is temptation. I've thought of finding him, confronting him for so long now, and so much more lately, I even wonder if I . . . if I did."

"Matt . . . you'd know."

"Would I? Denial is a magic cloak. Only it doesn't make *you* invisible, it makes things you don't want to see invisible. I remember a tragic case at my first parish, a newborn infant found in a toilet at the grade school." He shut his eyes at her gasp of shock, but didn't look up when he opened them again. "Umbilical cord attached. Dead, of course. Drowned at birth, perhaps during birth. It was a several-cubicle facility, children were coming and going in gangs of thirty. Certainly, she was in there at the same time, the mother. The scandal was hushed up. The church was better at that in those days. They finally found the mother, the murderer, the victim. One of the youngest nuns. She had no memory of the act, or any act that led to it. No memory. All of it was so foreign to her religious commitment that she blotted it from her mind. She couldn't blot it from her body. Call it a form of hysterical psychic blindness. Apparently a lot of clergy are capable of that. Something about trying to be holy blinds one to ordinary evil. Look what I did to my apartment. I barely remember doing that."

"That, but not your stepfather," Temple broke in, horrified. "You're not delusional, Matt, and neither am I. I know you didn't do it! You didn't kill him."

Matt smiled, wearied by his self-examination, yet amused by her defensive nature.

"Tell that to the skeptical Lieutenant Molina. She'll point out that you didn't know Kinsella was an IRA terrorist, either."

Chapter 19

Phone Alone

Matt sat by the telephone, home alone.

The phrase "days off" meant more to him now. Working nights made every day an "off" day, in a sense. It freed normal business hours for his abnormal pursuit of the truth—the truth about Father Rafael Hernandez and perhaps about himself.

He had been derelict. His personal life and the crazy way his past and present was intersecting—Temple and the Gridiron hijinks at the Crystal Phoenix, his stepfather's shockingly odd death in the Phoenix casino, so bizarrely reminiscent of the Mystifying Max's dramatic exit—had distracted him from this unpleasant mission. No more.

Now the phone receiver was pressed to his left ear again, while his right hand—hardly knowing what it was doing—scribed circles within circles on his note pad.

"Who did you say was assistant pastor when Father Hernandez was at Holy Rosary? Frank Bucek. How could I reach him? I know it's been a long time. . . . St. Vincent Seminary. Indiana."

Matt dutifully repeated the information. *Pretend.* Pretend that he was writing it down, dealing with unfamiliar syllables.

He wasn't. He most decidedly wasn't, which was why his insides cramped in a cold, iron grip.

Father Frank Bucek. Once upon a time, long ago, assistant pastor at Holy Rosary in Tempe, Arizona. And many years after that . . . Matt's spiritual advisor at the Indiana seminary.

An image of the man floated on the pale blank wall of Matt's bedroom. A spare man in a black cassock with knife-keen gray eyes and a receding hairline. Devoted, energetic, another apparently perfect priest. And, long before the seminary, he had been Father Hernandez's assistant pastor in Tempe. The trail from Our Lady of Guadalupe had led right back to Matt's own ecclesiastical roots.

Father Furter, the older guys in seminary had called Bucek. Matt didn't know why until later; the nickname came from Frank N. Furter, the cross-dressing protagonist of *The Rocky Horror Picture Show*. These days, Matt knew what that film was about, sort of, from popular repute. He suspected that the Legion of Decency would have condemned it back in the fifties. Now, it was a cult film precisely because it was naughty, not nice.

The nickname had no significance but to display the seminarians' rebellion and harmless irreverence. Lives steeped in study and prayer need a healthy dose of mischief. Father Frank had been a straight arrow, Matt remembered; he would swear to that. He recalled the man's other nickname: Father Furtive. Matt smiled at that one, which *did* mean something. Father Bucek seemed to have as many eyes as an Idaho potato. He always knew when mischief or a seminarian's defenses were up. A hard man man to fool, Father Furtive.

Matt didn't relish trying to smooth-talk him into revelations about Father Hernandez. He didn't like the idea of contacting him at all. If there was anybody in the world harder than parents to tell you were leaving the priesthood, it was your spiritual advisor, the one person who knew you inside out—or at least knew you as well as you had to know yourself then.

Calling Father Bucek, confessing his present status, would be the hardest thing Matt had done yet to disengage from the priesthood. It would be worse than disappointing a parent. It would be like disappointing a good father, which Matt had never had in a family sense. *The* good father, who was, after all, only a few steps removed from the Heavenly Father Himself.

Cliff Effinger was dead, Matt told himself, his hand still clenched on the plastic receiver long after he had hung up.

That didn't mean that Matt had run out of father figures to worry about hurting, one way or another.

Twenty-four hours later, Matt sat in the same place, his worn address book open to the long-distance number of St. Vincent Seminary. That was just a formality, a crutch. He knew the phone number by heart.

In twenty-four hours, he'd had endless opportunities to practice his presentation. The process reminded him of agonizing mental rehearsals for childhood confessions. No one is as scrupulous as a terrified ten-year-old, toting up selfishness and lies and assorted "unkindnesses to others."

Those confessions had been a variety of well-intended lies in themselves; nothing of Matt's true home life had come out. Nothing resembling it was covered in the catechisms the children pored over to prepare for each new sacrament.

Matt picked up the receiver and dialed the number, once more familiar than his home phone number in Chicago.

A man answered. "St. Vincent Seminary."

"I'm calling for Father Frank Bucek."

"Father who?"

Matt smiled. The voice was deep but young. Some raw recruit was stuck with switchboard duty.

"Father Bucek," Matt repeated. "He's an instructor and spiritual advisor."

"There's no Father Bucek here."

Was that a slim warm filament of relief coiling in the clammy pit of Matt's stomach? Relief tightened into disbelief, and almost exploded into anger.

"Check the roster," Matt suggested, an edge in his voice he couldn't quite control.

"Just a moment."

The moment became many. Matt hung on, hating the ambiguous silence of an empty phone line. The distasteful task had become imperative. Now that he had committed to contacting Father Bucek again, he intended to get it over with, or know the reason why.

"Can I help you?"

Matt started. This voice sounded older, even venerable. Though the timber faltered, the tone was confident. Matt felt like a green seminarian again, caught behaving less well than he should be.

"I'm trying to reach Father Frank Bucek," he said. This old bird would know the name, Matt was sure.

"I'm sorry, but Father Bucek is no longer at St. Vincent Seminary."

Not there? Of course he was there! He *was* St. Vincent Seminary, as far as Matt was concerned. Human monuments don't walk away from their chosen environments.

"Where did he go?" Matt blurted, hating his clumsiness.

"I'm not at liberty to say."

Another curve ball straight into the solar plexus. Matt remembered the voice now. Old Father Cartwright, the sacristan. How could this ancient still be there and Father Frank gone? And why the secrecy?

"Gee, that's too bad." Matt was sounding his ingenuous, bland phone self again. He went into the well practiced song-and-dance about Father Hernandez's "This Is Your Life" tribute. He was even beginning to believe it himself.

"And," he finished with glib flair, "Father Bucek was Father Rafe's assistant at his first pastorate. It would be so great to have Father Bucek here for the tribute. The parish would pay the transportation . . . unless it's somewhere prohibitive, like Hawaii." Matt laughed engagingly at the improbability of that notion.

"Not quite that far," Father Cartwright conceded . . . gave away . . . a dry smile apparent in his voice. "But—"

Matt frowned. This was very odd. Had the church grown paranoid with all the current charges against priests? The whereabouts of transferred clergy had not always been a state secret.

"Tell you what, young man—" Matt could almost see Father Cartwright's lips pursing in doubt. "I can contact him, and give him your address and phone number, if he wishes to call you."

"Why the rigamarole?" Matt asked bluntly.

An awkward silence. "Sorry. It's just that it might be difficult, and not appropriate for the 'This Is Your Life' program you're putting together. Father . . . Frank is no longer with us."

"But where is he assigned now? Surely you can tell me that."

"That's just it. He's left the priesthood."

Now the silence on the line was thunderous: the rush of blood pounding in Matt's ears sounded like a faulty connection.

Matt stumbled automatically through a rote recital of his address and phone number. He wasn't sure he got the still-unfamiliar numerals right, and he didn't care.

The drone of a broken connection was Muzak to his throbbing ears. He hung up with a slam that mattered to no one but himself. A bang, not a whimper.

Not there? How dare he? Now that Matt had mastered himself and was ready to confront the past, a big chunk of it had mysteriously vanished. Father Furtive, all right. The other guys had been righter than they knew. Sneaking off like a truant. Beyond reach, like the Pope in Rome or something. Father Oh-so-high-and-mighty now Father Nothing. Left. He left. Too. Why?

Matt felt his hands itching to seize the phone, hurl it across the room at the wall, at the chintzy crates that served as bookshelves.

Instead he looked inward at the flushed face of his rage.

He saw his own face, only an infantile version of it, round and unshapen, yet empurpled by some toddler tantrum.

Of course. Matt released the breath that had made his chest into a prison and his ribs into iron bars containing the explosion. He rubbed his chin, to assure himself his adult face was in proper place.

What he felt was infantile rage for his natural father's mysterious defection, transferred to Father . . . ex-Father Bucek. Frank, now. Just Frank.

Matt's hands slapped his thighs. He should be pleased. If his spiritual director, his personal role model from seminary, had also left the priesthood, it validated Matt's action. Father Bucek had seemed decades older than he, but young people always divided folks into Us and the Ancients Over Thirty, one undifferentiated decaying clot. Thinking about it, Frank Bucek was probably only in his late forties. Young enough to make a career change.

Would he call? Did it matter? Yes, in terms of testimony about Father Hernandez, who had not yet left the priesthood, and probably never would. In terms of Matt's own peace of mind . . . ? He shook his head at the phone, as if it were a sentient thing that could hold an opinion.

He didn't know. His falsehood about the tribute certainly hadn't given Bucek a pressing reason to call.

"It's not important," he softly told the phone. "I don't need to know his story."

He smiled to recall Temple's recent lecture on the abuse of the "need to know" principle.

"And I doubt that Father Furtive needs to know mine."

Chapter 20

Dis-guys

Some may find it odd that I am not home at the Circle Ritz ingratiating myself with Miss Temple Barr during her hour of need, but I was never cut out for the nursing profession.

My talents are best put to use removing vermin from the mean and dirty streets, rather than from the sterile environs of a sickroom.

Not that Miss Temple is sick in the classic sense, but I am sure that a bum hind-paw is no fun fast, especially since it will make wearing her trademark high heels difficult for a time.

So I do not scamper home to the Circle Ritz to throw my two cents and tongue-licks into the feeding frenzy of concern flurrying around the invalid. Miss Temple Barr is a lady whose care for others wins her an avalanche of tending when she is in need herself. Surely she will prefer the tender attentions of Mr. Matt Devine far more than my sandpaper-brand of succor.

No, I can better spend my time tracking down the heinous handy-men who sent my little doll tumbling down a hill of concrete stairs like Jill on a roller-coaster ride with a pail of sand instead of water.

Fortunately, I know just who to look for: one Vito, surname unknown. (Now there is a luckless sire with a pressing reason to get lost.)

Unfortunately, I have not spied Vito or his ilk around the Crystal Phoenix of late, though this trick with the loosened stair-rail brackets has his no-doubt-well-documented fingerprints all over it.

So I hunker down in the Crystal Phoenix basement, with which I am well acquainted. Some of my most cherished moments occurred in the dressing rooms here: my tender rendezvous with the Divine Yvette; my quite literal nailing of the Stripper Killer; the TLC I received from the Phoenix showgirls when I was only a down-and-out street dude without a reputation as a world-class shamus.

My long-stemmed gals from the good old days remain in full feather, I discover as the clock ticks toward the evening hours and showtime nears.

"It is Louie!" they chorus when I make my rounds of the dressing rooms.

"Ooh," says Miss Darcy McGill Austen, lifting me atop a makeup-cluttered dressing table. "You have gained weight!"

I do not make a practice of sweeping people off their feet and commenting publicly about their supposed avoirdupois.

"Then it is lucky that we have no treats on hand," Miss Midge Mancini responds quite carelessly. She flourishes instead the wire brush for polishing my topcoat to black satin. I produce a half-hearted purr as I undergo this massage, being most annoyed that the eats are absent.

Soon my flock of attendants scatter. Their hour upon the stage draws near. The busy, bustling underbelly of the Crystal Phoenix is suddenly silent and empty.

This is the way I like it. I jump off the red velvet pillow Miss Darcy McGill keeps for my visits and land soft as a powderpuff on the hard concrete. If evil is afoot down here, now is when it will stir.

Yet all remains still, except for a few feathered costumes trembling like aspen leaves in the air-conditioning vents' icy exhalation.

I prowl the hallway, seeing and hearing nothing. . . . Finally, I detect a familiar sound. Not the drip, drip, drip of a forgotten faucet, but the patter of high-heeled feet. Miss Temple Barr cannot be abroad! Perhaps a showgirl has left behind an essential item of dress, such as a g-string.

I duck into a dressing room doorway, then peek.

Sure enough, one of these long, tall tootsies is hotfooting it down the hall on silver size-eleven high heels, none too quietly . . . or gracefully. In fact, when one ankle twists she pauses to emit a few choice words, most of which would not be chosen by anyone who wanted to avoid an R-rating on a movie script. I am sorry to say that these dancing dolls sometimes grow a tad hardened from their gypsy lifestyle. My subject grabs the metal upright bar of a hallway costume rack, continuing her colorful cussing and yanking at the rhinestoned heel strap of her offending shoe. This gives me a chance to examine her full undraped glory.

Whew. Showgirl material must be in short supply. Despite rhinestone swags hanging off everything from headdress to feathered skirt, I have never seen such bony elbows, knees and feet, not to mention razor-stubbled legs that should be peach-satin-smooth. Despite the dim light, I even detect a smudge on her upper lip.

Imagine my amazement when my unattractive prey is joined by a man in a brown UPS uniform who is at least four inches shorter than she. Lili Marlene at her lamp-post she is not.

"God, I am dying for a cigarette," she mutters in greeting, her voice as grating as her appearance.

"Not on the job," he growls, eyeing her up and down with a leer. "Some snazzy outfit. Get any dates yet?"

"Shut up!" she growls, smashing her heel-clad shoe to concrete. "You will get a blind date with an incinerator if you keep up the smart remarks. Are you sure no one saw you come down here?"

Naturally, I am extremely interested in the turn this conversation is taking. I edge forward in the dark of the dressing room, closer to the door.

How am I to know that I am stepping on the trailing chiffon veil of a headdress gracing a white styrofoam headblock high on an unseen shelf?

This is how I know: the gruesome head and about twelve pounds of rhinestones come smashing down on my unprotected form, flashing and crashing like a Fourth of July firework all the way.

At least I have the sense to dive back deep into the room and burrow into a box of tap shoes—ouch! Those metal toe-stubbers hurt. Not the best shelter, but the pair at the door are too busy bickering to search high and low, which is the only place they would find a savvy customer like Midnight Louie.

"No one here," the UPS guy announces after a cursory search.

"Of course not," Lady Godiva says in a baritone grumble. "These damn outfits are so heavy the thing probably collapsed of its own weight and fell. I do not know how those broads manage to shake a leg, much less the good stuff, in this body-armor. Let us get to work before intermission comes and somebody spots us."

The high heels click away like they are being worn by Chester Goode from "Gunsmoke." Now is that not a mental image to cherish?

But I have no time to dwell on vintage television shows, for I have finally seen through the sawdust and the glitter to spot the five o-clock shadow and the gut beneath the rhinestone facade, skimpy as it is. That is no showgirl, that is Vito in the flesh, if you can call it that.

I scamper to the doorway and poke a cautious muzzle down the hall.

I cannot believe my eyes, ears and nose. I am too late. The pair have vanished like the Cheshire Cat, not even leaving a grin behind.

I thoroughly reconnoiter the area. No dice. No dudes in showgirl skin. Even my ever-faithful nose loses the trail when I pause by the costume rack. In sneezing at a noxious aroma of powder and sweat, I inhale a pink cloud of tiny ostrich feathers and ruin my sniffer for the nonce. Done in by a dead bird.

Of course my investigations are over for now. Sometimes life is a drag.

Chapter 21

Unauthorized Landing

Some call a flock of songbirds an "exultation of larks."

Some call a crowd of carrion birds a "murder of crows."

What does one call a full complement of Fontana brothers?

Temple pondered this intriguing question. A press of pastel suits? A bulk of bodyguards? A huddle of hoods? A muscle of mobsters? Or just a mob of undirected motive and opportunity?

The brothers Fontana, a uniform six feet tall, surrounded Temple on her triumphal return to the Crystal Phoenix, forcing her to ponder another fine point.

Could even the most optimistic public relations specialist call limping along in silver metallic sneakers (one loosely laced to accommodate an ankle the size of a breakfast bagel) . . . "triumphal"? Temple didn't have to worry about answering her own question, for a Fontana brother spoke.

"We are here to render assistance," said one tall, dark and striking brother.

Another offered a supportive arm with a mute smile.

"We are here to protect you," a third corrected threateningly.

"And to protect the hotel." A fourth spoke with equal ferocity.

"Where would you like to go?" a fifth asked.

"Would you prefer to be carried?" suggested the sixth.

"She is little," the seventh said. "We could put her in a chair and easily tote her to and fro."

"Is there anything you need?" The eighth cocked a helpful head in her direction, the better to display a single tasteful pewter earring in the form of a chain saw.

"No, thank you, Ralph," Temple said, relieved to recognize one familiar face, no matter how luridly accessorized. "Except maybe . . . name tags for you guys?"

A flurry of Fontanas dispersed, leaving Temple alone with Ralph and a naked-ear clone who swiftly introduced himself.

"Giuseppe. Nicky said we was responsible for nothing going wrong with you or your work for the hotel. You can expect us to stick to you like a mudpack from now on, whenever you're on the premises."

Ah. A mudpack of mafiosi . . . only we all know The Family doesn't exist, and besides, the Fontana brothers are not it, Temple reminded herself. Great. A high-profile escort of dubious types was likely to get Temple arrested. All she needed now to keep her from getting any kind of job done anywhere was a tail of tall lieutenant on her track.

Temple cautiously examined the glittering Crystal Phoenix lobby. No obvious police present. Not a soul in the vicinity who looked even faintly authoritarian, except for the burgundy-uniformed security personnel with gilt phoenixes embroidered on their breast pockets.

Oops. And a pale-suited flock of returning Fontana brothers. Temple swallowed a smile as they came close enough for her to read. Each expensive lapel now bore a stick-on name label outlined in a different color. Red for Rico, green for Giuseppe, blue for Aldo, lavender for Ernesto, yellow for Julio, orange for Armando, fuchsia for Emilio, and purple for Eduardo, the brother who had stayed behind. Ralph, of course, was readily identifiable by his earring . . . and also by a new pink-bordered nametag that decidedly clashed with the earring.

"Now," Ralph asked, "where would you like to go?"

"To the Gridiron rehearsal. Didn't that move to the actual stage yesterday?"

"You are correct."

"No more dark, damp, dangerous basements," said Emilio.

"You will be safer up here," Ernesto announced.

"Uncle Mario's men are patrolling the lower regions," Julio added forbiddingly.

"And the railings are fixed . . . with concrete," Rico put in modestly.

"Is there nothing we can do?" Eduardo demanded with a note of pleading. "Nicky will be mad if we don't make ourselves useful."

"Mad *again*," Ralph said.

"Well . . ." Temple hated useless people, too.

She eyed the brothers. Why did she get the impression that each bore a bulky something under his left arm, except for Ralph, who sported a suspicious lump under his right arm? Ralph must be a lefty. Why did Lieutenant Molina never look like she'd used a wad of wet newsprint for deodorant? Surely the police went armed in a town where a gat of gangsters packed more iron than a team of manic mangler-operators?

Temple lifted her obligatory tote bag crammed with everything essential to her working life—in other words, almost everything portable she owned.

"Could one of you carry my bag?"

Several brothers dove for the privilege, converging on Temple, a flapping phantom of albino crows. . . .

Half an hour later, Temple was ensconced front-row center on a banquette in the Crystal Phoenix's Peacock Theater, the smaller of its two performance facilities.

Her injured foot lay elevated on the crimson velvet banquette seat as if awaiting a glass slipper. She hoped it was a Weitzman plastic and Plexiglas pump. She certainly faced no shortage of Prince Charming candidates. One had recently deposited a short-stemmed goblet of sparkling mineral water before her. Another had opened a lined notebook. Three gold-trimmed Mont Blanc pens, produced in an instant by three different Fontana brothers—did that make them "Fontana pens"?—lined up at her right hand like well-decorated soldiers at her service.

She had never been so organized, so ready for something, and so incapable of doing much of anything.

Temple began doodling in the notebook, trying to organize details about her plans for Phoenix Under Glass. On the raised stage, set construction and lighting crews were banging away while the mostly amateur actors recruited from the news business stood around in the wings, frowning at scripts and mumbling unmemorized lines to themselves.

Danny Dove darted from tech crews to the wings like a manic dragonfly with a case of schizophrenia.

"No, no, no! That's all wrong," he would shriek over the din. "Over *there!*"

"Yes! I adore it. *Magnifique*," he would carol encouragement a moment later.

The crews, used to directional mood swings, kept their blasé expression no matter the reaction. They were, after all, union labor.

"That's where the mob would have a handhold in Vegas today," Temple muttered. "Nothing glamorous anymore, just grunt work at a going price higher than the loftiest baby-pink spotlight in the house."

"How're you doing?" asked a voice so unexpectedly near that Temple jumped.

She knew her visitor was not a noxiously solicitous Fontana brother before she turned to look. The voice was girlish, though underlined with a gritty touch of Western twang.

Turning, Temple confronted a tomboy version of herself: an elfin, red-haired woman wearing a plaid cotton shirt, honestly frayed blue jeans, freckles and sandblasted Western boots.

"Jill Diamond." She extended a tanned hand for a brief but firm shake, then nodded at Temple's bum foot. "You're lucky you only twisted a hock on that basement stairway. Nothing's more dangerous than backstage areas. I don't know why they have all them showgirls on their stiletto shoes charging up and down those concrete stairs all night."

"Tradition. That's why they call them hoofers; no stage elevator service, except for inanimate props. Oh. You must be Johnny's wife—"

"Yup." Jill tossed her rusty braids over her shoulders as she smiled. "I'm also Eightball's granddaughter."

"Eightball O'Rourke?"

"How many 'Eightballs' do you think there are, even in this town?" Jill grinned. "I guess you're keepin' my granddaddy out late nights again."

"What do you mean?"

"Isn't he working another case for you?"

"Not that I know of."

Jill tossed the straw Western hat in her right hand onto the tablecloth and sat gingerly on the velvet seat. "Well, shoot. He's been out and about more than an old soldier like him should be lately."

"What made you think he was working for me?"

"He did before. And . . . he said it was for someone at the Circle Ritz. I didn't expect him to name names. Professional discretion and all, you know. It isn't you?"

Temple shook her head. "It could be my landlady, Electra Lark. She hangs out with that crowd."

"Crowd." Jill shook her head while she watched the hullabaloo on stage. "Those old galoots think they're still in their prime. Running Glory Hole as a tourist trap isn't enough for them. My granddaddy not only has to make like a Sam Spade on Medicare, but now Spuds Lonnigan is opening a bar and grill at Temple Bar on Lake Mead. Calls it 'Three O'Clock Louie's.' That Glory Hole bunch should be napping at three o'clock in the afternoon, not remodeling some late-night dive."

"*The* Temple . . . Bar?"

Jill's clear eyes turned to Temple. "That's right; 'Bar' with one r. Say, with your handle, I'd think you would know about Temple Bar. It's a landing on the lake. Boats and excursions. Can't figure why Spuds didn't name his place 'Spuds'.' "

" 'Three O'Clock Louie' has a certain . . . seedy charm," Temple conceded, with another nocturnal Louie in mind. "Van mentioned that I had a namesake around here, or vice versa. I've also got one in London. A boat dock on Lake Mead isn't quite as toney as Queenhithe wharf on the Thames in London, is it? So your grandfather didn't say what kind of case he was working?"

Jill shook her head. "He was tracing some shifty character he had no business messing with, 'cause he was keeping later hours than an old guy should, I know that."

"You worry about him."

"Blame it on my upbringing. When the Glory Hole Gang was still hiding out, I was their only contact with the outside world. They took care of me, and I took care of them."

"Eightball struck me as someone who can look after himself."

"Maybe." Jill smiled. "I'll see if Johnny is done rehearsing on the big stage; then he'll come here and run through your number."

"Oh, that sounds so good. 'My number.' "

"I hear it's a stitch." Jill rose and retrieved her hat. "Everybody's talking about it, but no one will give away the ending, not even Johnny under pain of lethal tickling."

"Really?" Temple was pleased. Crawford Buchanan had acted like he was doing a favor for a half-wit friend by simply including Temple's piece in his one-man show.

"Oh, yeah, they're even buzzing at the other hotels. What do you expect if you needle half the big outfits in Las Vegas?"

"That's what Gridirons are for."

"Just remember that elevators are for avoiding stairs in future."

"I'll be careful," Temple said, amused. People her own size and age like Jill Diamond were seldom this solicitous.

"I'm the mother of a willful toddler," Jill confessed with a wry smile. "With me, worry is as contagious as measles."

"I'll be all right. Nicky's brothers are looking after me to a faretheewell."

"Now I'm *really* worried."

Jill slapped her hat on her blue-jeaned thigh out of long habit, then stomped back up the aisle on her petite cowboy boots.

Temple looked down at her notebook, on which she had continued to doodle. *Temple Bar*, it said in big letters. *Three O'Clock Louie.* Maybe she should offer this Spuds Lonnigan Midnight Louie as a mascot, and she could do PR for the place. Naw, she had her hands—and feet—full with the Crystal Phoenix and the Gridiron already. Then, again . . .

But who the heck at the Circle Ritz was Eightball working for? And working for hard enough that his granddaughter had time to notice, and to worry?

"Don't worry," a deep male voice urged seductively at Temple's left side. "We haven't cut your skit—yet."

"Crawford!" Temple scrambled to sit up straighter, the better to prepare for battle.

"Gout?" he asked with an automatic leer at her extended leg.

"Clout," Temple answered shortly. "I had to kick some crude dude who was staring at my legs." Despite the discomforting throb, she whisked her defenseless limb under the table.

"Rehearsals are going okay," he volunteered.

Buchanan gazed toward the stage, his akimbo arms pushing back his summer suitcoat the better to reveal his puny physique in a pale yellow shirt. Spending time around the male strippers at the Rhinestone G-string competition had spoiled Temple for the muscularly challenged.

"I don't know about Dove, though," Buchanan said in his usual basso grumble. "He doesn't seem to recognize a good skit when he sees one."

From this Temple gathered that Danny Dove was not bowled over by Crawford's own material. No wonder the director was making such a big deal of her one and only number.

"I hear you've lined up some celebrity bits," she said, determined to turn the conversation to a subject more distracting to Crawford: himself.

"Yeah." His already deep voice went subterranean with self-satisfaction. Temple imagined a panther purring in the Grand Canyon. "David Copperfield is lending us his awesome assistant-babes to lead the Lace 'n' Lust chorus line for my 'Vegas is Bustin' Out All Over' bit."

"Crawford, that's so sexist it's got balls and chains as well as cobwebs on it."

"Hey, this used to be a purely stag event in the old days. If I don't cater to the good ol' boy element, we've got no show."

"I thought the Gridiron had matured, outgrown randy jokes and raunchy skits and scatological language. Isn't Vegas catering to the family trade now?"

"You know better than to believe press-agent hype, T.B. This town has always run on three things and always will: betting, booze and boobs."

"If you are typical of the boobs, I doubt it."

He made a face, but Temple didn't linger to study it.

Instead she struggled out of her cushy seat, then limped to the short set of stairs leading up to the stage. Two Fontana brothers were at her side before she could murmur "organized crime." They gallantly assisted her up the steps, which lacked handrails. They also cut a trailing Crawford Buchanan off at the pass with superior tailoring and stern Italian faces as beautifully stony as Michelangelo's David.

"Little Miss Curlytop!"

Danny Dove greeted Temple with such a radiant smile that she couldn't have her usual hissy fit when compared to the adorable Shirley, which happened all too often due to her petite size, wavy red hair and first name.

"I knew we'd have you back up on your toes in no time flat," he went on. "Speaking of flats, how do you like your 'Las Vegas Deluxe' set?"

"Looks great. Very Busby Berkeley."

Danny frowned so severely that even his perfectly marcelled blond hair seemed to pucker under its trendy retro-pomade. "Busby Berkeley is too awfully camp these serious, pre-millennium days, darling. Shall we say very mock-Memphis, like the Luxor?"

"Whatever, it's splendid, Danny." Temple eyed the exaggerated Las Vegas skyline etched in colored chalk on stretched black velvet panels that fenced the back of the stage. "How are your special effects coming?"

Danny rolled his eyes with delight. "Orgasmic!"

Temple had not meant to inquire into Danny Dove's private life, but before she could utter words to this effect, he went on in living color and full plume.

"Only—please, dear Miss Temple!—enough of these naughty no-no's like your backward tumble down the stairs. We're using the stage elevator from the magic shows for the end of your skit. Then we drench the whole chitty-chitty-shebang with an absolute oh-my-miasma of dry-ice mist, tinted passion-fruit crimson. The *pièce de résistance* prop will drop from above; the most tacky *deus ex machina* of all time. *Voila.*"

He pointed high into the murky stage flies to a huge, hovering silver disc.

"Thanks to my percolating purple-crimson mist," Danny promised, "our UFO will appear to rise from the nether regions, with forty glamorous chorines dancing the Watusi around its spiral ramp—a bit of the old Busby, there. Then we yank the bloody thing upward in a finishing flourish . . . all lights blinking and smoking like mad, with the girly chorus singing their little glotti out. Smashing."

Temple craned her neck upward and nodded politely, trying to picture the effect. Mentally she added glittering fairy lights and neon constellations to the black-velvet-painting night-sky backdrop. Danny was right. Smashing.

"Looks cheap to me," a sneering voice said.

How did Crawford Buchanan get up here? Temple wondered with irritation. Where were her upstanding body guards when she really needed them?

"This is stupid." Crawford obviously enjoyed standing behind the pair and carping. "You're making a big mistake, Dove, putting big bucks into this dumb number. Who wants to see the Goodyear Blimp on stage besides opera-goers?"

For emphasis, and to demonstrate his disdain, Buchanan jerked a cable that trailed to the stage floor, part of the intricate network that hoisted the big silver blob.

Danny Dove turned on Crawford Buchanan as if he had been talking pig swill. "I am the director. You are the bureaucrat who stapled a few skits together. I make this garbage work, and most of it is, especially *your* scripts."

"What would an effete toad-dancer like you know about entertainment?"

Temple, PR instincts to the fore, edged between the two men, truly a showdown of pygmies. She was too much of a pipsqueak herself to act as an effective buffer, especially balanced like a stork on one leg. But matters were desperate. Veins were standing out on Danny Dove's forehead, and Crawford's dark-lashed eyes were venomous slits. Another kind of Dove was called for, the peace-keeping female of the species.

"Guys, please!"

Crawford brushed her aside, literally, the better to face off with Danny Dove.

Ordinarily a soft shove wouldn't have damaged more than Temple's dignity. With the weakness of her ankle, though, it pushed her into a flat-footed stumble. Temple grabbed for the nearest stable object (other than the testosterone-tempered Dove and Buchanan).

Her hand curled around the hanging rope. Temple heard the pound of running feet: a herd of heroes to the rescue, she presumed. The Flying Fontana Brothers should have kept Awful Crawford offstage in the first place.

The rope jerked her upright again. Then, just as she grabbed for a shred of balance, the entire length of cable dropped past her in punishing coil after coil, like a whipsnake.

"Watch out!" a man shouted.

Temple looked up to see a sky of silver collapsing down upon her, upon them all.

A flying tackle of Fontana brothers—pale as Cool Whip—rushed forward in a wedge formation. Temple, Danny, Crawford . . . all were swept away, wood chips in a water drain.

Temple had enough wits about her to see that the two arguing men had toppled like bowling pins under the force of Fontanas leveled at them.

She herself—oh, my—was levitated in the manner of a musical comedy vamp, so she perched on the impeccably padded (and probably impeccably pecced) shoulders of Fontanas twain. She couldn't lean over far enough to read their name tags and find out who her rescuers were, specifically. Too bad.

In the wings, frantic tech crew members male and female were swinging from various ropes. Under their combined weight and quick thinking, the footloose UFO had halted in mid-air just three feet above the stage.

When four Fontana boys applied themselves to the ropes like dapper but demented bell-ringers, the mechanism lifted slowly into the darkness of the flies where it belonged.

"Oh, my God." Danny Dove had forgotten spats with obnoxious show chairmen. "Dear girl!" He leaped up to look up at Temple with devastated eyes. "You could have been killed."

"*We* could have been killed." Crawford Buchanan was rising from the floor with far less grace and speed than Danny Dove. His prized ice-cream suit looked as if it had been double-dipped in soot. He glared accusingly at Temple.

"Don't look at me," she said, pleased to be in a position to stare down at Crawford as if he were a bug. "I didn't write this unauthorized landing into the script."

"We were all in jeopardy, but our dear Miss Barr was in the direct . . . line of fire, so to speak." Danny extended a hand, which Temple took.

She found herself wafted to the floor like a thistledown ballerina. Danny's looks were deceiving; the dancer/choreographer was as strong as piano wire.

"That UFO weighs a ton," he fretted. "I don't understand—"

A Fontana brother—Ralph—came swinging down from the flies like Flynn to the rescue, only on a rope and a hope instead of a wing and a prayer.

"Cut," he pronounced, displaying the end of the fallen cable.

"Sabotage," Danny instantly diagnosed. His eyes narrowed at the descending Adonis in Armani. "I love your earring."

"It's nothing," Ralph said modestly, missing the point and Danny's proclivities, if he had not missed the significance of the sliced rope.

Temple again felt an overwhelming urge to intervene. Interpret. Peacemake. Oh, blessed are the seriously straight, for they shall be politically incorrect until death do them part.

Until . . . death.

She looked up at the UFO rising jerky foot by foot to the rhythm of the stage ratchets, rather like bad poetry.

"Danny, do you think—?"

"I definitely do, darling." His demeanor was utterly serious now. "First the stairs. Now the . . . alien object. I'm dreadfully sorry, dear lady, but I fear that you are the subject of a nasty objective. I always thought that this show would be murder."

Chapter 22

Skits Ahoy!

"I don't get it," Temple said. "Why are you making a federal case out of this? It was just a stupid stage accident."

She looked from Lieutenant Ferraro to Lieutenant Molina, fervently hoping that this was a nightmare induced by a conk on the head with a fake UFO: not one but two homicide officials interrogating little old her. Again.

Molina smiled, and when Molina smiled at something Temple had said, that usually meant trouble.

"You are batting a thousand today," Molina told her. "First you avoid being squashed like a ladybug by an unanchored UFO; now you've anticipated the actions of two branches of the law."

"Huh?" Temple didn't mind playing dumb when she was feeling thoroughly stupefied.

Besides, she was still reeling from the close call with the runaway UFO, not to mention the threat of imminent demise while in the company, however unwanted, of Crawford Buchanan. Imagine ending up next to that creep in the morgue!

Temple remained puzzled. Why had hotel security hustled her to this secluded office right after the mishap? She hated being pulled untimely away from the sight of Crawford Buchanan whining and threatening law suit. Dousing that legal fire was a lot more important than submitting to another police grilling. Large portions of her anatomy would soon show permanent parallel tracks, she was sure. . . . And what was this gruesome twosome doing at the Phoenix so conveniently, anyway?

When Temple remained silent, Molina nodded at Ferraro—great, they were in cahoots—who went to open the door into an adjoining empty office.

Except the room wasn't empty until the man inside it walked out to join them. He struck her as a nondescript middle-aged man in a nondescript gray suit from Men's Waerhouse, with a tie equally as off-the-rack, but his blue-striped shirt had a sparkling white collar. Another cop? With a subconscious urge to make a fashion statement while taking hers? Oi, her aching ankle!

Despite his snappy shirt, the new man didn't bother to say hello. He came right up to her with a grim expression, pulled a leatherette case from his inside breast suitpocket, then flipped it open in front of her nose.

Darn. Temple was too curious not to look. An unflattering head shot. An impressive seal. Lots of tiny print.

"FBI." Temple read the big blue initials aloud to make sure that she wasn't having a dyslexic episode and it really said IBM. She wasn't. "You've got to be kidding!" She glanced to an impassive Molina.

The man shook his head so slightly Temple hardly saw it. He wheeled a secretarial chair over the tiled floor, then sat opposite her.

"We need to talk," he suggested.

"I can do that. I could even do a song-and-dance until a couple of days ago." To demonstrate, Temple hefted her still-swaddled ankle, which reposed on a pulled-out desk drawer. "So how have I offended this time?"

Amusement flickered behind the stiff, burglar-bar eyelashes shading his steel-gray eyes. Flickered and went out.

"Apparently you're a repeat offender around this town," he said dead-pan.

"Only at being innocent," Temple replied.

"Unfortunately, she is. So far." Molina had vouched for Temple out of the blue, sitting on the edge of the desk. "Harmless, I mean. Miss Barr's only crime has been acting as a magnet for trouble."

"Murderous trouble?" the FBI man inquired.

Molina nodded.

"Is this about that dead man that fell on the craps table?" Temple dared to ask.

Lieutenant Molina pounced like Midnight Louie on a trespassing cricket unwise enough to announce its presence with a friendly chirp. "You understand something about that we should know?"

Of course Temple did. However, she wasn't about to announce to all and sundry that the second casino murder victim was also connected to a man of her acquaintance. In fact, the Crystal Phoenix victim was much more certainly attached to Matt Devine than the long-dead unidentified man at the Goliath was affixed to Max Kinsella.

While Temple stonewalled, internecine rivalry saved her.

The FBI agent shook his head at Molina, as if to shut her up, before concentrating the full power of his drill-press gaze on Temple. "The murder is . . . under control, Miss Barr. This interview concerns that skit you wrote for the Gridiron."

"My Gridiron skit? You've got to be—" She decided not to accuse the man of kidding again. He didn't look like he had a sense of humor large enough to permit a discreet chuckle.

None of them looked particularly amused. Temple glanced from one sober official face to the next, searching for a quirk of the humanity that she knew had to be there. It was absent without leave in every case.

"My Gridiron skit?" Anxiety had pushed her voice into its froggiest register. "It's just the usual satire."

Ferraro edged closer, until he hung over the FBI man's gray wool-blend shoulder. "What's so funny about the mob taking over a major Vegas hotel?"

"I made that up. I was playing on tired Vegas clichés."

"You and somebody else," Molina put in darkly.

Temple jerked her head in that direction. Maybe she could get a little female solidarity going here. "That's what I do. I'm a PR person. I make things up. Based on the facts, of course, but I slant 'em and spin 'em and shake 'em up until they stand up and sing

'Dixie.' My skit merely exaggerated that sort of thing. Humor is exaggeration. Nothing in that skit is reality-based in the slightest."

"We're pretty sure," Molina said ponderously, more for the benefit of her colleagues than Temple, "that the Goliath murder a few months back was part of whatever caused this later murder, part of the same conspiracy."

"Conspiracy?" Temple squeaked. She knew that racketeering and conspiracy were charges that fell under FBI jurisdiction.

The agent nodded, watching Temple like a hawk would if she were a rainbow trout skimming too close to the surface. "I understand that you were associated with the suspected mastermind of the Goliath . . . incident."

Max? Oh, come on. "So then I went and spilled the whole scheme in a Gridiron skit, which the entire town will see in a couple of weeks? I don't think so."

"You're working at the Crystal Phoenix now," Molina pointed out helpfully.

"Yes, I am."

"Where another dead guy," Ferraro growled, "dropped from the Eye in the Sky like a crocodile tear."

Temple frowned. Same M.O., all right. "You . . . think whatever was up at the Goliath is gonna go down"—God, what a trendy expression!—"at the Phoenix!"

Her last supposition brought nods all around, whether of agreement or simple satisfaction that Temple had committed her thoughts to incriminating sound bites was debatable.

"Somebody up there"—Lieutenant Molina's luxurious eyebrows lilted toward the ceiling—"certainly doesn't want your skit, or you, doing business as usual."

"This skit is harmless fun," Temple protested again, truly confused, not to mention worried by this triumvirate of solemn law enforcement types.

"You haven't lived in Las Vegas very long," Molina informed her, "but let me assure you that 'fun' here isn't always as harmless as you and twenty-four million other tourists would like to think. Las Vegas isn't Wonderland, or even Disneyland. It makes its money from the art of separating ordinary people from an extraordinary amount of money by wrapping the process in expensive, glitzy paper. All of these architecturally overblown hotels, the acres of neon, the new virtual reality amusement attrations add up to a multimillion-dollar carnival midway that stays in one place. And that gives the sideshow operators very high stakes in the Las Vegas image, especially now that family-rated entertainment is becoming the name of the marketing game. You don't survive in this billion-dollar melee without a lot of brass, especially on your knuckles. And *you* don't tweak the tails of these sacred cash cows without risking an annoyed kick or two. In this town, you don't kick sand in the Sphinx's face and you don't step on an Elvis imitator's blue suede shoes.''

Temple contemplated the blank white ceiling to which her attention had been drawn by the notion of a "Somebody Sinister Up There" who didn't like her. That "Somebody" apparently hadn't liked the two dead men, either. She frowned.

"So something in my skit riled some power-that-be in the bottom line?"

"Could be," Molina folded her arms. "Or it could be that whoever's behind these hotel deaths is making the accountants nervous and your skit is the straw that broke the camel's back."

"Whoever's doing this serial hotel killing is certainly fond of heights," Temple admitted. "So you believe the plunging UFO was cut loose by the same person?"

"Person," Ferraro growled, "or organization."

"The Mafia?" Temple felt numb with disbelief. "That's another cliché so antique it could be marked up quadruple and furnish a national landmark."

"Not necessarily," Ferraro added. "The notorious godfathers may be an endangered species nowadays, but that doesn't mean that crime kingpins don't exist. They just don't get the colorful press they used to. The newer gambling areas are having the kind of trouble with organized crime we licked years ago. Then there's always the flashy foreign models—the Japanese Yakuza and the Russian mob are real bad news."

"Who would take my spoof seriously except somebody who was seriously disturbed?" Temple persisted.

"There's that, too," Molina conceded.

"You mean a nut case—?"

Molina turned to retrieve a sheaf of papers from the desk behind her. "A nut who's decided to follow the plans you so thoughtfully laid out in your sketch." Molina slapped the papers to the desk again, close enough to Temple that she could recognize the familiar lines of her Gridiron skit. Who had given the cops a copy? Did the initials "C.B." ring any bells, Quasimodo?

Temple shook her head, a mistake. The gesture brought her glance to the FBI agent, who was leaning forward in his borrowed chair. His no-nonsense eyes focused on Temple as if they hoped to rivet her to the wall.

"What about your veiled allusions to all those classified black projects at Nellis Air Force Base?" he wanted to know.

"Just that. Veiled allusions to what every TV tabloid show has been dredging up for years. Next you'll tell me that someone's trying to resurrect Elvis, too!"

"Well . . ." Ferraro began.

Temple couldn't stand it.

"Not . . . yet," he conceded with reluctance.

"I can't believe that you people are getting all excited about something I made up. Okay." She eyed Molina. "My mob takeover scheme does seem a bit close to your speculations about the deaths of the two men in the casinos, but it's pure coincidence. Can't you see that I went through a catalog of all the old fish stories about Las Vegas and put them together into one big, unlikely bouillabaisse?"

"And can't you see, Miss Barr," the FBI agent answered her, "that Las Vegas is a crux city where a ton of money and motives meet every day? Can't you see that an international clientele moves in and out of this town like a plague of locusts. The opportunity for big-time crime here is nothing to joke about. If you had any sense, you would jerk the skit from the show."

"What are you all? Shills for that miserable Crawford Buchanan? He'd love to cut my skit at the last minute, but Danny Dove would go ballistic if he lost his major number."

"Danny Dove?" The agent repeated the name with distaste as much as disbelief.

"An eminent local choreographer," Molina explained, "now directing this comedy of errors."

"A stage name, surely," the agent persisted.

Molina shrugged, but Temple jumped to Danny's defense.

"Absolutely not. He got that handle when he was born in Norman, Oklahoma, longer ago than he's willing to put on a résumé. I happen to know that for a fact, because I did freelance PR for the Sands when Danny was setting up the original staging for their big 'Sands of Time' floor show.''

The agent blinked, obviously flummoxed by the nitty gritty of Las Vegas entertainment.

''Whatever Danny Dove's antecedents or reaction to losing your literary efforts,'' Molina put in, ''it's pretty clear that your imagination has irritated somebody besides the local constabulary. We can't force you to do as we suggest, but we can cover this production like a London Fog shrouds a flasher. And we will have to, if nobody else is to get killed, especially you.''

''You can't believe that these backstage mishaps were meant to harm *me?*'' Temple was incredulous. ''How could anyone determine *when* I would go up those steps, or that I'd use the handrail?''

Molina's eyes dropped to the site of Crawford's continuing inspection, for a quite different reason. ''Anybody familiar with your footwear could figure that you would hang onto something when climbing those steep, concrete stairs in high heels.''

''What about the footloose UFO?'' Temple asked. ''That thing could have smashed half the chorus, too. Isn't that overkill, even for Las Vegas? And who was to know that Crawford would be up on stage, and make me play bellringer, the jerk?''

''There could be two scenarios,'' Ferraro suggested from his corner. ''One to take you out, and one to disrupt the production itself. Maybe they coincided. Either way, someone besides us doesn't much care for your script-writing.''

''I invoke my freedom of speech.'' Temple folded her arms. ''Besides, I think you're paranoid, which was part of my point in the skit. Pretty soon you'll hatch some notion that Elvis was secretly freeze-fried at death and is being brought back as an assassin for Castro.''

Nobody smiled. That was the trouble with pursuing a career in law enforcement, Temple decided right then; all that martial arts practice destroyed the funny bone. She'd better cut back, fast.

They could do nothing, of course, even with the mighty FBI on the case, except interrogate, suggest and warn.

By the time Temple limped out of the barren office, a crowd of worried supporters had mustered in the narrow hallway. Actually, it was composed mainly of Fontana brothers, but they added up to a crowd all by themselves.

Danny Dove was eyeing Temple's limp. "More ice, more rest," he decreed.

Temple nodded meekly. Her ankle was throbbing almost as much as her head.

"We'll see her home," Ralph declared, promptly bending to hoist her like a Barbie doll.

Van von Rhine stood next to her husband, her arm threaded through his, her porcelain brow ruffled with worry. She walked out with the airborne Temple and her flock of Fontanas.

"Temple, that woman lieutenant had some rather worrying words with me. I told her that the hotel had been the victim of malicious 'pranks' before, but she thinks this outbreak could be much more lethal. She pointed out that it already has been, in fact."

Temple could only agree. "Do they know anything more about the man who was killed?"

Nicky broke his polite silence. "Some small-time low-roller. A drunk and a woman-beater. In other words, a loser hardly worth killing, unless he knew something uncomfortable to somebody. I'm thinking the cops are right about a possible takeover scheme."

"Oh, Nicky, no!" In her distress, Van stopped walking.

Fontana, Inc., too, stopped on a dime, which meant Temple was jerked to a halt that was rather hard on her ankle. Though elevated, it was not stable enough to withstand sudden changes in direction.

"Ow!" she complained without thinking.

Everybody tsked in concert. Danny would have been proud of them.

"It's not for us to do the police's work." Van patted Temple's shoulder. "You go home and get a good rest."

Temple nodded, unwilling to debate everybody. She had some heavy thinking to do, anyway.

Nicky and Van peeled off. Temple was left wafting along in her flock of Fontanas. They cut such an impressive swath through the casino that slot junkies actually stopped their button-pushing long enough to look up.

Temple felt like Snow White among an unnaturally elongated

squad of dwarves. Yet she liked the new vistas afforded by being carried along at a tall man's chest height, a mobile and human Eye in the Sky.

My, she could look down rows of slot machines, spot Hester Polyester and the Leopard Lady working the few one-armed bandits left, like laundresses chained to shiny chrome wringer-washers.

She could literally oversee the craps tables, and eyeball the balding heads of the ardent worshipers at the temple of snake-eyes and naturals. Had anyone ever done a study: craps and male-pattern baldness?

She could gaze into the hotel's lobby area, to view hordes of tourists lined up to check in and then check out the tables, the shows, the what-have-you, and in Las Vegas, you could have almost anything . . . legal or ought-not-to-be.

She could even overlook the lobby bar's indoor greenery, laced with garlands of twinkling fairy lights, and glimpse a dark head weaving among the towering ficus trees with a certain, unmistakable liquidity of motion, like a tiger through the jungle . . . no, more like a panther, black and stalking, with unearthly green eyes—

"Hey!" Temple tried to climb the current Fontana brother's broad, broadcloth shoulder. "Hey, you there!"

You there, you with the stars in your eyes.

That was her. Blinking. Seeing fairy lights. Thinking. Thinking that she had seen . . . no . . . glimpsed—Max. Max Kinsella, don't you know? Alive and moving, bold as brass and as big as a Broadway opening when there's standing room only.

Temple discovered that she couldn't stand on a Fontana brother's shoulder, despite the awesome padding, not with her weak ankle and deluded eyesight.

"Miss Barr?" Her custodian was confused, and his suit was getting wrinkled. "You don't want to scramble around like that. You could aggravate your foot."

She could aggravate her entire life. Temple settled down and smiled apologetically at her forehead-puckering escort squadron.

"Sorry. Thought I saw someone . . . suspicious."

"Where?" they demanded en masse, noses lifting like bloodhound muzzles.

Fee, fie, fo, fum, I smell the blood of an Irishman. Be he live or be he dead, I'll follow his trail from A to Zed.

"I was wrong," she apologized hastily, though she was not sure that she was. Even Max Kinsella deserved a less public unmasking than by a baying flotilla of Fontanas on his heels.

"I suppose," she said with maudlin determination, "I need to go home, to Tara, and rest until tomorrow, which, we all know, is another day."

And frankly, my dear, she added internally to the fleeting image she had perhaps seen, I don't give a damn.

The Fontana brothers, with the exception of the one toting her, clapped politely.

Temple's Vivien Leigh imitation had been spot on.

Chapter 23

Louie of the Lake

What could a woman with a weak ankle, frazzled from an interrogation by two homicide detectives and an FBI agent, better wish to carry her home than a silent, gentle glide on a magic carpet? Swing low, sweet chariot.

But this was Las Vegas and Temple was in the custodial care of Fontana, Inc.

Once Ralph had stopped the black, low-slung and decidedly unsweet Dodge Viper in front of the Circle Ritz—no one was present today to witness this exotic landing—Temple remained seated and experimentally tugged a tooth to see if they were still anchored.

The teeth were secure, which was more than could be said for the alignment of her vertebrae. When Ralph came around the car to carry her in, she made no objection. Besides, her voice had probably developed a stutter in the forty seconds flat the Viper had permitted to elapse between the Crystal Phoenix, a mile away, and the Circle Ritz.

"Cool digs." Ralph grinned at the lavish neon of the Lovers'

Knot Wedding Chapel beaming purple and pink good cheer down on the Strip.

He turned to cast a last possessive glance upon the lethally spotless Viper, shining like fresh hot tar in the sunlight. He aimed a small remote device at its darkly mirrored surface, then blipped on the security system. Apparently the car was community property of the bachelor Fontana brothers, allotted where needed. Apparently, Temple's welfare and whereabouts was a matter of swift concern for them all.

Somehow she was not comforted, being in the mood to brood about her assailed skit, her assailed self, her perhaps-glimpse of a Max clone, and her current, ignominious state of physical dependency.

Ralph shouldered the lobby door open and braced it with one Italian loafer toe as he turned to edge Temple through without any rude brushes with the doorjamb.

The Circle Ritz's always tepid air-conditioning greeted them like a tropical zephyr, humid and half-hearted. The door hushed shut to banish the traffic hiss-and-squeak reverberating from the ever-busy Strip.

Temple sighed.

Ralph smiled with the knowledge of a job well done.

In the dim, black-marble paved and lined lobby, someone cleared his throat.

A figure stepped from the interior shadow before either one could react.

"Sorry to intrude on such utter solitude, but I have come, I fear, to beg a most receptive ear."

Ralph was not amused. "This bum must have a speech impediment. He doesn't make sense. Is he trying to rip off my earring?"

"He makes perfect sense," Temple dared to disagree. "Nostradamus is no robber, he's a bookie."

"Same difference," Ralph growled, lowering Temple to the floor in preparation for battle.

She braced a hand on the cool marble facing the elevator and attempted to put weight on her bad ankle. It declined to buckle, so she stepped slightly ahead of Ralph to keep him from charging Nostradamus in defense of his treasured earbob.

"I take it that you came to see me, not Ralph Fontana."

The bookie doffed his hat, a sweat-stained straw number pungent with nostalgia, especially in its pleated paisley band.

"Sure fine to see you on your feet again," he said. "It's glad I am that we could meet again. I hope to lure you to Temple Bar, to see a friend who's under par. Spuds Lonnigan has opened a new bar, and he could use some clever PR."

"Spuds." Temple tasted the name, which was familiar in a warped sort of way. Time-warped, probably. "You mean one of the geezers in the Glory Hole Gang?"

Nostradamus's face screwed up in disapproval despite the lurking presence of Ralph Fontana. "Geezerdom, like beauty, lies in the eye of the beholder. Someday even youngsters like you will find themselves . . . older."

"True. I feel it already. I just meant . . . well, what does Spuds want? To talk to me?"

"If you could repair to where his place is, you two could discuss some nice biz."

Ralph, still playing bodyguard, toyed with the pewter hacksaw dangling from his left lobe. "Sounds fishy to me," he told Temple.

Nostradamus turned to him with ready politeness. "Indeed, young sir, you have hit it on the nose. The landing at Temple Bar teems with those."

"Fish," Temple translated promptly for Ralph's benefit. "I've heard about this new . . . restaurant. Jill Diamond's grandfather Eightball O'Rourke is an associate of this Spuds Lonnigan."

"That don't cut any gray poupon with me," Ralph insisted.

"Carp," Nostradamus explained. "Carp swimming ashore in a golden greeting." He turned to Temple with a bow. "Shall we say two tomorrow for this meeting?"

"I may not yet be able to drive—"

"A car will conduct you to this dive."

"Dive?" Ralph frowned, then turned to Temple and laid down the law like an overprotective husband. "You're not going who-knows-where to God-knows-what alone, today or tomorrow."

" 'Dive' is just an expression," Temple said hastily, "and it rhymed."

Nostradamus shrugged apologetically, but said nothing.

Temple mused on the mental effort it must take to improvise rhymes day in and day out. One would think figuring odds for bettors would be taxing enough. A master of both math and meter; Nostradamus was indeed a Renaissance bookie.

Ralph might have made more objections, having settled as deeply as a Method actor into the role of grim guardian, but just then the Viper shrieked from the street outside.

Ralph was barreling across the lobby and through the door, reaching into his flapping suitcoat, before Nostradamus could come up with a rhyming couplet.

Temple hobbled after, Nostradamus taking her elbow, for all the good that gesture did her.

Outside they found Electra Lark, her hands lifted so sky-high that her muumuu had hiked up well beyond the dimples in her knees. Given the landlady's Technicolor dress and her lime-and-pink sprayed hair, it wasn't hard to notice that her face was Liquid-Paper white.

Maybe the source of Electra's shock was the shiny black Beretta that matched the screaming Viper so nicely. The semiautomatic fit Ralph Fontana's fine Italian hand like a steel gauntlet and was pointed straight at the turquoise bird-of-paradise on Electra's muu-muu.

"I was only . . . petting the fender," Electra said in a gush, "when the dang thing started yammering. I barely touched it."

"Better be the truth." Ralph holstered his firearm and settled his jacket into smooth lines again. "Better not have a fingerprint on it. That's a fresh, hand wash-job, lady. This baby's been buffed by genuine shimmy cloth."

Temple refrained from telling Ralph that chamois was pronounced "shammy," not like something a topless dancer does.

As Ralph came around the hood to examine the streetside fender, Electra, hands still raised on high, edged around the car's rear until she stood on the sidewalk with Temple and Nostradamus.

"I barely brushed it," she complained again.

Ralph silenced the alarm system with a punch on the remote control, then bent deeply over the fender for a close inspection.

"The alarm is set on super-sensitive," he muttered with satisfaction. "Look wrong at this baby and you're siren-meat. This is Fontana brother property. Look, and lust, but don't touch."

Electra examined the speaker and made a face that Ralph was too intent to see.

"Well, excuse me for window-shopping." She turned to Temple, finally lowering her limbs. Armfuls of garish titanium bracelets jangled from forearms to wrists like the rings of Saturn coming in for a landing. "You okay, dear?" She eyed Nostradamus with more mother-hen suspicion.

Temple nodded, weary of such high doses of solicitude. "Nostradamus came here to discuss business, and Ralph drove me home from the Phoenix. I admit that I could use a little peace and quiet, though."

"You shall have it." Electra appropriated Temple's elbow to guide her back inside. "We shall all have it when the nasty man with the noisy car departs."

Ralph, squinting into the dazzling, dark mirror of the Viper's sun-warmed fender, heard nothing.

Nostradamus topped his balding head with the straw fedora and tipped its brim to the two women vanishing into the Circle Ritz. He looked well satisfied.

Temple was waiting—feet wisely shod in tennis shoes, tote bag loaded for bear over her left shoulder—in the Circle Ritz lobby less than twenty-four hours later.

In the interval, she had taken a long, hot bath, followed by a long, cold application of ice to her ankle while she read her way through one-twenty-secondth of Mark Helprin's *Winter's Tale*. Temple kept an always-mean-to-read-someday shelf of eclectic books, most of which she never got to. Helprin's lyrical yet epic fairy tale bewildered but bewitched her, and totally made her forget Fontana brothers, police officers and Crawford Buchanan, which was a sizable achievement.

In the morning she cut her toenails, another always-mean-to-get-to chore, did her nails, and read the paper with Midnight Louie.

Reading the paper with Midnight Louie meant that she opened a section wide in preparation to concentrating on a story. Then Louie walked across the paper and her lap. He finally settled in a large, lumpish mass on her thighs, the paper betwixt them, so that he was comfy and she could not read, move, or even breathe. She could not, in fact, do anything but stroke his glossy, Viper-black fur until he purred like a hive of bees.

When her legs were asleep to the hip and the paper was crushed beyond legibility, Louie would yawn, stretch, rise and go elsewhere. Often his farewell leap would leave a prick of braced hind claws in her thighs as he vaulted away. Sometimes, Temple thought, a cat was not unlike a live-in lover who left suddenly.

Despite Louie, or perhaps because of his inadvertent numbness therapy, Temple's ankle felt almost normal in the morning. The swelling was down, and by noon she was itching to return to the scene of the crime. Maybe this mysterious car that was to waft her to Temple Bar wouldn't show up, she thought hopefully as she buckled on her oversize watch.

Once a watch was on her wrist, she was ready to simmer, cook, parboil and rock and roll. She was no longer chilling out at home, she was primed to do business.

So she paced, despite her ankle, waiting to go down to the lobby. There she would consult some old guy about a Lake Mead restaurant at an obscure site that coincidentally bore her name, minus a terminal "r."

When she rode down in the rickety elevator, every clack and clank seemed to chide her for deserting the action at the Crystal Phoenix. Why had she agreed to this bizarre side trip, other than the fact that a freelance PR person always can use another client and she had been eager to disarm Ralph, the human Doberman, who seemed ready to rend the flesh of any harmless being who crossed her path?

But maybe Ralph was right, Temple thought in the deserted lobby. She was about to ride—with a stranger—to meet a strange man somewhere she had never been, on business she wasn't sure of. Maybe the police were right, too, heaven forbid. Maybe she was dangerous to somebody. Maybe that somebody would stop at nothing to stop her. Nostradamus could be an innocent shill, thinking he was acting for this Spuds Lonnigan. It could all be a—famous phrase from detective stories—a *set-up*, with her as the *patsy*. Well, she didn't play the patsy for anyone. . . .

A cranky car engine idled outside. A heavy-metal door slammed. A shadowed figure was framed by the doorway, the blazing afternoon sunlight etching only a shapeless silhouette.

Temple braced her feet and clutched her tote to her torso, six pounds of shoulder-numbing sandbag.

The door whooshed open, admitting a shaft of heat that sliced the Circle Ritz's tepid coolness like a warm knife dissecting a stick of butter.

Temple cursed herself for being too trusting.

"Hi," said the newcomer's familiar, desert twang. "I'm your chauffeur to Temple Bar."

Temple babystepped over the sleek marble floor until she was close enough to see features.

"Jill? Jill Diamond?"

"Yup. I'll run you out and back. A drive in the desert will be fun. Hope you don't mind a ragtop."

Boy, did Temple feel silly. Jill Diamond was almost smaller than she was.

And the vehicle that waited at the curb was almost smaller than the Storm, but not quite. Jill's unlikely set of wheels was an ancient Jeep, painted a baby-blue that sand and sun had buffed by to a muted, matte finish like a beloved pair of time-faded blue jeans.

Temple climbed gingerly into the rough-and-ready vehicle. The seat was about as upholstered as a rock. Jill did equally rough-and-ready things with the stick shift, and the Jeep jolted into motion. Temple felt rather like someone riding a baby-blue bucking bronco. She jammed sunglasses onto her nose and dug for the sun-screen in her tote bag as the Jeep sputtered onto the Strip, then onto the highway.

Wind rushed by as if late for somewhere. Talk seemed too much trouble. Beside Temple, Jill's braids whipped behind her like pennants, while she squinted into the distance without benefit of such sissy accessories as sunglasses, aiming the Jeep for the farthest wrinkle of the horizon.

Steel-gray highway, blue sky and sage-green land streaked by. Mauvish mountains ringed the horizon like the jagged edge of tomorrow, a distant barrier to keep the pinball of the Jeep from shooting right off the map into Maybesville.

Temple laughed suddenly.

Leaping lizards, but a change of scenery . . . and locomotion . . . was exhilarating.

"Sorry the ride was so rough," Jill said when she finally jerked the Jeep to a stop before a ramshackle wooden building on the shore of blindingly blue Lake Mead.

"No problem. Not much out here, is there?"

"You visit Lake Mead much?"

"Not really. It's . . . well, for tourists."

After dismounting the Jeep—that's how Temple thought of it, for the step-up was higher than she was used to—they ambled to the water's edge.

Without the engineering feat of Hoover Dam only miles away, none of this lucent water would lie here, as rich as lapis lazuli against the red-rock roughness of the surrounding land.

The lake glimmered in the sunlight, a hundred-carat sapphire set in an unforgiving rocky rim of desert landscape.

"It's almost unearthly," Temple commented.

Jill smiled. "You're not the first to think so. Remember the scene in *Planet of the Apes* when the astronauts' capsule crash-landed in water? That footage was shot here. This place could pass for another planet, if you look at it right."

Temple turned to her. "You don't seem—"

"Like a late-night lounge singer's wife? Nope. I grew up on this desert. I only went into town to play poker—professionally. What are you smiling at? The idea of a woman poker player?"

Temple shook her head. Jill was sure touchy on the subject. "No. I'm smiling at the idea of calling Las Vegas 'town,' as if it was someplace you went to buy feed for the stock."

"You can," Jill said seriously, wrinkling her turned-up nose. "Heck, you can even buy the stock there. Las Vegas is a lot of things, but to me, it's just a gaudy belly-button in what really matters. This land all around here, and what's on it, what time and tradition stamped into it."

Temple turned back to the building of unpainted boards. Despite its sand-blasted look, it now had a mystique, thanks to Jill's insight. "What was this?"

"Oh, some boathouse/roadhouse long ago. Crazy as a bar and grill out here looks, I think Spud's onto something. The boys have plans for this area, maybe even a paddlewheel gambling boat on the Nevada side of the lake and a water park, all in the weathered-wood ghost-town look . . . natural, you know?"

Temple smiled again, this time at the Las Vegas idea of "natural." Such effects invariably took unnatural amounts of time and money.

"I know what you're saying," she said finally. "I'm creating a similar theme-scheme for the Crystal Phoenix."

"That's why I thought you could help Spuds out. He's a hell of a cook, let me tell you. And my grandfather's old bunch, they spent too long alone on the desert. It's time for them to get into the mainstream."

"Eightball has certainly gone mainstream, and then some. Doesn't it worry you, a man his age playing private investigator?"

"Hell, yes! It worries me, and I spent my younger years worrying about these old coots while they were fussing about me. But them doing nothing worries me more. They're like lifers, you know, in prison, whose sentence just got commuted. It's a new world, so they might as well live in it."

" 'The boys,' " Temple repeated ironically.

Jill nodded seriously. "They are that. Come on and meet Spuds."

Jill's bootheels dug into the soft sand as the pair edged around the sprawling building to the lakeshore side. The weathered wood was a soft, ashen gray, Temple noted with favor, and a broad deck edged all four sides, a perfect site for al fresco dining.

Up front, a crude hand-lettered sign over the door announced "Three O'Clock Louie's." Smaller printing beneath promised "Around-the-clock fun and food for the entire family."

From inside came, not the aroma of food or the chatter and laughter of fun, but the sound of hell-bent hammering interspersed with the occasional curse.

Jill doffed her cowboy hat and sprang up the shallow steps to the deck. "Hey, fellas, cut your cussing. There's a lady present. Not me, gents, but the lady who shares the name of this landing, Miss Temple Barr herself."

Temple was not pleased to have to live up to that introduction, especially in tennis shoes. She soft-footed it over the wood planking and inside Three O'Clock Louie's.

Bare light bulbs draped the perimeter of a cavernous room filled with sawhorses, lumber, table saws and older men working away like the Seven Dwarves.

"This is what you call starting from scratch," said one, wiping a sawdust-covered hand on his baggy jeans, then coming to shake Temple's. "That's the way I cook, and that's the way I cook up a restaurant. From scratch."

"It does take a lot of scratch," put in another fellow.

They all stopped what they were doing to ogle Temple, which was most unsettling. She had met them briefly at "Les Girls" strip club, where they also had a financial interest, but she had not had time to put faces and names together.

Now, here she was again, confronted *en masse* with a pack of males, trying to tell one from the other. Besides jeans, they all wore kerchiefs around their necks or foreheads, and suspenders, but some were portly, others lean. Some bald, some still hairy.

She recalled shards of the local legends about the Glory Hole Gang, who were a PR person's dream in a golden oldie package: how these senior citizen fugitives, then mere whippersnappers, had hijacked a shipment of silver dollars before World War II and buried the loot in the desert. How they could no longer find Lost Camel Rock, that marked the buried treasure. How they hid out for decades at a ghost town called Glory Hole, with Eightball's grand-daughter, Jill, growing up there. How Jill learned to be a crack poker player and supported the entourage when she was old enough by playing professionally in Las Vegas. How the lost silver dollars were found by some curious tourists, but the statute of limitations had run out on the old boys' heist by then, so they went scot-free after their long exile in the desert. How they turned Glory Hole into a tourist attraction and now were rich enough to expand their empire in other directions. Such as an eatery at Temple Bar.

All this flashed through Temple's mind in the wink of a butter-fly's eye. History was fine, but her immediate problem, as with the brothers Fontana, was how to tell the Glory Hole Gang apart.

"You must be Spuds," she began, addressing the fellow who was still wringing her hand.

"Smart as a whipsnake, Jilly," he commented. "No wonder she catches all those murderers red-handed." He turned to Temple again. "I'm mighty pleased a big-time operator like you would bother with my little down-home restaurant. It's nothing fancy."

"That's good," Temple decreed, stepping over strewn two-by-fours to get an impression of the place's size. "It's called 'atmo-sphere.'"

"Oh, we got atmosphere," another fellow said. "At our age, that's all we got, 'cept arthuritis. Pitchblende O'Hara, at your disposal."

"Don't use that word, Pitchblende," put in yet another man. "Spuds plans to install a big, stainless steel maw of a disposal. You don't want to go down it by accident."

"Pitchblende," Temple said. "What a colorful nickname!"

"Mining term, ma'am. We all used to do a bit of prospecting when we was younger." He shyly ducked his bald head. "Pitchblende is uranium ore—dark, brownish-black stuff, the way my hair used to be."

"When you used to have hair," guffawed a fourth man, whose own snow-white shock emphasized Lake Mead-blue eyes.

"Wild Blue Pike!" Temple guessed. At least this Glory Holer matched his name.

"So they've called me since Adam's apple was a pippin. I like to fly a bit when the weather's good."

"Yeah," Spuds suggested with long-time raillery. "Pilot that table-saw a little more, brother, and the work'll get done faster."

His words sent everybody back to their appointed tasks, which, as far as Temple could see, involved making as much noise as possible to little effect.

Spuds stuck a gnawed yellow pencil behind his ear and escorted the two women to the front porch, away from the racket.

"Jilly says you got your hands full at the Crystal Phoenix," he told Temple when all three were gawking politely at the lake, trying not to be distracted by the hammering, yammering, sawing and offkey whistling drifting from inside the building behind them. "But if you get inspired about any ways to promote this little enterprise of mine, I'd be much obliged. And we Glory Hole Boys pay well."

"Nothing much is out here," Temple said, gazing at the lovely view. "Getting people to come here will be a trick. I like the name, though—not yours, the restaurant's. It's folksy but implies life after dark. How did you ever come up with it?"

"Simple." Spud's grin showed off impeccably bright false teeth. "I did what all clever entrepreneurs do: I borrowed it."

"Oh, dear." Temple prepared herself to explain the facts of commercial life. "Not from anything copyrighted or trademarked, I hope."

"Not unless you call me a copy-cat." He pointed to a corner of the deck.

A large solid-black cat sat there, doing his nails.

Actually it was grooming its feet, toes spread, teeth pulling at the fine hairs between the pads. Temple had seen Midnight Louie do that a dozen times, and she was seeing it now.

"Louie! How did you get all the way out here?"

The cat looked up, revealing his trademarked green eyes. He twitched a full set of whisker-white barbs, lifted his hindquarters from the planking, then sank into a belly-down stretch.

"How did my cat get out here?" Temple asked someone who would answer this time, namely Spuds Lonnigan.

"That's your cat? I don't see how that could be. This animal belonged to a war buddy of mine, who gave up the fishing business in Puget Sound and retired to Fiji. He wanted a good home on American soil for his old seagoing mascot, but near water. So I was elected. This here's Three O'Clock Louie."

"Are you *sure?*" Temple demanded. "He's the spitting image of my cat, Midnight Louie."

"Old Wayne came through and handed him over not six weeks ago. Must be one of those Koppelgang situations."

"Doppelganger," Temple corrected absently.

The huge black cat had risen and was ambling over to inspect the visitors.

"What does he eat?"

"Every one of these dang goldfish they planted in the lake to entertain the tourists. I can't keep him away from 'em, not even with my best cooking. 'Course, Wayne did run a salmon trawler, so I guess this old boy's used to some pretty fancy fillets of fish."

By now the cat in question was rubbing itself against Temple's calves as if they were old friends, purring like a motorboat.

"It certainly does like you," Jill noted. "I see what you mean about a resemblance to Midnight Louie, but this must be a different cat."

"You know Louie?"

"Sure. From the Phoenix."

Temple squatted down to scratch the animal's chin. The green eyes slitted, just like Louie's, but close up his muzzle looked dipped in milk.

"No, it can't be Louie. The muzzle is grizzled."

"Just like us," Spuds said, chuckling as he ran a palm over the pale stubble dotting his jaw. "Been working day and night on this barn, no time to shave."

"Never had much time for it in the desert, either," Jill added fondly.

"Don't have ladies calling often. Think you can do something for me and Three O'Clock Louie, Miss Temple?"

"Sure. We can hatch some plans later, when the renovations are done. In the meantime, I think I better get back to the Crystal Phoenix, pronto."

"Why the hurry?" Jill asked, sounding anxious. "There's plenty to discuss here."

Temple suddenly saw through Jill like she was plate glass. This expedition to Temple Bar had been planned to distract Temple Barr herself from the ugly business at the Phoenix. But it hadn't worked; seeing Three O'Clock Louie in the flesh and fur had fixed that.

"I've got to get back and make sure Midnight Louie is in carp heaven and all's right with the world, for one thing."

"And for another?" Jill pressed her.

"For another, I better defend my skit from the forces of law and order, evil and Crawford Buchanan."

At her feet, Three O'Clock Louie seconded her announcement with a piercing meow of approval.

The Good Father

Matt left ConTact preoccupied, his ears ringing with the multi-voiced, remote misery of the phone lines.

The drug overdose was all right; Matt had heard the ambulance siren wailing to a stop on the line's other end.

The suicide was another matter. Like alcoholics, suicide-prone people promised reformation, then recanted barely after the telephone was hung up. They were also addicted to sudden terminations of calls, and of counseling: volatile, tortured people craving both attention and the numbing safety of anonymity.

How easy, Matt reflected, to deal with woe in a generic sense, to label people by their maladies. The distance of a counseling line worked both ways. It kept the caller from revealing too much, committing too much. It kept the counselor from feeling too much, bleeding too much.

No matter how specific the caller's anguish, it always fit into a universal mold, seen and shaken out onto the table to study a thousand times before: the suicide; the addict; the alcoholic.

Matt smiled wryly.

The Shoe Freak.

At least she fit a one-and-only mold, God-only-knew what size. Her obsessive documentation of the downfall of women's feet through the ages via the fiendish agency of high heels made for welcome comic relief. He must consult Temple about some of the Shoe Freak's complaints. Did she exaggerate, in the way of all obsessives, or was there a grain of truth, stubborn as a grain of sand rolling around inside a shoe, to her mania?

Only the sound of his footsteps interrupted the faint night music, the sawing wing-work of cicadas and the gliding passage of unseen cars a block or two away.

But . . . Matt's shoes had rubber soles, he shouldn't be hearing the faint, gritty scrape of leather soles on sidewalk.

He mentally shrugged off his reverie, reflecting that he would rather be trailed by a stranger in a car than a stranger on a street.

The man in a car was visibly dependent on the accoutrements of civilization—tires and car keys, gas pumps and street lights. The man on foot seemed a more sinister figure, a throwback: the stalker, the hunter, convinced he needed nothing against the night but himself, and what he could carry. What *would* he carry?

Yet . . . someone as innocent as Matt could also be out walking. At three-fifteen A.M.?

Matt thrust his hands into his pants pockets—to imply he carried something else in them beside his fists and some small change, and turned.

A man scuffed along the street fifty feet behind him, moving purposefully, a man in a suit, oddly formal apparel for this deserted shopping area at this time of night. Lauds.

Still, a suit was better than more Gothic garb, say a cowled monk's robe.

Matt grimaced at his religion-ridden imagination and turned, unwilling to have a stranger gaining on him along this lonely street, loath to challenge or to flee.

Instead, he drifted closer to the dark storefronts, until he reached an expanse of plate glass that was bathed in a reflected streetlight.

Now Matt himself was the Gothic figure, with the strong overhead light washing his features in skeletal shadows.

In the makeshift mirror of a dry cleaning establishment Matt watched the figure appear in the window's far corner, move within ten feet, and stop.

Oh, Lord. Matt turned to look, suspicious but not unduly alarmed . . . yet. The suit could be a decade old, and the man could be a homeless panhandler. He certainly wasn't a gang member.

"You're pretty hard to track down," the man said.

The particular vocal timbre plucked a long-unused string of Matt's memory.

"Not really," Matt said carefully. "I just work late."

"Luckily, so do I. Sometimes."

Matt could have sworn that a smile touched the voice, but the man was all shadow, and still a stranger.

"Why are you tracking me down?" Matt asked.

"You wanted me to."

Matt shook his head in annoyance. This conversation was going nowhere. "Who . . . ?"

"How soon they forget." The man stepped into the brighter light near the window, nearer to Matt than he liked.

Matt studied a lean, fit figure, one not to mess with, but an older man, he sensed. Was this was an associate of his late stepfather's, who had heard Matt was looking for Cliff Effinger and wanted to know why now that the man was dead? Maybe this person thought that Matt had something to do with that death. . . .

"Hey," the man prodded, "I can't decide if you're too trusting, or too wary. Which is it?"

"Unless you want to find out, don't come any closer until you identify yourself."

"Ah, Matthias, and I was supposed to be such a permanent influence on your life . . ."

Stupefaction froze Matt just when he should be most alert.

The voice, the use of his full given name evoked a mental snapshot of a bland office, of cluttered bookshelves, of a tree-dotted campus outside the single window, quite beautiful really.

"It's Bucek," the man said abruptly, ending Matt's misery in racking his memory.

"My God, Father, I forgot! I left a message at St. Vincent, but they were so unforthcoming. I didn't expect to hear from you."

"You wouldn't have, except business brought me to Las Vegas, of all places, and your message had been forwarded. Why don't we keep on walking; the Circle Ritz isn't getting any closer."

"You know where I'm going?"

"You left your address."

"My home address, yes, but not ConTact's. How did—"

"I travel a lot, so I check things out rather thoroughly. For my job."

Matt fell into step with the slightly taller man, his mind flashing between similar walks on that bucolic Indiana campus and this shadow stroll some . . . ten years later.

Despite the other seminarians' edgy discomfort at Father Bucek's acerbic manner and stern intellect, Matt had always admired him. Until . . .

"You left," Matt said. Accused.

"So did you," Bucek shot back. "I must say I was surprised, Matthias. Surprised and sad."

"It's Matt now, and save the guilt trips for somebody with a ticket to ride."

"Humph. Back there just now. I couldn't decide if you were up to facing off a possibly dangerous stranger, or just a nice Catholic boy about to get creamed."

"I can take care of myself. No one's ever bothered me on my walks home. Before."

"Martial arts. You were a veteran even in seminary. What was it? I didn't pay much attention then. Tae Kwon Do? Karate?"

"Whatever feels right at the moment, and I don't mean just that I've had martial arts training. I had that then. I mean I can take care of myself now."

Bucek nodded.

Father Bucek, Matt's mind kept insisting. You expect certain things to stand: the parish church you grew up near; the Pope in Rome; the priest who was your spiritual director in seminary. *You* might fail, might deny like Peter, might end your oath at the ironic age of thirty-three, but these things stood. Bucek the sometimes-terrifying, the always-wise, with his intellect so acute he seemed to see through excuses. Father Furtive, who knew what every seminarian was afraid to confess.

"There's a Burger King a couple blocks down," Bucek said now. "Want a cup of coffee?"

"I don't drink caffeine this late at night."

"There's a bar three blocks down."

"You do check things out, but I don't want a drink."

"The Burger King then. It's a more wholesome arena for a couple of ex-priests than a bar, anyway."

The fast-food joint was also more brightly lit than a bar.

Matt almost cringed under the interrogation-level lighting, but he stood in line with Bucek like a good prisoner, collected his tray, and ordered the usual burger and fries.

Bucek had a chicken sandwich, which he liberally sprinkled with pepper and smothered in mustard.

They sat at the sleek table and seats, designed to slide people in and slide people out in endless rotation.

Around them customers chatted and chewed, clattered and came and went. Want privacy? Go slow where everybody's in a hurry.

"You look good. Matt." Bucek had immediately adopted Matt's preferred civilian form of Matthias, as if glad to inter one more reminder of their former relationship. He slowly masticated his chicken sandwich, his forehead corrugated, not with worry, but by his upward glance and perhaps by curiosity.

"It seems . . . sacrilegious to call you Frank."

"Do it. We spent all those hours dissecting theology, vocation, holiness, ethics . . . I guess I never knew you very well, did I?"

"Nor I you." Matt dragged a limp French fry through a puddle of ketchup he had squeezed out of several small plastic pouches, like coagulated blood. "When did you leave? Are you . . . married?"

Frank's mouth twisted as if he had just bitten down on a chicken bone. "Oh, shortly after you left seminary. I'm a veteran 'ex.' Yup, married. Eight years now."

"Is she—"

"Catholic? Yes. A high school music teacher. Widow. Three teenaged sons." Bucek laughed, as Matt had seldom seen him do in seminary, loudly and at himself. "I'm still a spiritual director, Matthias—Matt. I guess."

"You have no children of your own?"

"No." He spoke abruptly, subject closed.

Can't? Matt wondered. Or won't? None of his business, no more than the ins and outs of his own life—and soul—were Frank Bucek's business anymore. They both had graduated.

"And you?" Frank sucked on the straw spearing his plastic-topped paper cup of Diet 7-Up.

"I left within the year. The phone counseling job is the first thing I qualified for. I've been at it for six months. I like it. It's not so different from confession, especially the way it was done in the old days, in darkened booths with veiled shutters. I hope I'm doing some good. What kind of job did you end up doing? We're puzzlers for employment agencies, we ex-priests, you know. Over-educated and under-experienced."

"I managed something," Frank said gruffly. "But tell me what you wanted to talk to me about."

"It's . . . ah—" Matt shoved his brown plastic food tray aside, leaned his elbows on the slick, Formica tabletop. "Private. It's none of my business, really, except my conscience is kicking up. It's about Father Rafael Hernandez."

"Good man. Pretty good priest."

"Glad to hear it. Unfortunately, I had to hear something else about him, from a compromised source, but still . . . the charge of child molestation has been made."

"Publicly?"

"No. That's my problem. Father Hernandez obviously knows about it. And the man who made it does. And I do."

"That's all?"

Matt nodded glumly.

"Surely the man's bringing charges, if he's a victim."

"That's just it. He's not a victim. He's a blackmailer, an embittered blackmailer who hates the church and anyone who's a part of it. He killed his elderly great-aunt to get her estate, crucified a convent cat, made obscene phone calls to an ancient, and luckily stone-deaf nun—"

Frank Bucek winced at this litany of evil-doing. "But he won't press the molestation issue against Father Hernandez?"

"No. He's in jail, awaiting the outcome of a sanity hearing. He seemed rather viciously sane to me when I saw him, hoping to wring the truth out of him."

"Bitter people don't tell the truth, Matt, not even to themselves. They have too much to lose."

The wisdom of that struck Matt like a breath of fresh menthol. He leaned closer, lowered his voice even more.

"That's just it. This man won't admit that these charges were part of his harassment tactics against his aunt's parish. I saw him in jail, and . . . I tell you, Frank . . . it was like interviewing the Devil. I can't claim the church is perfect, or that any one of us in its service is without sin, but such anger and enmity, such scalding . . . despise. I know the man's half-mad. I know he's violent, and vicious. I just don't know if he's a liar in this case. And he taunted me with that uncertainty. He wants me to squirm."

"You've told no one of this charge against Father Rafe?"

"No. I've been . . . oh, blast it. Frank, I've been 'investigating.' I concocted this story that the parish wants to honor Father Hernandez with a 'This Is Your Life' tribute and I've been calling good, earnest Catholic ladies at diocesan offices wherever Father Rafe has been assigned, trying to find his associates and grill them without their knowing."

Matt suddenly realized that Frank was grinning at him over the remains of his chicken sandwich.

"I've *lied*, Frank. White lies, for a good cause, but I feel like a skunk. It's too easy. I had no idea I was so believable."

"It's all that good-boy training. The veneer remains even when the foundation has cracked. Welcome to the real world, Matt."

"You're not shocked?"

"Who am I to be shocked?" Frank inquired gently. "Matt, I never had a seminarian under my direction who was so sincere, so scrupulous, so promising and so damned self-deceiving. I always sensed that you would make a terrific priest, and that you had no business being one."

"You always knew? Then why didn't you tell me? Why let me work and muddle and sweat my way through . . . ?"

"You can't tell someone what to do. Not even God can do that. You have to let them find out for themselves; otherwise, they're never free. And . . . I didn't know it, but my own vocation was built on sand. It will take other men, Matt, to follow in the shoes of the fisherman now. A new generation."

"Maybe other women," Matt added, remembering the dedicated minority with no rational hope of ordination, taking theology at the seminary for themselves alone even in his day. They must number more now, and they would be demanding more equity—even Holy Orders, despite the Pope's recent, hope-smashing decree.

Frank's hands lifted from the table, then slapped down.

"Listen, Matt, put your overactive Catholic conscience at rest. It so happens you've come to the person who can help you out of your moral quandary. Call it a last spiritual direction from a man whose own spiritual direction has taken a radical change of course. First, I can swear—swear on any saint's name you care to mention—that Father Rafael Hernandez showed no signs of pederasty when I was his assistant pastor at Holy Rosary twenty-five years ago.

"And," he added, as Matt stirred restlessly, "I am also in a position to prove it. I can have him quietly checked out, his entire roster of parishes. If there's any taint clinging to Rafe, I'll find it. You see, I have an obligation, too. I knew him years before you did; I shared parish work with him. Now I have a pressing need to know, and I'm in a position to find out."

"Why? How?" Matt felt a hosannah of relief rising in him, even as he didn't quite dare believe in such easy deliverance.

Frank smiled. "Fear not. I'm in the FBI now, buddy."

Then he winked.

Father Frank Bucek, Father Furtive, ex-Father Frank, winked.

Chapter 25

Midnight Louie Eats Crow with Caviar

With more fishy things occurring at the Crystal Phoenix, I am forced to eat and sleep on my old turf. I would much prefer my literally cushy spot at the Circle Ritz, but too much is afoot (including the little doll to whom I owe so much, and *vice versa*) at the Phoenix to leave the premises.

Fortunately, I can do both (eat and sleep, that is) in the same spot: under the tropical green leaves of the calla lilies that edge my own private pond. One might argue that since the funny business is being transacted within the hotel and casino, what I am doing lounging about the grounds outside?

First, a fellow must have a retreat in which to ponder. Plus, I must keep an ear to the ground, and that is hard to do indoors. Second, it behooves me to keep myself undercover. I am a well-known, perhaps even a notorious figure around and about the Phoenix. To flaunt my familiar profile would cast discretion to the wind. I am also in something of a quandary. Not only must I conceal myself from the nasty types committing sabotage and savagery inside the Phoenix, but I am not anxious to draw the attention of the lovely Caviar.

She has shown a lamentable tendency to haunt the place while hunting the poor sod who sired her. Had he but known, he would have thought twice about any hijinks with her mother, I can tell you. Since I am he, I speak with authority.

By some happy kink of Miss Caviar's brain, she does not suspect me of being this irresponsible dude, though I match the description in every respect. My most delicate task is to keep Miss Caviar from seeing me in the company of anyone who might let slip the dogs of revelation and call me by my name. This is not easy to do around the Phoenix, where I am known and loved by all, from the owners to the chorus girls to Nicky's bevy of brothers, who are all over the place these days, up to their Armani lapels in strange doings.

Needless to say, an ace detective who is forced to hide like a craven mouse most of the time is more than somewhat handicapped.

So the calla lilies provide my sole reliable cover, though I sneak out every now and then to kipe a carp to keep the old hide going.

This, however, is becoming less likely.

For some reason as irritating as it is mysterious, little Miss Caviar has also chosen the carp pond as her favorite retreat. She does not even have the innate feline grace to slink around it, but sprawls openly on the flagstones framing the pond, tail fluffed and fanned.

For a female who supposedly knows the ways of the back alley and the Dumpster dinette network, this is astonishingly naive behavior. I feel an unselfish urge to warn the poor sap, but restrain myself. Frankly, the young often need to be taught a harsh lesson, and Miss Caviar more so than most. Offering lip, teeth and claws to one's elders (not to mention one's forebears) is not something that should go unpunished.

In fact, I must have been leading a pretty angelic life lately, for even as I drowse in the dirt under the calla lilies, unnoticed by all, even and especially by my unacknowledged offspring, who should come striding into the sunlight, resplendent in executive whites, but Chef Song himself.

The sizzling Las Vegas sun glints off the broad steel rectangle of a formidable cleaver. Usually these cleavers are used for such yummy tasks as cutting meat, but, Chef Song being of Asian ancestry, it is also used extensively on vegetables as well. In fact, I spot a sliver or two of mushroom still adhering to its slick, razor-edged surface.

If Chef Song walks softly and carries a big stick (or cleaver), many the time I have run before it with a juicy carrot in my mouth. My carrots are often orange and tasty, but wear fins and scales. No one is more devoted to the welfare of these imperial koi than Chef Song. And no one is more dedicated to extricating the most tender among them from under the very eyes, nose and cleaver of Chef Song than Midnight Louie.

So Miss Caviar has made a severe error in judgment in displaying her languid length to the oncoming chef. It is true that she considers herself too refined for raw meat, preferring the pulverized, putrid-green pellets of Bast-knows-what that pour from a Free-to-be-Feline box.

But Chef Song does not know that. All he knows is that our kind are enemies of his plump, pampered, piscean pets. He especially knows that Midnight Louie is the master of the game. Let Chef Song see black, and he sees red.

Even now he stops, focusses on the flagrantly visible Caviar, and hefts his cleaver with a curse.

I cannot bear to look. Caviar is chopped liver. And kidney, and other essential organs. I would advise discriminating diners to avoid the main restaurant at the Crystal Phoenix for the next few days.

When I hear nothing more—no frantic yowls, no ring of cleaver on flagstone, no more curses, I unsquinch one peeper.

Miss Caviar has risen at the chef's approach and replied to his opprobrium with a plaintive mew.

Oh, please! This innocent act will get her nowhere.

Chef Song narrows his eyes and looks Miss Caviar up and down. I cannot blame him. She is a trim piece of pussycat.

"Skinny," he pronounces.

I prefer them plump myself.

"Eyes . . . gold. Not green."

Not my fault.

Miss Caviar sits again, neatly, with her feet and tail all tucked together like she wouldn't mash a mayfly.

Chef Song edges to the pond and does a quick fin count. The greedy-guts in the fish suits do a mass schooling at the pond rim, all expecting a fistful of their favorite snack, an unwholesome pellet available for a quarter from a dispensing machine installed there for the hotel guests.

Chef Song, being the boss, knows a way to get the machine to hand over without feeding it a quarter. He dribbles these unappetizing nuggets over the bubble-blowing fish-faces in the water.

A few fall to the flagstones and roll away.

Miss Caviar gives a dear little cry and bounds to retrieve one, crouching beside it to chomp away.

Chef Song straightens in wonder. "You strange kitty. You do not want fish, you want fish *food!*"

She looks up with her big carp-gold eyes and gives a miniature meow.

"Nice kitty." He is patting her satiny little head, which is as black and sin-smudged as her larcenous soul, with the hand that does not hold the cleaver.

She sniffs delicately at the lingering odor on his fingers and licks one.

My stomach turns. So does Chef Song. He is retreating rapidly back into the hotel, as would any self-respecting person confronted with such an unnatural feline.

Still, the minx's fish-hating act has probably saved her skin. I can give the devil her due.

She does not rest on her laurels, or sneak a spare carp and get out of there, as I would. No. She sits facing the door through which Chef Song has vanished as if bereft. Cut the act, kiddo; you've lost your audience, except for me, and I am not impressed by such a turntail to the feline creed.

In fact, she has outstayed her luck, for the door springs open and once again Chef Song advances on the carp pond.

I wince. If he suspects that she has hanging-around tendencies, he will make even shorter work of her.

I do not see the cleaver, but perhaps he will resort to a trap of sorts to remove her to the animal pound.

Even as I think this, he is bending low before her. For an odious moment, it almost looks as if he is worshiping her. In fact, he has left an offering; two in fact. I spot rice bowls of blue-and-white porcelain.

Miss Caviar digs into one urged on by untranslatable coos from Chef Song.

Poison. It is worse than I thought. I rise, ready to do my duty, however odious, and warn the little skunk away.

Chef Song straightens, uncrosses his arms, and reveals the cleaver at the ready.

What can I do? Risk an extremity? These are vital to my work and leisure activities. I recall needing an antidote to poison in an earlier case of mine involving some unsavory characters from the fringes, coyotes by name. So I know a noxious plant that will make the victim throw up the tainted food. It is unpleasant to down, and even more unpleasant to upchuck, but Miss Caviar obviously needs a lesson.

As soon as Chef Song skedaddles, I will point out her error and play the hero by leading her to the nearest stand of Desert Tobacco, which is guaranteed to make the heartiest eater repel any toxic substance.

The chef, nodding and grinning like a homicidal puppet, leaves the scene at last.

I am about to do as planned, when Miss Caviar rises and trots after him. After performing some nauseating leg-rubs in the doorway, she is invited in.

Will travesties never cease? I always had to break or sneak my way in to the Crystal Phoenix. That is the way it should be done. That is the way it was always done.

I stalk over to the abandoned bowls. Ugh. Free-to-be-Feline salting a well chopped mixture of white chicken meat, shrimp and . . . caviar. The other bowl holds clear liquid. I sniff it, expecting to inhale turpentine or some other deadly libation. Water. Just water. Smelling faintly of minerals and other healthful natural additives. Bottled water! What kind of decadent dishes are these? Not poison, but bribes. What is happening to the species?

I stalk to the pond edge and gaze into a dozen fish eyes as glassy as marbles, all those carp pushing eagerly to the pond's edge as if dying to leap into my grasp.

Unfortunately, I have lost my appetite.

Chapter 26

Old King Coil

The cursor on Temple's laptop screen blinked faster than a racing pulse.

Nothing is more aggravating to a writer than a blank mind to match that blank screen, all while an agitated cursor itches to be off and running down the invisible pixels, spitting out letters.

She had meant to dream up a Three O'Clock Louie campaign. Every new exposure generated a flurry of new ideas. Now the flurry had flitted to the back of her brain. What dominated her mental foreground was the Jersey Joe Jackson connection to the Glory Hole Gang and the Joshua Tree, the hotel that became the Crystal Phoenix. The Ghost Suite had been his; some said it still was.

Disconnected ideas were running around her unconscious like gerbils in an exercise wheel. The Phoenix and ghosts, ghost towns and the old days, digging for gold and silver dollars, theme parks. Nothing coalesced.

When the phone beside her rang, she snatched the receiver off the cradle, eager for distraction.

"Temple?"

Oh, no, this wasn't distraction, it was penance.

"Yes, Crawford."

"Glad to catch you at home."

"I'm glad one of us is."

"Stay there. We don't need you nosing about the show anymore. Besides, it's dangerous."

"Danny Dove invited me to drop in on rehearsals, and he's the director, not you."

"Well, I'm uninviting you. In fact, I'm warning you."

"Warning? Is this a threat?"

"You bet. If you set one bum foot in the theater, I'll file the suit I've been considering."

"I thought all your sweat-stained suits were at the cleaners."

"Just jibe away. I'll up the numbers. I'm serious here. I've had chest pains ever since your UFO went AWOL and nearly flattened me and half the cast."

"It's not 'my' UFO, it's a stage prop. How can you blame me for a set piece that came loose because your hysterical shove forced me to jerk one of its anchoring ropes?"

"I can blame anybody, but I *will* sue those who have the bucks to be worth it—the Crystal Phoenix, Van von Rhine and Nicky Fontana. And Danny Dove. For negligence."

"Get real. The police think the 'accident' was arranged."

"Doesn't matter how it happened, only that it did. I figure about six mill ought to cover it."

"Crawford! Don't be an ass. Sorry. It's impossible for you not to be one. But don't be dumb, too. You'll sink the Gridiron and all your wonderful skits."

"No, I won't. Danny Dove is tossing them out right and left, anyway, and what he's keeping he's mauling into mindless mush. That little twerp is acting like Hitler in high heels, stomping all over my best lines, my best pieces. He claims they 'won't play.' What does a toad dancer know about good writing?"

"Danny Dove does jazz and tap mostly nowadays, plus he's designed and mounted several of the Strip hotel's most successful shows."

"Sure, defend him. If you're the best attorney he can get, he'll be easy pickings in this suit."

"So that's why you called . . . to threaten me?"

"No, I called to tell you to stay away from the Gridiron. If you call that a threat, that's your privilege."

"Crawford, you dragged me into it against my better judgment in the first place."

"Yeah, but then I thought I could dump your skit and that would be that. I had no idea Dove would jump on it like a frog on a lilypad."

"You . . . planned to dump my skit? Why?"

"Because this is my show. I was gonna write all of it."

"Then why ask me, beg me, to go over to the *Las Vegas Scoop* on a Saturday and write my fingernails to the bone all day?"

The phone line was suddenly, tellingly silent.

"Maybe I just wanted to see you," Crawford said in a sullen tone at last.

"See me what?"

"Sweat," he admitted. "There you were, hogging the Gridiron's big opening and closing numbers year after year. This time you were gonna show up for the big night and find it was a big bust. Only that damn wrist-waving Danny Dove wouldn't go along—"

"What a dirty trick, but then, why am I surprised? I guess I doubted even you were that rancorous."

"Listen." Crawford's voice had gone deeper and softer, so it hummed like bass static over the wires. "Maybe I was planning on playing the jerk, but it's not so funny now. Some big muscle around town isn't happy about what's in your skit. They've been sending plenty of messages—to me, like I'm responsible or something. I've got some of those messages on my answering machine. Anonymous. They want your skit out of the show. Maybe they want you out of the picture. I'm telling you to stay away from the Crystal Phoenix and the Gridiron. If you don't, and it's curtains, don't say I didn't warn you, which is more than you did for me when the E.T. special was crashing down on my head."

"Crawford, are you saying someone's trying to close down the show because of my skit? Why? What's in it?"

"Obviously it isn't very funny, which was what I told Dove, and now the powers that be have noticed that. So, stay away. That's what I'm going to do, until the coast, and the cast, are clear."

He hung up without saying goodbye.

Like maybe there was no point, like maybe she was dead already.

Temple stared at her computer screen with its paltry sprinkle of words: "The good times never stop at Three O'Clock Louie's."

Underneath Crawford's usual bluster Temple had sensed genuine fear. In his own craven way, he was warning her to do as he was doing and desert the Gridiron.

So. It was his project. So what if Danny Dove was left in the lurch? He'd get something mounted. And the Flying Fontana Brothers Security Syndicate was crawling and clambering all over the place. Johnny Diamond was set to sing Temple's medley of satirical show tunes, surely he'd be all right. Nobody would dare to mess with a big name like that. But what on earth could be so threatening about her skit?

And if the accidents were intended to discourage the production, whoever was arranging them didn't know the old maxim that "the show must go on." Troopers like Danny and Johnny and the eager semi-amateur cast weren't about to bow out because of some dubious accidents. Unless those "accidents" included the murder of the man in the ceiling, Matt's missing stepfather, Cliff Effinger.

Temple saved the gibberish on her screen and gave it a name: 3Louie. No wonder she had mistaken the black cat at Temple Bar for Midnight Louie; she'd seen so darn little of him lately that she'd forgotten exactly what he looked like. In fact, the last place she had seen her Louie was at the Phoenix. . . .

Temple retreated to the DOS C-prompt, then turned computer and screen off. The last, small luminescent letters vanished.

The same could not be said of the string of bright, pulsating question marks on the screen of Temple's mind.

Eightball O'Rourke's neighborhood was as shabby as ever.

Temple glanced back at her aqua Storm poised at the curb like a brilliant blue butterfly that had just landed. She hated to leave it unattended, that shiny bluebird of happiness in this neighborhood of rusted-out heaps of trouble.

She paused at the front door, then pushed the scabrous bell. Its surface was rough with coats of overpainted green enamel.

While she waited she studied the peeling paint patterns of the front forest-green screen door. Then she rang again.

Should have phoned first, she told herself, but she hadn't even known where she was going when she left the Circle Ritz.

A third ring was equally unable to stir the low stucco house with its gravel roof. The swamp cooler at its core grunted mechanically from the so-called peak of the shallow roof.

The door was shaded by scrawny eaves-high bushes too insect-eaten to declare a type. Temple waited, shifting from one tennis shoe to the other, watching little red ants dance a conga line up the cracked sidewalk to her feet.

The big wooden front door creaked, then gaped open.

Eightball stood there in his undershirt, blinking.

"Should have phoned first," he said. "I been working late, sleeping days. I'll get me a shirt."

He vanished, leaving Temple to pull open the rickety screen door and edge inside.

The house broadcast the same musty smell of her last visit, the deep-down halitosis of an old house. Eightball appeared, buttoning a short-sleeved polyester shirt of indeterminate color.

Temple followed him down dim halls, through shadowy rooms into the same sparse office with the billiard-table-size desk and narrow band of windows under the ceiling.

He flicked on an overhead light and sat at the desk. "So what's up?"

Temple sat on the lumpy green leather chair, escapee from some fifties-vintage office—or dump—and tried to come up with a reasonable explanation of why she was there.

"I visited Three O'Clock Louie's the other day."

Eightball nodded, fussing to fasten the second-to-the-top button on his shirt. It was pale green.

Undershirt, Temple thought. Who wore undershirts anymore, especially in a hot spot like Las Vegas? And this wasn't even your Sears Catalog model with the short sleeves and v-neck, but a tank-type sleeveless undershirt that smacked of pre-Clark Cable and *It Happened Last Night* innocence. That was Eightball and the Glory Hole Gang, all right—1930's kind of guys in a nineties world hung up on Calvin Klein's Obsession instead of old standbys like undershirts and B.O.

Maybe, she thought, Crawford Buchanan wore pale yellow undershirts to match his cowardly streak.

"What did you think of it?" Eightball asked. He lit a cigar that looked like a Doberman turd with gangrene.

Temple restrained herself from fanning away the smoke; the smell was more lethal anyway. "Think of what? Oh, the restaurant! Interesting. Not a bad name. Needs a lot of work."

Eightball nodded at each of her inane comments.

Temple edged forward on the chair. "It has a lot of possibilities. Especially . . . well, if I—you guys—drew on your Glory Hole background."

He squinted as he exhaled a storm-blue thunderhead of smoke. "You mean . . . tie it in with the ghost town concession?"

"Thematically, yes. Let's face it. You fellows are enough local color for a megacity like Los Angeles, much less Las Vegas. Just the name of the place: 'Three O'Clock Louie's.' It reeks of speakeasies and jazz, bathtub vodka and guys with shoulder holsters and cigarette holders, dolls with garters and gats."

"Bathtub gin."

"Did I say something else? Sorry, I'm . . . distracted."

"We were all just kids during Prohibition," Eightball said doubtfully.

"Sure, but you were there. And wasn't Jersey Joe Jackson there too?"

"That skunk." Eightball was so agitated that he stubbed out his cigar in the tray-size olive-green glass ashtray on his desk.

Temple thanked whatever gods may be.

"Skunks can be ver-ry colorful," she pointed out with singsong significance.

"If you like black-and-white, as in prison stripes."

Temple beamed. "See what I mean? Convicts in stripes. You fellows are soooo colorful. About Jersey Joe Jackson—"

"He's dead, and we ain't."

"So much the better. We can . . . er, exploit his, ah, colorful legend without treading on any living toes."

"We?"

"Well, think about it. Wasn't Jersey Joe an original member of the Glory Hole Gang?"

"Yeah, sure . . . but not for long."

"Why not?"

"For one thing, he ran off with half the silver dollars we lifted off the train in that heist. Then he hid them around town—and Vegas was mostly brush and bobtail in the forties—in all his private little hidey-holes.''

"Didn't you Glory Hole guys bury what was left in the Mojave, so successfully that even you couldn't find the cache for forty years?"

"Yeah, but that was because the terrain shifted. Desert will do that, you know. Skitter around on you like a sidewinder rattler in a windstorm. Wind, gully-washers, they all scrape the face off the desert floor, the way time erodes people's faces. Look at mine. Can you even imagine what I looked like at your age, girlie?"

Temple shook her head.

Where did it come from, the seaming and searing? The eyes sinking like burned-out suns and the ears and nose growing wild. She thought of the sand-eaten features of the real sphinx and shivered a little at the notion of the cosmetically enhanced one at the Luxor. Behind Eightball's wizened visage, she glimpsed a muscular, wiry young fellow tanned the color of Corinthian leather in a white undershirt, sweating in a shipyard somewhere, working for Uncle Sam.

"The thing is," she said, "we're interested in *your* age. Your Age. A time when watches ticked and ladies' nylon stockings had seams and we all had a kinder, gentler view of everything. When even shady ladies were classy and guys could shave with straight-edge razors and wear hats. Fedoras. That's the ticket. That's the ambiance. That's . . . jazz."

"I don't get it? Why are you spouting this stuff to me?"

"Because I want to pick your brain, Eightball. I want to bring back the Glory-Hole days. Out on Lake Mead at Temple Bar. Here in town, at the Crystal Phoenix." And I want to bring a boys' band to River City. Right here. Do you buy that tuba? How about a French horn? A PR person is always one dance-step removed from a conman. Buy the sizzle, not the steak; the shining brass band, not the song; the surface cha-cha-cha, not the underlying instinct. The song-and-dance woman, not the amateur detective. . . .

"You've got some scheme—" he began, sounding uncertain.

"Not a scheme . . . a theme! For the Phoenix, for Temple Bar and Three O'Clock Louie's, even for the Glory Hole Ghost Town. And the link is . . . Jersey Joe Jackson."

"A guy who gave sewer rats a bad name when he was alive!"

"But he's dead now. We can use him with impunity. As he used you, as he made you poor fellows parboil in nowhere while he lived it up at the . . . what was the Phoenix called in the old days, before Nicky and Van revived it?"

"The Joshua Tree," Eightball said with venom. "A common, stingy kind of cactus with big ideas and lots of stingers."

"Joshua Tree." Temple shook her head in distaste. "If he named the place, he didn't have much flair."

"Jersey Joe didn't have flair, he had nerve. That's what ended up on top in those days. Like Bugsy Siegel and the Flamingo. Nerve. We were kids, Spuds, Wild Blue, Encyclopedia and the rest. We were schmoes."

"Schmoes?" Temple was lost.

"Stand-up fools made to knock down. But schmoes always come back for more, bounce back, and we did, one more time than Jersey Joe, in the end. In the end, that's all that matters."

"Why was Jersey Joe such a successful con man? What did he have?"

"Besides nerve? He had half our silver dollars. Somehow he cashed them in to buy the land and put up the Joshua Tree and still bury this stash of silver dollars in his mattress. Can you believe it? The guy owned his own hotel on the Strip. He had his own suite in it, like a poor man's Howard Hughes, and he stashes a hoard of the stolen silver dollars in his *mattress*. Then he hangs on, and loses everything and the hotel is a wreck and a ruin and deserted, and he dies. And years later someone bounces on his broken-down mattress and out tumble a king's ransom in silver dollars."

"No," said Temple quite sincerely. "I can't believe it. Why did he stay in those rooms when the hotel was such a wreck?"

"He'd become a derelict, that's why. A derelict at the heart of his own lost empire. And—" Eightball lifted the butt of his cigar from the ashtray to regard it fondly, as an old friend that had died, and therefore, quite naturally, stank. "There were rumors."

"Rumors?"

"Guy like Jersey Joe always is better at rumors than reality. They say he was sitting on a gold mine. That the Joshua Tree was built on a hidden vein of glory-gold so thick and long and bright it would take you to Oz and back. They say the dirt and desert beneath the hotel is eaten away by earthworms. Tunnels. Secret passages. Gold for the taking, if you can find it. That useful? That suit your theme-scheme, Missy?"

"Oh, yes," said Temple. "To a Tee and that rhymes with B to Z and that stands for Truth. Oh, yes, thank you very much."

Temple shoved her tote bag back on her shoulder and stood.

"By the way, who at the Circle Ritz is keeping you up past your bedtime these days?"

Eightball picked up the dead cigar, flicked his Bic and sucked on it until the tip reddened in the steady flame. "You know that information is confidential," he offered on an exhalation of putrid smoke.

Temple backed up, but not off. "Nothing's confidential to a PR person but her client's business. I suppose the same is true of a P.I.?"

Eightball nodded, still puffing away poisonously. The room was clogging with smudge.

"Just tell me this," Temple pushed. "Are you still working for someone at the Circle Ritz?"

"Maybe not."

"I guess you wouldn't be averse to helping Electra out in a jam," Temple suggested.

"Guess not, but maybe not."

She frowned. Eightball hadn't flickered an eyelash at mention of her landlady's name. Was that a sign of iron control, or of ignorance? Who else would employ him, if not her or Electra . . . ? Temple recalled the phantom figure she had glimpsed at the Crystal Phoenix. An aura of Max was settling ever lower on this whole muddled landscape, from the Crystal Phoenix to the Circle Ritz.

"It's not . . . couldn't be . . . Max . . ." she thought aloud.

Mention of that name alarmed Eightball as nothing else had.

"No!" he said quickly. "Not *him*. Never laid eyes on the guy."

Except that Eightball's emphasis had been on *him*.

So he had been hired, not by Max, but by another "him" who was associated with the Circle Ritz.

Temple nodded slowly. "Goodbye, and thanks for the information."

Eightball watched her suspiciously, not sure to what "information" she referred, which was just the way Temple wanted it. Let him stew for a while.

Temple wove her own way out of the house, bumping gently against dim walls. She was also beginning to see her way out of the current maze. *Not him, but a he.*

Was it Matt, who had been so busy and distracted lately? Matt, whom she had worried was pulling away from her because she had been too pushy? Maybe Matt was simply pushing in another direction.

Maybe not.

Maybe they were both headed in the same direction from two different places. And maybe the collision point was the Crystal Phoenix.

Lou Who?

Although I am used to undercover operations, it is more than somewhat galling to be forced to slink around my former digs like a
criminal.

But this is exactly the lot that is mine at the Crystal Phoenix Hotel
and Casino, now that Caviar, a.k.a. Midnight Louise, has taken over
my turf. Normally, I would not sit still under the nearest topiary tree
chewing my nails while some upstart usurps my territory.

However, in this instance my tongue and tail are tied.

This does not suit my larger goal of sniffing out what foul forces
are afoot and endangering my devoted roommate, Miss Temple
Barr, and her current project, the Gridiron show.

Miss Caviar, in the meantime, shows no shyness whatsoever
about swaggering around the grounds and hotel interior, gathering
compliments for her resemblance to yours truly, albeit in a somewhat slimmer and younger form.

The more the unsuspecting humans mention my name, the more
they ensure that the relentless Caviar remains in the vicinity. I even
spot her interrogating the occasional canine that lopes around the
fringes of the hotel, hoping for some Dumpster dining.

The first such ugly customer she broaches has me covering my eyes with my mitts as I lurk in the ever-convenient oleander clump near the service entrance.

The browsing dog is a pit bull–shepherd mix, no type to trifle with, believe you me. My forbearance with the young upstart may have given her too high an opinion of herself, for she sashays up to this truly terrifying dingo without a qualm.

"Pardon me, sir," I hear her say as he rips open a body bag with expert slashes of his canines.

He looks up. One eye has a squint and the opposite ear is semi-chewed. "Get lost, cupcake. I will be ready for dessert soon and you would do nicely."

"Funny you should mention 'lost,' bud," she replies without stiffening a single hair. "I am looking for someone who is apparently missing."

"We are all missing in action, babe." His staple-gun jaws wrestle what's left of a t-bone steak out of its plastic wrapping.

Caviar sits on her cute little tail and applies a prissy paw to her whiskers, no doubt offended by her subject's crude dining habits. "The object of my search is somewhat notorious around here. Have you ever heard of Midnight Louie?"

"Heard of him?" The dog spits out a few splinters of bone. "I am the first one in this town to pin his ears back. Has the big bully been bothering you, cupcake? I am the one to knock him into next week, even the next world, and if you tip me off when the goodies are about to hit the buffet table"—his scrawny tail bangs once on the Dumpster side—"I may even let you live a while longer."

"That will not be necessary," says she. "I do my own knocking. So he is afraid of you. I thought he was big and tough."

I cringe in the bushes, my tail beating up a cloud of dust. The reason this dingo dude squints is due to the number three shiv on my right mitt. Yet I am forced to grit my fangs while I hear him libel my battle prowess, not to mention my courage.

"Big and tough," the dirty dog repeats with a growl. "Hearing news like that is what makes a hyena laugh. This Midnight Louie was a creampuff, cupcake. Big, maybe, but it was all lard and laziness. I for one am glad to hear that the old layabout is off the premises. It improves the neighborhood."

As if this scrounger adds some elegance to the environment!

Apparently Caviar is not buying this bozo's story. "Why would Midnight Louie leave such a cushy job, if he is as lazy as you say? A position of house detective at a major Strip hotel does not open up every day. And the staff—with the understandable exception of Chef Song—seems fond of him. I have even heard him credited with rescuing the manager, Miss Van von Rhine, from a mob of musclemen."

The dog snorts, which is what you can expect from the breed while eating. "People are easily misled by milk-sucking parasites like him. He has done nothing for this hotel except decimate the fancy fish supply." The animal snuffles among a selection of orange rinds and apple cores before pulling out the butt end of a hot dog. "Besides, from what I hear, he has moved on to another establishment."

"Oh?" Caviar says in a way that begs for answering.

I have got to hand it to the kid. She manages to sound supremely uninterested just as the dumb cluck is spilling the info she wants the most.

He scarfs up some odds and ends I would not deign to bury, then feeds her the info while his mouth is full. "New place. On Lake Mead. Eatery called 'Three O'Clock Louie's.' Sounds like your friend has found a new gig with a better water view and more carp, where he can stay up later these days."

"He is not my friend," Miss Caviar is quick to establish.

"Then why do you want to find him?"

"Personal business," she answers, flexing her hardware.

The dog eyes the glint of her front claws stretching and retracting in a rhythm no one could mistake for expressing contentment. He backs away, dragging some of his ill-gotten gains with him.

"Yeah, well, I do not intrude in vendettas, lady. I doubt you could do more than nick a few loose hairs off his chinny-chin-chin, but I would like to see that lout get his comeuppance, so I will let you get off easy this time. Now get out of here before I lose my appetite and forget I swore off cats!"

He lunges, feet braced, ears back, his loud and uncouth barker at full cry.

Caviar lunges too, fluffing her hair into a fat black aura, and arching her back like a midnight rainbow.

"I have had enough of you, too, fellow," she says in a tone between a growl and a hiss. "You should know that I am the new house detective at the Crystal Phoenix, and I do not welcome passersby of the wrong sort. You will have to do your snacking elsewhere from now on.''

''Or else?'' he snarls.

I tense, readying myself for a leap to the rescue. Much as Miss Caviar deserves a lesson, I cannot allow even maybe-kin to lose all nine lives to a dirty dog in my presence.

''Get back to the Araby Motel where you belong,'' she screeches, executing some swift and subtle moves she probably learned off an Oriental shorthair, which is exactly what that breed of cat usually get their opponents by.

The dog's threatening growl has escalated to a howl. He is backing away in big, bounding jerks, rubbing his long ugly snout in the dirt. Four dark furrows now tattoo his nose. Even as I watch, they well with bright red blood.

He dashes off, leaving a trail of droplets a near-sighted wombat could follow.

The triumphant Caviar drags his leavings back to the Dumpster, pantomimes burying the mess and ambles off, no doubt to attend to her beauty routine and cadge another disgusting hand-out from Chef Song.

I remain in the shade, mulling the cruel twists of fate. I am not only rumored to be living elsewhere under a pseudonym, but I have lost my old job to a female. What is this world coming to?

Chapter 28

Missing Connections

The water, warm and velvety, felt like partially set Jell-O.

Matt pulled himself through the pool's turgid length, rhythmically angling his shoulder and face toward the overhead sun as he took a deep breath every other stroke.

Swimming was always a surreal experience. Immersed in an alien element, he battled to remain part of it, yet apart from it, moving with a shark's constancy.

His every breath came on a smelling-salt slap of chlorine. Through blue-tinted goggles, he glimpsed the world moving in a way that couldn't be sensed by walking on Mother Earth. A slash of palm frond waving against a blazing blue sky. A flash of the Circle Ritz roof spinning away as he made a splashy turn at the pool's far end. A black dot oared across the sky just as he rolled for a gulp of air, then submerged again.

Doing the Australian crawl was a fractured experience united by the water's tepid, seamless presence, an amniotic fluid buoying a rather restless fetus.

On the twenty-third lap, Matt's routine twist for air showed a man's face masked by sinister wraparound sunglasses hanging over him.

Matt wrenched himself into a full roll and came upright, treading the gelatinous water, trying to focus through droplet-spotted goggles.

"Frank!" he said, as much with relief as recognition. Temple's tales of shady characters and dark doings at the Crystal Phoenix had gotten to him.

With a wry grimace of acknowledgment, the man retreated to the shade while Matt drew himself, dripping, onto the hot concrete bordering the pool.

"What are you doing here?" he asked.

Matt's wet feet left Friday footprints on the concrete. He collected his towel from the elderly lounge chair beside the one Frank had settled upon with gingerly reluctance.

"Quite a quaint place," Frank said instead of answering, pocketing the intimidating sunglasses to squint at the Circle Ritz's black marble bulk shining like a mausoleum in the sun. "Even a little sinister looking."

"Speak of the Devil." Matt looked Frank up and down, from the gray suit and tie to the wing-tip shoes resting so incongruously on the cement.

"Unwritten FBI dress code." Frank loosened the utterly unimaginative tie. "Out of the church and still in uniform."

"Still on duty?" Matt asked, throwing his damp towel on the lounge seat before sitting.

"Always. You still keep in good shape."

"Always. And swimming is so routine, it's good for meditation."

"Yeah," Frank said, "routine has its uses. Once we go the suit route in the hot, humid Virginia summers, the heat elsewhere doesn't bother us. And priests are used to overdressing."

Matt self-consciously dabbed chlorine-perfumed droplets off his shoulder. His damp bareness suddenly symbolized the vocation and past that he had thrown off like an itchy black suit.

"I still can't believe you're an FBI agent," Matt said.

"You'd be surprised how many ex-priests end up in law enforcement. Makes sense. We've acquired the education, the people skills, plus a highly overdeveloped sense of right and wrong. We know how to knuckle under to rules and authority. We believe we can change the world, or at least the dirty undersoul of mankind."

"Speak for yourself. So what brought you here besides rank curiosity?"

Frank laughed apologetically as he pulled a packet of cigarettes from his suitcoat pocket. "Bad habit. Every good celibate deserves, or develops, a compensatory but less condemnable vice—food, drink or these. Mind?"

Matt shook his head, actually enjoying the acrid odor of the freshly lit cigarette Frank soon inhaled as hungrily as a man breathing air through a straw.

"What are *your* vices?" Frank wanted to know.

"Nothing. Yet. My greatest weakness was always my lack of weaknesses."

"Granted. Everybody is entitled to a weakness," Frank mused. "Makes us human. Maybe your apparent perfection was why you could leave with laicization. Few of us need apply for that rare status, because we won't be granted release from our promises."

He regarded Matt with piercing, almost painful curiosity. "Besides, the only allowable conditions are so humiliating. Either admit lacking free will and maturity at ordination, or confess to such insatiable lust for women that you can't live without one, or be dying in an unauthorized married state and facing eternal damnation without emergency laicization. Ugly, bureaucratic word, isn't it?" Frank eyed Matt. "You don't look like you have terminal anything, and didn't have a wife already. You certainly don't strike me as possessed of a manic lust for women as the church defines it, and you were the most mature seminarian in your class. How did you manage it?"

Matt stared at the pool, an emerald-cut liquid aquamarine glinting under a ceaseless spotlight of sunshine.

"I made my case, and they accepted it."

Frank hissed out an exhaust of smoke. "It's none of my business; I'm just a little envious. Of course I wondered what you were doing in the seminary, as everybody must have. Seminarians are always misfits of a sort, like raw recruits in the Army. You were so smart, so smooth, so self-contained. And you looked like a movie star. I wondered if your vocation was revenge, to drive some girl—all girls—crazy."

Matt laughed. "My vocation was to save my own sanity, and it did. That's why it was misdirected. Too selfish."

"Laicization is seldom granted. Most ex-priests exit into a moral limbo of sorts. I had to marry in the Episcopal Church, but you're free to be Catholic—"

"I'm not free yet," Matt said abruptly. "When you married. Was your wife the first woman—?"

"No. I wasn't a virgin bridegroom. Went a little crazy after I left. I didn't know how to do it at my advanced age, have relationships. So I . . . experimented before I got it right."

Matt felt himself flushing. "I wasn't asking that. I just wondered if she was the first woman you dated. Usually former priests begin—and end—with ex-nuns, but you said she was a widow."

"Sandy's no ex-nun, for sure. Listen, Matt, if you're going to go around asking questions on any level, you better figure out how to phrase them exactly so you learn what you want to know." Frank's sideways glance was embarrassed. "Then you won't learn more than you need to know. Here we go again, me offering direction and you listening. At least I've been through the mill first. That's the worst, learning to socialize with the world of women in a whole different way. That, and overcoming all the avoidance therapy we get in seminary."

Matt nodded. "What about coming to terms with church doctrine? Now that I'm out here, it doesn't seem possible to live by it."

Frank's hearty laugh came like a burst of machine-gun fire. His heavy shoe ground out the cigarette on the concrete, then he picked up the flattened butt and wrapped it in a fast-food napkin he pulled from his pocket.

That was Father Furtive, terminally tidy, Matt thought. How had he made the awesome transition between the priesthood and the secular world?

"Feel a bit more compassion for confused parishioners during confession?" Frank asked. "No, it's damn hard. We exit the priesthood as we entered, awkward ugly ducklings no matter the outward sophistication. We're overeducated, over-ethical and underexperienced. Haven't you learned by now that there's no way *not* to sin, not without losing our humanity, and certainly our humility?

The secret is to select sins that do the least damage, to others and one's self."

" 'First, do no harm,' " Matt quoted the Hippocratic oath taken by doctors. "Isn't that a principle of the Tao?"

"Yup. We grew up on a culture and a church that insisted we must do good, even if it meant imposing our notion of good on people who didn't subscribe to it. I've concluded that in matters of spirituality, the absence of malice is more important to the human soul than the presence of some rigorous system of perceived rectitude. More people have been hurt by being forced to fit someone else's notion of 'good' than by being allowed to be human."

Matt absorbed his words, realizing that Frank had become an automatic outcast by leaving the priesthood. His renegade marriage was just that, unsanctioned by the church in which he had grown up and made his promises to the priesthood. Matt still could be perfect, if he did things according to Hoyle and the Holy See.

He could marry in the Church, if he could find an undivorced woman. If he was lucky, he would find a perfect life partner the first time out, commit only a few venial sins of longing and lust, and enter matrimony as virginal as Mary, avoiding the pitfalls of sexual trial and error. But then the onus would be upon selecting the right partner in the dark, and both of them would go half-blind into the most important alliance of their lives. Failure would push him into the divorce trap, which would forever enjoin the perfect ex-priest to lifelong celibacy again.

Matt began to see what Temple had meant when she had asked him what on earth he would do. Temple was shrewd, but she was also trouble. She wasn't Catholic, and didn't understand or kowtow to the culture. Maybe that was why he liked her so much.

"Theology and human behavior mix like oil and water, don't they?" Matt said finally.

Frank nodded. "Human behavior is always a conundrum, but inhuman behavior is worse."

"Are you counseling me again?"

He shook his head. "Warning you. It's not easy. Compared to this, checking out Rafael Hernandez was a snap."

Matt held his breath. "That's what you came to tell me?"

"He's clean, Matt. I used my contacts from twenty-five years ago, I used computers. I even used some pull in the various dioceses.

Nothing. Not a word of scandal or complaint. I interviewed several ex-altar boys by phone. Hernandez can be a bit severe, even a little pompous, but misconduct—never."

"You're absolutely sure?"

"Certain enough to stand up in a court of law and swear that I was unable to unearth a scintilla of evidence."

When Matt said nothing, Frank pulled out another cigarette and lit it in disgust. "What do you want, Devine, a chorus of archangels announcing the news from on high? I did my best, and I'm satisfied. Why can't you be?"

"Sorry, Frank. I appreciate the favor. It's just that the price of being wrong is so high."

"It always is, we just don't notice it in every case."

"So." Matt bent to pull his canvas shoes on dry feet. "Now you can concentrate on what really brought you to Las Vegas." He shrugged on a shirt that still clung damply to his shoulder blades.

"Hinting? I'm not about to talk about that. Seal of the professional," he punned with one of his rare flashes of humor as he stood with Matt.

"I'll walk you to your car. Maybe you could leave your phone number."

"Sure." Frank pulled out a card, scrawling his home number on the reverse with a ballpoint pen. "I travel a lot, but messages reach me everywhere. You have any questions, call. If you don't, let me know how you're doing. I'm curious to see what you end up doing."

"Professionally or personally?"

"Both." He opened the wooden gate to the parking area.

Matt tucked the card in his shirt pocket, spying Frank's car right away. A rental Taurus, forest green. Perfect for a priest, or an FBI man. He began to see the logic of Frank's new profession.

Pulling up next to Frank's authoritatively nondescript car was Temple's lurid little Storm.

He watched her car absently, thinking about what he and Frank had discussed.

Frank was opening his car door when Temple came clicking around behind it, grocery bag in one arm, tote bag on her opposite shoulder, oversize prescription sunglasses slipping down her narrow, upturned nose.

"Hi," she began, then glanced at Frank and stopped cold.

"What are you doing here, Miss Barr?" Frank's recent affability had hardened into alertness.

"I could ask the same of you. I live here."

"Do you?" Frank turned to Matt with surprise, as if wondering why Matt hadn't volunteered this fascinating fact. "You know each other?"

Matt was momentarily tongue-tied. More was going on here than the obvious. How did Frank know Temple? Had he been checking on Matt?

"We're neighbors," Temple said into the growing conversational gap. "Matt teaches me martial arts."

"Are you trying to say we shouldn't worry about your safety, Miss Barr?"

"I'm trying to explain how Matt and I know each other, although I don't know why." She shifted the bag. "I've got some frozen yogurt. I'd better get inside."

The paper bag was slowly slipping down her hip.

"I'll get it," Matt said. He turned to Frank. "Thanks for stopping by."

Frank was eyeing the grocery bag in Matt's arm, then Temple, speculation running visibly wild.

"We'll talk again," he told Matt. He nodded at Temple in a way that was not quite farewell, got in the car and drove away.

"Well." Temple was eyeing Matt with equal curiosity. "How do you know FBI Agent Bucek?"

"I went to school with him." Matt didn't feel like unreeling chapter and verse of the connection at the moment. "And you?"

"He's the government goon who interrogated me along with Molina and Ferarro, the homicide twins from the LVMPD." She preceded him to the wooden gate, and pulled it open for him. "Hey, just kidding about the 'government goon' part. He was perfectly polite, but I got the impression he can be formidable when he needs to know something."

"He can."

"Sounds like the voice of experience, and isn't he a little old to be in your class?"

"I didn't say we were in the same class, just at the same school."

"Curiouser and cursiouser." Temple clattered into the building ahead of him.

Matt could feel the condensation on the frozen yogurt carton seeping through the brown paper, softening it to pulp. It wasn't the only thing that was sweating.

They were silent in the elevator, both facing forward as if the cubicle were crowded and they were on their best, most indifferent behavior.

"Matt," Temple said suddenly. "Did you hire Eightball O'Rourke to protect me?"

Chapter 29

A Ghost of a Chance

Temple surveyed her new home away from home. The first pair of high heels she had been able to wear in days sank past their plastic heel caps into plush carpeting the color of *café au lait*. Beige grass-cloth wallpaper was interwoven with silver strands. A computer screen cursor winked encouragingly from a neatly petite laptop floating on an otherwise empty sheet of inch-thick glass. A laser printer in the same ivory-color casing rested atop a nearby cart.

Against the wall, a row of walnut-veneer two-drawer file cabinets awaited the opportunity to conceal any clutter that Temple could generate.

Atop one file cabinet, steaming discreetly, sat a black coffee mug emblazoned with the gilded, feathered form of a rising phoenix.

Temple peeked into the cup. She had asked Van's secretary (male, but not a Fontana brother) to bring her coffee with milk. Yup, the mixture within perfectly matched the color of the carpeting.

Temple sighed wistfully at her magnificent blank slate of an office. She would make it the clutter capital of America in a just day or two, she thought, unloading the essential contents of her tote bag onto the glass desktop.

She owed her elegant roost at the Crystal Phoenix to two people. Danny Dove had insisted that Temple rewrite the absent Crawford Buchanan's "abysmal scripts," his phrase, not hers, in front of Van von Rhine. And Van von Rhine, in turn, had insisted that Temple needed an office in which to mastermind the Crystal Phoenix resurgence, as well as any little promotional project she might dream up for "dear Spuds"—Van's phrase, not Temple's—"and his offbeat lakefront fast-food emporium."

Temple suspected that the office served another, unspoken purpose. It would help everyone at the Phoenix keep an eye on her, since she was the suspected target of the mischief now abroad. She frowned, remembering how Matt, hot, bothered and indignant, had denied any intention to protect her, other than by teaching her martial arts. He had not denied hiring Eightball O'Rourke. Interesting.

"All right," Temple told her gorgeous but empty office. "As long as I'm being kept after class for my own good, I might as well do a little homework."

She hit the intercom button on the desk, jumping when a disembodied masculine voice answered. For all she knew, a Fontana brother could now be manning the outer office. Or Crawford Buchanan.

"Could you find out if Van has the Crystal Phoenix renovation blueprints? I want to see a set."

"Yes, Ma'am," the young man, who answered to Yancy, replied. "Be right back."

Temple's coffee had barely cooled to drinking temperature when a light knock resonated on her door.

At her invitation, Yancy entered, bearing armfuls of rolled architectural drawings. They tumbled to the desk like blueblooded bones. Temple uncurled one, anchoring one corner with her coffee cup, another with a china dish of paperclips. They were the only possible paperweights in the sleek office.

Sighing, she took off one red leather Margaret Jerrold pump, then another, and laid them across the remaining two corners.

She had seen architects' renderings before, but she had never tried to interpret them. She broke a nail while excavating her tote bag for her glasses case.

"Will that be all, Ma'am?" Yancy wanted to know.

He was a slight young man with a well-scrubbed face and dark, collar-dusting brown hair moussed into an oddly antique-looking pompadour.

"For now," Temple said grimly.

She sat on the desk chair and rolled it across the plastic carpet-protector until she could rest her elbows atop the slick glass surface and absently sip coffee.

Zillions of fine blue lines zigged and zagged across the plans' expansive surface. She had enough sheets here to paper her condominium, if living inside the veins of someone else's walls appealed to her.

Hearing the door shut, she glanced up. Yancy was gone. She was alone with her secret treasure maps at last. Yo, ho, ho and a bottle of rum-flavored continental coffee.

"Here they are, dearest dumpling."

Danny Dove had knocked before entering, Temple wasn't sure exactly what with. Both arms were loaded with sheaves of coffee-stained papers. But, after all, he was a toe- and tap-dancer, so he must be digitally dexterous with all limbs.

"An office to die for," he said with a melting look around.

"Not *in*, I hope."

"Of course not. You're far too important to knock off now."

"How can we—I—rewrite these skits at such a late date? Won't the performers go crazy if they have to relearn changes?"

"They would go crazier delivering Mr. Buchanan's garbage to an audience. Most of this mess"—Danny dumped the lot atop the desk as if unburdening himself of rubbish—"is salvageable with some editing and a modicum of real wit."

"I happen to have my modicum right here with me." Smiling, Temple reached into the ever-ready tote bag sitting at her feet.

Danny watched her extract a blue fine-line ballpoint pen, then eyed the tablecloth of architectural plans beneath the precious but putrid scripts.

"Riveting," he said. "Architects and editors always use blue pencils, or pens. It must mean something."

"They are probably just depressed. Looking over these skits, I can see why. Crawford's only funny bone is in his left elbow."

"Too bad *he* didn't dive down those steps and break it."

"There haven't been any more rehearsal accidents?" Temple asked anxiously.

"Not since you've taken all the sunshine and yourself away."

"Hmm."

Danny braced his hands on the curling edges of the architectural plans and leaned forward for emphasis, reminding Temple of Michael Caine in one of his spy films. "Listen, ducks. I don't know what's going on around this hotel, but it's not normal. Watch yourself, love."

"Oh, I will," Temple promised. "I will."

Danny nodded and bounded, Gene Kelly style, to the door and out it.

By mid-afternoon Yancy had run the edited skits through the handy-dandy full-page scanner in the corner—nothing but class for the Crystal Phoenix, even in the office furnishings department.

Her blue pencil busily checked off skits that were already read into the computer memory. Now she could correct the blue screen of the color monitor, sharpening Crawford's dull wit and lopping off leaden lines, adding her own impromptu spin. He would be furious, but she was having fun. Such nice, messy raw material he provided! Temple loved operating on club-footed prose.

She was so busy she hadn't even noticed when the office door opened.

But it must have opened, because Midnight Louie was now serving as the fourth corner paperweight on the plans, his black muzzle nestled deeply into the toe of her red shoe.

She noticed him with a start, then saw that the door had been nosed ajar. Apparently the secretary was off secre*tarrying*.

"Glad to know you're alive," she told him. "I guess you're sorry you ever moved to the Circle Ritz. If you miss my shoes so much, I can leave a pair with Van von Rhine for your future delectation."

But the cat was not about to go quietly on a guilt trip of Temple's making. He yawned and rolled over to display his impressive underbelly. Temple gave the black fur a good scratch and also tickled his chin for good measure.

"We both have been spending a lot of time at the Crystal Phoenix," she admitted aloud. "I hope your sojourn has been less traumatic than mine."

At that Louie blinked solemnly, as if to sympathize.

He stretched out a fat paw and patted the curled corners of the hotel plans.

"No messing with the floor plans, fellah. I haven't even had time to look at them yet."

Temple turned back to her computer. She was in the process of integrating Crawford's tasteless "June Is Bustin' Out All Over" number into her grand finale. Her remodeling would require a new wardrobe of complicated costumes, but the effect would be socko. Shocko! Boffo! Psycho! Danny Dove wouldn't mind. After all, she wasn't kicking the Lace 'n' Lust ladies out of the show, she was simply giving them a whole new platform, a fresh facade, a free face-lift, so to speak.

She snickered wickedly. Crawford would be finger-flaunting furious.

Her office door cracked open, hitting the wall. The sudden inrush of air sucked the papers on her desk into rustling rearrangement.

Temple spun to face the door and found a brace of Fontana brothers frozen in an action pose worthy of a movie poster, guns in hand.

She decided not to hit the floor. People with glass-topped desks have nowhere to hide.

"We saw your door was ajar and suspected an invader," the nearest brother explained, eyeing the empty office with displeasure.

"Just something the cat let in . . . the cat."

She pointed to Midnight Louie, still hunkered atop the crinkled pile of hotel plans, his significant overweight the only thing that had kept the whole shebang from scattering. Her shoes lay at opposite corners of the desk. Paperclips glinted everywhere like solid silver rain.

"Sorry, Miss Barr," Ralph offered lamely. "We thought that crack in the door was suspicious." He holstered his semiautomatic and bent to join his brother in picking up the pieces.

"Kinda wrinkled," said the other brother, probably Julio, as he plopped the disheveled pile of Crawford's scripts back on the desk.

"Hey, our suits will be fine with a fresh pressing," Ralph said. "That's nothing compared to making a mess for Miss Barr. You don't have to mention this to anybody, do you? We'd look a little . . . trigger-happy."

"I appreciate the protection, but right now I could really use some peace and quiet while I work."

They left, drawing the door shut so slowly and quietly that it took twenty seconds to close it. Temple counted.

She sighed and regarded Midnight Louie, who was stretching luxuriously on his favorite snoozing surface—papers. Architectural plans were almost roomy enough to accommodate his full length.

He began pulling up the corners to construct a nest.

"Enough. You're as awkward as a Fontana brother doing flying tackles. You're as clumsy as a kitten up a tree, and it isn't even spring. Oops. I've been writing too many song satires lately. Get off the papers; they're bent out of shape enough already!"

Temple shoved Louie's lolling weight aside and tried to stack the plans like a giant deck of cards, but the sheets were too battered to push meekly into one pat pile.

Then she saw the problem: they weren't single sheets, but pairs, stapled together at the upper left corner. No wonder they were so cumbersome.

She stripped off the first pair and held them up in her arms, which barely stretched from edge to edge.

The top sheet showed the remodeled Crystal Phoenix entrance and lobby, complete to a small square indicated dead-center. That must represent the Plexiglas plinth that upheld the gorgeous Lalique glass sculpture of a phoenix.

She struggled to flip over the huge page so she could see the next drawing.

Not much to see. More marshaled lines going every which way in rectilinear precision, like Mondrian in a blue period. Except that . . .

Temple frowned and set down the plan, reaching for her shoes to act as corner anchors again. The paper underneath had an ocher cast, and the drawing style was different.

She studied the plan. It was like trying to create a jigsaw puzzle, breaking the design into pieces that would tell her more than the whole.

For one thing, this layout was the same general shape and size of the top sheet, only there was no square placed dead center for a mythical bird.

She flipped back the top sheet, then flipped it away again to study the bottom sheet.

They were the same, but different. Then she saw it: the bottom drawing must be the plans for the original hotel that Jersey Joe Jackson had built in the early fifties, the Joshua Tree.

Temple sat down, studying blue lines until an orange grid remained before her vision when she glanced up at the pale grasscloth walls.

She grabbed a second set. Midnight Louie yowled his displeasure as another layer of paper was whisked from under his sprawling limbs, torso and tail.

Examination revealed the same system. The remodeling plans overlay the original construction plans.

"Kind of neat, huh, Louie? Past and present in one tidy package. The basement-level plans should be the most revealing. You can bet Jersey Joe Jackson never built in the elevator stage and all the neat technical stuff."

But when she got to the bottom set of plans—by then Louie was lying on cold, unforgiving glass, his ears back and white whiskers twitching—there was only the top sheet,

Temple riffled through all the other sets, accompanied by enough crackles of stiff paper to simulate a fire on a radio show, but found no original of the hotel's lowest level.

So she picked up the phone receiver and punched in Van von Rhine's extension.

"Temple here. Yes, I adore the office and Midnight Louie looks very dashing against the pale motif. Yup, he showed up. Apparently it's not me he's avoiding, but the Circle Ritz, I can't imagine why. Anyway, I've got the remodeling plans and each page is stapled to the original plan for that area, except the basement. Why is that missing?"

Temple turned her blue pen upside down and rapped gently on the glass desktop as she digested Van's explanation.

"You never found a set of plans for the basement? Then how did your architect . . . ? Remeasured every inch, huh? Ouch. That must have played havoc with the budget. No, no real reason, just curious. You know me. You're sure? . . . I see. Thanks anyway."

Temple replaced the phone on the console and continued tapping her pen, until a big black paw swiped it sideways.

"I'm not playing, Louie. I'm thinking. Why is the plan for that one floor missing? That would have all the important mechanical areas and everything. Granted that Nicky and Van's architect worked around it, why did he have to? The plans for everything else were intact, and in order."

She leaned back in the ivory leather chair, which leaned back with her.

"Oh! It even tilts and swivels. How nimble of it."

Temple's comment was not to inform the cat of the attributes of her chair, but to calm her nerves. At the sudden motion, her stomach had wrenched with a sudden fear of falling, probably a flashback to her bad tumble down the stairs. To the basement. To which there was no extant set of original architect's drawings.

Jersey Joe Jackson's basement.

All that was left of Jersey Joe's hotel now was his former rooms during the days of his decline and death, the Ghost Suite. Room 713. Where Jill and Johnny had discovered a hoard of stolen silver dollars in a mattress just a couple of years ago. What else was stuffing the mattresses in Jersey Joe's former suite?

Temple smartly tapped the intercom button.

"Yes, Ma'am?"

Good, Yancy was back.

"Can you get me some room keys?"

"All the rooms are entered with cards nowadays, Ma'am."

"Not 713, I believe."

"I'll have to check with Miss von Rhine."

"Fine."

Oops, she had made a Nostradamus-style rhyme. About time.

Temple had a feeling. Temple had an itch in her instep. She grabbed her pumps off the table and donned them. While she waited to hear from Yancy, she tapped her toe instead of her pen, impatient to be off. Temple had an idea running around the back of her mind like a gerbil hunting for an exercise wheel.

Soon there came a tapping, as of someone gently rapping, rapping on her chamber door.

"Yes?"

Yancy appeared, in his hand a genuine brass hotel key attached by a chrome beaded chain to a wooden oval with the number 713 carved into it.

"Great!" Temple stood to take custody of the key.

"The boss was out of the office, so one of the Fontana brothers dug it up for me."

As Yancy passed it over the desk, Louie bestirred himself to leap up between them and bat at the dangling wooden plaque.

"Always so playful," Temple said jovially as she jerked the key well beyond his reach.

Yancy did not leave the room.

"Is there something else?" she inquired.

"I've heard of that suite," he said darkly. "It's haunted. Miss von Rhine won't rent it; she won't even have it mentioned. It's like the place is not supposed to exist."

"Then we'll pretend that this key doesn't exist, and I'll return it directly to the appropriate Fontana. Which one gave it to you?"

"I don't know!"

"And you work here full time? Tsk-tsk."

Temple sallied past the young man before his misgivings could get the better of his inertia.

"Don't worry. It's my job to come up with marketable angles on this hotel. Ghosts are very popular right now. Maybe I can cut a deal with this one."

She exited, twirling the key around her little finger.

Yancy, she hoped, would put his scruples on hold until she had some time to do a bit of serious snooping into the deep, dark past of the Crystal Phoenix.

Chapter 30

How Suite It Was!

Temple did not believe in ghouls, ghosts or even ghostwriters.

Still, as she jiggled the big brass key in the doorplate of suite 713, she was reassured by the warm, furry rub of Midnight Louie's solid sides along her calves.

The cat had leaped to follow her so fast that the architectural plans had half-spun off the desk.

She had been pleased to see him show a little pet-like loyalty after unaccountably deserting her and the Circle Ritz for the Crystal Phoenix these past weeks. Of course, she was spending a lot of time at the Phoenix herself nowadays, despite warnings to the contrary; perhaps Louie was simply following his meal ticket.

Temple had frowned as she hopped on an Up elevator and held the Door Open button while Louie sniffed the threshold, peered down the deep, dark slot between lobby and car, then ambled inside.

Several passengers had looked annoyed by the delay, or unnerved by the final passenger, but that didn't bother Temple. No, what gnawed at her conscience was worry: what was he eating instead of his Free-to-be-Feline nowadays? It wasn't good for a cat to lose access to his regular and nutritionally balanced to a fare-thee-well food.

Louie had left the elevator with much more speed than he had entered when the car paused at the seventh floor. In fact, he had led the way down the hall, while Temple lagged behind to squint at the room numbers indicated by the directional arrows.

Sure enough, Louie had taken the proper heading.

Temple hadn't liked that.

Cats were reputed to possess some special sixth sense, a kind of animal ESP. Why was the cat suddenly bent on keeping her such close company only now that she was about to enter a set of rooms purported to be haunted?

Temple looked down at her feet.

Midnight Louie's limpid eyes were gazing up, the irises as big as black marbles in the soft-lit hotel hallway, the green only a halo around the fathomless darkness of his expression.

"Ridiculous!" Temple told herself—or him. Or the so-called ghost. She wrenched the key right and turned the knob at the same time.

The door eased open with a truly corny creaking sound.

Oh, please.

She stepped inside, feeling her high heels sink even deeper.

The room was dark, its windows shaded. A scent of stale lemon-wax perfumed the dimness.

When Temple's palm patted down the wall for the light switch, all she felt was the slightly rough pattern of wallpaper.

Louie was no longer brushing her ankles.

A clock ticked with a showy sharpness of sound no longer allowed in battery-operated models of today. Apparently something in this room was plugged in, so maybe a lamp was too.

Temple shuffled her feet over the carpeting, wary of unseen barriers. Her eyes were adjusting enough to distinguish horizontal bars of faint light on the right wall.

Shadowy things shaped themselves to the dimensions of the room: a sofa in the center. *Or a coffin* . . . A tall narrow cabinet against one wall. *Or a mummy case* . . . A chair skirt snagging on her instep. *Or the brush of spectral fingers at her ankle* . . .

She glimpsed a shoulder-high shape near the sofa. Either a lamp shade . . . *or a Chinese peasant in a coolie hat.*

Hey, there was nothing spooky about a Chinese peasant in a coolie hat.

Temple delicately touched the silhouette, feeling her fingernails scratch taut-stretched taffeta . . . *or the papery skin of a seated corpse!*

She pawed below the brittle fabric, found the cool, urn-shaped outline of a porcelain lamp base . . . *or the smooth bronze sides of a funerary urn containing ashes not quite cold. . . .*

She clutched at the phantom of a light switch, something plastic that would click. What she found was the shape of an ornate key, but it turned. Cherry-tinted light flooded down on her hands like diluted blood, but her fingernails looked gore-black.

A sudden rattling sound—*the clatter of skeletal bones?*—made her start, nearly overturning the lamp shade. The sound came from the shuttered windows, and then a broader streak of daylight broke through.

By its narrow band of brightness, Temple navigated her way to the window, where Midnight Louie was perched on a fragile-legged blond Hepplewhite table, one massive paw thrust into the light.

The window wasn't covered by shutters, Temple saw, but blinds—broad-vaned, industrial-strength wooden blinds that made thoroughly modern metal miniblinds and micro-miniblinds look like effete little toothpicks.

Blinds were nothing. Temple edged to the side, found the cords and pulled until the vanes stood up and took notice of the sunny day outside.

In the greater light, she marched to the next window and performed the same chore, then dusted her palms. There wasn't any grit between them, but there should have been.

Temple surveyed the living room where Jersey Joe Jackson had wheeled his last deal. By the time of his death, he had lived here in sufferance, according to some, a penniless, aging has-been tolerated only for the memory of his own legend.

She toured the last living arrangements of the late Jersey Joe Jackson, pausing at the lamp to shake her head at the shade's whimsical form—that of a crimson-laced corset. Surrealism, she recalled had influenced late forties decorative accessories, however funky the form.

The apple-green satin drapes framing the windows fell in still-shining cartridge pleats, fluted like a classical column. Padded valances were upholstered in the same satin, and curled on the ends like huge Ionic capitols, or an upswept forties hairdo. Given their formality and height, Temple couldn't help thinking of Lieutenant Molina.

Midnight Louie, having successfully drawn her attention to the blinds, had retreated to the chartreuse-upholstered sofa. There, the green of his eyes shone to advantage in the flattering daylight that shrank his dark pupils to mere slits.

Temple analyzed the room, understanding why it was part of what was called a "Ghost Suite."

The forties-style furniture was an odd albino amalgam of modern lightness of color and traditional eighteenth-century furniture forms. The graceful blond mahogany legs of sofa, tables and chairs seemed almost gilded in the afternoon light, but they were actually silver-white in tone, except for the frankly blond cabinet between the windows.

The carpeting was dark, the better to show off the ashen-legged furniture. Temple stared down at a matted ocean of forest-green leaves and exotic maroon blossoms. She felt she was walking on Monet's water lilies.

A pale Sheraton desk hugged the wall by the door. Temple trod water lilies to the desk, then switched on the green-glass-shaded banker's light hunkering over a gold-tooled, green leather deskpad.

She wasn't surprised that everything worked here. The place was untouched, but not untended.

The effluvia of thirty years or more floated in the shallow central desk drawer. Old bank books bound by rotting rubber bands. Stamps so outdated they were worth only a penny. Unused stationery as yellow and brittle as autumn leaves. Some of it was imprinted "Joshua Tree Hotel & Casino," with smaller block letters underneath announcing "Las Vegas's biggest little hotel."

Temple was surprised by the number of stubby pencils in the drawer, a collection formed before the dawning of the age of ball-point and felt-tip pens. The gaudy barrel of a fifties Esterbrook pen rolled under her fingertips as she probed.

She found a letter to Jersey Joe Jackson on faded rose stationery signed "Mona." The contents were almost deliberately bland and there was no return address.

Temple pulled out the delicate desk chair and sat on its bold maroon and forest green satin stripes relieved by a pinstripe of chartreuse.

Dust fuzz hobnobbed in the drawer corners with rusted paper-clips. Someone had lined the drawer with the same bamboo and jungle growth wallpaper that swathed the walls. Not Jersey Joe, Temple would bet. Anyone nicknamed Jersey Joe would not be the drawer-lining type.

She found a string of tiny keys, the type shaped for hard-sided suitcases of another era, for ladies's little jewel boxes and diaries, for strongboxes and secret cabinets. They jangled like jewelry and would have looked swell—that was a forties expression, wasn't it, along with jeepers creepers and mairsy doats?—silverplated and dangling from a chain bracelet today.

What did these fascinating Lilliputian keys open once? Why had a two-timing crook with a penchant for squirreling away ill-gotten goods kept them? Didn't anybody at this hotel have a curious bone in their body?

The room's silence was utter, to the point of rebuff. Temple fished out something caught in the crevice of the drawer—a holy card edged in gilt, picturing some pastel-tinted female saint or other looking sappy under a coyly tilted halo. The back text marked the passing of one Harold Lynch on October 8, 1943. Poor Harold had only been thirty-three. In the drawer's right back corner, a white satin garter coiled like a deflated balloon. Several dull red wooden gambling chips lay scattered amid the dusty papers like lost coat buttons.

The deeper but smaller drawers on either side held plastic boxes filled with paperclips and rubber bands, a deck of well-thumbed playing cards bearing the image of a robust pinup girl with very long hair and legs.

"Ouch!" Temple had found a hoard of thumbtacks—rusted.

She slammed the offending drawer shut and squeezed her finger-tip until she had produced a Sleeping Beauty drop of blood as crimson as a Ceylonese ruby cabochon.

She rose and went through an ajar door, looking for the bathroom. She found herself in a dim bedroom and stumbled her way into a black-hole-of-Calcutta closet before trying another doorknob with her good hand.

This time there was a wall switch. It flooded the room with a funhouse-mirror-view of Temple holding her right wrist and blinking.

The bathroom was smaller than it seemed. Tiled in large squares of mirror, none of which matched reflections perfectly with their neighbors, it created a fractured, surreal multiplicity of images—maroon porcelain pedestal sink, commode and built-in bathtub; black octagon-tiled floor and—surprise!—a silver-leafed ceiling that softly echoed the reflections below.

Temple went to the sink and turned a massive porcelain handle.

Water flowed, not fast, but it flowed. She guessed that even the original plumbing to this suite had been left intact during the remodeling.

The water washed away her blood, its brightness lost against the sink's maroon bowl. Temple pinched forefinger and thumb together and hoped the pressure would stop the bleeding. She wasn't half done here and it would be tacky to drip blood on the furnishings. Presumably that grisly privilege would be left to the ghost of Jersey Joe Jackson when, and if, he decided to show himself.

Leaving the bathroom light on, Temple moved back to the bedroom and opened the blinds at its two windows. She turned to face twin beds covered in chartreuse satin . . . and one of them was doubly upholstered, since Midnight Louie was now sprawled in jet-black array on the becoming background.

"Oh, you think you look like the cat's pajamas on that poison green color, don't you?" she chided Louie, glad nevertheless for his company.

"Now. The silver dollars were hidden in a mattress. If I were going to hide something as large as an architectural plan, a mattress would do fine."

Temple squatted by the twin bedframe bare of lounging cat to pull up the coverlet. The white cotton sheets were scratchy. No ironing-free miracle-fiber blends in the forties, and no color but white.

She untucked the generous bottom sheet—no fitted sheets then,

ɔ unveil a modern-looking mattress. Digging
ə bed, she finally revealed an appalling label:
d that brand dated to the forties, and
t this cloud-pattern fabric did. Nothing
⸺ike about it.

⸺ squeaked a protest when she jerked the bottom sheet free
on the neighboring mattress to find the same disgusting, spanking
new, modern-day fabric. When Jill and Johnny had discovered what
they had been sleeping on—a mound of stolen silver dollars, and
what were they doing in this supposedly never-rented room anyway?—the old mattress covering must have shredded. Van von
Rhine, tiptop hotel manager that she was, had replaced it with a new
one, and its mate, so the two beds, however unused, would match.

Temple made obeisance to the beds—and indirectly to Midnight
Louie, who had not moved so much as a hair as she wrestled the
linens—then retidied the sheets.

She rose and studied the bedroom, finally going to a bureau. She
jerked open its reluctant drawers in turn. Each was lined with the
living room wallpaper. Under each lining was bare wood.

She returned to the bathroom, gazing pensively at its accouter-
ments and herself lost in a sea of semblances. No place to hide paper
here; besides, it would have rotted by now.

That left the living room.

Midnight Louie anticipated her by jumping off the bed and trotting back to the main room. Temple followed, wondering what had
stirred his sluggish soul.

She entered the room just in time to hear a faint clicking. Aha!
Superior feline hearing strikes again.

Temple eyed the open blinds at the windows, welcoming the
bold bars of light striping the floral carpeting. No self-respecting
spirit would deign to appear against such a well-lit background.
Then her own ears traced the snick-snick sound to its source.

The keyhole. Someone very physical was attempting to break
and enter.

Louie stood by the door, stretching his considerable length up it
until his paw patted the doorknob, which was beginning to tremble
preparatory to turning.

Temple looked around. No place to run, no other exit. No place to hide. She darted to Louie's side and flattened herself again wall, hoping the cat would divert whoever entered long enough her to brush by and escape.

Unless it was a hotel maid. The rooms were amazingly dust-free.

While Temple stood in closer communion with the atrocious wallpaper than she would have wished, Louie retreated from the door and gave a welcoming meow.

Traitor!

The door swept open at last, ending the suspense and nearly smashing Temple behind its solid bulk.

Keys jingled. Someone moved a couple steps into the room. Temple held her breath, wishing she'd brought the shield of her tote bag from the office below.

The form pushed farther into the room as Louie turned around in the middle of the carpet and flopped heavily on his side.

Good distracting tactic, Louie! Play the friendly pussycat. Temple edged around the door and stopped as the intruder turned.

"What are you doing here?" they shrieked at each other in unsettled unison.

Van von Rhine put one hand to her breastbone and one to her pale blond French twist. Temple wasn't sure whether she was more protective of her heart rate or her hairdo.

"You!" she exclaimed. "I'd heard Chef Song mention that the blinds were open in this room. They're never open."

"So you came up, alone, to investigate?" Temple sounded as incredulous as she felt.

"Apparently you did too."

"Apparently . . . not. I'm the distributor of the dust, the barer of the blinds."

"Why?"

"I had a wild idea."

"That's what you're paid for, but why have them in this suite, of all places."

"Because, of all places, this is the one where Jersey Joe Jackson was liable to hide something. He'd done it before."

"Hide what?"

"The missing original plans to the basement."

"I didn't know any plans were missing."

"Neither did I, until a couple hours ago. I decided to take a look for myself."

Van's piercing blue eyes flicked to the doorknob. "How did you get in?"

"Pass key." Temple flourished her open sesame.

"How did you get a key? They're only kept in my office."

"Yancy got one from a helpful Fontana brother."

"Which one?" Van's voice was sheer steel.

"Who can say for certain with Fontana brothers? Listen, what's so awful about my trying to track down a lead from the past? I'm supposed to dream up a dynamic new theme for this hotel. I have to dig deep for that."

"Not here." Van looked around, then clasped her hands over her bare upper arms and shuddered. "It truly is haunted. I can hardly bear being here, but in a sense, I'm the guardian of this place. There's nothing here, Temple, but things we shouldn't disturb."

"Did you replace the mattresses?"

Van looked startled. "Yes, but how—"

"Then there's nothing in them. What about the old ones?"

"Destroyed. They were broken down."

"Did anybody examine them first?"

"Of course. After the silver dollars came tumbling out, you can imagine that every spring and piece of cotton batting was torn apart."

"So it never was there."

"This . . . missing plan, you mean? It's only the basement, after all, and that was extensively remodeled two years ago."

"Why is it the only floor plan missing?"

"Because it wasn't important!" Van answered, exasperated.

"Or because it was the *only* important one."

"Can we leave?"

"This place really makes you nervous."

"Doesn't it spook you?"

"No," Temple replied stoutly, completely forgetting her earlier heebie-jeebies, another vivid forties expression.

She turned to regard the room again. "Only the bedroom bureau drawers are big enough to hold an architectural plan, and they don't. The closet is dead space, empty as a tomb. Sorry," she added as Van shivered again. "The desk is too small for anything. The only possible other place to look would be inside the walls. After all, Jersey Joe built this place. He could have easily concealed something in the construction."

"I am not," Van said grimly, "tearing the walls apart. I refused that option even to hunt for more blasted silver dollars, though everyone pooh-poohed my notorious superstitions. The point of leaving this suite alone was preserving whatever . . . ambiance it had and respecting whatever . . . influence the dead Mr. Jackson still has. Had."

"A pity"—Temple glowered around like an interior decorator with indigestion—"this wallpaper design is so busy. Who could tell if it had ever been tampered with—by anyone? Or anything."

Her eyes fell on the desk again, with its perplexingly ordinary contents. The banker's lamp beamed down on the rich leather surface. Something, a dust mote perhaps, danced in the lamp's narrow, bright beam of light.

Louie catapulted to the chair seat and atop the desk before Temple could blink at the motion. He began pawing at the lamp, pushing it askew.

Van uttered a strangled scream, but Temple saw the reason for Louie's attack.

"A moth," she said, watching its small gray form flutter upward as Louie stretched three feet up the wall—and then jumped upward another foot—to capture it. "Just a moth."

"There is no such thing as 'just a moth' in a hotel," Van replied, the starch stiffening her voice again.

Temple pulled Louie down with little resistance, getting her nose right against the wallpaper in the process.

"Wait a minute. The paper is faded over the desk."

"I told you. Except for the mattresses, this room has not been touched in thirty years. Of course the wallpaper is old and faded—"

"But *more* faded here. See? A big oblong over the desk, like something had hung there."

"Something did hang there." Van was speaking through her teeth now. "Could you please close the blinds so we can leave? These rooms are bone-chilling."

Temple saw that Van's massaging hands were raising goosebumps on her arms, and hastened to undo the damage that she had done: letting new light shine on an old environment.

"I didn't know they had colored bathroom fixtures in the forties," she yelled to Van from the bedroom blinds.

"The rich did, and Jersey Joe Jackson was filthy with lucre when he built the Joshua Tree. The bust came later," Van caroled back. "Please hurry!"

Temple was just as glad to have another human being present as she returned the bedroom to its eerie, perpetually dimmed state. She charged into the living room to shut the blinds there.

"What is this blond cabinet, a radio?"

"Early t-t-television." Van's teeth were chattering now. "Don't you feel the c-c-cold?"

"No, I'm running around too fast. Television." She remembered the blond model in Electra's penthouse. "Jersey Joe was fond of the latest technology."

She hesitated at the corset lamp shade, then turned off the light. Fascinating as the Ghost Suite was, the living faced deadlines of a less final nature, such as an imminent Gridiron show.

The room returned to the twilight that had swallowed it for decades. At the desk, Temple paused before turning off the last light.

"What *did* hang here?"

Van was truly upset, Temple saw. It was cruel to keep her here another instant. Temple needed an answer to every anomaly. Sometimes she could be cruel.

"An old blown-up photograph! Black and white. Of the desert. That's where Solitaire Smith found the map to the Glory Hole Gang's hoard of buried silver dollars . . . in the frame backing. Now let's go!"

Temple grabbed Louie in one arm—ooh, he was heavier than her tote bag, and that was going some, clutched the key in her other hand, and headed for the door, Van in front of her.

As she turned to give the room one last glance, she saw a glint of something at the drapes. Perhaps the hallway light reflected on the high points of the satin pleats.

"Shut it!" Van begged, backing into the hall.

Temple obediently dropped Louie to the floor and drew the door shut. A breeze—cool and sharp, rather than musty, fanned her as the door closed. She used the key to lock it, then tried the knob.

"As tight as King Tut's tomb—oops, sorry again."

Van, now as pale as the ash-blond furniture within the rooms, was recovering herself against the far wall.

"Did you see anything odd?" she asked.

"Only the hall light reflecting off the drapes."

"The hall light isn't that strong."

"Van, you don't really believe that the ghost of Jersey Joe Jackson is inside there?"

"I've seen it. Him. I've seen him pass through that door. Let's leave!"

Temple hurried her down the passage, taking Van's arm and finding it ice-cold. Funny, there had been no air-conditioning in the rooms.

She turned to see if Louie was following.

He was still sitting in front of the Ghost Suite, busily grooming his coat as if he were at home on his own—her own—bed.

If there had been anything *outré* to sense, Temple told herself firmly, one would think a black cat would be the first to know.

But Louie just sat there, twisting to lick the hair on his spine, which had lifted into a series of dinosaur notches all the way to the base of his tail.

He would have to work quite a bit on the tail, too, Temple noticed. Swollen to twice its size, it was a kissing cousin to a radiator brush.

Must be an awful lot of static electricity in the Ghost Suite, she thought. Um-hmm.

Chapter 31

Kung Phooey

Here it is, the dawn of the day of my little doll's greatest triumph, the Gridiron show. I should be present in my always-elegant black tie and tail.

As luck would have it, and as is usual of late, my personal matters are interfering with my professional prowess.

I cannot claim that I planned on attending this Gridiron dinner and show. Satire is not my strong suit. Still, I planned to be about the premises for moral support and even had intended to show my puss at the Circle Ritz when Miss Temple Barr was dressing for the grand event.

She needs me to press her best duds when they are laid out on the bed prior to donning, though she has a cute habit of pretending to protest my help. Then, too, I am adept at weaving in and out of her legs and leaving my calling cards—tiny black hairs—on her pantyhose, usually a pale color that will benefit from some dash and contrast. I also help Miss Temple locate her missing evening bag by lying on it until she notices me, shoos me away and discovers the absent purse right under my nose.

My many adventures down Life's meanest streets does not mean that I have lost my delicate domestic touch. Even the most macho dude will benefit from tending to the care and coddling of the human companion.

However, the day begins with a revolting event at the Crystal Phoenix that rockets me into an entirely different direction.

I am innocently enjoying the late morning sun among the calla lilies, especially since I do not detect the inhibiting presence of Miss Caviar. I am not to be left alone for long, though.

I hear a scrape of long nails on flagstone, then a disgusting snuffling sound that would serve well on the soundtrack to *The Hound of the Baskervilles.*

Who is sniffing around the imperial koi pond?

In a moment I have parted the calla leaves with my face to view a sight to turn a Samoyed a whiter shade of pale. The dog from the Dumpster is back and he is playing kissy-face with my carp!

I bound out on all four rollerblades. "Take a hike to Pike's Peak, scavenger, or you will be feeding goldfish, instead of vice versa! What makes you think you can intrude on Crystal Phoenix grounds?"

He backs up, belly dragging over the rough stones.

"Do not be so testy. I thought you were . . . gone."

"Why would you think such an unlikely thing?"

He whines a little and rubs his nose on the ground. I can see that Miss Caviar's lesson has made a humbler hound out of this hard case.

"I heard that you were taking a dip in Lake Mead."

"From whom?"

He sits back and hefts a hind leg, thereby showing all sorts of unmentionables, to scratch thoughtfully at his freckled chin. "Chihuahua named Chi-Chi. Hotel guest. Says the resident black pantheress overheard his mistress chattering about some new joint on Lake Mead called Three O'Clock Louie's. She jumped him a few minutes later while he was doing his business in the dog-walk and forced him to give her the whole poop on this Lake Mead location, Temple Bar. She must have outweighed the poor little blighter by a full pound. Only his mistress coming along with the doo-doo bag and scooper saved his hide. Anyway, this feline Rambette took off, vowing that this Three O'Clock place had something to do with her rotter of a father and that a floater would soon be found in Lake Mead if she had anything to say about it."

"Her . . . father? Why would she think that?"

He pauses to bite a flea on his shoulder. I begin to wish I could don latex, like the cops, when interrogating lowlife witnesses.

"Seems the joint on Lake Mead has a mascot—black dude just like you. Guess they are related. At least she seemed to think so."

"That may be," I say, letting my shivs click to the stone all at once. "But I still patrol these grounds. In future, think twice before you figure that Miss Caviar's absence gives you trespassing room. Now beat it, before I decide to make mincemeat of you."

He growls a little to show yellowed teeth, but I hold my ground. He backs away before turning tail and hieing back to the Dumpster where he belongs.

I remain, triumphant but disquieted.

This Three O'Clock Louie is nobody to me, but he is obviously about to pay for the sins of the father, merely because his name bears an almost actionable resemblance to mine. I admit that I am annoyed to learn of a dude of the same color treading so close to my own, unique moniker. Time was when black cats were considered unlucky in this town and I alone dared to show my puss, and then some. Still, being a copycat is not a capital crime. I cannot knowingly let my own offspring commit murder of the wrong guy.

My duty lies with Miss Temple on the day of her grand night out, but this happy association is not to be. If my choice lies between Temple Barr and Temple Bar, I am forced to pursue that headstrong alleged offspring of mine. Someone must preserve some poor, unsuspecting dude from a date with the feline equivalent of a jackhammer.

Whoever this Three O'Clock Louie is—and the name has a splendid resonance, despite its more than somewhat imitative ring—I cannot let him take the fall for my fault, i.e., fathering Midnight Louise the Terrible.

I know how this little black banshee learned of this establishment: via the usual methods—making herself invisible, keeping her ears perked and her mind percolating. I do not know how she will get herself to Lake Mead and the appropriately named landing of Temple Bar, but I have no doubt that she will accomplish this feat, and pronto. She has the genes for ingenuity.

As the vulture flies, and he often does in this desert, Temple Bar is eighty-five miles from Las Vegas proper, if ever a city of such character can be considered proper.

Temple Bar is also in Arizona.

It just so happens that the bottom half of Lake Mead runs through the southern border of Nevada and Arizona. Most folks know that Lake Mead is the artificial result of Hoover Damn, which plunked a long, narrow, forked body of bright blue water shaped like a double fishhook right in the middle of a knot of mountain ranges.

What most folks do not know is that the Nevada/Arizona border runs right through it—through the east-to-west horizontal, hook-part of Lake Mead. This means that opposite banks, at times close enough to shout across, are in different states. The border runs from Hoover Damn in the west right to Iceberg Canyon on the east.

Why people would want to put something as essential as a state border right in the middle of a body of water where no one can see it boggles the feline mind. Those of our ilk know a thing or two about marking territory. Although we also employ running water to do it, we make sure that such benchmarks are on otherwise dry land, where they can be seen, and more important, smelled.

Still, it is not for me to decipher the mysteries of human behavior in other than criminal matters. I only know that I have a long, challenging journey to Arizona ahead of me, for Temple Bar sits on the south side of Lake Mead.

All is not lost, for I have certain contacts that I use when it is necessary to cover vast distances in a hurry and I am forced to rely on motorized transport.

So I hike over to the Gray Line Tours building, a low, nondescript structure most notable for launching a fleet of long, looming vehicles with an exhaust system that could singe the hair off a porcelain Chow. In addition to their size and power, these buses have a sinister look due to tinted wrap-around windows. I am reminded of limousines carrying a whole convention of shady characters.

Luckily, these buses chauffeur tourists around Las Vegas and beyond, and tourists are no more sinister than a chocolate Easter bunny.

In fact, before I had landed a place of my own, I used to hang out here quite a bit. The exhaust fume fog greets me like an old friend, rushing to fill my ears, eyes, nose and throat.

I amble among these idling behemoths, looking for the nine o'clock run to Lake Mead. This will ultimately get me to Temple Bar, hopefully before mayhem of the cat kind has been visited upon this innocent Three O'Clock Louie individual.

"Well," notes a bus driver of my acquaintance, bending to look me over. "So you're back again. I gave you up for a grim statistic. How are you doing, Blackie?"

(At times I have found it convenient to work under a *nom de guerre,* which is to say whatever someone chooses to call me. Usually such names sadly lack imagination, but have the advantage of applying to dozens of dudes.)

"Like some lunch?" The fellow sits on the high first step to his bus and offers me a bite of summer sausage on rye.

I wolf it down in the name of building rapport among contacts.

My host is Red Kimball, a veteran driver whose pale thinning hair still boasts a scarlet thread or two among the gray. While I nibble on another piece of his sandwich, another set of Hush Puppies squeegees over.

"Look who's back," notes another old pal, Gloria. She squats to stroke my head. "This old boy doesn't look much the worse for wear."

"He's eating like he's been locked in a closet for a decade or two," Red says, more with admiration than pity.

"You want to ride to the Valley of Fire with me today?" Miss Gloria inquires solicitously.

I have trained these drivers to the notion that I relish the occasional joyride, and their clients always find my presence on board, eagerly staring out the windshield, "cute," so no one has yet reported me to the company as a stowaway. See what I mean about cultivating contacts for a rainy day?

Not that it is about to rain today or any time soon.

After disposing of the last crumbs on the parking lot asphalt, I scamper up the rubber treads of Red's bus. (What an obnoxious smell to encounter after lunch, but none of the odors broadcast by a bus are what a discriminating nose would call five-star.)

"Guess the old boy wants to go to Lake Mead with me," Red concludes with admirable logic.

He dons his visored cap and follows me up the rubber-mat road. Over the next half hour, we are joined by a straggle of tourists, all wearing short pants, short-sleeve tops, and sunglasses and cameras on cords around their necks.

I take my usual alert pose alongside Red, forelegs braced on the dashboard, my profile pointed toward the unknown future.

"Oh, look, Lucy! That cat looks just like the figurehead on a ship. Isn't that cute?"

(My unerring instinct for "cute" when it will do me the most good is almost as strong as my nose for news and penchant for crime.)

Soon our party is lurching out of the depot and onto the open road. Well, the road would be open if we did not have to navigate Las Vegas traffic until we turn onto Highway 95 and head for the wide, open shores of Lake Mead. Highway 95 whisks us through Henderson (the site of one of my more outre adventures involving a pack of coyotes) and then past such Lake Mead landmarks as Las Vegas Wash (I thought the only wash in L.V. was at the crap tables) and Boulder Beach (which will give an idea of the quality of the shoreline sand hereabouts).

The difficulty of relying on transportation other than one's own four feet is that the route may be circuitous, or even involve pesky pauses. Thus when Highway 95 hooks upward through Boulder City (it is not; a city, that is), our bus pauses on the brink of a fearful dropoff point. In this steep mountain defile that only goats can traverse with any illusion of dignity rises a sheer cliff of concrete, a towering monument to the ingenuity of man. Hoover Damn. (I believe it is so called in tribute to all the cussing the massive construction job caused. Why it is also named after a vacuum cleaner, I cannot say.)

I am forced to remain aboard while the gaggle of tourists clatter and chatter off the bus to swarm around and into the impressive concrete-slab face of Hoover Damn. Myself, I do not give a Hoover for heights of this magnitude. Besides, the bus remains air-conditioned.

Red doffs his cap to swipe his forehead with a Kleenex, then extends me the hospitality of the second half of his sandwich. I do not wish to appear rude, so we have a nice little picnic there on the brink of the drink, so to speak.

After forty minutes and a chance to see a slide show about Hoover

Damn on a giant screen (why they do not project the slides upon the multi-story pale facade of the damn itself I do not know), our merry crew is on its way. Through the Black Mountains to the White Hills we go, taking a sharp left to head north past Virgin Basin and then east again right to Temple Bar, which sits in the protected curve of Heron Point. Beyond us await a marina, ranger station, campground and trailer hookup facility, not to mention a restaurant, the so-called Three O'Clock Louie's.

Soon I am stretching my legs alongside a wooden dock while tourist tennies trod over the planking to a restaurant that projects onto the lake's frilly blue waves.

I am also watching dozens of carp school by the tourist walkway, making a solid gold, glittering carpet of scales punctuated by round, staring fish-eyes and round gaping mouths.

It is too easy to snag carp when they are begging, and they are shameless beggars. No finesse. Just gimme, gimme, all day long. I watch them wistfully, but dare not linger. These carp have waxed fat on tourist bounty; if I pause to ingest one, I risk seriously slowing myself down.

In the name of my rescue mission, I must travel on an empty stomach. (Although the summer sausage and rye are doing a rhumba in my stomach, I only indulged in them to win Red's regard. Nothing gives a human such vicarious pleasure as overfeeding an animal.)

The moment I separate from the tourists, I make good time sniffing the surrounding terrain. The rocky shore of Lake Mead is seldom washed by rain, which means that scents ferment in the scalding heat for a good long time.

Away from the gadding crowd, the shoreline is mostly deserted in more ways than one. I bear south on the sandy rocks, the morning sun massaging my left shoulder with welcome heat. I may need my muscles loose for the coming fray.

The dainty Caviar, aka Midnight Louise, may be a hard case to trail. Since she has had the dread surgery to prevent offspring, she will leave no rich, siren smell in her wake. As for this Three O'Clock Louie who is so bold as to make light with my name, I am not familiar with the dude and must separate the scents of my species from others, such as fox, skunk and the aforementioned coyotes.

But it appears that the skills of my merciless nose are not required. My ears perk to the sound of hissing and scraping.

Either a nest of rattlesnakes is holding a limbo contest over the next rise of rock, or I have come upon a contretemps between two of my own kind.

I bound atop the ridged red rock, lashing my tail to announce that someone to reckon with is on the scene.

I am not a split-second too early.

Were I not prepared for the event, I would think I was seeing double.

Two black cats circle on the barren soil below, backs humped, tails spiked like cactus, heads hunkered down beneath predatory shoulder blades.

Low moans and growls echo from the surrounding rocks. This is either an embarrassing private moment or a rumble of the first order; with my kind such distinctions are sometimes hard to make. Each stalks slightly sideways, the better to keep an evil eye on the other. Neither gives ground, nor growl, nor glance to my arrival.

The piquant Caviar I have seen in full battle fluff before. She is petite by virtue of her gender and her tender age, but manages to swell to the impressive size of a sheared beaver muff.

The dude who has commandeered a portion of my name (and I really think there ought to be a law against such trespassing) is altogether a huskier sort, as one would expect of the male of the species. In full battle bristle, he is the size of a tumbleweed and has command of an impressive array of snarls, wails, belly-whines and cat curses.

I cannot help feeling a pang of anxiety for the well-being of my impudent offspring. She may have strange modern ideas; she may not respect her elders as she should, especially me; she may be in the mood to commit particide, but she also may be my own flesh, fur and blood. I am proud of her for facing off this seasoned dude three times her size.

Everyone knows better than to interfere between two felines in a state of such savage fury, but Midnight Louie makes his own rules, and his path is clear. I must preserve from harm the innocent dude who is about to be turned into instant sushi merely for being mistaken for yours truly and the sire of the lion-hearted little minx below. I must also spare this idiotic offspring of mine the fruits of her misguided vengeance, which could be a fatal dose of the cactus known as "catclaw."

I dart down the rocks, adding my own guttural wail to the proceedings.

I have forgotten the impact of sudden movement on an eclectic lunch, and pause. To burp.

Luckily, the contestants do not appear to hear this decidedly unwarlike sound.

With a bound, I flare my own magnificent coat into a state resembling Phyllis Diller's coiffure and land dead center of the quarreling cats.

Furious at having their unshakable glares so rudely disrupted, they snap their eyes to me, theirs hisses reaching an apex of hysteria.

I turn slowly, as a martial arts master surrounded by uppity students.

I speak even more slowly, selecting my syllables carefully, choosing a hypnotic lower register to disarm the combatants.

"You must . . . control yourselves," I suggest in my deepest baritone, a combination of a purr and a growl.

"Who do you think you are?" the purported daughter demands in a raspy voice. "Kitty Kong?"

I bow. I am not the figure purported to rule all cats, but I will masquerade as anyone to avoid a tragedy.

"Listen, layabout," she adds in the disdainful tone that is native to her. "Get out of the way. This is a family matter, a blood feud. I do not need any overage hotel hang-around telling me what to do. This dude is my runaway father."

She scowls at the individual beyond me, whom I confront next.

Well. He is a large son of a bitch. (I am not using bad language here, as this is a breeding term among the canine species, and this dude is larger than your average lapdog!) His bile-green eyes spit figurative sparks at me while his mouth makes with the real spitballs.

"Listen, whippersnapper," he snarls. "Get out of the way. I was baldly attacked by this back-alley scrapper, and no one keeps Three O'Clock Louie from administering a well-deserved licking."

I whirl to confront Caviar. "You see? His name is Three O'Clock Louie, not Midnight Louie. This is the wrong dude."

"He could have changed his name," she spits, not a single hair going limp. I would like to know the name of her grooming products. "He might have heard I was looking for him. One thing was sure, he wasn't hanging out around the Crystal Phoenix any more."

"Crystal Phoenix?" Three O'Clock sounds confused. "What is that, a glass bird?"

"Sure, play innocent," Caviar says. "No doubt that is how you ensnared my poor deluded mother not a year ago. She may not be here to call you what you are, but I spit upon your whiskers! You are a faithless, irresponsible, dog-livered layabout I would be so ashamed to call my father that it is better to wipe you off the face of the planet."

"Mother? Father?" Three O'Clock lets one dog-eared ear lift a little. "Am I hearing this right, young lady? You think I am the poor bloke who fathered you?"

"I expected you to deny it," she growls.

Three O'Clock shakes his massive head. I notice a scar running down his cheekbone. His muzzle is grizzled with years of knocking around an arbitrary world.

"I am not the dude you wish to denude."

"Your name is Louie!"

"True, and it always has been."

"But not . . . Midnight?"

He shakes his head again. "Nope. Midnight has never been my best hour. Besides, Miss, I could not be your much-hated sire. A year ago I was not even in Nevada."

"Prove it."

He sits down on his haunches. "That would be difficult. I would have to extract testimony from Mr. Spuds Lonnigan, the owner of Three O'Clock Louie's, and humans are decidedly dense when it comes to answering feline-cross-examinations."

"Then you are history, mister."

"What made you think I am your father?" he asks.

"I was named Midnight Louise when I was born, and my mother said I was the spitting image of my father. I figure him to be Midnight Louie, and such a personage is notorious around Las Vegas for begging a free meal, chasing every fluffball that came along and consorting with humans."

"Hmm." Three O'Clock relaxes enough to lift a paw and give it a considering lick. "Not a bad life. But who is this interloper who has dared to come between us?"

Caviar lets the gold of her glance flick over me. "Some has-been no-account house kitty. Harmless if a bit meddlesome."

I am so speechless I cannot even muster a decent spit. Here I leap where wildcats fear to go, between two battle-mad combatants, and neither thinks much of my intervention, or myself!

"Listen—" Sister, I am about to say, but that is not quite correct under the circumstances. "Listen, you little lynx. If you had half the brains of your old man you would not be here accosting the wrong dude. You would have figured out already that *I* am Midnight Louie! Midnight Louise indeed. Your mama was sadly mistaken. You have not got the class for such a name."

"You!" She looks me up and down and back and forth as if she had never seen me before. "You are just some overweight, would-be gumshoe with pretensions of grandeur. My father is a heavy dude. My father is the terror of the back alleys. My father is a rat, but he saved the Crystal Phoenix and Johnny Diamond's life—"

"And fingered the ABA killer, and saved Baker and Taylor—the corporate kitties—even though they do have crumpled ears and awful accents, and nailed the stripper competition killer. There is a lot that has happened since your mama and I have parted ways."

"Parted ways! You deserted her, and all us kits."

"She wanted it that way. Said she did not like the hours I kept, or the danger of my job. Said she and the kits would be safer on their own. Would she have named you after me if she hated the sight of me?"

"She . . . did not know what was best for her."

"Apparently you do. Listen, kit. My old man ran out on us kits, too. That is just the way it is. It is better for everybody. I am not looking for him. I hold no rancor. In fact, I know where he is, and should I choose to be snarly about it, I could hunt him down and hand him a few swipes myself. After all, he is leading the sweet life on a Pacific Northwest salmon trawler, living on the high seas, sucking all the tuna and salmon and shrimp he could want, without a thought for me and my siblings, or you and yours. But do I blame the guy? No. We must all do what we must do."

All of a sudden I feel a tremendous swipe on my shoulder. I turn around, my temper ripe for a fight. I am saving this dude's neck, torso and toes, and he has to attack me from behind?

"What is your problem?" I ask.

Three O'Clock tilts his big, battered head and gives me the green eye. "Just saying hello. Son."

Chapter 32

Confidence Man

Matt sat staring at his phone. He had to consider the case of Father Hernandez closed, but another matter was not. He knew he was avoiding a last, unpleasant call in a life that was now half-lived on the telephone.

The number looked so innocuous, written in his compulsively legible grade-school hand on a mini legal pad. Blue ballpoint on pale yellow. Yellow pretty much described his mood of the moment.

He picked up the receiver, punched in the numbers. A soothing computerized female voice instructed him to punch more buttons to route his call. Matt usually used the phone to deal with raw human anguish. To him, voice mail was obscenely remote and cheerful, especially considering that many callers of this particular number would be far more anxious than he was at the moment, to say the least.

When he finally got a human voice, he asked for Lieutenant Molina. He was not relieved to be promptly transferred.

He gave her his name, which earned an infinitesimal pause.

"What can I do for you?" she asked.

"I need an appointment. There's something you should know."

"There is lots I should know, Mr. Devine. What about right now?"

"Fine." Now he felt relief; it would soon be over. "Are you . . . is the police department located downtown?"

"Right on top of the Mint. But you're calling from the Circle Ritz?"

"Yes."

"I'll come there. Fifteen minutes."

"I'll meet you by the back door."

"Why the back?"

"To avoid the late afternoon crush at the wedding chapel up front."

"That's right, Electra Lark's cottage industry, 'The Lovers' Knot.' I forgot. Back door, fifteen minutes."

She hung up, leaving Matt smiling ruefully at her brusque efficiency. She wasn't going to make this easy, but then, he supposed, that wasn't her job.

Matt went down by the pool to wait. That was one reason he loved the Circle Ritz, this peaceful pool area hedged by greenery. Maybe it reminded him of a monastery.

In a few minutes, he heard Molina's car idle up to the parking area outside the fence and went to open the gate.

She was wearing her usual casually formal outfit: solid-color A-line skirt and blazer, buff today, with a cream camp shirt. Matt wondered if she realized her mode of dress resembled a Catholic girls' high school uniform, except for the pale colors needed in hot climates.

Molina's emphatic eyebrows lifted as she viewed the scenery. "Shangri-La on the Strip."

"Let's sit here." Matt headed for the white plastic chairs planted on the shaded concrete.

Molina didn't budge. "I'd rather talk inside. What's wrong with your place?"

"This is just as private." Her eyebrows lilted again. "And—" Matt produced the smile he used when he wanted to be disarmingly honest "—in my former . . . profession, my room was the only private place I had. I guess I still feel that way."

"Too bad." She reluctantly moved to one of the molded chairs. "I prefer to see people's surroundings."

"I spend more time out here than in my rooms. Frankly, I don't have much there to see."

She looked away, to the pool, embarrased. "You swim?"

"Thirty laps every day. Terrific form of meditation."

She nodded, relaxing her posture in the chair. Matt blessed his institutional instincts. Molina used her brusque antisocial manner to maintain control. This pool party atmosphere would soften her hard edges and make it easier to tell her something he didn't want to tell anyone in the world, least of all the authorities. And, he saw now, she was madly curious about him.

She eyed the round, black marble bunker that was the Circle Ritz. "This place is quintessential Las Vegas! Neon and instant weddings out front; out back, the round residential building that's run like a zoning department's nightmare, half apartment, half condominium."

"I love the building. They still built quality in the fifties. And I'm lucky that Electra's flexible enough to take renters."

"Not to mention the interesting neighbors," Molina added laconically.

"This has nothing to do with Temple," he said quickly.

"Why so touchy?"

"You and Temple seem to have trouble relating."

" 'Trouble relating.' That's counselor talk for you. She has trouble telling me everything she knows about Mr. Mystifying Max, and I have trouble relating to that."

"I think she's told you everything that she feels is relevant."

"Police work thrives on what most people consider irrelevant, Mr. Devine. They aren't allowed to be the judge of that."

"They can be the judge of what they consider private."

"Like rooms? You know you've made me curious."

"Maybe you don't realize how touchy Temple is about Kinsella's disappearance."

"Do you?" Her tone was challenging.

Matt realized that she was beginning to enjoy herself.

"She hasn't said much about him," he admitted.

"When a woman is mum about the former man in her life, she's interested in the man she's with. Beware, Father Matt."

He closed his eyes at her mocking tone, at her reminder of his special status, his former life.

"Sorry. That was . . . tacky." Her voice was brusque again, as she flicked a red thread from her skirt. "But I see you strolling in where devils fear to tread. I couldn't help noticing that you and Miss Barr were fairly cozy at the Blue Dahlia the other night. From the way she acts when I bring up Max Kinsella, he's a hard act to follow. I don't know if you're up to it."

"I don't know if I'm in the running."

"Oh, she likes you."

"And I like her, but I don't know if I want to be in the running in the way you mean."

Molina shrugged. Clearly, she didn't believe him.

"You're a wonderful vocalist, by the way," he said.

"I sing a little."

"What you do isn't just singing, it's art."

"Thanks, but I don't have much time to rehearse and less time to perform. Most people don't know I do it."

"Not even one of your co-workers?"

Molina's laugh was as rich as her contralto singing voice. "Cops could not care less about scat and all that jazz. The Blue Dahlia is the one place they'd never find me. But you've changed the subject, very smoothly. Since you're dictating the place for this interview, I'll direct the subject."

"What subject have I changed?"

"What it's like to be an ex-priest."

"That has nothing to do with this meeting."

"Maybe not. But I'm the judge, remember? And I like to know milieus."

"While keeping your own secret."

"Investigator's privilege."

"You grew up Catholic; you can guess what it's like."

"Guesses don't cut it in my game."

"Why are you so curious? It's almost personal."

Molina looked down, twisted the ring on her right hand. Matt noticed that it was the only jewelry she wore, that it was large and a trifle garish, though genuine gold. A class ring, meant to announce a school affiliation to all and sundry. Why was it so important to her?

"I'm divorced," she said abruptly. "You know what that means. A failure. The Catholic Church doesn't allow for failures."

"And I'm a failed priest? Sorry, but I don't feel that way. God called me to the priesthood and God called me to leave. When I left, it was with laicization, if you know what that means."

"No. I never heard much about leaving religious vocations in grade school, only about entering."

Matt smiled. "Me neither. Laicization means that I was officially freed of my promises. I didn't just walk away one day. I went through the paperwork as well as the angst. Most ex-priests can't qualify to do that. They feel driven out, in a sense. I don't."

"Then you're bound only by what the average Catholic is?"

"Isn't that enough?"

"A joke." Molina noted his humor, but her smile was pale. "Not for me. I've got Mariah to think of. My ex-husband was a jerk. We're well rid of him. But to the church we're an irregular family."

"Are you so sure? Is anyone at OLG bringing it up to you?"

"No. No one except Pilar, the parish housekeeper. But my family is, in spades. You know how it is in ethnic Catholic communities, the parishioners pride themselves on being holier than the Pope. Every large family—and every family is large if they aren't using birth control—is supposed to provide at least one child for a religious vocation, a nun or a priest. In turn, all their married kids will be fruitful and multiply like lemmings. And stayed married."

"*Supposed to's* can strangle a person. Sure, I know what you're talking about. Irish, Polish, Hispanic, the dynamic is the same. I don't suppose"—Matt smiled at his inadvertent use of the word in question—"we'll ever see families like we grew up in again. I can't claim that I'm the child tithed to the church, because I was an only child."

"Why?" she asked in surprise.

"My father died when I was an infant."

Matt was treading close to the real point of this meeting, but for now he preferred to play counselor, to learn Molina's mental milieu, so to speak.

He wondered if she knew the tables had turned, if she realized that she was casting him in the role of priest, and herself as troubled parishioner. He could see that someone in her position could hardly unburden herself to her pastor, especially when that pastor was the starchy Father Hernandez.

"Your father died," Molina said softly. "I'm sorry. Sometimes my forever family drives me nuts, but at least they're there."

"Why do you call them your forever family?"

"They're always in your face, your life. They always know better, and there are so damn many of them. No Molina ever heard of the Pill except from the pulpit. Luckily, they're all in L.A."

"That's why you're in L.V."

"Maybe. And maybe, being divorced, and being a maybe-Catholic, I want to warn you. You say you're free. I presume that means free to marry?"

"If I would want to."

"Were you a bad priest?"

"No."

"That's too . . . bad."

"I don't think so."

"In other words, you didn't leave because you broke any vow, or were about to."

"No." He left it at that, and saw that she knew that's where it would stay.

"Tell me something," she asked with sudden animation. "How can they do it? The bad priests? I was reared to respect priests and nuns, and I saw a lot of good ones. Some priests liked their liquor too much, or their food, but that was an understandable failing. I . . . we, people then, never suspected that we were sheltering priests who violated their celibacy with women, and men. And children."

"I could tell you that their unconscious needs are so great, and so garbled, that they deny the wrong in what they're doing, but you'd call that psychobabble. I think that some people who set themselves up as religious leaders suffer from a deep sense of unworthiness, of hypocrisy. Some of them may feel compelled to commit sin so they'll be found out for what they think they are. Look at television evangelists. The abusers probably came from abusive families. How they can stand in church on Sunday and preach, or say mass, is a form of denial I can understand intellectually, but not from the gut. I never had to make that choice."

"In the seminary, didn't you ever suspect? I mean, with your looks—"

"I got a lot of curiosity, and more crushes." Matt found himself recalling those days almost with nostalgia for his fiercely ingenuous self, who had so readily dismissed the easy admiration of others. "I noticed the crushes from women and girls, of course. I was scrupulous not to encourage them. If another seminarian had tendencies . . . I was too naive to notice. We hardly knew what we were and we were there to control biological urges. No, it didn't crop out much in seminary. Once out in the real world, I had developed an invincible shield against 'temptation.' It wasn't hard; I wasn't really tempted, so it was no credit to me."

"You'd be surprised, but I know what you mean. As a woman working in a man's field, I have to create this invisible shield around me. My actions, my clothes are neutral. I don't send any signals, and I rarely receive any. It works."

"Too well, maybe. Your stage persona releases all that subdued femininity, but you're safe up there in the spotlight, still distant, tempting but still untempted."

"As the priesthood was safe for you?"

"*I* was safe in the priesthood. The world out here . . . I don't know."

Matt was amused to see Molina's expression grow gruffly maternal.

"If you're the innocent I think you are, you're not free at all. Just like me. I'm divorced. That means I can't marry again, not in the church. And that means I have to answer to Mariah, whom I've sent to Catholic schools because I want her to have a good, safe education. I would have to justify myself to my family, to the whole damn neighborhood, 'if I would want to' marry, as you put it so well. Again. As for an affair—" She laughed bitterly. "There goes the neighborhood, and here comes the Bad Mother."

"There are annulments."

"Not everybody qualifies, as you said, or has the patience for the endless paperwork and waiting."

"Do you want to marry?"

Molina laughed again. "Hell, no. With this all-hours job and a child to rear? Not to mention the kind of men I come in contact with. The quandary is theoretical, Mr. Devine."

"Call me Matt. This conversation is too personal for honorifics, Lieutenant."

She blew out a frustrated breath. "I usually know where I'm going and how I got there, but not at the moment. Don't expect me to reciprocate by telling you to call me 'Carmen.' I hate the name."

"Because of the associations?"

"Because I was a fat little kid in a Hispanic neighborhood who sang a lot and you should hear what other kids can do with a name like Carmen. I tried to go by my middle name in high school, but that was a disaster too."

"I hate my first name too."

"What's wrong with Matt? It's simple and the only mass association is the marshal on 'Gunsmoke,' not some slut or a fruitcake-head with an atrocious accent."

"My name's 'Matt' now. It was Matthias all through school."

"Oh, an old-fashioned saint's name. Still, that fits a priest and isn't so bad for a layman." Molina smiled encouragingly, as she would with a child, maybe her child.

Matt didn't want to further explain why he had come to loath his given name. That was another room he wanted to keep private. It was bad enough that Temple knew.

"What's your middle name?" he asked.

She shrugged. "Regina."

"Latin for 'queen.' Not bad either."

"Regina Molina? You see. Nothing goes well with Molina. I hated to hang Mariah on the poor kid, but it's pretty—"

"And it isn't a saint's name, but it's close to Mary as in 'Ave Maria'; you were walking the line between Catholic and not-Catholic even then, when your daughter was born. So Molina was your family name. Why aren't you using your married name?"

"What are you, a detective? Or a frustrated shrink? Role reversal stinks."

"Knowing about people used to be my job, too."

"Why'd you leave it?"

"Because I needed to know about myself."

"Why'd you call me?"

"Because I have a confession to make."

"Funny."

"Not to me. Listen, Carmen." He used the name firmly, as he would have with a rebellious grade-schooler. She made a face but said nothing. "There is something you need to know about me, because it has to do with your job." Matt gathered himself. "I heard about that man who died at the Crystal Phoenix, or who was found dead there. I think that I . . . knew him."

"Temple told you," she noted sourly, but she sat up to take literal notice of his revelation. "So you knew Cliff Effinger?"

"You could say that. He was my stepfather."

Carmen Molina's blue eyes scintillated with shock, pleased speculation and curiosity as deep as the navy-dark waters of Lake Mead.

"Gee whiz, Matt, I'm so glad we had this little talk. I desperately need someone reliable to identify the body."

Temple backed away from her bed.

It didn't look much like a bed at the moment, being draped with every cocktail dress in her possession and bordered by endless pairs of glitzy high heels.

Why couldn't she ever decide what to wear to a special event until it was time to get ready? Maybe her theatrical background was the cause. Even in civilian life she always felt like an actress who had to make her grand entrance without any idea of what part she was playing or how to dress for it.

Then again, maybe she was just nervous because this was her first official special event with Matt Devine for her escort.

Whatever the reason, she felt flustered and dithering and hot under whatever collar—if any—she decided to wear.

In exasperation she turned to the window for a calming view of the pool—so still, so placid, so well dressed in its eternal costume of chlorine-treated azure. . . .

This afternoon the view was not calming at all.

Not with Matt Devine sitting in the shade of the lone palm tree. Not with one Lieutenant C.R. Molina sitting right there beside him.

They looked like a bloody ice-tea ad! Prim, proper and on, oh, such jolly, pleasant terms!

Temple pushed as close to the glass as she dared without being seen, wardrobe dilemmas forgotten.

What was *this* tête-à-tête about? Devine and Molina? Matt and, and . . . Carmen? Acquaintances? Friends? Buddies? Or worse?

Now don't get paranoid, Temple warned herself, to no avail.

Perhaps Molina was just interrogating Matt, using him to dig into Temple's background to get to Max. Temple nodded soberly, glad she had kept pretty much mum on Max when she was with Mr. Devine.

Matt might not mean to give away anything about her that Molina could use—and abuse. Still, he was pretty naive about women, even when they were cops, relationships and life in general. He might blurt out something that she would regret. A good thing that she knew how to keep the past in an airtight compartment if she had to.

Temple watched Molina rise, smooth her stupid, bland skirt and walk to the gate. Matt accompanied her, hands in pants pockets, the afternoon sun glinting off his hair-gilded forearms.

Obviously, nothing momentous had happened during the conversation. Yet the scene had reminded Temple never to underestimate Molina's bulldog nature, or the possibility that she might use Matt, and Temple's interest in him, to pursue her obsession with Max.

No way, Lieutenant, Temple swore as she watched the woman vanish behind the closing wooden gate. Matt checked his watch, glanced up at the Circle Ritz—Temple flattened herself against the wall for a few seconds before she peeked again—and hurried into the building.

Temple released an anxious breath. Really time to get ready now! Eyeing the bed again, with its crazy-quilt of choices, the decision seemed simple. Temple swooped up one perfect dress and one perfect pair of shoes. Humming happily, she installed both by the closet door where the poster of Max Kinsella had once hung.

Chapter 33

Three O'Clock Rock

I wish I could say that this unexpected family reunion resulted in a good deal of mutual grooming and purring, but the fact of the matter is that we each face a formidable generation gap, not to mention the gender stretch.

Still, discovering unsuspected blood ties does force a truce of sorts. We withdraw under the deck surrounding Three O'Clock Louie's to hash out our various grievances. If, from time to time, the occasional tidbit from the diners above slips through a gap in the boards, none of us can object as long as each gets a lick at the booty.

The old man regales us with tales of his life at sea. Even the hostile Caviar finds herself hypnotized by the details of life on the *Bounding Maine*. (Personally, I remember the *Maine* being lost at Pearl Harbor, but apparently this vessel is a namesake.)

"Does not all that heaving and sinking make you seasick?" Caviar asks Three O'Clock.

"No, Ma'am. Not in the slightest." The old fellow tidies his whiskers as his eyes soften with a nostalgic sea-green glow. "Has a soothing effect, as when we were rocked in the cradles of our mother's bellies. They do not call it Mother Ocean for nothing. And I soon got my sea legs—especially when I saw all that North Pacific silver tumbling to deck. Ah, that is a sight . . . mountains of piscine delight, fresh and gleaming with saltwater. The captain would often offer me a nip of his best brandy after the catch was in and we were relaxing from our labors in the cabin.''

"What labors?" I ask. "You did not even have to snap a whisker in the pursuit of this prey. Their heads were handed to you on a platter, so to speak."

"True, my lad, but the thrill of the chase is overrated, to my mind. At a certain age one grows wise enough to find a situation where one's meals are home-delivered. Did I not understand you to say that you had found a domestic situation at a place called the Circle Ritz?''

I do not miss the slight sneer at the notion of "domestic."

"I have retired to a condominium with room service," I admit, "but before that I was self-employed as a house detective at the Crystal Phoenix Hotel and Casino, the classiest joint on the Strip."

"Hmm, joint." The old man lunges into the shadowy twilight of our retreat and snags a fallen piece of fried chicken.

"That fried food is bad for one of your years," I point out. "Full of fats and salt."

"You may be right," he says, chowing down the find without offering to share it with his long-lost descendants. "I will sacrifice myself and eat it all to spare you youngsters any health problems."

"Spare me the blarney, Grand-daddio," Caviar puts in. "You and your boy here have all the paternal feeling of a trash compactor."

I am still stinging from hearing my present situation described as domestic. "Miss Caviar has done well for herself," I say. "She resides just above me at the Circle Ritz with Mr. Matt Devine, a most genteel fellow and a friend of my own associate, Miss Temple Barr."

"He is a bit hard on the furniture for such a genteel person," she replies cryptically. "I have spent most of my time of late at the Crystal Phoenix. I perceive a need there for an agile, youthful, full-time house dick."

"You cannot be a house dick," I shout.

"And why not?" she demands in a low purr.

I am not going to stalk nose-first into that trap. "I have not officially vacated the position. You will notice that I have been staking out the grounds of late. Events of a dark and sinister nature are afoot there, and I am ready to pounce at the right time."

"Oh, please," Caviar beseeches me in weary tones. "The stray dog population is up and what have you done to address it? Nothing. Next thing we know, coyotes will be venturing up to the Dumpsters for a nighttime snack."

"I am not worried about a few coyotes when there is bigger game to hunt."

"Such as?"

"I cannot answer, as the case has not entirely come together."

"In other words, you have not got a clue." She turns to the old man. "Do you perform any other function out here, besides adding to the atmosphere?"

He sticks his neck out from under the deck to snag an errant shrimp.

"Drenched in butter," Caviar sniffs. "The cholesterol count must be astronomical."

The old man is not about to be dissuaded from any seafood surprises. I watch him munch away, my stomach growling in sympathy.

"Hush!" Caviar snarls. She stretches up on her lithe little legs to press her ear to the planking above us. "I heard someone mention the Crystal Phoenix. I am on eavesdropping duty now."

Three O'Clock rolls his eyes but does not desist smacking his lips.

I sit up and take notice. I am always interested in the odd conversation, especially when I recognize one of the voices.

"Never mind asking why," Crawford Buchanan is hissing to someone seated directly above us. "All the poker chips in Las Vegas would not get me anywhere near the Crystal Phoenix tonight."

"But you are show chairman," a female voice objects.

This voice I have never heard before, but under the down-trodden quality I read a dogged weariness as it goes on.

"I do not understand you, Crawford. This Gridiron show was so important to you. You were hardly ever home for two months, yet this last week you act as if the entire event were poison."

"Everything he touches is poison," puts in a third voice—young, bored, bitter and female.

"Quincey!" the older woman reproves.

The man's voice lowers. Above me a deck chair frame creaks as he leans forward. "This show *is* poison. Those so-called rehearsal mishaps are no accidents. That stupid PR woman has really cooked her goose and her gizzard this time."

"You mean that Miss Barr who visited you in the hospital when you had your heart attack? She seemed real nice."

"Nice is not enough in a town like this, Merle, you should know that by now. Temple Barr will be lucky to see the sun come up tomorrow. The signs have been there all through rehearsals and neither Temple nor that high-handed Danny Dove have glimpsed the writing on the wind. Somebody Very Big is mucho upset about this show, and about Temple's closing skit in particular. Buchanan predicts that when the curtain falls tonight, it is going to take a few people with it, including that uppity pair. That is why you will not find me near the Crystal Phoenix tonight. Not on my life!"

A warm drop of bloody water drenches my forehead as Crawford bites into whatever live bait he favors. I hope that it is dog, rare, but restrain a shudder of distaste and keep an ear cocked despite the bio-hazardous material dribbling down.

Caviar has minced back from the mess, but her own ears remain fanned like furred satellite dishes to catch every syllable. She does show some investigative promise, were her attitude not such a handicap.

"Should you not warn them?" the woman asks.

"What, and risk my neck? I am not going within spitting distance of that sitting tinderbox. Besides, who would believe me? They do not even respect my scripts."

"Crawford, if you are irked about your show and neglect to warn somebody—"

"Forget it. I am only guessing, but I *am* dead serious. Something major is going down at the Crystal Phoenix tonight, and all I want to know about it is what I read in tomorrow's *Review Journal*."

"You mean that you do not want to scoop the competition?" the younger female jibes.

"I mean, Quincey, that I do not want to be scooped up in a spoon. Now shut up about this. You never know who is listening."

Enlightenment has come too late for Crawford Buchanan.

With swift lashes of my rear member, I herd the others away from our inadvertent listening post. Caviar is more than ready to move on, but Three O'Clock seems inclined to remain reclined and suck up any descending goodies. I tap him politely on the shoulder and nudge him along.

In seconds we are twenty feet down the decking and able to have our own discussion without fear of eavesdroppers.

Caviar is all fired up. "We have got to get back to the Crystal Phoenix pronto."

I frown. "I can see that I must hustle to the aid of my personal associate, but I do not perceive any reason for you to cut short your visit to your grandpa at the lake shore. You two have a lot to talk about."

"Hah!" she responds in her usual tone of disrespect.

For a moment I pity Crawford Buchanan, with such a sullen daughter. No wonder the mother's milk of feline kindness does not surge through his veins.

Three O'Clock is frowning now, especially as Caviar has positioned herself under a knothole where one might expect even larger bounty to trickle through. "I do not know why you two find it necessary to skedaddle so soon just to take care of some humans."

"Professional pride," I growl. "I owe it to my domestic partner."

Three O'Clock rolls onto his side and begins to tidy up his black bib.

Caviar and I exchange a look of perfect concord for once. The old man will be of no use on a mission of such urgency.

We wriggle out from under the decking, eyeing the tourist cars.

"How will we get back in time?" Caviar muses.

"How did you get out here?"

She drops her eyes coyly. "Spuds Lonnigan dropped by the Phoenix to visit Jill Diamond. I hitched a ride."

I nod. "Not bad. But he will be out here cooking until Three O'Clock Louie's closes—at three A.M., I presume."

She pulls a sour face, which is not hard for her to do. "I fear so."

"Then my mode of transport is the best bet."

"What is that? Donkey cart?"

"You are sarcastic even in a crisis, but, no. There is my vehicle."

I nod at the Gray Line tour bus, which is belching exhaust as its passengers mount the high steps. "We can just catch it for the trip back. The driver, Red, is a friend of mine; he will let you aboard too."

The doors remain ajar, but we can hear the screech as Red puts the bus into gear.

With a mutual look, we race toward the huge silver bus. I tell myself that timing is everything, even as I urge Caviar to greater speed. Together we sink our claws in sand to keep from shooting under the bus. I smell hot rubber and diesel fuel, and—somewhere near—something dead.

"Get on!" I yowl, unsheathing my claws to give her a spur in the flank.

She shoots up the stairs so fast that Red will think she is me.

Even as I watch, the accordion doors snap shut, grinding their rubber buffer strips like toothless gums.

I hear Red on the microphone, announcing the rest of the itinerary.

"Now that you have had a tasty lunch at Temple Bar, we will head back up north, folks, for a leisurely tour of the Valley of Fire, with dinner at Echo Bay. Hope you enjoy."

I back up as he turns the behemoth and it starts lumbering for the access road.

An old lady in a baseball cap at a nearby window jumps, then I see Caviar pasted to the tinted glass, her green eyes focused on me with furious disbelief.

"It is better this way, kid," I tell her, though she cannot hear me. Maybe she can read lips.

She is too young and inexperienced to lay her life on the line in case of such dire necessity. And she is blood kin, after all. Plus, this is no job for a dainty little lady who is as green as a twenty-dollar bill.

Besides, I work best alone.

I dash around the back of the restaurant and breathe a sigh of relief.

A big white truck is idling there, its back doors as wide open as heaven's gate.

HARRY THE MEATMAN the side lettering reads. LAS VEGAS.

Here is my ticket to ride. I leap up into the dark cool interior. Ah, at least the ride back will be air-conditioned and considerably more direct than the tour bus. I chuckle to think of Caviar seething amid a busload of tourists all calling her "Kitty, Kitty." I just hope that she does not bite the hand that feeds her. Red might bear me a grudge.

I hunker down behind a carton of wieners and curl into as tight a ball as I can manage. Not only could I be accused of attempted assault on a side of beef if I am found, but if my calculations are wrong and we do not speed back to Las Vegas post haste, I could end up on ice, permanently.

I shiver as I contemplate the long odds facing me. At least if I die it will be in a meat locker.

Chapter 34

Girded for the Gridiron

Matt jerked down the sleeves of his black dinner jacket for the third time. He wasn't used to white cuffs showing.

He winced to glimpse himself in the makeshift mirror of Temple's French doors. Twilight's soft sable fog was pushing against them, so his rented suit vanished into the oncoming night. He looked like a dark-cloaked magician standing against the illusion of concealing black curtains, only his pale head, shirtfront and disembodied hands visible.

The black satin bow tie perched at his throat looked frivolous, even oddly sinister. It was such a different symbol from the plain notch of white linen he had been used to wearing. Black tie was the last vestige of the peacock in modern male dress, and, ironically, also the closest thing to clerical garb.

He could hear Temple moving in the other room, the click of her heels telegraphing unread messages onto the hard tiled bathroom floor and then the bedroom's quieter walnut parquet.

She was late; she wasn't quite ready; she was as nervous as a barefoot cat on a batter-ready waffle iron.

In two hours the curtains would sweep back on the Las Vegas Gridiron show. Temple's sole, show-closing skit would be on the line, not to mention the others she had doctored at Danny Dove's invitation.

Matt had never glimpsed that opening-night edge in Temple before. It must date back to her amateur theater days, he mused, even to her time before the cameras when she had worked as a television news reporter.

Tonight she broadcast an air of energy and suppressed excitement that made him edgy. He remembered that Max Kinsella must have shared that singular exhilaration; that they had understood and suited each other very well; that he was a stranger, an uneasy intruder in an arena he hardly knew.

"Where on earth is Louie?"

Temple came trotting out from the bedroom, trying to screw a rhinestone dangle into her left ear.

"Not here. Nor is Caviar at home upstairs. Trouble?"

"Ouch! Oh, I'm all . . . thumbtacks . . . tonight! I seldom wear these blasted glitzy things. I can't find the hole."

"I didn't even know—notice—that you had pierced ears."

"It's this rusty mop. Distracts everyone."

"I'd help if I could." The Matt in the French doors lifted uncertain hands.

"Just look and tell me when I get the prong through."

Temple came over to present her earlobe, all the while jabbing at it like a mad jackhammer.

Matt squinted at the operation, then lifted his hands. "There. Looks like a picture nail went through."

"Good." Temple slapped a tiny clip over the prong and smiled. She pulled a small chrome purse paved with rhinestones from under her elbow. "Hope I've got everything. I'm not used to Lilliputian evening bags . . . say, you look fabulous."

"You think so?" Matt pulled his sleeves down again. The shirt cuffs seemed wrong.

"Perfect." Temple pulled his cuffs up a half-inch. "What about me? Anything off?"

He supposed married couples performed this mutual inspection ritual on evenings out, a thought that made him even more nervous.

"Perfect," he repeated for lack of originality, not so sure. Temple's gown was a slim, short beaded length of glittering silver—shapeless yet slinky, as liquid as a mercury fountain.

"How do you like my latest Stuart Weitzmans?" She turned to present him with a cocked, pale-hosed calf. "My first dressy high heels since I did a double axle down the Crystal Phoenix stairs."

Matt studied the mysteries of a black suede high-heeled pump with an ankle strap. Its gravity-defying, curved Brancusi sculpture of a steel heel was sheathed in white rhinestones.

"A masterpiece," he pronounced with confidence.

Temple sighed with edgy content. "Shall we go?"

Matt checked his watch, an inexpensive Timex that looked shoddy against the rented finery he had been advised to wear. "We're only twenty minutes late."

"I know!" Temple rushed to her door, then hesitated; she wasn't waiting for him to open it. Her subtly madeup face fell. "Louie's been gone so much lately. Where can he be? It's not like him to desert me in my hour of need."

"You think the show is going to be that bad?"

"I don't know! I'm too close to it. You tell me after you've seen it. I don't think I can bear to watch."

Matt laughed and opened the door for her anyway.

Temple certainly knew how to prolong her misery.

Despite the delay, they had arrived at the Crystal Phoenix early enough for her to conduct an antsy tour of the stage's underbelly. She led Matt to a frill-free freight elevator that whisked them down a floor in silent, motionless magic. He couldn't help thinking of a magician's vanishing cabinet, which people entered to disappear and emerge from again on cue. Despite the elevator's impression that it had gone nowhere, the stainless steel doors slid open on vast warehouselike space, the antithesis of the meticulously decorated atmosphere above.

Matt was treated to more clicking heels on a hard surface—concrete in this case—more pre-performance jitters and the sight of amateur chorines in exceedingly careless states of undress, which made his ears overheat. He had been an ordinary citizen for eight months now; when would he become blasé about the simplest signals in a world that emphasized, rather than ignored, boy-girl interaction?

Of course Temple proudly introduced him to one and all; he was her date for the Big Night. This was far more adult stuff than their pseudo-prom, Matt quickly found, disliking being on public parade. The women in the cast, her professional sisters, lifted their overdrawn stage eyebrows and cooed. The men eyed him with a touch of unspoken competition he found unnervingly new, and Danny Dove effused over him like he was the Second Coming.

"Isn't she wonderful, our Miss Temple! Nothing fazes her. And fast with a rewrite, let me tell you. What is your line?" Another appraising glance, underlined by a disconcerting glitter of appreciation. "Aren't *you* the cat's meow? Are you an actor?"

"No," Matt said. "A shrink of sorts."

"Oooh. Better watch out, Miss Temple. He'll have you psychoanalyzed and on a couch in a second flat."

With a fanfare of bawdy laughter, Danny Dove bounded off on innerspring ankles to supervise a dozen different things.

"Danny is truly taken with you," Temple noted with amusement. "He's so protective of me that he usually glowers at my escorts like a Victorian father. The Fontana Brothers were subjected to a constant barrage of insults."

"He's . . . different."

"Well, he is gay, and if you weren't with me—"

"Oh, my God," said Matt, glimpsing yet another pitfall of the theatrical world.

"Don't worry. He'd never hustle a straight guy. But he can look. He's been really sweet to me, besides being the best director I've ever seen in action."

"Better than anyone at the Guthrie?" Matt asked in disbelief.

Temple thought. "As good as, in a different milieu."

"Very different." Matt tried not to stare as a sylph attired only in glitter and a chiffon scarf darted across the hall from one dressing room to another.

"You'd be surprised," Temple said, aware of his unease. "All theater people grow casual about the formalities. This stroll amongst our players should do you good. You've led a sheltered life."

"I know. But your dress is probably all the education I need at one time."

She stopped walking, surprised. "This? Glitzy Girl debutante stuff. It certainly doesn't show a lot of skin."

"But it . . . moves in a, an interesting way."

Temple quirked an eyebrow. "I'm impressed. You noticed. Poor Danny is doomed."

"It's not funny. I can't believe how oblivious I've been to so much. Is it any wonder that in seminary we never suspected sexual deviates among us? We were reared to be holy innocents."

"Now, instead of being wholly, you're just *partly* innocent," Temple said, "the best of both worlds. Everything's under control down here, as much as a backstage area ever is, and I see nothing that looks like Crawford Buchanan. Danny said yesterday that he had vanished into the wormhole from which he came."

"You don't sound properly relieved."

"No. Even if Crawford is sulking because the show is no longer all his, it would be like him to breeze in at the eleventh hour on performance night to claim all the credit. He may have a Alp of ego, but when it comes to honor, he is strictly in the molehill league. Come on, let's check out the house."

The same unnervingly smooth elevator transported them to the first floor. They threaded through the casino crowd until they reached a queue of people hedged into a line four-bodies-wide by emerald velvet ropes hung from Plexiglas-and-chrome posts.

Matt was beginning to understand Temple's enthusiasm for the Crystal Phoenix. It avoided the predictably posh cliché, such as red velvet ropes in brass stands, constantly reinventing itself and therefore the look of Las Vegas.

"Excuse me." Temple was blithely trotting outside the velvet boundary to the line's distant head, oblivious to proprietary frowns.

Matt followed in her wake, embarrassed. Good Catholic kids always took their turns in line, no matter how long.

She stopped so suddenly he collided with the beaded glass curtain of her back. Matt steadied her, and himself, by grabbing her upper arms. He hunted among a confusing array of unfamiliar faces for the source of her ankle-jolting pause.

Oh. There stood Carmen Molina, almost unrecognizable in a tall, floor-length column of maroon crepe and sequins that matched her age, beside a tall man in a dark charcoal suit. Frank Bucek.

"Lieutenant Molina!" Temple summoned a tone of arch surprise. "I didn't recognize you without that ear thingamajiggy." Her agile fingers pantomimed a growth at the side of her head. "What are you doing here?"

Molina's scant smile didn't bother stretching all the way to her eyes. "Not an occasion for flowers," she said. "I suspect the audience will more likely want to throw vegetables, uncooked. I am a private citizen. I *do* go out now and then. And the Gridiron is an annual exercise in civic satire. I need to know how the script writers are depicting the police department, and if anything libelous is being said about anyone." She finished by nodding "hello" to Matt.

Matt realized that he was still clutching Temple like the hero on a grocery-store romance and loosened his hands. Injured ankle or not, Temple was securely mounted on her favorite high horse as well as her favorite high heels, and was in fine fettle.

"Agent Bucek," Temple acknowledged next. "I do hope that if the script police find anything actionable, they'll wait until the final curtain to make any arrests."

"Give us a break," Molina said blandly. "We just want to see the show. I would say . . . break a leg, but that strikes a little too close to home."

Temple laughed and sailed on, dragging Matt behind her.

At the azure-and-emerald carpeted steps leading to the Peacock Theater, Temple finally confronted a guardian in the form of a Crystal Phoenix security woman.

Temple snapped open the tiny metallic purse dangling from her shoulder on a fine chain to present two salmon-colored passes.

They were waved into the auditorium.

"Everybody is going to hate our guts," Matt suggested, *sotto voce.*

"I'll limp then, legitimately." Temple did just that as they disappeared into the theater. "They'll feel so ashamed, begrudging a poor, disabled person her privileges. Oh, look! Isn't it gorgeous? Van and Chef Song have outdone themselves."

Matt surveyed the banquettes diminishing on a steeply raked aisle toward the shrouded stage. In the deliberately dimmed lights, the wine velvet seats glowed against black linen tablecloths set with gilt-edged white china. Dead center of each table a huge crystal brandy snifter held a pair of circling goldfish, their long, lacy fins and tails undulating through the limpid water.

Each setting, replayed by the dozens throughout the huge chamber, gave an impression of a continuum of exquisite and infinite beauty, of images repeated to the nth power in a funhouse of mirrors.

"Don't worry about skipping the line," Temple said. "All the VIPs coming tonight will be doing just that—the governor, the mayor, some mega-star performers." Temple thrust the salmon-pink tickets back in the metal bag swinging at her hip. "Danny gave me Crawford's show chairman set of tickets because he hasn't shown. Can you read the table signs? We're at number eight."

Noticing the white cards on their thin chrome stands, Matt scanned the numbers until he spotted the right one. He knew that Temple would die before donning her glasses in such a public setting.

"Down there." He pointed to a perilously distant banquette just right of stage center.

Temple sighed. "A mercy that I'm solid on my pins again. These endless shallow stairs aren't made for walking on."

Matt was relieved to notice other people threading their way into the glamorous emptiness, wondering who the VIPs in their black ties and glittering gowns were, though any viewer of tabloid television probably could have told him.

"How much do the tickets for this cost, anyway?" he asked.

"One hundred and fifty dollars."

"Each?"

"Don't sound so shocked. A sit-down dinner for eight hundred, plus a show with a union tech crew and orchestra doesn't cost peanuts. And, remember, my set of tickets is free, thanks to cowardly Crawford."

Temple expertly eyed the angle to the stage, then slid into the banquette. Matt edged in after her and exchanged stares with the serenely gliding fish.

"Do you think that's why Buchanan isn't here?" he asked. "He expects something bad to happen?"

"Probably." Temple cracked open her purse and snapped the tickets down, like aces in the hole, above each of their plates. "Doesn't mean it will. In fact, Crawford not being here guarantees that nothing bad *can* happen, Crawford himself being the worst thing that *could* happen."

"Your logic leaves a lot to be desired."

"Thank you. Now. Have you ever seen a Gridiron show before? Of course not. I should warn you. Situations and dialogue can get a tad naughty."

"I see."

"Oh, nothing as crude and rude as years ago when the Gridiron was a men-only show."

She picked up the white program brochure at her place setting. "Too bad they had already printed C.B.'s name as show chairman. All he did was make extra work for everybody else."

Matt studied the inside of his brochure: dinner menu on the left and satirical bill of fare on the right, skit by skit. Writers were listed without indicating which skit they wrote. Lo, Crawford Buchanan's name led all the rest—not that there were many, just Temple and two others.

Murmuring voices were filling the house with a buzz of anticipation. Waiters that remarkably resembled Matt in dress and demeanor darted about the languid scene like penguin-fish, taking drink orders.

"Won't it be hard to eat and applaud at the same time?" he wondered aloud, as two other couples settled into their banquette from the left.

"The show won't start until desert is cleared," Temple said. "No scraping forks to interfere. Except for the celebrity cameos, the cast is amateur, most of them newsies. Their fragile stage presence would shatter if they had to fight a filet mignon for the audience's attention."

As the one person present with the least to lose, being neither the perpetrator nor the subject of a Gridiron skit, Matt settled back to enjoy dinner and the panorama of the audience. He had to admire the waiters' deft ballet. Once the preset salads were eaten, the glass plates were floated away and a dinner plate of fish fillet, steamed squash, peppers and broiled tomatoes was presented to each diner.

Temple eyed the generous whitefish fillet, then glanced at the goldfish pirouetting in their glass globe. "What a pity Louie isn't here. He would adore the ambiance. I don't understand it. He's been hanging around the Crystal Phoenix all week and now—just when things get interesting—he's gone."

"What interests a cat differs from what intrigues a human being," Matt noted, squeezing a lemon slice onto his entree.

The during-dinner chatter increased in noise level as the liquor flowed and the waiters whisked. Dessert was a black-and-white slice of chocolate-and-cream-cheese pie. Temple tried to pass her portion to Matt, claiming pre-show nerves and a diet.

"This is rich enough to have its own secret bank account in Switzerland," she complained. "No wonder the Swiss are famous for chocolate. No?"

She watched a trifle wistfully as the waiter wafted away her untouched dessert plate.

At last every table was cleared except for wine and low-ball glasses. Temple nursed a white wine spritzer and Matt had called for coffee. By this hour he had usually had consumed two cups from ConTact's huge communal pot.

Orchestration swelled from the stage lip, hushing chattering voices and clinking glasses. A show-tune medley blared with brass. Matt leaned forward to view the orchestra and saw none. Then heads hairy and bald began elevating into view, baton and bows waving, brass blasting.

"The whole orchestra pit is an elevator," Temple bent near to explain in a stage whisper.

Matt nodded. He remembered her saying the Peacock Theater's stage had all the latest equipment. He wondered if she knew because she had researched the hotel, or because the Mystifying Max might have performed here once.

The thought was unsettling. He concentrated instead on Temple's fretting about the missing Midnight Louie. Caviar had been AWOL a lot lately, too.

Could the cats' absent ways be related?

No. Cats walked alone, according to Kipling, and liked to wander. Matt momentarily envied their freedom. He would rather be with Caviar and Midnight Louie, wherever they were, than sitting here in rented formalwear about to see an elaborate but mainly amateur show.

Besides, he thought, running a finger under the newly irritating starched white cotton at his neck, with all these people in the theater, he was getting fairly hot under the collar.

Chapter 35

Midnight Louie's Icecapade

No doubt in some obscure scholarly circle a debate rages as to whether cat whiskers are susceptible to freezing.

I realize that this subject is abstruse in the extreme, but it so happens that I am in a unique position to present empirical data.

When I leaped into the back of the meat truck, it was my theory that refrigerated goods would be swiftly sent on their rounds, to avoid rotting in the hot sun. Apparently I underestimated the need for speed, what with modern refrigeration techniques.

The truck I have selected soon grinds into gear and rattles over what passes for road around Lake Mead. Not long after that it hits a smooth satin ribbon of asphalt and slips into high gear. I curl tightly into myself, husbanding enough warmth to generate a puddle of melted frost. Some, like that flaky Karma, would call it an aura. Others, like that hypercritical Caviar, would call it something far worse and more earthy, but I know the exact effect that produced this phenomenon. My own body heat is fighting the encroaching chill of the Big Sleep.

Above me, large and frozen-stiff pieces of dead meat swing to the rhythm of the road. I am keenly aware that my present condition, alive and sneezing, is the exception to the rule around here. So I am most relieved when the truck stops after a few minutes and a good deal of gear-screeching.

I wait, my frozen joints instructed to bound toward the slightest slice of light through the vehicle doors.

No dice. Just Louie on ice.

I do not get it. Is this truck parked for the night, or what? Do they leave all this prime pork just hanging around? The hour can only be three or four o'clock in the afternoon. This meat should be on its way to all the restaurants in town. How has my usually infallible knowledge of human habits failed me?

More important, how long will it take for Midnight Louie to become frozen fillet of feline?

At last the truck body shudders as one of the beefy (excuse the expression) drivers bounds into the seat up front. The motor vibrates to life, which massages my chronic shivers into something resembling apoplexy.

Then the vehicle jerks forward and we are moving again. But not me, personally. No, I believe that I am fast-frozen to the truck bed. Somehow the thought of Caviar taking the scenic route through north Lake Mead is no longer so amusing.

I am wondering if I will be preserved long enough to be thawed in a kinder, gentler century when something lances needlelike into the swollen pupils of my eyes. Perhaps I am being cloned for posterity.

No, my frozen orbs slowly contract. Light!

I leap, employing the memory of motion to propel me in one splendid vault to the door. I scream, as several body hairs adhere to the semi-frozen slush in which I was lying.

Two hammy hands clutch me in midair. I glimpse the stupefied faces of the drivers and smell their beery breaths. Stopping at a low dive on the job, the cads! Somehow I manage to spring my icy claws from their stiff sheaths and give them both a parting pat on the cheek.

Now *they* are howling, but I have touched pad to ground. My stiff muscles and joints go through the motions I remember so well until they melt at the instant contact of warmth and sunshine.

I am halfway down an alley and I still hear the drivers arguing whether I am a skunk or a bear cub. Either guess stinks, but I am not about to linger and educate these clods to the scents of the animal kingdom, not when I smell like a loin of lamb ready for barbecuing.

Once I am moderately thawed, and my sprint for freedom has assured that, I take my bearings, then head toward the Crystal Phoenix. Even my chilled tail tingles at the prospect of once again saving my favorite hotel from the forces of evil—and all by myself, without that nosy Caviar on the scene.

Some ends are worth the means, even if it was my personal end at risk.

In a hop, skip and crouch, I am inside the hotel and following my instincts. These lead me directly to the basement.

Some people may think I have an unfortunate fondness for basements. True, I did end up bagged in the basement during my most recent adventure. Yet that was merely a minor basement in an old house, suitably creepy and damp but not worthy of Cecil B. DeMille.

It was also in a basement that I last rendezvoused with the Divine Yvette, that silver sweetheart of a Persian who guards my heart with her little lacquered toenails. In that same Goliath basement I pounced on the Stripper Killer, thus saving my other little doll, Miss Temple Barr, from a fate almost as bad as death. Miss Temple Barr's little lacquered toenails are not too tacky, either, and I speak from experience, or at least close observation.

At any rate, if some deviltry is afoot on cloven hooves tonight, I suspect it will stem from the below-stage area while the hundreds of innocent humans in the house above gaze rapt upon the refined onstage shenanigans. I have never seen a Gridiron show, but I am certain that any event in which Miss Temple Barr is involved must be the model of good taste and innocent fun. Perhaps that is why I hear the faint roar of hearty laughter from above.

What I also hear from above is the stampede of elephant feet. I duck under a corridor costume rack just in time to avoid sixteen pairs of silver-dyed character shoes tippety-tapping down the stairs at a terrifying clip. Worse is the chorus of high-pitched squeals and laughter from the amateur chorines that accompany the shoes. One might almost wish for the bannister to break again.

I slink farther down the hall, looking for the right scent and wrong sight. If something besides the Busby Berkeley Retirement Home Follies is afoot, I will know it when I see or smell it.

Indeed, I pick up the whiff of dirt, an interesting substance to find inside the sealed environs of the hotel, where dust is public enemy number one. This is fresh dirt I smell, not the usual sandy stuff up top I so often mistake for the miserable contents of Miss Temple's thankfully untouched bathroom litter box. This dirt is not decomposed of desiccated, stale, almost odorless grains. No, it is prime stuff, rich as Colombian coffee with earthy odors. In fact, it is giving me ideas I am in no position to act upon, and I realize that I have gone some time without . . . going.

Oh, well, the experience-hardened operative is not one to dawdle for sanitary reasons. I follow the sniff, bringing all my senses and my formidable experience to bear on the trail.

It leads me past dressing rooms humming with between-act panic attacks. I ignore clouds of talcum powder and the sickening reek of underarm deodorant, which seldom works. Will these humans never learn? Smell is good. Smell is free. Smell surrounds the ape family.

My nose is so close to the ground—concrete in this case—that I walk forehead-first into an iron garment frame. I am knocked back on my tail. Perhaps I pass out for a moment, for when my senses focus again, I am seeing double.

Well, not exactly double. What I am seeing is what should not be there, and what should not be there is what I am seeing, *capiche*? Perhaps not.

Let me put it this way. I am a large enough dude that my collision with the rack has jarred the unit and knocked some costumes askew. I can now see a portion of the wall behind it. Now the walls in the underbelly of a major entertainment facility are fairly predictable things: concrete blocks enameled an uninspiring shade of tan or pale green.

But this garment rack stands before a darkened door. Not only darkened, but smelling like Juan Valdez and all his bags of rich Colombian coffee *and* his donkey and its accumulated mementos of meals past are gathered there.

Naturally, I slink under the swinging skirts of the rack and into the fragrant dark. It will surprise no one with any nose at all that I am not in some accidentally concealed dressing room, but an earthen cellar. Do I smell a rat? Oh, yes! Several.

My claws curl into raw dirt as I glide through the dark. My nose leads me deeper, until I know this is no secret chamber but a tunnel. All that is lacking is the drip of water on some stagnant rock trying to become a stalactite in a thousand years or so, and that is just as well. Given the state of my bladder, the dripping of any liquid on rock would be Chinese water torture.

Drafts of clammy air riffle my fur. I find myself following them, and thus bearing right, then left, then right again. By now even my superb sense of spacial placement, otherwise known as direction, is confused. I know only that I traverse some vast, curving network of unsuspected subterranean channels. After the first flush of discovery, however, I find the dark and the damp somewhat boring. I fondly envision the amateur performers singing and dancing their heart-and ham-strings out under the dry, bright beam of the spotlights far above.

No doubt Miss Temple Barr is thoroughly enjoying herself as I belly-crawl through the bowels of the Crystal Phoenix, pushing my poor, quick-thawed body to its limits. . . .

I pause. Another entity shares my darkness.

How I can say this? I do not know what it is, only that every hair still left on my spine has stiffened.

Rats I can handle. A chorus line of rats . . . would be more difficult.

I twitch my whiskers. I circle in the blackness, knowing my cover is perfect. I see nothing.

And then a light comes wobbling from the distance, a feeble, focused light, like the beam of a flashlight. That spells one thing: *homo sapiens.* I am not exactly afraid of a run-in with any sample of the species, even to the twelfth power, but I also wish to keep my anonymity.

I debate possible moves as the distant light bobbles closer. By its oncoming brightness I make out another hunched form on the opposite side of the tunnel. Or call it a Chunnel. It is big enough, and stinky enough.

Speaking of big and stinky, I cannot yet make out the species of my roommate, save that it is four-legged, smaller than myself and almost as dark.

The nearing light strikes a spark from its narrowed eyes: pure, venomous green.

For a blinding instant we are both caught in the unwanted glare.

I stare into the gilded eyes of Caviar.

Then we rocket out of there, dodging the light like vampires avoiding a dagger of sunlight.

"Hey," grunts some yahoo down the tunnel. "I think there's rats down here. You never said nothing about rats."

Caviar is boxing her ears with a damp paw as if she would like to be boxing my finer points, such as my face.

We are recovering ourselves outside the tunnel entrance and crouch under the swaying costumes.

"Some dirty trick," she comments.

"How did you get off the bus and back this fast?"

"Did the sunstroke routine at the first stop. Some tourist in a Rent-a-Rustbucket took pity on me and drove me back to Las Vegas. I ditched her at the first gas station, while she was inside buying me a Perrier water and some beef jerky."

"You are a most ungrateful date."

"And you are so typical of your type, what can I say? Just what I expected. Devious, cowardly—"

"What do you mean 'cowardly?' I wanted to spare you the danger."

"You never told me who you really were, Fatso."

"I did not deem you ready for such a revelation."

"Right. Who is protecting whom? Okay. As to this. What's the scam, Sam?"

"Now that you know my real name," I say with great dignity, "you might as well use it."

"Okay. No more hooey, Louie. What's up?"

I examine the dirt underneath my toenails. "I am not quite sure yet—"

"Then what is our next move, so you can be sure?"

"We have to investigate the tunnels systematically."

"What are we supposed to do, leave a trail of yarn?"

"Well, for starters—" I rise and peer down the opening that we have exited. "No one is coming this way. I suggest that the action is farther down the tunnels. I should go back and investigate. You wait here in case the authorities need to be called."

"You think they would pay me any mind?"

"It can be done." I stand and use the advantage of my great height to pontificate. "I have found methods."

"All right," she says, switching her tail. She gives me a sideways glance that I do not like. "Go back and be a hero. I will stay here and keep watch for any suspicious behavior."

"Fine," I say, wishing I had a moment to myself. I will just have to make do with the dirt down the tunnel. "Stay put, and there will be nothing to worry about."

"That is not encouraging," Caviar says, rolling her eyes. She settles onto her haunches like a good little girl, though. I do not for a moment believe that she will still be there when I return from my explorations. I suspect she wishes to make explorations of her own. "Bye-bye, Daddio."

Chapter 36

Offstage Acts

The huge stage curtain, panels of alternating emerald and turquoise velvet, drew back and the first skit was underway.

Matt watched with some wonderment. The cast numbered at least forty. Despite the lavish professional surroundings, these were indeed skits. Tap-dancing choruses might fade in and out, but the dialogue was mainly snappy repartee about local projects, failures and personalities, with a few digs hurled at national figures.

Matt hadn't lived in Las Vegas long enough, or paid close enough attention, to understand every gag. From the serial guffaws surrounding him, most of the audience did. Sometimes they even applauded a well-aimed line. During such pauses in the onstage action, Temple often leaned close to whisper, "That was mine," against the neighboring din.

Matt applauded when the audience did, but was beginning to wonder why all the pomp and circumstance and men in cummerbunds for what could have been a pleasant show in a high school gymnasium. Then he remembered that Crawford Buchanan was responsible for most of it, and that Temple thought poorly of his qualifications for the job. Still, the audience seemed delighted by spoofs of its power and glory and goof-ups. Matt suspected that these people would have applauded a Three Stooges version of this show, just as long as their names were mentioned, no matter the context.

When the curtain closed between major skits, blackouts involving only two or three actors dominated the apron while the stage was readied for the next big scene.

During such an interlude, Temple pulled her program so close to one of the candles that Matt was afraid that her hair would catch fire.

"What is it?" he whispered over the microphone-amplified lines.

On stage, a supposed Steve Wynn of the Mirage Hotel held off a duo of disgruntled Las Vegas Lions—literally the MGM Grand Hotel's oversized Leo and the Luxor's giant Sphinx—with Siegfried and Roy's famed white tigers. Since all of the big cats were portrayed by people in fuzzy suits, the skit had a surreal *Wizard of Oz* quality.

"This hokey 'Line Tamer' skit shouldn't be next," Temple fussed. "Not according to the program. Why are they playing for time? My big number is coming up. Must be a snag. I'm scooting backstage to see what. Excuse me."

"Whoa." Matt caught her arm as she prepared to shimmy impetuously down the banquette seat. "Maybe they don't want you there."

"Are you kidding? I know this show almost as well as Danny Dove. It never hurts to have help in a crisis."

Matt slid over the resistant velvet—the soft nap acted like flypaper—to let Temple out. The velvet was even more resistant to her beaded dress, but she wriggled out and then tried to tiptoe unobtrusively up the stairs.

Matt watched her as he took his seat again. Unobtrusive, sure, in that Christmas-tree tinsel dress and those glitter-heeled shoes. Someone else far back twisted to watch her exit. He recognized Lieutenant Molina, lifting opera glasses to her eyes from the far left rear of the house to follow Temple's exit. Beside her, Frank was bending his head to fuss with his watch. The opera glasses snapped to the stage, but the score was Lions 3 and Tigers 6, if you were counting laughs instead of stuffed tail thumps.

Matt glanced at the strangers next to him on the banquette big enough to seat six. Their profiles were intent on the stage, anticipatory smiles pasted to their faces. They sensed nothing wrong.

Yet now that Temple had left, Matt noticed the occasional curtain bump and bustle backstage, as if the crew were struggling. He glanced at his watch, first impatiently pulling back the cumbersome formal cuff.

Nine-thirty. The show would be working its way to the wind-up. Maybe he should have gone with Temple. . . . He turned to gawk at the closed doors leading from the house, not knowing what he expected to see.

What he did see surprised, then shocked him. Molina and Frank were gone, leaving a wine velvet hole in an audience of wall-to-wall glitter and penguin contrast.

Matt stood and made his hopefully discreet way up the long shallow ramp of carpeted steps. Around him the amplified voices on stage traded mots, bon and not-so-bon. The audience laughed.

Bursting through the exit doors, he was taken aback by the usual bustle of milling gamblers in the casino beyond. He had gotten used to the theater's programmed give-and-take of show-and-clap.

Temple was nowhere to be seen, which did not surprise him, but Lieutenant Molina was, which did.

He approached her. "Where's Temple?"

Molina kept her voice and her eyebrows level. "Isn't that your job?"

"Is something going on? Where's Frank?"

"*Frank.*" Her tone did not imply a question, but Matt knew he better explain.

"We . . . ah, used to know each other. In school."

Molina looked intrigued, but lifted the large, forties-style evening bag she carried, a large, encrusted envelope that bristled with gilt metallic curls and leaves until it more resembled a weapon than an accessory.

"I'm here as a civilian, honest. This is not my bailiwick."

"Then there *is* something going on!"

Molina tossed her head impatiently. Before she could say more, Van von Rhine and Nicky Fontana came rushing over, both attired as formally as he and Temple. Matt had noticed them slipping in and out of their seats at the very back of the house like nervous hosts double-checking arrangements every five minutes.

"What happened?" Nicky demanded in his turn, and much more impolitely than Matt. "All the undercover cops took off down the Strip like Godzilla was after them. Are we on our own here, or what?"

Molina glanced cautioningly toward Matt, then shook her head. Her short, thick hair swung back to reveal heavy vintage earrings that gleamed like brass knuckles at each ear. Matt was willing to bet that industrial-strength clips and not fragile posts held those earrings on.

"It's a wash," she admitted. "They were wrong. There's a heist on tonight, all right, but not here. The Goliath just got hit. Eight hockey-masked men in the back room."

"All the cash?" Van asked, her face ashen.

"Reports are sketchy, but they supposedly hauled it out on the collection carts."

"But the Phoenix is okay?" Nicky asked.

Molina nodded. "The Phoenix is fine. All the pre-show hanky-panky here must have been a diversion to make us think that this casino was about to get robbed. Slick," she admitted. "Well, at least we had heavy personnel committed here, and the Goliath is just down the Strip. Believe me, they'll never get away with it. That much money is much too cumbersome to move out fast. I suggest we leave the work to the people who are on duty and go back and enjoy the show. I don't want to miss Miss Barr's supposedly scintillating final act." She turned to Matt. "Maybe she skipped out early because it's a bomb."

He frowned to find his fingertips poised on the plastic dial of his watch as delicately as a waterbug's legs. Ten minutes. Temple had been gone for ten minutes, and the countdown for her skit's big moment had begun. Where was she and why hadn't she come back?

Molina had taken her own advice along with Nicky and Van. Matt glimpsed the trio's backs as the dark theater doors hushed shut on them and a faint burst of laughter.

Nothing was going to happen at the Crystal Phoenix but the Gridiron. Maybe something bad had been expected, but that impression was part of a ruse. Here, everything was hunky dory. Matt had that on good authority. Police authority.

Why was he worried?

Maybe because it was too quiet at the Phoenix and everything was a little too normal to believe. He was beginning, he realized, to think like Temple.

He was acting like an amateur sleuth.

Chapter 37

Midnight Discovery

"Everything's fine," said the Luxor Hotel, adjusting the blue-and-gold horizontally-striped headdress of the Sphinx that fronted her gold leather bustier. In fact, this Sphinx had an unusually prominent set of cheekbones.

The Luxor bent to straighten the seams on her net tights—a glittery string of Egyptian hieroglyphs.

"Except it's hot as hell down here," complained the MGM Grand, tossing the spangle-tangled blond mane that streamed over her bare shoulders. *Her* bustier was warm and fuzzy and a perfect likeness of Leo the Lion's blunt-featured feline face, except that he too had awesomely pronounced cheekbones.

"We are going to have to tap like hell to keep our balance on that puny ring-of-Saturn ramp around the UFO," the Treasure Island added in turn.

Perhaps she should have been called the Treasure Chest, for her bustier ranneth over with golden pieces of eight spilling from a brass-bound box unto the ninth power.

Temple had to admit that the night shift at the Lace 'n' Lust had perfect figures for her Living Hotels tableau. Modest proportions would not have adapted so hilariously to the overblown images of Las Vegas's latest hostelries-*cum*-theme parks.

The amateur chorus girls in their battered silver-painted tap shoes and sequined body suits gathered around to ooh and aah the Strip Hotels and their stripper impersonators, who each wore twenty-some pounds of folderol.

"You look fantastic," Temple told them all, meaning it.

Beyond the milling performers, the huge silver bulk of the grounded UFO glimmered matte-silver in the understage dimness.

Two dozen local print and electronic reporters paced in more prosaic outfits. The men portraying gangsters wore brown zoot suits with neon-colored shirts and white ties; the G-men wore gray suits with pinstripes so exaggerated that they resembled convict stripes.

"Oh, and wow!"

Temple turned to regard the array of Elvis imitators.

Never before had she seen so much white satin Spandex, so many nickel-size rhinestones, so many glitz-ridden belts wide enough to be mistaken for wrestling trophies or even freeway on-ramps.

Temple gazed rapturously at sideburns as long, black and fuzzy as tarantula legs, at slicked-back pompadours and sweat-stained scarves, at rings even bigger than Liberace's collection of pinkie pianos, at boots that looked like they were cut from the concho-studded hide of a country-western singing cow that consented to chew only a rhinestone cud.

"Cosmic," she sighed with the satisfaction of an artist who has attained a particularly elusive vision.

"Danny wanted us to surprise you," the Luxor said with a pout. She fiddled with the battery-powered azure laser-beam atop her pyramid headdress, which gave her the look of a blue-light special at a K-Mart store. "He'll be so upset that you peeked."

The MGM Grand nodded soberly, almost unseating her own towering headdress—the operative initials seven inches high surmounting the keyboard of a glossy black piano—a grand piano, naturally.

"Danny wouldn't want you down here now." She absently patted Leo's nose, which covered her belly button, but not much else. "You might miss our grand entrance."

"I just wanted to ensure that nothing is going wrong," Temple said.

"It isn't," an Elvis growled. "God, this elastic pajama-suit is stifling, and so is the stuffing."

"That stuffing is *you*, Mitch," a svelter Elvis, but not by much, suggested. He tugged at the ten-inch-wide rhinestoned belt girding his loins. "You can bet that I will stick to writing obituaries from now on, instead of reversing them."

"You look adorable, every one!" Temple reassured the nervous Elvii, hard-boiled newsmen all who would writhe at her choice of adjectives.

Half the humor of a Gridiron show was seeing newspeople and public personalities forced to play against type. And most of the men sweating in the costumes required by Temple's skit had made the casual condescending comments they made to all women who were small, young and decent-looking.

Temple pinched a fleshy cheek that happened to belong to a cigar-smoking assistant news editor of the *Review-Journal* who had once called her "dollie."

"Just too cute for words," she enunciated in her treacliest tones. "You'll be a biiig hit."

"True. Now you shoo." The Treasure Island had gyrated as close as she could with the model Spanish galleons afloat on each shoulder. "We'll whip these amateurs into getting their cues right." The assorted men shivered in delight. "Danny's walkie-talkie signal for the crew to board should come in a few moments. Next the dancers take their positions on the ramp. Then we hotels hop aboard for showtime and we all twinkle and do our thing in four-four time."

Temple nodded, grateful for the professional presence of the Lace 'n' Lust ladies for the first—and last—time. This was a complicated production number. The performers would need all their wits about them to cram twenty-some people inside the UFO on cue and get another two dozen hoofing around the outside as the stage elevator slowly levitated the silver saucer.

She was just being a mother hen, Temple told herself, clicking away on her Weitzman heels that were almost glittery enough to whisk her away to another world. No, she recalled, the ruby-red slippers were supposed to take Dorothy home, and Temple had no intention of clicking her heels three times to end up in Minnesota

. . . and miss the pleasure of viewing her big production number.

The halls were deserted. Below-stage was often like that when a major show was unfolding upstairs. The cast was either up on stage, in the wings waiting to go on, or huddled around the UFO waiting for the final number. The agape dressing room doors made this a hall of mirrors in which Temple glimpsed her passing figure—a slender silver flash, hardly recognizable as she trotted past. Didn't want to miss the skit's beginning, and poor Matt must be wondering by now what ladies' room she had disappeared into. . . .

"Louie!"

She stopped on the double dimes of her skinny metal-tipped high heels.

Sure enough. The big black cat was lying in the middle of the broad hall, so perfectly still and centered that he seemed an illusion.

"Louie?"

Temple found herself tip-toeing closer. How odd! First Midnight Louie virtually leaves home. Then he shows up like a poster cat for the Mystifying Max.

"I'm taking you home tonight," she resolved aloud. "You can stay put in my office until the show is over. And if dealing with you makes me miss my big number—"

The cat stood, stretched, yawned wide enough to show every shark-white tooth in his cherry-pink gums . . . and ambled to a rack of costumes along the wall.

"Oh no, you don't."

Temple scrambled to intercept the cat before he vanished into a curtain of clothes, her steel heels practically striking sparks from the concrete.

Too late. Just his tail showed beneath a froth of feathers and bejeweled hems. Temple bent to capture it and felt a furry plume elude her grasping hand.

"Louie! No games. I'm late for a very important date. I'm *leaving* a Very Important Date sitting alone like coagulating chili. Get out of there!"

Of course he didn't. And of course Temple had to bend down in a bead-encrusted dress not designed for bending, then thrust her head among the powder and mothball and deodorant-saturated costumes to feel frantically for what had become a Cheshire Cat, without the visible grin. She didn't feel much like grinning either, except in frustration.

"I could kill you," she threatened, hearing a few precious beads clattering to concrete and feeling her silver pantyhose stretching beyond even the endurance of Spandex-blend.

And of course she didn't find him, couldn't feel him and had to go down on her knees, which would make her pantyhose bag if it hadn't already burst. Then she had to crawl on all fours, banging her knees on the rack's low metal support pipes and getting her hands filthy with God-knows-what floor fungus and her hair churned into a Raggedy-Ann mop and—the final indignity—inhaling a faceful of—spit and sputter—stage-dusting feathers.

And still no cat.

Temple was angry now. She back-peddled out of the costume patch on hands and knees, hoisted herself upright by grabbing the rack's vertical pipe, then braced her precariously shod feet to wrench the entire rack away from the wall.

Ooof!

It didn't move. Temple glanced down. The frame was bolted to the floor. She stared, aghast. The entire point of costume racks was that they be mobile. They all had wheels. Who would bolt one to the floor?

Very well. She would expose Louie in another way.

Temple positioned herself at the rack's middle, then reached out and jerked the heavy, hanging costumes to either side. Louie should be easily visible cowering against the naked wall.

Uh . . . what wall?

Temple stared at an oblong of black. It was not a cat. There was no cat in view. Louie had pulled a Max and utterly vanished. So had the wall, the concrete block wall painted a pale, pukey color.

Temple stared at the matte black rectangle she had revealed. It looked like a mirror-backing spray-painted on the wall. Maybe the mirror was on the other side. Maybe she should go through and find out.

She stretched out a hand, surprised to see a rhinestone bangle sparkling on her wrist. That's right. That hand was supposed to be applauding a Gridiron dinner show, right now!

Her hand passed through the mirror backing into the dark. She saw no reflection, not of her silver self, not of a glint of green from a black cat's eyes.

Temple's shoes scrapped concrete as she stepped over the rack frame to edge into the wall. Alice had followed a white rabbit down a rabbit-hole. What would happen if Temple followed a black cat into a black hole? What if it was a hell-hole?

But Louie had never led her ashtray before. Her groping hands found a metal frame inset into the thickness of the concrete blocks. This opening wasn't a hole, then, but something built into the structure of the building.

"Louie," she whispered.

The small sound echoed.

Wherever she was, it was big enough to throw her own words back at her.

Oh, Louie. What had he quite literally got into now? She couldn't see just leaving him here. Nor could she see, period.

Temple sighed.

The space mocked her with a faint hiss.

Turning, she saw a slit of light where she had drawn the clothing aside. Her eyes were adjusting now, and the area was revealing limits, a thin trickle of light glinted off walls.

The suspicion of light seemed to thicken and solidify farther on.

This was it, Temple suddenly knew all the way to her arched insteps. This was why the basement plans were missing! Her groping hand touched a wall as her fingertips traced a familiar surface of concrete blocks held together by depressed lines of mortar. Her heels sank into some sandy surface broadcasting an earthy perfume.

This was the underbelly of the old Joshua Tree Hotel, Jersey Joe Jackson's place as he had meant it to be, and as he had meant it to be forgotten.

Visions of silver dollars danced in her head. Who knew what was down here? Who knew what wealth lurked in this hidden labyrinth? Midnight Louie did.

Temple squinted at an apparent movement near the floor where light so soft that it whispered seeped in. The moving thing could be Midnight Louie. It could be the Giant Rat of Sumatra. Or it could be the ghost of Jersey Joe Jackson.

She edged deeper into the darkness, her mind churning with

great expectations, with notions of a lost past heritage shaping a profitable future.

One thing she was sure of, one way or another: Midnight Louie had hit paydirt.

Chapter 38

Track of the Cat

Matt lingered outside the Peacock Theater, not sure which sin was the greater: to risk missing Temple's skit, or to hunt for her as if she were a lost three-year-old incapable of taking care of herself.

Still, he knew how much that one production number meant to her. Why would she risk missing it?

While he debated, he noticed a dark-haired man who resembled a department-store floor-walker in a tuxedo eyeing him suspiciously across the crowded room.

Matt realized that standing still and thinking could be construed as bizarre behavior in a gambling casino. He hesitated for a last moment, torn between returning to the banquette, where Temple would expect to find him when she returned, or trying to find his way below-stage.

"Something wrong?"

Matt glanced at another dark-haired man in a tuxedo who had sidled up beside him, then looked for the first man. Still in place, and still watching Matt curiously.

In evening dress, the two men looked like twins, but now he understood. He turned to the stranger beside him.

"I was with Temple. I wondered where she'd gone."

The man frowned and cocked his head at his distant clone. The other man began walking over . . . another who looked just like him came from the left and yet another deserted his post leaning against the cashier's cage to advance on Matt.

The sight of the converging sober men in formal dress might have been intimidating, except that Matt had recognized the species from his encounter with the owner of the Crystal Phoenix: Fraternitas Fontanas.

"Temple is missing?" the first man asked incredulously. He toyed with a gold cannon-shaped earring in his left ear. "Can't be, man. The alert here was a false alarm. The Phoenix was just a diversion. All the action is over at the Goliath." He sounded truly sorry about that. "Now is no time for Miss Barr to flee. This place is safer than Al Capone's vault was from Geraldo Rivera."

The identically dressed brothers had circled Matt, giving him an unnerving impression of confronting a stranger's face in a funhouse chamber of mirrors.

"She went to see about backstage matters." Matt waved toward the service elevators. The brothers' overwhelming presence had made evasion devoutly to be wished. "I'll tell her the bad news about everything being okay here."

The brothers nodded morosely, twitching the armed portions of their anatomy in reckless abandon: shoulders, hips and even ankles. All that hardware was now redundant. Pity.

Matt broke their charmed circle and headed for the service area. Temple was going to miss the Gridiron finale unless she showed up pronto. What could be keeping her?

He didn't bother with the elevator, instead clattering down the empty stairs once so unexpectedly threatening. The handrail felt as solid as Gibraltar, but he didn't trust any weight to it.

The downstairs, where only hours before performers had dashed and chattered, was eerily silent. He peered into abandoned dressing rooms, inhaling the oily chemical scent of open stage-makeup tins. Askew chairs, scattered pencils and jars, carelessly tossed items of clothing gave the place a Twilight-Zone feel, as if the cast had truly been wafted away in a UFO, leaving everything behind.

When Matt reached the understage area, he saw a hushed crowd huddled around the strangely compelling form of the UFO, and stopped. A muffled din filtered down from the stage above like smothered Musak. No sense disturbing the cast. Temple wasn't here. She probably had returned to their banquette by some arcane backstage route and was now wondering where *he* was.

Matt retraced his steps, enjoying the echoing silence. He began to understand Temple's fascination with the theater's big, rumbling underbelly. The atmosphere reminded him of a team locker room while the big game was played elsewhere. Full of past and promise, for now it was a place where time stood still.

Then Matt stopped. He had heard something, faint but accidental-sounding. A clang of some kind. And the sound came from ahead, away from the understage area. A clang like a cell door slamming, and then—a shriek. A thin, tiny scream, so distant it could have been the squeal of an unoiled wheel.

Except that nothing moved here, not even a ceiling fan. He stood and listened to the building breathe; the air conditioner's constant drone became a white noise to ignore. He looked back down the hall toward the now-invisible UFO. No, not from behind . . . from ahead.

But nothing waited ahead—only the stairs and elevator at the left, the empty dressing rooms on the right. He glanced at a spooky rack of hanging costumes of every type and color. It looked like Halloween had been lynched. The stuffed black cat with a fear-arched back planted at the hems of the tawdry costumes only added to the macabre impression.

The cat hissed as it saw him, then lowered its back and stepped forward tentatively to greet him.

"Caviar!"

Matt was shocked to the soles of his black wing-tips. The little cat had been off on her own of late, and he had worried about that, but his own multiple anxieties had overridden any other concern. He was surprisingly relieved to see her. Now if only he could pinpoint Temple. . . .

Caviar was rubbing frantically back and forth on the swaying costumes, her nervous turning, pacing and tail-waving lashing them into an eerie imitation of live-action.

"What are you doing here?"

He neared the animal cautiously, knowing the idiocy of asking a cat anything, but the creatures responded to vocalizations. He had learned that much.

Caviar meowed plaintively. At his approach she transferred her rubbings from inanimate clothing to his pant legs. At least she was also black.

He bent to pick her up, but she eluded him. Mincing over the costume rack's bottom metal support, she nudged between the hanging curtains of costume.

"Hey, kitty! Don't do that."

He bent lower to retrieve her, and that's when he heard the distant echo of scuffles and muffled shouts. Caviar was disappearing where the costumes gaped in the middle like a carelessly closed stage curtain.

Matt reached into the narrow aisle of space and thrust back the costumes as far as he could force them.

The faint noises he had heard were louder. He was facing a black velvet curtain where the wall should be. Caviar nosed right into that dark barrier, her front half vanishing except for the glow of her golden eyes.

She looked back at Matt with that patented feline gaze of calm expectancy: *You know what I want. Now do it, ignorant human.*

The wall was obviously absent without leave here, Matt thought with new anxiety. Since Temple was truant, being Temple, she must have gone where the missing wall went.

Sure. Matt stepped over the rack frame and into instant darkness. Looking back, he saw the costumes had sprung almost closed again now that he was no longer holding them apart. Temple could have performed the same vanishing act, and no one would have been the wiser had Caviar not played lookout and attracted his attention.

Who—or what—Matt wondered, would attract attention to where *he* had gone? Maybe his guardian angel, he thought, hearing Caviar's gentle purr of satisfaction and feeling her rubbing pull on his pant legs.

The smothered racket deep in the darkness intensified. Was this some theatrical storage area? Was a crew moving unneeded Gridiron props? Whatever, Temple was even more likely than he to explore such an interesting anomaly. She really was as curious as a cat. He was not, but he had another bad trait: a bulldog sense of responsibility to and for others.

Matt plunged into the unknown territory, his hands a buffer zone before him in the blackness. His fingertips bounced off the paint-smoothed roughness of concrete blocks. He quickly discovered that the space was a broad tunnel, and that it *curved* as it continued. Light gleamed off a turn far ahead. When his reaching hands found an empty space that proved to be another arm of the tunnel, he began to doubt his wisdom in being there.

"Caviar?" he questioned the dark.

There was no answer, not even a tug against the satin side seams of his rented trousers. He weighed alternatives and decided that feeling his way in a dark so dense he couldn't even see a black cat was idiotic.

He retreated while he still sensed the way, despite a plaintive meow from the abyss. Fools will rush in where even guardian angels fear to tread. He couldn't guarantee any angels, anywhere, anymore. But he could keep at least one fool from further folly.

Chapter 39

An Uplifting Escape

Temple wasn't sure how far she had walked.

In her high heels, it felt like blocks, but how could that be? The Crystal Phoenix grounds weren't *that* extensive.

Farther into the tunnels the occasional bare lightbulb provided periodic gobbets of light. She guessed that they were on the same line as other lights at the Phoenix; the same circuit as the dressing rooms, say. Maybe this had once been storage space for casino and theatrical equipment.

Now the space was utterly empty, but not deteriorated. At least this was Las Vegas, and the walls weren't damp and discolored, or covered with lichen and slime, she thought as she skimmed along the tunnel wall with her hand as a guide.

She could still hear the faint sound of stage machinery. The tunnels were curved, not straight. She may have circled back behind the stage elevator for all she knew. Still, she hadn't found another exit yet, and she didn't even have a humble trail of bread crumbs to lead her back.

She knew she should have turned back long before, but Midnight Louie kept eager pace with her. Every time she stopped, she felt him brush against her calves. Occasionally his upright tail tickled her thighs, the naughty boy! He acted like a dog in a Disney movie; he had something to show her.

Besides, Temple's mind was spinning a public relations web from the network of tunnels she traveled. She could see it now: the Glory Hole Gang mine ride: *rocket like Indiana Jones through the darkest bowels of a treasure-laden earth!* The Jersey Joe Jackson desert diorama and treasure hunt, with a silver dollar at the end for every ticket holder.

Of course, this motherlode of invention would cost Nicky and Van a fortune, but, hey, half the groundwork had been done. The Crystal Phoenix already had a pre-excavated, dark, dramatic underworld ripe for development, repositioning and exploitation. Plus, Temple thought happily, the *mystique!*

Jersey Joe Jackson—Action Jackson!—had hacked this secret network of tunnels from the desert in his heyday, perhaps for a dozen mysterious purposes. Pick your passion. Treasure-hoarding. Escape routes. Disposing of rivals. Oooh, creepy. Any minute Temple expected to stumble over a body, no . . . a skeleton. Oh, holy fright night! They could offer a Halloween special with a holographic "ghost" of Jersey Joe haunting the rides and displays.

Temple was thinking so hard she stumbled over something, and hoped it wasn't Louie. The steel heels on her shoes were more than somewhat lethal.

She bent down to feel for the cat and found her hands shaping a long, lumpy hummock of burlap sacks.

Oh my gosh, maybe this was her dead body!

Temple crouched beside whatever it was in the dark, unwilling to probe further, yet unwilling to turn around and give up.

Midnight Louie began massaging her jackknifed legs, his enthusiasm threatening to topple her.

The sounds that Temple had thought were behind her increased. The stage machinery was running full tilt now—darn, she was missing the debut of her very own UFO. She could hear the subtle squeak of the pulley wheels turning and the grunts and gritted-teeth curses of the stage hands . . . getting forty people and a humongous prop positioned for an elevated entrance was not easy.

She must be very near the staging area, Temple thought, looking back over her left shoulder for the narrow, lighted crack of an exit.

Light came, but it fell on the right side of her face.

She looked ahead, hearing some machine grinding toward her, some truant *deus ex machina* wheeling down the abandoned tunnel's curling length toward her like a runaway ore car in an Indiana Jones movie.

Temple stood, sensing that she needed to get out of the way. Watery light was leaking down the tunnel ahead of the noise, pale but indomitable. It fluttered like candle flames, jerked up and down.

"Damn!" a man protested.

"Shut up!" another whispered. "Sound carries down here. Just a bit to go and then we can dump this load."

But the unseen vehicle's wheels continued protest in soprano squeaks while the men's guttural grunts provided a percussive base.

Temple now could distinguish Midnight Louie's outline against the dawn of light warming the tunnel sides. His halo of uplifted hair made him resemble a hedgehog. He was retreating on stiff legs, adding an intermittent hiss to the sound effects echoing off the concrete walls.

"You hear anything?" a desperate voice whispered hoarsely.

"Just us," came the answer. "Keep movin'."

Temple glanced to her feet. The soft light played over the shape of a sleeping transient at the tips of her black suede shoes. She jumped back, then saw that she viewed not a body, so much as . . . body parts. Bags of camouflage-colored canvas grouped into the accidental semblance of a human form.

She bent again, worked one stiff draw-cord open and felt inside. Her fingertips touched the damp, limp linen of well-used legal tender. Paper money. A cache of cash.

At that moment a spear of light bounced off the opposite wall. A man was backing into her sight, a man in dark clothes, with something shiny, dark and bulky jammed into the back of his pants. He held flashlights in both hands, hoisting and waving them as an airport worker guides a grounded airplane into the gate.

After him came the grinding, squealing sound, swelling as a stainless steel cart nosed into view. It could have been a hospital cart, or a food cart or a dozen other carts, but it looked just like the carts casinos use to transfer slot machine and gaming table money to the collection center hidden at their cores.

Now Temple was backing up, and so was Midnight Louie. Her hands were behind her, on the smooth cool wall. She kept her feet shuffling along the hard-packed dirt floor so her steps wouldn't be apparent. Thank heaven the cart sounded like the Tin Woodman before he got a lube job! Its shrieks would surely drown out little her. Louie, of course, made no more noise than a quartet of Q-Tips on parade. . . .

The tunnel was finally curving enough to begin concealing the oncoming men. Temple could only glimpse one bag of the pile that was their goal. She let her breath ease out while inching and shuffling backward.

The lead man twisted his head over his shoulder to gauge the distance to go.

She saw a bone-white face punctured by a machine-gun pattern, and gasped.

He didn't hear her over the din, but he saw her.

The twin flashlights swept her way like dueling lasers.

She turned and ran, the rat-a-tat pound of her heels a surprisingly heart-stopping burst of noise. No point tippy-toeing now. This dress was a sterling silver target.

"Stop her!" someone shouted.

The cart noise died in an instant, replaced by pounding soft-soled feet and huffing breaths.

Where was Louie?

Temple had no time to look. She had successfully plunged into the deeper darkness, her hand scraping along the sandpaper surface of the concrete blocks.

A feeble glow of light ahead signaled one of the overhead bulbs. She paused to snatch off her shoes and ran on, dreading the light. They wouldn't shoot her, no. They didn't want sound. But they could catch her; their big feet pounded relentlessly behind her. She didn't know the way out, only that tunnel branches might lead to dead-ends.

And she knew that the occasional lightbulbs would act as fingering spotlights. She was barreling into the wincing light of one now.

Temple ran faster as she neared the light, holding one steel heel high. She imagined she must look like the Statue of Liberty bearing a rhinestone torch. As she streaked under the light, she leaped up and swatted up with the heel. The glass bulb shattered, then scattered to the floor, its filament winking out in an instant.

Pleased to discover she had not electrocuted herself, Temple sprinted on, her strides hiking her hem up to mid-thigh. Between the rough floor and her beaded hem sawing against her thighs like a diamond-edged blade, her pantyhose were history.

Temple hoped that she was not.

Then an oncoming overhead light developed an alarming mobility and began probing the darkness with relentless intelligence. Temple, huffing and puffing, dared not slow down or be overtaken, but she was surrounded! Someone was ahead of her, maybe a confederate who planned to meet the money-movers in mid-tunnel.

Or could these people be legitimate casino employees? Had she stumbled on where they discreetly processed the take? Maybe they took *her* for a crook, an unauthorized person at least, and all would be well.

Maybe Oprah Winfrey and Geraldo Rivera would get married.

A stitch in her side was giving Temple the contrary impression that it had split open. Or her dress had.

With her last rush of adrenalin, she hurtled straight for the barrier flashlight. If whoever held it wanted to shoot, so be it. Her dress was a goner, so she was going to aim a karate kick right where the unseen arm would be.

She aimed, leaped, kicked . . . and felt a countering hand intercept her instep with a force that stopped her in mid-thrust.

She would have twisted and tumbled flat on her face, except that the arm holding the flashlight moved in front of her as she collapsed on it.

"Temple, what on earth—?"

"Matt! All right. Come on, run! They're armed."

The flashlight snapped off. "Who?"

"Miners. The Seven Dwarves. The ghosts of the Glory Hole Gang. I don't know! Look!"

The twin flashlight beams blinked into view.

Matt's third beam flashed on again, aimed at the middle of that bullet-ridden white face. It was impossible to read surprise on a mutilated mask, but the flashlight beams drooped with surprise, and then Matt was a shadow interrupting the light.

The pursuer fell with a grunt of surprised pain, his flashlights rolling from limp hands and crossing beams on the floor. Too bad an "X" wasn't the mark of Zorro, Temple thought with irrelevence, maybe Zorro could put in an appearance in the J. J. Jackson underground theme park.

Footsteps and fresh light came from beyond the first man's fallen form.

"Come on," said the dark that rushed back to Temple, taking her arm. "It's a good thing I went back for a flashlight."

They ran together, Matt using the flashlight intermittently to scout the tunnel's curves. No more overhead lightbulbs betrayed their position. After the sounds collided with the fallen man, there was a pause, then renewed pursuit.

Suddenly Matt was pushing Temple ahead of himself.

She stumbled forward, stubbing a toe on a steel rod, flailing through a fabric curtain she thought she'd never see again, beating her way into the light and familiar surroundings of the basement hallway.

Matt bounded through after her, throwing down the flashlight to turn and pull the costumes closed. He snatched up the flashlight again, answering her questioning look.

"Found it in a dressing room."

They glanced around. Temple saw that the hall was still deserted, drat it.

Costumes trembled and swayed.

Matt and Temple bolted down the passage, peering into deserted dressing rooms.

"Hey," a voice shouted from down the hall.

They ran faster.

"Hey, Miss Barr, what is the big hurry? You're going the wrong way. Your skit is gonna start any moment."

Temple looked over her shoulder. The voice was calling from the foot of the stairs, where a flotilla of Fontana brothers in penguin colors was gathering in puzzlement. Twenty feet ahead of them, a horror of hockey-masked felons were streaming out of the wall and between the costumes.

"Fontanas," Temple gasped to Matt. "The odds are even."

But the pursuers were aware of nothing except prey. Temple heard the same pounding feet that had set her heart's tempo for the past six minutes: about two hundred beats per minute.

Like a vision from a dubious television documentary, the huge prop UFO loomed ahead of them.

The show was over, Temple knew with a sinking heart. The show was over and there was no place to hide.

Matt had twisted his head back and glanced at her, shaking it. "Out for blood," he warned.

There was no place else to go. They charged up the plywood ramp and circled the UFO following the upward spiral. On the other side, the floor was a full fifteen feet down, with no ladder.

Footsteps were vibrating the ramp as six or so pursuers jumped aboard. Matt and Temple exchanged a stunned look, then she dived for the only exit . . . an oblong door into the UFO.

After the normal light of the hallway, the UFO interior was blackout-dark. Matt had Temple's wrist in a firm grip, but as they pushed into the interior they encountered resistance. A wall of resistance.

A human cordon, in fact.

"Hey, watch it!" a woman's voice grumbled. "That's my foot."

"Yeah," a man objected, "you're creasing the knife-pleats in my zoot suit. If you're not in the cast, get out."

Little did he know. The UFO doorway darkened, both actually and metaphorically. One hulking, goblin-faced man after another bounded inside. The population explosion pressed everybody further into the dark, crowded and somewhat pungent space.

Temple and Matt were jammed into a wall of flesh.

"I didn't know anyone was still in here," Temple whispered. "They could get hurt."

"Not in this mess."

Mess indeed. Barely had the inadequate light streaming through the door brightened, then a new storm on the horizon darkened it. Fontana brothers piled onto the UFO like a team of football players.

People were complaining and elbowing and mixing it up as one aggravated anonymous mob.

"Shut up," a woman's authoritative voice rang out. "Anyone

who ruins this entrance is ground round. Now settle down, people. We'll straighten this out later."

Her words ended with a bang, rather than a whimper, when the UFO door slammed shut at the prompting of some mysterious outside force.

Temple huddled against the hull, Matt shielding her from the front. He still had her wrist in custody and could no doubt take her pulse, which was now about two hundred and forty. The crowd, the overcrowding, the uncertainty, the heat had everyone crammed in like sardines.

"Where are the dancers?" Temple wondered in a whisper she meant Matt only to hear.

An unsuspected male voice at her ear, evidently belonging to an Elvis, answered.

"The UFO was too heavy for the elevator to lift the whole cast, with the addition of those hotel babes, whoever's bright idea that was."

Temple did not volunteer her own identity, under the circumstances.

"Danny Dove decided at the last moment tonight that the chorus line will enter from the wings, under the cover of the crimson mist," Elvis managed to reveal before being shushed by the woman with an interest in raw hamburger.

Temple winced, in the dark, where no one could see her.

A full load of Fontanas and the tunnel people made the UFO overweight again. Lord knows what would happen when the stage elevator tried to uplift them.

"Hold on," Matt advised softly as a motor whined and they began to rise ever so slowly.

Temple sighed. Whoever these tunnel people were, they were ruining her grand finale. What a disaster! What a quandary—forty-some innocent people trapped in a UFO with armed thugs.

Gridirons were supposed to spoof the news, not make it.

Somehow, she decided, it was all her fault. Perhaps she had been too mean to Crawford. *Mea culpa. Mea maxima culpa. Mea Max.* Right. It would take a magician to get them all out of this safely. She pictured the spectacular conclusion of the Gridiron: an on-stage shootout between the Fontana brothers and the forces of underground evil. Innocent bystanders dropping like swatted flies onstage and off. She might as well fall on a spike heel right now and get it over with. Even if she survived, she would never live down this ignominy.

At least she would perish with Matt Devine holding her hand. Sort of.

Chapter 40

Louie's Last Bow

Naturally, I have not been a slug-a-bed during all this hullabaloo.

The instant I detect that Miss Temple and I are about to encounter unfriendlies in the tunnel, I improvise a brilliant plan.

Since I am in perfect camouflage gear for the situation, I huddle in the shadow of the sandbags.

Once the interlopers spot my dear roommate in the glare of their twin beams, they head right for her. I must say that the males of her species certainly are crazy for Miss Temple, with the lamentable exception of Mr. Max Kinsella, who has been all too successful at keeping well away from her.

So everybody streams past me, while I have plenty of time to size up the predicament with my specialized infra-green night-sight equipment.

Certain inalienable facts are self-evident. One, the lads on Miss Temple's tail are a gang of thieves. The hockey masks are the first tip-off. The second is the cash cart, which I study for a half-second in their flashlight beams, especially the affixed steel plaque that is engraved with the tattletale words, "Goliath Hotel."

After the crowd has galloped down the tunnel, I pause a moment in the contemplation that so becomes my kind. We are not about to bestir ourselves to no avail. Perhaps I would better serve my beleaguered roomie by following the tunnel forward to whence these villains have come. I could then lead the forces of law and order—who are no doubt well aware of the missing cash cart, if not this underground escape route—after me . . . and the crooks, thus saving my little lady's hairless skin yet once again.

Or I could follow the evil-doers and Harry their arrears, but the fact is that, though I possess the heart of a tiger and the liver of a lion, I am slightly outnumbered here, not to mention outweighed, despite my finest efforts in the eating department.

Clearly my superior brain is the best means of insuring that all ends well.

Now that I have selected my weapon of choice, I am all action.

I rise, carefully concealing my razor-sharp shivs about my person, and race down the tunnel after the absconding *dramatis personae*. I am not so over-concerned for the safety of my little doll, for she is light on her feet and quick with a kick, thanks to lessons from Mr. Matt Devine.

However, she is not bullet-proof. I see my mission as insuring that no lead poisoning pollutes the air around my little doll and the Crystal Phoenix. Given my superior bursts of speed owing to a Cheetah strain a few thousand years ago, I am but a whisker behind the perpetrators by the time they wrestle their way through the costume curtain into the full light of the Phoenix basement. I am relieved to see no sign of my lovely assistant in crime, assuming that she has maintained her lead in this race of life and death.

When I cautiously peek my snout out from under a white feather ruffle, I am rudely battered about the head and face. I was not expecting thugs and draw back with a snarl.

"Pantywaist!" a too-familiar female voice hisses. I view the sour little kisser of the supine Miss C. "Why are you slinking along in the rear guard? Is that the best you can manage? What are we going to do about those gangsters?"

It is, of course, my darling daughter, here to cheer on her old man. I peer out and down the hall.

"Leave it to me," I inform Miss Caviar in no uncertain fashion, giving her a love tap on the nose. "I have a plan."

"And?"

I eye the disappearing heels of six thugs of unknown identity pounding after the fleeing forms of Mr. Matt Devine and Miss Temple Barr. At least my poor roommate is not alone during her hour of need. The company of Messrs. Derringer, Colt and Beretta would no doubt be even sweeter comfort, and while Mr. Matt Devine brandishes a flashlight, I doubt that he is packing blue steel.

However, I do see a hardware factory on the horizon in the personages of Fontana *Frères,* who are gaping in surprised indecision at the foot of the stairs.

This must stop.

"Run when I do," I growl at my errant apparent offspring, "and stay down."

I take off down the center of the hall, hoping that Miss Caviar is on my tail.

"Hey," opines a brother Fontana in an aggrieved tone, "that looks like Midnight Louie. Louies. Am I seeing double?"

"Something is up," another brother concludes. "Could it be that all the action is not at the Goliath? Let us go."

They do, hallelujah!

I sprint after the bad guys and arrive in time to see them hurtling into the silver-painted UFO that has been built with much expense for Miss Temple Barr's Gridiron skit.

"Under the ramp, kid," I order my offspring.

We leap into the shadow and soon are panting in the welcome shade while thundering black patent leather loafers pound up the ramp.

"You seem to spend a lot of time under decks," Miss Caviar notes.

I do not pause to answer, but romp up the ramp behind the last Fontana and bound at the open door, thus sealing one and all inside the UFO. It is true that I have shut my foxy lady in with her hounds, but I figure that being confined in the dark will confuse these bozos enough to allow the good guys to get the upper hand.

There is a flaw in my reasoning, and that is that it depends on the Fontana brothers doing the right thing at the right time.

I strut down the ramp, well aware that I look particularly awesome against a silver metallic background.

Little Miss Carp-spurner is waiting at the bottom.

"Now that you have canned them all like sardines, what will you do? Send in the boiling oil?"

I hear gears grinding and sense an imminent upheaval.

"Off the ramp," I order gruffly, "unless you want to be trampled by a herd of human hoofers."

The floor beneath us rises like a piston. She jumps off and makes a perfect four-point landing on the basement concrete. The platform on which I stand is now five feet about basement level, and rising.

"What is the scam?" she demands. "What are you up to?"

"About six feet now. Too high for a youngster like you to jump back aboard. I am off to see the stars and give my regards to Broadway. See you later."

She is dwindling to a small, uncertain figure as I levitate like a legendary god into the black sky of a darkened stage. I could get used to such dramatic exits, not to mention the forthcoming surprising entrance.

An eerie orchestration of computerized music is swelling above me. I run up to the ramp's highest point, then scale the UFO's silver-bubble top with a trio of well-chosen leaps. I now sit atop the vessel, with a 360-degree view of everything, which at the moment is a lot of nothing.

High above me sabers of blue, red and green light stab the darkness and a rising cloud of stage mist—dry ice by the bucket. When the UFO jolts to a stop, and it does, a stream of happy hoofers flows from the wings under the fog cover and ankles up the ramp on tiptoe. Unseen at the back of the ramp wait the number's surprise packages, which I am privileged to preview before the audience. I gaze down on a ludicrous trio of headdresses incorporating elements of the town's latest theme hotels, the Luxor, the MGM Grand and the Treasure Island.

There is not room enough for me and two ersatz pussycats up here, I think, eager to pounce on the likenesses of the Sphinx and the Leo the Lion. We will see whose stuffing will fly in such a set-to. But I control my temper, well aware of the boiling temperaments that must be erupting within this plywood prison.

As the stage lights come up, the ramp vibrates to the tapping of two dozen size six-to-nines equipped with silver metal soles and heels. From the audience on whom this spectacle is slowly dawning,

I hear gasps, then laughter and smatterings of surprised applause.

Ah, if only Miss Temple were present to hear this! Well, she is present, but not within hearing range.

I wait with interest, bending my attention to the UFO door that I have shut. It occurs to me that if the people inside were able to open it they would have done so already, so that part of my plan is proceeding nicely.

By now the tapping chorus is singing a parody of "It's a Small World After All."

The ladies caparisoned as the featured hotels strut their stuff at the front of the UFO, each earning thunderous applause mixed with uproarious hoots.

I lash my tail. With all the fireworks, no one has noticed me. Of course my coloration blends into the black velvet curtain backdrop, but that is no excuse. One would think a modern audience who was forewarned by numerous national touring companies of *CATS!* would be more discerning.

Two actors on the fog-choked ground to whom this UFO has appeared approach our happy, dancing little craft crammed with surprises.

"Ah," says one in a stagy mike-amplified voice reminiscent of the fake Wizard of Oz, "I was right. These are the latest out-of-state investors in Las Vegas."

"And I was right," says his companion. "Elvis is not dead, but kidnapped by aliens. They have cloned him and been performing liposuction at a secret government laboratory under Nellis Air Force Base. See for yourself."

She points with a broad stage gesture. Two chorines stop ball-changing long enough to whisk the UFO door open and proudly stand at attention on either side.

Out pours (and I do mean pours) a plethora of Elvii. They leap to the stage and their knees and begin singing "Heartbreak Hotel."

"I told you the mob is behind the alien takeover," claims the Chamber of Commerce shill on the ground.

Out jump about eight guys in zoot suits and key chains long enough to leash a Bengal Tiger. They begin jiving with the jitterbugging Elvii.

"No," says the second Chamber of Commerce type. "It is G-men."

And out leap the guys in the pin-stripe suits.

By now it is obvious to the audience that the UFO contains an obscene number of individuals, none of them particularly alien to the planet.

They hoot and clap and stomp.

While they are doing so, a spate of masked men squirts out like an afterthought.

There is a moment's silence as the audience wonders if they are regarding the real aliens at last. Can you imagine a gang of crooks popping out of concealment to face the house of a theater filled with several hundred happy show-goers?

The perps stand there gaping and gulping just long enough for the first four Fontana brothers to pop out of confinement. Naturally, in their snappy tuxes they look like a phalanx of Fred Astaires. They leap down to the stage and disarm the robbers before the bad guys even have the wits to know what is happening.

By now the audience is rolling over in their seats and clapping, especially when each Fontana brother puts a crook in custody by the simple method of forcing him to the stage floor and sitting on him.

The Elvii are hip-swiveling, the chorus girls are posing on the ramp and the applause is deafening. These amateur actors do not know quite what to make of the additional cast members, but someone has sternly told them to go on with the show no matter what, so they are dancing and singing as if their lives depended on it. Which they no longer do, thanks to Fontana, Inc.

The most satisfying moment is when Miss Temple Barr pokes her curled red head out of the UFO to observe the scene, particularly the corralled tunnel people. She then eyeballs the audience, expresses shock and is about to dive back in, when something comes caroming out of the wings like a white tornado.

It is Mr. Danny Dove in white duck pants and cotton shirt. He sprints up the ramp to bow into the UFO and extract Miss Temple Barr in spite of herself, who looks quite in costume in her cosmic silver beaded dress.

"Ladies and Gentlemen," Mr. Danny Dove announces over the portable mike in his hand, "the creator of our fabulous finale, Temple Barr."

Miss Temple Barr looks as if she wishes she could levitate to another planet. Her face begins to compete with her hair and the crimson mist for color. She rolls her eyes up at the flies and down at the ramp, but nothing goes away, particularly the clapping, so she finally takes a deep bow and finishes with both hands above her head, in each of which is clasped a shoe with a rhinestone-studded heel, but I imagine from the audience they look like bowling trophies or appropriately alien artifacts.

I choose that precise moment to leap down to the ramp beside her, which causes a burst of fresh laughter. I cannot imagine why, as I have always felt I maintain a dignified demeanor at all times and in all crises.

"Louie!" Miss Temple screeches, forgetting herself and clapping her hands together, only the steel heels ring on each other like iron bells. "I was so worried about where you were."

Unfortunately, all the offstage hullabaloo drowns out the tender moment of our reunion. Leave them wanting more is an old theater maxim, and that is precisely what happens when the curtain comes down.

Only then does Mr. Matt Devine emerge from the UFO. He and Miss Temple Barr confer feverishly with Mr. Danny Dove, who has wisely turned off his mike, while the cast buzzes with confusion and the Fontana brothers ask plaintively when they can get off the floor and their captives.

I am not the center of attention that I should be, given all my accomplishments, but then it is a crowd scene. I notice that Miss Caviar has found her way backstage and is watching me from the wings.

When I leap airily off the UFO ramp to approach her she has one word for me: "Showboaters," she sniffs, "cannot bear to share the spotlight."

"There are no bears here. And all is well," I quote the Bard, always a good port in a storm onstage, "that ends. Period. Especially a Gridiron show."

With my tail as upright as a flagpole, I give up the theatrical life and amble offstage into a mist of crimson fog.

Chapter 41

Midnight Special

They met, as hastily planned, in the Ghost Suite of the Crystal Phoenix at midnight on the dot.

Van von Rhine had broken the house rules—her own—to import a jeroboam of Dom Perignon to the desk. The huge bottle, diapered like a baby in white linen, lay cradled on a crushed-ice bed in a sterling silver bowl. Ranks of crystal champagne flutes surrounded the bowl like a besieging army.

Leaning against the floral wallpaper behind the desk was a framed hand-drawn map of a particularly underpopulated section of the Mojave desert, whose presence Temple had requested.

The Ghost Suite itself was uncharacteristically overpopulated at this pivotal hour between one day and another. The Gridiron show, ended just two hours before, was becoming history.

Besides Nicky and Van, Temple and Matt were there, along with Johnny and Jill Diamond. Eightball O'Rourke had missed the Gridiron but not the mopping-up action afterward. Here, he represented the Glory Hole Gang, the only person present who had actually known the late Jersey Joe Jackson in his corporeal form.

Nine Fontana Brothers fiddled with the forties television set against the wall, fascinated by the ceiling-aimed screen reflected in a pop-up mirror in the cabinet lid. The brothers were of a generation used to in-your-face media exposure, not discreetly indirect images.

Midnight Louie reclined in state on the chartreuse satin love seat. Despite adapting a forelegs-forward pose reminiscent of the disdainful miens (if not the manes) of the Luxor Sphinx and the MGM Grand lion, Louie was not too dignified to refrain from eyeing with disfavor another black feline form lying on the aggressively floral carpet.

Unfortunately, nobody much noted his regal displeasure, so it was largely wasted.

"This oversized bottle of bubbly has 'Las Vegas' written all over it," Nicky was saying as he struggled to wrestle a gigantic cork from the gargantuan bottle.

"What's a jeroboam?" a Fontana brother asked disingenuously.

"Four-fifths of a gallon," Van answered, while her spouse grunted manfully over the cork.

"All right!" came a Fontana, Inc., chorus.

Matt went over to steady the champagne bottle. Conversation, sporadic as it was, stopped, until the show was over. Nicky's forehead sprouted tiny beads of sweat to match the condensation dewing the bottle's green glass sides.

When the cork gave up the ghost, it popped like a Fourth of July firecracker.

Van jumped as if she had *seen* a ghost, and nervously eyed the room.

"Whooee!" Nicky jumped back to avoid a foamy burp that quickly subsided. "Reminds me of delivering a kid. What shall we christen the bouncing baby bottle now that it's open?"

"How about . . . history?" Temple quipped.

"Exactly." Nicky accepted the first delicate flute from his wife's hands and tipped the massive bottle enough to nurse a pale trickle down its crystal throat.

Soon sixteen flutes filled sixteen hands. Van presented Nicky with the last empty flute for filling.

He frowned as he eyed the assembly. "Mine's already on the desk, thanks anyway, Van. I guess you ordered an extra glass."

She shook her champagne-blond head without speaking.

"It's for Midnight Louie?" Nicky asked.

She shook her head again, mysteriously. "Maybe it's for our host."

"Oh." Nicky looked embarrassed as he filled the last flute to the brim.

Van carried it carefully to the small, cabriolet-legged end table between a pair of upholstered chairs, and set it down.

Everyone observed this gesture in silence, either touched . . . or shocked.

"If anything of Jersey Joe Jackson remains, beyond his actual remains," Eightball said out of the wild blue, "that glass won't stay full for long."

"Amen." Nicky lifted his champagne flute. "And now a toast, to—"

"To the Crystal Phoenix's newest entrepreneurial mastermind," Van broke in. "To Temple for envisioning a future Phoenix that will bring our hotel into the twenty-first century via the nineteenth and twentieth. Your underground theme park plans are stunning!"

Temple, regarding the uplifted flutes and faces turned her way, smiled her edgy pleasure. "It's only logical—"

"And," Nicky added, "to Temple for cleverly writing the capture of a gang of crooks into her script so that no breath of scandal will touch the Crystal Phoenix. That could have been *our* cash collection chamber that got knocked over, with the robbers escaping the underground tunnels via the Goliath, and no one the wiser."

"Even Lieutenant Molina couldn't complain this time," Matt added with a smile at Temple.

"Yes." Van frowned in memory. "What did the lieutenant say when she visited you backstage?"

"It wasn't her case, you know," Temple said quickly. "She was just an onlooker like everybody else, although she still does suspect that"—she glanced at Matt—"the dead man in the Phoenix ceiling was a scout for the gang. I'm not so sure—" Temple straightened her shoulders and looked around. "Hurry up and drink; I don't get any until the next toast."

Under the cover of their obedient sips and laughter, Matt walked over to touch glass rims with Temple . . . and to ask a discreet question.

"We need to talk about that . . . dead man. Why do you think that Lieutenant Molina's suspicions aren't history, like this champagne?"

"Because," Temple said under her breath, eyeing the crowd to ensure no one was listening, "Molina came up to congratulate me on the skit . . . and to say that the scheme of setting up the Phoenix as a diversion, the hitting the Goliath smacked of 'stage illusion.' She said that she wouldn't be surprised to see the Mystifying Max come out of that UFO, and maybe he did, in the guise of Midnight Louie! I was supposed to think she was kidding. Molina kid?"

"What did you say?" Matt asked.

"I said the only person left lurking in the UFO was you, and that I doubted you were Max in disguise."

"And?"

"She said, I quote, that she 'would have to look into that interesting theory' since I was such a canny crime-solver, but that she was 'glad I seemed to know the difference.' "

"Merow." Matt winced. "She doesn't let a subject go, does she?"

"Not when he's missing in action. Maybe I should let her think that Max is a shapechanger and that Louie is a magician in pussycat's clothing."

They turned to the lounging cat. His eyes had drowsed almost shut, but a faint green glimmer betrayed the fact that his cat nap was a very light sleep.

"Midnight Louie," Van said fondly, "deserves the next toast."

"Hear, hear!" Johnny Diamond's glass was already raised. "The best surprise entrance I've ever seen. Just when it looked like not even a gnat could exit that clown car of a UFO, Midnight Louie jumps down from the top into the spotlights. An inspired moment."

Eightball added a postscript. "Don't just make a speech, buster. Give the old boy some of that French soda-water. Van, here's an empty ashtray. Jersey Joe wouldn't mind, believe me."

Nicky poured a couple ounces in a big glass ashtray while his brothers watched possessively, then Van bent to place it on the floor near the sofa.

Before Louie could perform the proper preparatory-to-moving ritual: yawning, stretching, examining his nails and rising as slowly as bread dough, Caviar had leaped up to lap the sparkling wine.

Louie pounded to the floor, tail switching. After a feline stare-down, Caviar edged back to let Louie have a sip.

"That cat's been spending a lot of time at the Phoenix," Van said. "Who does it belong to?"

"Me," Matt said, "by default. Caviar's a Humane Society stray Temple brought home from the cat show."

Van regarded Caviar with almost-maternal fondness. "She's like a little, thin, female version of Louie. Seeing her around the hotel has reminded me of Louie, and of my arrival at the Crystal Phoe-nix."

"And of meeting me, no doubt," Nicky put in.

"And your whole family," Van added with a sigh. "Caviar is cute, but I think we should take Temple's cue and rename her Midnight Louise."

Everybody who had not yet heard the name laughed at the idea.

Louie looked up from his champagne with a baleful glare, but Caviar only rolled over on the carpet and stretched luxuriously.

A knock at the door was barely heard over the hilarity, so Temple ran to answer it.

The winsome au pair girl stood there holding Cinnamon, who was swathed in a yellow flannel jumpsuit. "Madame said to bring the infant if she was awake."

"Oh, she's adorable!" Jill Diamond crooned, running to take the baby. "I haven't seen her for a month."

Once on the scene, Cinnamon became the star of the party. Even the brothers gathered around, Ralph asking Van when she was going to have Cinnamon's ears pierced.

"Not until she makes me," Van answered sternly, eyeing Ralph's swinging cannon earbob with disbelief. "Perhaps age fifteen or six-teen."

Cinnamon passed from person to person, gurgling until she began fussing.

"Put her down," Van suggested.

Once on the rug, the baby began practicing her crawl to oohs and aahs of praise. She crawled right over to Midnight Louie and grabbed his tail in one chubby hand.

A sudden gasp stirred the crowd.

Louie edged sideways, twitched his tail free and resumed lapping champagne. Cinnamon watched him for a moment, then spotted

the newly named Midnight Louise. She crawled the two feet between them at top speed, then reached out for the cat.

Midnight Louise sat up and leaned her face toward the baby.

Van edged nervously nearer, the au pair girl behind her.

Cinnamon fell back on the cushion of her diaper, much to her
own surprise, flailing an arm toward the cat. Midnight Louise
sniffed the baby's hand, then stepped closer.

Cat and child were nose to nose, silent and curious. Midnight
Louise delicately sniffed the baby's face, no doubt detecting milk.
Cinnamon turned to gaze up at her mother with an expression of
vacant delight.

"She likes her!" Van said, although who was "she" and who was
"her" remained uncertain. Van turned to Matt, some of that wide-
eyed babyish joy still brightening her expression. "I shouldn't ask
this, but if you got the cat by default—"

"You're welcome to her," Matt said quickly, "if she wants to
stay. I work nights, and I haven't been home much days lately." He
glanced nervously at Temple, as if he had revealed a clue she might
pursue. "It's not fair to the cat."

Van watched cat and baby absorbed in each other, while Midnight Louie finished the last of the champagne. She picked up
Cinnamon and handed her to the nanny. "Enough excitement for
now. It appears that the Crystal Phoenix has a new house kitty, if
Midnight Louise deigns to stay."

"I hope Midnight Louie deigns to come home now that he's the
one and only cat at the Circle Ritz," Temple put in.

Louie, busy cleaning his whiskers, stopped to give her a piercing
look, as if he thought she meant more than she said.

Temple was getting unsettled. Everybody was looking at her like
she was Lieutenant Molina or something, always on the job. Was
she missing something here? Probably a lot, she concluded.

"When will you have a draft of the master plan for the hotel?"
Nicky asked Temple during the conversational lull.

"As soon as I can get all my scattered ideas on paper. It seems
idiotic not to use the tunnels now that we know they're there. And
I have—I hope—a small surprise already."

"The Goliath link will be sealed as soon as possible, of course,"
he said. "Why do you suppose the tunnels' only exit led there?"

"No mystery." Eightball came over to Nicky for a refill of champagne. "You young folks forget that only a few decades ago this was all desert. Ole Jersey Joe probably put the tunnel exit at the edge of his property. When he hit hard times, he began selling off land on the fringes of the Joshua Tree Hotel until all he had left was the hotel grounds. Then he sold that. It just happened that the Goliath was built atop the tunnels' end."

"By the way." Temple lifted her glass. "When we talk about the heroes of the tunnels, I'd like to toast my personal rescue team, Matt Devine and the Fontana brothers, every one."

"Amen," said Eightball, gulping down the exquisite champagne as if it were beer.

The brothers smiled with modest restraint, and Ralph fidgeted with his earring.

"All I did was find a flashlight and follow Midnight Louise," Matt objected.

"Trust a cat to find a new place to hide," Van said.

"Why was that entrance to the tunnel left open anyway?" Matt asked.

Everybody paused to consider. Except Nicky.

"I examined the scene with our security supervisor after the show. The door itself has a heavy metal frame to support the weight of the concrete block facade. When it swings shut, the fit is perfecto; a government inspector couldn't see it."

"It must have been shut all these years," Van added. "What opened it, and who discovered it?"

"All I know is the how," Nicky said. "We found this phoney electrical outlet nearby. If you pry off the cover, you reveal a button that operates a motor inside the tunnel. My security gal says that the costume rack was bolted to the floor recently, so nobody checked it. The robbers must have planned to leave their loot in the tunnel, seal up the entrance from the Goliath as fast as they could, then carry the cash out through the Phoenix in small amounts over time. Those guys were coming and going around here for quite a while setting this scheme up."

"And setting up the disruptions," Van put in, "to focus attention on the Gridiron and the Phoenix so all the suspicion and the police personnel forces would concentrate on us."

"Then they'd slink up from the basement in their own sweet time," Eightball said, "laughing up their sleeves at us the whole while. That's the kind of scheme Jersey Joe would have dreamed up. Almost makes you think the dirty double-crosser is still kicking."

"I hope not!" Van clasped her champagne flute to her chest as if it were fire and she was cold.

Nicky put an arm around her. "No more superstitious hokum. This hotel—and this suite—harbor nothing intangible but history and memories. Hey, Van, I thought the whole idea of holding this party up here was to banish ghosts."

His wife's smile was tremulous. "I know. I want to be big and brave, but when I look at those two black cats and this suite—"

A knocking resonated in the room, startling everyone.

"Just the door," Temple said calmly, going to it. "Who else are you expecting—?"

She opened it in mid-sentence, instantly getting her question answered in 3-D and Technicolor. "Lieutenant Molina. What a surprise. Do come in."

"Miss Barr. Don't mind if I do."

Van von Rhine stepped away from her husband, the picture of a collected hostess. "I'm so glad you had time to drop by, Lieutenant. I didn't know how long that . . . business downstairs would take." She went to the table to collect the untouched glass of champagne.

That's Jersey Joe's, Temple wanted to shout, but didn't. Instead she glanced at Matt, who was watching Molina with the same guarded suspicion that Temple usually had.

"This isn't my case." Molina's smile was purely social as she accepted the champagne and looked around. "What an . . . amazing room. What's the story?"

Awkwardness had settled on the party despite Molina's formal gown and informal question. The brothers Fontana particularly looked like mongeese into whose midst a cobra has suddenly slithered. They began adjusting their tuxedos as if instantly infected with a plague of fleas and ticks.

Temple supposed that there were enough concealed weapons in the room to arm the LVMPD's tactical squad.

Molina, however, did not seem in the mood for police matters. She strolled the room's perimeter like a visitor to an art museum, studying each piece of furniture, the carpet, the blinds, the draperies, with quiet reverence.

"Jersey Joe Jackson's suite," Van explained, pride of possession overcoming fear of another kind of possession. "He was—"

"I know who he was," Molina interrupted in that official way of hers.

"This was his last residence before his death," Van continued without a hitch. "When the hotel was redone, nothing here was touched."

Molina turned with a radiant expression. "Brava! It's wonderful . . . and look at that—" she swept toward the television set, Fontana brothers scattering like ultra-formal bowling pins at her approach "—it's a television set, isn't it? Very early." Molina caressed the lid rim as she stared down into the oval screen. "Fabulous."

Temple was torn between wondering why on earth Van von Rhine had invited a police lieutenant to this informal gathering and pouting because the setting so appealed to Molina. Worse, it enhanced her. Her size and height, her floor-length, crimson vintage gown, the simplicity of her hair and makeup fit the Ghost Suite like an old elbow-length kid glove.

Something touched her arm. She glanced up to find Matt smiling down at her. "The Blue Dahlia looks right at home, doesn't she?"

His reference made her smile too, but Temple couldn't help feeling that this was her night, her skit, her discovery in the tunnels, her friends and her cat to the rescue, her hotel. Molina was stealing some of Temple's stage-thunder, just by being here.

"Frank couldn't come?" Matt asked suddenly.

Molina turned with another one of those disconcertingly serene smiles. "Unlike myself, he was on duty. He had cleanup work to do." She turned to Nicky and Van. "Frank is an FBI man. You'll be happy to know that he thinks the thieves were not local talent. With other states now allowing legal gambling, criminal elements driven out of Las Vegas years ago are making inroads elsewhere. Some not-too-bright factions decided to bring their ambitions here." Molina paused, as if undecided about continuing. "That's one theory. Then again, foreign elements might be backing native hoods; either gangsters or terrorists who need money and Las Vegas has a lot of that."

"Foreign gangsters? Terrorists?" Van grew stern. "What kind?"

Nicky answered. "I think the lieutenant is referring to the Russian mob that has sprung up since the Soviet Union collapsed. Am I right?"

"You're right about the Russian mob, but they were not what I had in mind."

"The Yakuza?" Nicky asked, doubtful.

Van was not reassured by this dialogue. "Russian mobs, terrorists, the, the . . . Jacuzzis. At our little Las Vegas hotel?"

"Don't worry, Mrs. Fontana." Molina was still smiling at Van's original nickname for the Japanese mob. "My own theory involves a much more reassuringly familiar portion of the globe."

"The Middle East?" Van asked tensely.

"More like the North Atlantic," Molina answered cryptically.

Everyone kept blank silence at this perplexing notion, but Temple felt a sudden chill.

"If the masterminds of this scheme are foreigners, how did they know about our tunnels?" Van asked. "Even we had no idea."

"Ah." Molina placed her champagne glass on the linen tablecloth that temporarily covered the desk. She lifted the big, bold, brassy envelope purse she carried and withdrew a large plastic baggie filled with something white.

"They had local assistance. And I do have a teensy bit of relevant evidence with me, in hopes you could help identify it. This was found in the tunnel. It appears to be an architectural plan. I know it's folded, but—"

"The basement floor plans!" Temple came over in high indignation. "This must show the tunnel system. It was missing from the set of plans Van gave me, and I had my own suspicions about where it was. Where did you get it?"

"In the tunnels. We'll have it examined, of course," Molina said, "but it appears to be a copy."

"Can I see it?" Temple asked.

Molina's hesitation was just long enough to be mildly insulting before she handed Temple the plastic bag.

Temple leaned over the desk and held it up to the wall behind it. Despite her high heels, she had to stretch to touch the folded plan to the wallpaper.

"There! Can you see the darker oblong on the wallpaper? That's where Van said a photograph of the desert hung for a long time. This folded section covers about a fourth of it. I think this plan was in the frame. Somehow someone saw it when the frame was disassembled to retrieve Jackson's map to the cache of silver dollars."

"Come to think of it—" Van looked at Nicky with dawning surprise. "There was something on the back of Solitaire's treasure map, but we didn't pay any attention to it."

"Just as I thought. That's why I asked you to bring this." She touched the framed sketch. "Is that the map you had framed?" Temple asked.

Nicky and Van nodded as one, seeing the light.

"Can you take off the paper later and see if it's drawn on the basement plans?" she requested. "I believe that the original plan is still there, but maybe someone else got a copy long ago."

With a shrug, Nicky turned the frame and ripped the brown paper backing off. Inside was a piece of matboard he managed to pull away from one corner with the tip of his car key.

Faint blue lines made patterns like the furrow-scribed Peruvian plains that were supposedly an alien airport. *Voilá!*

Everyone crowded around to see, but Molina was unimpressed. "I said that this was a copy. That's what matters."

"Did Jersey Joe have out-of-state friends or relatives?" Temple asked Eightball.

"Who knows? Jersey Joe was a human fox. He didn't like folks to know who he knew or where he lived, and he liked to have a lot of emergency exits out of everything. I'd guess his relationships were as extensive and hidden as those tunnels. He sure took us Glory Hole Guys for a ride. If we're around, some of his other associates from the old days could be too. Maybe we weren't the only ones looking for his loot."

"Hmm," was Temple's only comment. She was dreaming up twists in the Jersey Joe Jackson theme park again. Everything she learned about the man lent itself to commercialization. And with Jersey Joe dead, it was public domain. What a find!

"Hmmm," Lieutenant Molina echoed in a far more dubious tone.

She collected the evidence from Temple and returned it to her purse, then picked up her champagne glass and toured the room again, savoring its ambiance.

Molina paused before Matt.

"Was the man who fell from the ceiling an associate from Jersey

Joe Jackson's past?" she asked rhetorically, facing only him. "I doubt that, but it's possible. Will we ever know who he was, or why he was killed?" Her head twisted over her shoulder to regard Temple. "Or about the dead man at the Goliath? I can only promise that I will never stop trying to answer those questions."

She moved a step or two to replace the champagne glass on the table where Van had set it. It was still half full.

"Thank you for the inviting me up here," Molina told Van and Nicky. She glanced at Temple, then the others. "A most interesting . . . show."

She glided to the door.

Temple reflected that this was one of probably only two rooms in the whole world in which clunky old Lieutenant Molina would glide like the spider woman.

"You will tell us," Matt said abruptly, stepping forward, "if you find out anything about the dead man. Men."

"*When* I find something out," Molina corrected, "I may have another question or two to ask some of those here. Good night."

In the silence that prevailed like a dropped curtain after she had left, Nicky Fontana shrugged. "I feel like I've just survived the Last Roundup scene in a Charlie Chan movie."

"That is one spooky dame," a Fontana brother suggested. "I mean, police officer."

"Don't mention spooks in this room, please!" Van said with a shudder.

"I suppose the lieutenant has to be cryptic," Matt said, but he didn't look happy about it.

Temple didn't know what to say, except that it was time to return to the Circle Ritz.

She looked at Caviar—Midnight Louise, rather—and found her peeking out from under the chartreuse love seat. Louie still occupied the cushion. Temple sighed. She could hardly force the hero of the hour from his satin-pillowed lap of vintage luxury. Maybe he wanted to be the Phoenix watchcat again, along with his new namesake, Midnight Louise.

Louie himself wasn't talking, but he was watching. Intently. Temple realized that his hair had stiffened into an ebony aura. He was staring askance, as if to inquire "Who goes there?"

Temple followed his absinthe-green stare to Molina's abandoned glass, then looked again, committing a classic double take.

The champagne flute, half full only seconds before, was now utterly empty.

Chapter 42

Templetation

Temple wasn't sure which part of the sight that greeted her when Matt opened his door was more startling: the vision of a docile Midnight Louie in Matt's arms, or Matt's intriguingly bare upper torso that Louie was obscuring all too effectively.

"I called because, after moaning all the way home about Midnight Louie's apparent defection, I figured you would be relieved to know," Matt said. "Not to worry. Apparently, he's come home."

"Why to your place, and not mine?"

Matt scratched Louie under the chin while Temple practically purred. Ah, the advantages of being a cuddly kitty cat.

"Maybe," Matt said, "it was there, and maybe he forgot which floor you were on after his prolonged absence. The bathroom window's still open for Caviar."

"Midnight *Louise*," Temple corrected him. "I think it's kinda cute."

"I wonder if Louie does." Matt regarded the cat, who blinked solemnly at his scrutiny. "He's one Zen dude; we'll never know what he's thinking. Maybe he's here reclaiming territory a foreign cat had tainted, or maybe he just knew I had a particularly rough day."

Matt bent to put Louie on his own four feet again.

"Cats can be comforting, when they want to be," Temple agreed. "You want me to take him back to my place?"

"No." Matt had straightened again and so had his expression.

Temple watched Louie stalk around the sparsely furnished living room, sniffing this and that. She was trying not to feel flustered and failing miserably.

For one thing, she and Matt were both so undressed, and not ready for it. She had rushed up to see Louie barefoot, wearing a terrycloth romper. Matt had obviously been in bed when Louie arrived, and had time to pull on only trousers in honor of her imminent arrival.

Why hadn't he pulled on a t-shirt while he was at it?

Sure, she had seen him in swim trunks by the pool, but that was outdoors and public. This was indoors and . . . intimate.

It didn't help that Matt looked so good without clothes.

Louie jumped on the sofa and began sniffing all the corners, no doubt discerning the traces of his new namesake. Temple wished she could smell motivations as easily.

Matt went over to evict him, then turned back to Temple. "I know it's late, but I thought we needed to talk."

"Sure." Talk was cheap, if nothing else in human relationships was.

Temple edged over to the couch. They both stood awkwardly before it. At night, with the room so bare and the overhead light so bald, Matt's living room felt like an empty bus station, impersonal and chilly.

"Sit down." Matt followed his own advice and sat first.

Temple perched on the adjacent cushion. Lord, she was acting like an idiot!

"I went to the morgue today," Matt began. He laughed at his own opening line. "You're a bad influence. I never used to get involved in such macabre matters. Anyway, I wanted to make sure that the dead man they found at the Phoenix was my stepfather."

"And?" Temple was relieved that things were back to normal and they were discussing less stressful things like bodies and murder, even if the body in question was related to Matt.

He shook his head. "I expected sheet-covered gurneys or stainless steel drawers, like in a horror movie. Instead, they have this 'viewing room,' a cubicle actually. It's about as homey as the visitors' room at the jail. Beige walls and a picture window with a short drape over it. They pull the curtain and the star of the matinee is lying before you, actually several feet below, on a gurney, covered by a sheet to the neck, like he was sleeping. It's the oddest feeling in the world to look down on the dead."

"Especially on someone you knew."

Matt eyed her intently. "That's just it. I don't know if I knew him."

"What do you mean? Wasn't that why you went to the morgue, to settle this once and for all?"

"Yes. But I should have known better. He's escaped me again."

"You mean the corpse isn't Cliff Effinger's? Molina will have a cow."

"Hold on, Molina already knows about this."

"She does? This changes the whole complexion of the Goliath heist."

"No, it doesn't. I said I don't know if it's Effinger. That means I can't tell. I can't identify him."

"Of course you can. This is the man who made you and your mother's life hell for years. How can you forget a face like that?"

"Temple, you don't realize how death changes people, especially their faces. I should have known better. I've anointed the sick at the instant of death, after all. Our faces, our features, they're merely muscular . . . masks. When the attitudes and tensions that form them leave the body, so does the familiarity. In death, the face elongates, and gravity pulls the skin, even the eyes, to the side. It's instant and impressive. Life is gone, as if the Master Puppeteer had loosened all the strings at once. The more the strains of life have distorted the face, the greater the change."

"Gruesome! Most of the dead people I've seen, except for funeral home visitations, have been people I didn't know when they were alive. And all those people on television shows waltz in and identify the body just like that."

"You see my problem? I was so focused on finding Effinger I forgot about morbid transformation. And I haven't seen him for seventeen years. I didn't have a prayer of making a credible identification. Close the curtain and call it quits."

"It's like with Max," Temple said slowly. "You'll never know." Only Matt was facing lost hate, not love.

Matt shrugged. "Maybe that's better. Maybe that's God's punishment for my unforgiving need for vengeance."

"*Max's* disappearance isn't punishment for anything. Maybe God isn't that interested in you. Sorry, is that blasphemy?"

Matt's laugh carried only a touch of rue. "No, that's good old secular reality, and I deserved it. This theological angst of mine must be wearing. I can't stop looking for my stepfather, and if I have to start with a stranger's body, I mean to find out who he was and why he carried Effinger's I.D. I've discovered you can't drop unfinished business. That's why I wanted to talk to you tonight."

Temple waited, still nervous, while Louie prowled the perimeter.

Matt angled himself to face her more directly, so their knees—hers bare, his not—almost touched. His arm lay behind her along the top of the sofa's back cushions. She felt a little surrounded, by his seriousness as much as his position. Now she understood the lack of a shirt. Baring his body was an unconscious metaphor for baring his soul. She wished she had a seatbelt; she had a feeling this was going to be a Bette-Davis-style bumpy ride.

"A lot has happened in the past twenty-four hours, but I realized something," he said, "when I was standing there in that bizarre cubicle yesterday afternoon looking down on that dead body."

"About yourself?"

"That, and about you."

"Oh, great. I better get a different perfume. That's not the sort of ambiance it's supposed to evoke." Temple's fingernail was nervously tapping her teeth before she realized it.

"I know it's macabre, but you're not exactly unconnected with that scene." Matt's smile was self-mocking again. "What I realized is that I've been using my personal crises to avoid you, just the opposite of what I told you, and told myself."

"Yup. That 'Poison' has got to go. And I love the bottle, too."

"You're hiding behind humor again," he accused mildly, "but that's one of your most charming habits."

"Really? You think I'm charming?" Temple was pleased, even if she didn't think she was charming.

"I think more than that. I've been thinking a lot about that night on the desert, a lot about you, about . . . touching you again."

Here it is, Temple thought with despair, her nails picking at the lettuce-edged hem of her shorts, the moment I've been hoping for, and I'm going to sit here paralyzed with pleasure and fear, then say something dumb, or semi-funny, or say nothing at all, which will be the worst thing of all to do. Charming old me.

But this wasn't her scene; Matt was directing this one. She realized suddenly that playing stage manager gave her a sense of control she needed to function. Here, she couldn't be sure where Matt was heading—he wanted her madly; he was giving her up for Lent. This was her big opening night, the possible beginning of a real relationship with Matt, and she had a bad case of stage fright.

"Am I scaring you?" he asked.

Temple shook her head, forced herself to speak. "No. Never. I'm scaring me. I do it all the time."

"Funny. I never noticed. Too busy being me. Temple, I know you've gotten a few clues, but I'm kind of a mess. You're the bravest woman I know, but are you sure you want rush in where even archangels fear to tread?"

"Brave? Me?"

He nodded. "In every way it counts. Mentally, emotionally, spiritually."

"I'm not . . . spiritual."

"I didn't say religious. We're all spiritual, under the skin. And sexual."

Uh-oh.

Matt shifted position on the sofa. Temple tried not to jump. She succeeded.

"Okay," he said.

He was laying all this out very logically, like the good teacher he was. Temple wasn't fooled. Homework was coming due. She listened intently as he went on.

"You have to realize that you're dealing with an overage but classically confused adolescent male. You know the home life I grew up in, the abuse. You don't know how deeply that undermines self-esteem. No matter that my grades were good in school, my behavior preternaturally perfect, that the abuse didn't scar me, that my looks were above average. To me, all that stuff outside the home was a lie. When people said I was smart, or well-behaved or handsome, I didn't believe them, because I knew how I really deserved to be treated no matter what I did or was. I hated their praise. It struck me as phony. My looks I hated worst of all. I wished for zits, buck teeth. I knew that—inside—I was really the ugly picture of Dorian Gray in the attic."

"That's terrible! Horrible. That's like an anorectic, who has what every woman in the world nowadays is brainwashed to desire, supreme slimness, and still sees herself as fat in the mirror when she's skeletal."

"Same issue, different approach. I hated it when girls, even some of the lay teachers at school, started cooing over my looks."

"You became a priest because you didn't believe you were handsome?"

"No, it's more complicated than that. I didn't have a decent role model for sexual relationships. There was the dirty little secret of the violence at home. I was mostly terrified of becoming like him, Cliff Effinger. To me, sex *was* violence. The physical outlet of martial arts let me glimpse the rage beneath my gold-star deportment. I didn't want to risk a sexual involvement, because I might find rage there too. Most of all, I never wanted to have children, never wanted to risk doing what was done to me to someone else."

"People don't usually become what they hate."

"Except in cases of abuse. There are three routes for a child of abuse: become a perpetual victim, become a perpetrator and victimize others; overcome the past and do neither. The last path is the least taken, because the early patterning is so unconscious, so impossible to overcome. I'm right to fear my own rage."

"But you understand the process so well; you help others with it."

"Knowledge isn't everything. I'm still surprising myself. Look at what I did to this place when I heard Effinger might be dead."

Temple looked around the restored but barren room. "You damaged things, not yourself or others."

"Brave new Temple." Matt looked down, then took her hand, the one that was still worrying at her hem. "When I saw you take that in stride, I really got scared."

Oh, Temple thought, this is so mature. This is such important stuff. And, oh, rats, Temple thought again. Maybe Matt is right. Maybe this is too much for me. I'm walking wounded myself.

"So," he said, "the priesthood saved me from the family demons. I could hide from women and children, yet serve them, care for them from a distance. My real father vanished, my 'fake' father was a monster, but the parish priests were my ersatz fathers, and so encouraging of my vocation. By becoming one of them, I could become perfect as my heavenly Father is perfect, to paraphrase the New Testament. No one would think it odd that I avoided sex; it was part of the job description. The priesthood was a great place to hide out, and everybody praised me lavishly for my choice, especially since I was so good-looking, they said. Even that became palatable as long as I didn't use it."

"When did it fall apart?"

"When I grew up, grew more confident in my ability to function in an abuse-free environment. I started analyzing more than my spiritual state of grace, and my outward actions. I found some pretty corrosive, un-Christian buried emotions. By the time I applied to leave, I had built a case that clearly showed misguided motives. That's why celibacy was no problem for me. I'd learned to deflect even the mildest sexual message. A lot of priests are casual nowadays about wearing the collar, but I clung to it. It was my wedding ring to Mother Church; it warned women off."

"And challenged some, I bet, even some Catholic women."

"Teenage girls, and older women. I was the pet of the flower society ladies, who were all over sixty. Still, I kept it harmless. The last thing I was going to do was take advantage of it."

"Poor things," Temple said, thinking of all those starry-eyed women mooning over Father Devine, who was so nice and so handsome and so impossibly unattainable, by vocation and inclination. No, not by inclination, by upbringing.

"I agree. What a waste of everybody's energy, including mine."

"So now what do you do?"

"You asked that at the tacqueria after I administered the anointing to Blandina Tyler, and my answer is still as muddy. I'm trying to settle my anger with the old days. You're right, given my lifelong abstinence and fear, I'm finding celibacy a hard habit to break. It's so safe, isn't it? So removed. I can even feel superior in a secular way, because of AIDS."

"And," Temple added, "your religion looks on most sexual behavior as sinful in some way, as far as I can tell."

"That's another reason I left. I was having a tough time reconciling what some of my parishioners did—good people trying to lead decent lives—with the letter of church law. American priests have a particularly hard time with that; that's why we're called liberal."

"So you still don't know what you'll do?"

"No."

And he was still holding Temple's hand, which she was holding motionless. In fact, she was holding her entire body and mind in a state of suspended animation.

"No," Matt repeated, looking her hard in the eyes, "but now I at least know what I *want* to do."

Temple tried not to swallow, which was so obvious. "What?" she asked softly in a voice as hoarse as if she had laryngitis.

He answered with another question. "Would you ever consider . . . I'm not used to all these euphemisms . . . sleeping with me, making love?"

"That's easy. I have considered it. Often." Temple saw more in his eyes than the surface question. "But whether I would actually do it would depend."

"On what?"

"On what's going on with you, and with me, and with us."

"You wouldn't have to be married . . . ?"

She shook her head. "I never have been. I've had hopes. Especially with Max. I made it out of high school a virgin, and was most disappointed about that. I mean, it wasn't the done thing, even for Midwestern girls, who are a bit socially retarded. There was a guy my freshmen year in college. We were both desperate to become worldly wise, and didn't have much chance of that with each other. But we liked one another and accomplished the landmark initiation without any trauma. I had a solid but unexciting long-term relationship with a man in Minneapolis, before we agreed to split. Then along came Max."

Matt lifted her hand, kissed the top of it.

Temple's suspended animation melted like milk chocolate in a hot saucepan.

"Max was your Real Thing," he said, gently prodding the past out of her, as she had nudged it out of him.

"So I thought. I mean, he swept into the Guthrie for a weekend stand and he swept me off my feet—literally—and out of there so fast it made my whole family's heads spin. It was so flattering, and exciting, and, God knows, I was in a rut there. But when you're dropped to ground after that kind of rush, the downfall is brutal."

Matt kissed her hand again. His brown eyes were warm with empathy and understanding and the intense fascination of dawning infatuation. No one had seen him look like this, Temple thought. No one but her.

"That's my problem," she said. "You're not the only one with a conscience."

"You'd think I was," he broke in with the self-deprecating humor that was surfacing nowadays.

"You see, Matt, I've been kind of mad at myself for being attracted to you from the first. I thought maybe I was being shallow, reacting just to surface, or I was on the rebound from Max. And I felt guilty, like I was married to Max, and shouldn't be looking at another man so soon. But I've been looking, oh yes, and kicking myself, which is really punishing, considering my high-heel collection. And now that I know more about you, I can also worry if I'm interested because you're sexually inexperienced, and I can be in control, which is ego-building after the Max let-down, and if it's fair to follow up on my inclinations."

He frowned. "Relationships are hell, aren't they?"

Temple laughed. "You got that right. At best, we're all hoping to be honest and trying to be true. But we're only human."

"So," he said, "you haven't answered my major question."

"Women aren't used to saying these things first. It's more flattering that way. But, speaking from raw instinct, without letting scruples get in the way, yes, I'd sleep with you, especially if it didn't involve much sleeping. Besides, I feel an obligation."

He looked shocked for the first time during this rather shocking conversation. "Obligation?"

"Now that I know so much about you, I feel it's my duty to ease you into the real world. I wouldn't want you getting hurt by some-body else."

"I'm an act of charity? I don't think I'm flattered."

"Then we're even," Temple said.

"This is . . . hypothetical," he added. "I don't honestly know how I'll react to the pressure of an intimate adult relationship. The intensity of the feelings, the sensations, scare me sometimes."

"Yup. Typical adolescent male. Tell you what." Temple gently withdrew her hand from his.

Matt looked worried. He should. She was having another one of her bright ideas.

"Why don't we zip back into our handy-dandy time machine and go back to post-prom night. It's the last summer before we go off to college and nobody in the world is bothering us. But we're a couple of square kids from Podunk and we do have a few primitive rules. Just necking, no petting. Just nice romantic kissy-face, which girls are crazy about anyway, so you want to learn it right for the future anyway, and we have all summer to practice."

"Won't that be . . . hard on you?"

"It should be hard on you, and then some. But it's been done before and hasn't hurt anyone. This is the nineties. Fools don't rush in like they used to, and, besides, getting there is all the fun. Believe me."

Temple finally fulfilled one of her favorite fantasies. She edged closer and put her arms around Matt's neck, gazing deeply and playfully into his eyes. She wet her forefinger and ran it smoothly over his lips, upper, then lower.

"I promise," she swore tenderly in the instant before their mouths met, "to be gentle."

Chapter 43

Mass Approval

Temple awoke Sunday morning Scarlett-O'Hara style.

First she blinked at the creamy white ceiling dappled in morning light, aware of surfacing from a long, dreamless, restful sleep.

Second, she slowly absorbed where she was—safe in her own bed . . . as her mind dredged up memories of where she had been before this.

Her eyes fixed with fuzzy focus on the glittering clutter atop her dresser, then sharpened with returning memory. Oh, yes . . . Oh . . . my. All right!

Her mind backed up to replay surprising or particularly memorable moments. She was smiling. And giggling. And her toes were wriggling under the summerweight blanket.

Only then did Temple realize that a movie camera mounted on the ceiling would capture a fairly good replay of a famous scene from *Gone With the Wind*: the one when Scarlett wakes up the morning after Rhett had stormed up the crimson-carpeted staircase with her in his arms.

No staircase. No crimson carpet. No Clark Gable. Best of all, no overtones of overriding anybody's inclinations. Otherwise, Temple decided with a luxurious yawn and stretch, her own personal scenario from the previous evening was definitely movie material.

An annoyed growl interrupted Temple's state of lazy satisfaction. She peered over the rim of her covers to see the black blur that was Midnight Louie waddling across hummocks of blanket, head lowered and green eyes angled at a possessive slant.

Temple's inconsiderate stretch had dislodged him from a comfy position at her feet.

Unrepentant, she pushed her feet into the spot he had vacated, now toasty warm. Lazily, Temple watched him resettle on the other side of the bed, which was virgin territory, being unoccupied.

She frowned. Louie would not take kindly to additional bedpartners, not that any were imminent. Yet. Perhaps he had become a bit spoiled.

At the moment he was lounging on his side, fanning formidable claws as if to remind her of their recent usefulness on her behalf.

She sat up and leaned near to bring the big cat into focus. She admired the black velvet sheen of his forelegs, the almost steely pearl-gray-and-pink gleam of his talons as his cherry-red tongue darted between them to wash between his toes.

"You aren't the king of the queen-size mattress, Louie," she reminded him. "You are a guest, not a host. You happen to have hit me between engagements, but that doesn't mean that I intend to sleep alone for the rest of my natural life."

He looked up from his industrious grooming, the round green eyes staring at her as if to say, *You are not "alone" when I am here.*

She held her tongue. After Louie's heroic role last night at the Crystal Phoenix, he didn't deserve being reminded of life's cold realities.

Temple stretched again, restraining herself so the covers were not unduly agitated on Louie's side of the bed.

Honestly! Who ran this joint? Her, or the cat?

The bedside phone caroled as if in answer, an affirmative to the last alternative.

Temple squinted at the clock's red rectilinear numbers formed from dotted lines. She couldn't quite decipher these segmented numbers without her glasses, which were probably enthroned on the bathroom sink atop a pile of cotton balls bearing what was left of her makeup. Still, the numbers' vague, fiery configuration suggested that it was damnably early on a Sunday for anyone to call. Unless . . .

She snatched the red shoe phone from the table.

"Hello," she said.

"Hello," he said.

Amazing what such simple syllables could convey all by themselves. Temple's Scarlett smile revived as she snuggled down in the pillow with the phone.

"Did I wake you?" Matt asked, perfectly polite and patently anxious.

"Not at all."

"I . . ."

Mornings after were always awkward for all but the seriously jaded, Temple reflected. She stir-fried her brain looking for the just-right thing to say and help him out.

Before she could do more than lightly sauté her little gray cells, Matt went on without her.

"I wonder if you'd be interested in going somewhere with me today."

Temple wound the coiled red phone cord around her forefinger, speculating on their destination. "What did you have in mind?"

"Actually, I just remembered that I promised someone . . . Sister Seraphina at Our Lady of Guadalupe. Would you go to mass with me this morning?"

Mass. Temple blinked and wished she had her glasses on so she could see the ramifications more clearly. Church was not the destination with which she had been stoking her always suggestible (and now seriously sensual) mind. Not exactly . . . romantic. In fact, a Catholic mass was rather scary to one of her cheerfully agnostic temperament.

"What time is it?" she asked while whipping her errant thoughts into a totally unforeseen direction.

Was he guilty about last night? Did he need to make a pilgrimage of penance to the nearest R.C. church? Last night had been decidedly pleasant and even promisingly steamy, but hardly anything a reasonable adult would feel compelled to disown. Except . . .

"I did wake you," Matt was saying contritely. Or maybe he wasn't saying it contritely; maybe Temple was coloring his simplest statements with the lurid crimson haze of her own anxiety.

"No, I just don't have my glasses on," she said, fussing. And a good thing she hadn't had them on last night, speaking of steamy.

"Eight forty-five." He told her the time with as much emotion as a hotel wakeup computer voice.

"And what time is mass?"

"Ten o'clock is the next one."

"Holy . . . hallelujahs, we've got to get moving. Or I do. Matt, isn't this awful short notice?

"I forgot about it with all the excitement last night." A pause escalated the awkwardness. "The crisis at the Gridiron," he finally clarified. "I had promised Sister Seraphina that I'd attend Mass at OLG this morning."

"This is important to you, isn't it?"

Another pause, not nearly so awkward, merely thoughtful. "It's been hard for me to go, yes. Hard to see myself in a different role. Naturally Sister Superfine tuned in on that. She's right. I have to confront it."

"Are you sure that you want to go with me?"

"Yes."

"Even though I don't know much about mass?"

"Yes."

"Sure, I'll go. Um, do I need a mantilla or something?"

"No! Temple, that's ancient stuff. Women haven't had to wear head coverings in church since the Church modernized in the late sixties."

"Too bad. I've always wanted to wear a mantilla. So dramatic."

"You can wear one if you want to."

"No, I can't. I don't have one."

"You sound nervous. Maybe you don't want to go."

"Yes, I do. And, hey, you sound even more nervous than I do."

"Then I'll need the support. I'll meet you downstairs at nine-thirty, okay?"

"Okay," she repeated, not at all sure of that.

Matt hung up, thinking about Temple, not the imminent mass. As usual, she had read him right. He *was* nervous. How much did she have to do with it?

Did he need a buffer between himself and the church now? Temple's presence, as a non-Catholic, might help him view the sacrament of mass with some distance. Since leaving the priesthood, he had found himself reluctant to attend. Was that the result of guilt, or envy?

One thing he knew: how hard it was to watch other men perform the rituals learned by heart and soul so long ago. At the masses he had attended since leaving, he seemed to view the rite through the wrong end of a telescope, as if he were standing at the church door watching a distant puppet show. Attending mass only emphasized his unique and separate status.

So maybe he wanted Temple there as a partner in crime. After all, now he had "last night" to fret about. Despite himself, he felt the same overscrupulous sense of guilt and edgy self-justification he had suffered in high school about confessing sexual sins. Not that he had allowed himself many of those, but thoughts would come and demand to be classified as "impure" or not. Feelings came as well, and nocturnal emissions. They were all examined, agonized over, omitted from the confessional roster, then rejudged in harsher terms and presented with shame and self-disgust.

A few Hail Marys and Our Fathers usually sufficed to erase the errors, but Matt always felt that he had been lucky, that he had gotten off too lightly. In the triumph of time, he had erected such a barrier to these bitter failings that they seldom occurred.

Now the curtain of the temple—Matt winced at the aptness of that expression under the circumstance—had been ripped away, and then some.

Nothing . . . confessable, he devoutly hoped. He was so inexperienced, so armored against all sexuality, that he wasn't sure. One thing he was sure of: he was "free" now. Free to marry. Free to make the same impulsive mistakes other men did, free to take comfort in another's trust and tenderness. Free to reach out and touch someone, and call it wonder instead of weakness.

He was an ordinary mortal who had discovered that mutual compassion was the royal road to passion. Still the ancient anxieties stalked his mind, nipping relentlessly at every thought, every feeling, instilling savage terror. Would God strike him down if he received communion without confession? Last night he had violated the inner litany of no's he had obeyed—and hidden behind—since high school.

He knew that he must walk away from that ancient road in the name of mental health and healing, but old habits die hard, especially when being hard on oneself has become the strongest habit of all.

Matt smiled and stared almost fondly at his ugly old phone. He was lucky to have someone willing to walk new roads with him.

Temple was waiting in the lobby when the elevator cranked him down. She looked like a Sunday school kid in her beige linen short-sleeved suit, with matching pumps and a purse that wasn't the size of Communist China.

Matt was almost disappointed not to see white, wrist-length gloves on her hands, but the signature fingernails were uncovered, lacquered in a red as vivid as her unsuppressible hair.

"You're dressing the part," he suggested as they walked into the early morning warmth.

"Dressing what I think is the part. I still wish I had a cream lace mantilla." Her fingernails unconsciously both fluffed and poked at her curls. "I guess I'm not the Spanish type."

"What is your nationality?"

"Oh, bits of everything—English, Scots, French."

"Good Lord, your ancestors got around."

She shrugged. "And you?"

He shook his head. "Half Polish, and reared all Polish. What my . . . real father was I don't know. Mom didn't want to talk about him."

"Devine. It could be French: de Vine. Or Celtic."

"Whatever its derivation, it was always a pain to explain. I stood out like a sore thumb at St. Stanislaus School, and later—"

"I'll drive," Temple said as they arrived at her car.

She unlocked the driver's door, then leaned across the seat to unlock his door, before donning her prescription sunglasses.

The car started eagerly and once she got it in motion, she smiled at him. "And later . . . I bet you had a hard time living it down. No matter what role you played, that name was just too perfect."

He nodded. "Maybe. But I didn't mind it as much as you might think, the teasing. At least it wasn't 'Effinger.' "

Matt rolled down the window, since Temple hadn't put on the air conditioner. He decided not to tell her his new resolve: to pursue the enigma of the corpse that might be Effinger until every question was answered. A soothing breeze wafted into the car.

Temple's casual presence took an edge off the Sunday obligation, made him feel part of an audience, rather than a performer.

Her easy resumption of their ordinary day-to-day relationship released any clinging guilt. Life was a usually predictable, placid river with places to go; its whitewater patches were intermittent intensities—crises, pain, passion.

As they drove onto the school playground that functioned as a church parking lot, Matt studied the families trickling up the shallow stairs through the big wooden double doors of Our Lady of Guadalupe. He noticed the nuns greeting parishioners at the door, and felt self-conscious suddenly about being with Temple. How would Sister Seraphina construe this? As defiance, bringing a non-Catholic woman? As loudly and clearly announcing his ex-priest status to her?

"How nice to see you again, dear," she cooed at Temple when they had made their way to the top of the stairs.

Sister Superfine cooing?

Temple seemed to think nothing of it, she merely glanced with what she thought was surreptitious speed at the nuns' bare, grizzled heads.

"Matt." Sister Seraphina took his hand in her own cracked aged one. She squeezed, hard. "Good to see you here."

He breathed easily once past the gantlet of nuns at the gate, but Temple suddenly pressed his forearm, her longish nails biting into his skin.

"Oh, God. I mean, excuse me. Molina!" she whispered in throaty despair. "Does she always go to *this* mass?"

"I don't know." The homicide lieutenant was entering by a side door with her daughter, who was wearing jeans, t-shirt and a defiant expression.

Matt paused by the Holy Water font to touch his fingertips to the cool sponge and make the sign of the cross.

Temple waited, but eyed the yellow sponge stranded in its grandiose stainless-steel-lined white marble bowl as if it were something dead washed up on a beach.

He leaned down to her, automatically whispering in church. "These old Holy Water fonts were once filled with blessed water, but since the trick with the red dye, I think Father Hernandez capitulated to modern times and converted to a Holy-Water soaked sponge. It's less messy and more economical.''

"And it discourages pranksters," she added, nervously eyeing the impressive width and length of the central aisle.

For a split second he saw the familiar sight of a church interior through a stranger's eyes. The ranked pews gleaming with golden oak polish, the elaborately carved and plastered altarpiece, the altar, the hanging vigil light beaming its red greeting. He had always found this scene awesome, inspiring and calming, especially when the deep-throated chords of an organ swelled to fill every crevice and linger among each bit of holy bric-a-brac.

Temple teetered on her modest heels and bit her lip. Matt took her elbow and steered her behind the last row of pews, to a side aisle. Halfway down, he gestured her into one of the pews.

She slid in and sat quickly, looking around. "I'd have felt like a Miss America candidate or something worse—maybe a bride—going down that big aisle," she confided in the accepted whisper.

"Nobody's looking at anybody," he whispered back.

"Oh, yeah? Molina is giving us the Big Eye, or didn't you notice?"

Matt glanced around until he spotted the lieutenant and her daughter across the aisle. If she had been watching them, she wasn't now.

Matt pulled two paperback missalettes from the rack on the pew-back before them and handed Temple one. The corners were curled from previous use. They seemed so disposable, compared to the black leatherette-bound missals of his mother's day.

"Is there a lot of kneeling?" she asked anxiously. "I'm not good at kneeling—bony knees."

"You can always sit instead, and you should have seen the old days, at the Latin mass they held at St. Stan's. But the kneelers are padded, see."

She dubiously eyed the folded kneelers.

Then a small bell rang and the altar boys were entering—Matt winced, knowing few Catholics would be able to regard them with as innocent an eye now that several scandals had surfaced.

Everyone stood at Father Hernandez's entrance—why did he keep couching every action in the terms of a play? Matt wondered—

and Temple followed suit, playing her part like a diligent bit player.

Matt was suddenly glad for his instincts and her presence. She was the cautious stranger in his world now, as he had been in hers last night. Each had their uncertainties and strengths.

And then the ritual began, the words and actions that were as automatic as breathing, and Matt was watching, listening, thinking, partaking, released from being any more than what he was now, what he might become later.

Beside him, Temple read along and recited where the missal called for it; she sat and stood and—when called for—watched him flip down the kneeler and then settled upon it so gingerly that he almost laughed out loud.

Before Matt knew it, the central sacred part was unfolding as Father Hernandez held up the chalice and the Host. And he was able to watch, to participate in a passive sense where once it had been active. And, thanks to Frank Bucek, he felt his heart lighten and pride for Father Hernandez suffice this moment, a pride for himself that he had answered the ugly question without creating any more unnecessary ugliness. Like Christ, Father Hernandez had been falsely accused. Unlike the Savior, he had been privately found innocent and spared the public trial and crucifixion. Innocence is often hard to prove in life, Matt thought, and one's own innocence is the most ambiguous of all, but this case was closed. And, Matt knew, he would never have been able to act, to ask, had he not seen Temple refuse to leave unanswered questions lie like sleeping dogs.

So he saw it as a serendipitous circle: himself and his new life, the anguish of his old life, Temple a key opening locked doors in both. By Communion time to hesitate seemed craven, even insulting to everything and everyone he cared about.

Matt edged past a sitting Temple to the central aisle, where he jointed the two parallel lines shuffling over the rough tiles to Father Hernandez.

When his turn came and the priest placed the bland white circle of faith in his palm, saying, "The body of Christ," Matt looked into his raven-dark eyes without guilt or reserve.

He saw joy teetering on the brink of tears. Father Hernandez had never stood on the sacristy steps to judge Matt, but indeed had felt judged himself all during the terrible time at Our Lady of Guadalupe.

Seeing Matt before him, taking Communion, told the priest that Matt did not judge him and find him wanting. Matt did not see him as a priest who had buckled in the face of enormous pressure, nor as one possibly guilty of unspeakable sin, as charged by the bitter Peter Burns.

Matt knew all of Father Hernandez's secrets and could keep them in good conscience.

He returned to his place beside Temple in a daze, blessed with relief. He knelt, his face in his hands, in prayer.

Then this part was over. When Father Hernandez faced the congregation and instructed them to exchange the Kiss of Peace, Matt found himself shaking hands with people behind and forward. Temple did likewise, handling this assignment like the crack PR lady she was.

Finally there was no one to greet but the one in the same pew. Matt turned to her last, taking her hand, then bending to kiss her mouth.

He could feel her hand tense at the kiss, a quick, caring gesture. As he drew away, he saw she was terribly pleased.

Suddenly self-conscious, he glanced around for Sister Seraphina. Instead, he found himself exchanging glances with an unknown woman—well-groomed, her hair both silver by age and gilded by frosting, perhaps fifty-something. She was watching him with the look he had always surprised on women's faces, one of speculation, distance and unsettling ache.

Matt, feeling naked, wanted to look away. He had always looked away. Then, caught up in the moment, the mass, he smiled at her instead. For a moment her face was blank, confused. Then she returned his smile, sheepishly, shyly, as if to mouth that catch phrase of women in department stores, "just looking." The unspoken admission liberated him. Perhaps he had misinterpreted the women's eyes and smiles all the time. Perhaps it wasn't his looks they admired, making him feel phony and unworthy, but his instincts, his warmth. Perhaps they saw unlived life in him, and wanted to call it forth.

He glanced at Temple, who was pretending to concentrate on her paper prayerbook, but smothering a smile. She had seen the byplay and she wasn't threatened. In fact, she approved.

Matt realized such looks might not be invasive and judgmental, but wistful expressions of an other person's warmth or joy, or seeming self-possession.

Now that he had experienced this Kiss of Peace in the congregation, he pitied the priest in his lonely role at the forefront, the instructor who urged acknowledgement on others, but always held himself apart.

Matt felt the shards of his guarded, stainless-steel inner self drawing together as by a magnet. He felt a cooling inner bath, as if immersed in an immaterial font.

Like Father Hernandez, his swell of self-acceptance put him on the brink of tears. Instead of the altar boys, he saw his former self carrying the tall candelabra. The small boy from that house of shouts and sudden crashes, whose inner mantra was "I will never cry, never."

Matt had never before seen it as so adult to cry. He didn't know whether this moment's epiphany was a symptom of a fresh peace with the past, with his new role in his religion, or of falling in love with Temple, or something as simple as falling in love with life, with being alive in ways he had never allowed himself to be before.

He would need time to decide, to deal with these galloping new emotions and insights.

He and Temple filed out with the shuffling crowd, silent. He slipped past the clogged line waiting to greet Father Rafe afterwards; he was too overcharged to trust himself. Leaving church always meant a plunge into the bright of daylight. Here in Las Vegas, the sun was even more shocking, almost blinding as it bathed the pale buildings. The eyes hurt for a second, and he wanted to reach for sunglasses.

He waited for a moment, hoping the welling tears in his eyes would mimic a response to strong sunlight, but also not anxious to shield himself from too much illumination. He had done that for far too long.

"Father Hernandez seemed uncharacteristically upbeat at the . . . end," Temple was saying, digging in her tiny purse for sunglasses. Like all redheads with blue-gray eyes, she was sun-sensitive.

"I imagine he's relieved to have the parish troubles pretty much over." Matt was conscious of speaking on two levels. He took Temple's arm to guide her down the shallow front steps as she concentrated on searching her bag. "Let's go to breakfast."

"Great."

"How about that tacqueria—Fernando's?"

Temple stopped. "I don't know. . . ."

"Isn't it open on Sunday?

"Sure, I suppose so."

Matt was conscious of people streaming around them as they paused, chattering of family plans and food. He'd never been part of this exodus before, had always stayed behind, disrobing, putting away the artifacts of faith, thinking about his Sunday schedule of visits and duties and paperwork.

He felt as free as a schoolboy now, but Temple was looking oddly hesitant.

"Don't you want to eat out?" he asked.

"Yes, but Matt—isn't that hot Mexican food kind of hard on the mouth?"

What was she talking about, she had dived right into Fernando's hottest the last time? Then. . . .

Matt discovered that despite his recent epiphany of self-acceptance, spiritual release and preceding sexual sophistication, his ears felt hotter than Fernando's green chili sauce.

He started fumbling for his sunglasses too.

Chapter 44

Maximum Impact

Temple returned to her condo humming the only song from the service that she had recognized, "Today While the Blossoms Still Cling to the Vine."

She unlocked the door and welcomed the familiar quiet, broken only by the eternal hum of her air conditioner.

Today the hum was amplified, for who sprawled like a sultan on the ivory sofa but His Majesty, Midnight Louie in purrson?

"You look proud of a job well done," she told the cat, opening the French doors across the room to let a butter-warm oblong of sunlight spill onto the walnut parquet floor.

She stepped onto the patio for a moment, standing in the shade of the overhang, taking approving inventory of the wooden tubs of cheerful blooming oleander and her white wrought-iron café table and chairs. A perfect place for breakfast for two. The air was cool, and the afternoon still new enough for her to enjoy it. She reluctantly returned inside to sit beside Louie, careful not to make the cushions jiggle, and stroked his side.

Louie's big black head lifted. He allowed his ever-vigilant eyes to slit half-shut in tribute to the tranquility of home, sweet home. Temple continued to stroke the solid, soft-furred body as Louie's purr escalated to the level of a Hoover vacuum cleaner.

"Looks like your wandering days are over for now," Temple said. "About time. For a while, I wondered if you were running out on me permanently."

Louie's eyes shut completely as he twisted his face to permit Temple to scratch his chin a little lower and to the left.

He looked almost as contented as she felt.

She sat in the quiet of her rooms, full as a tick on IHOP lingen-berry pancakes with whipped butter, taking inventory.

Mass had not been as alien as she had dreaded. It was even rather inspiring, with the organ music, hymn-singing and sunlight seeping through the jeweled kaleidoscope of Our Lady of Guadalupe's stained glass windows. Best of all was the sense that Matt had crossed some threshold in accepting his new life that morning, and that he had invited her to partake in that transition.

He and Father Hernandez had also crossed some barrier between them, Temple suspected, one that had affected both men with a contagious sense of celebration.

She herself had plenty to celebrate, Temple decided. She kicked off her church-going beige medium heels, letting her stocking-clad toes explore the grass-long fibers of the synthetic white goat-hair rug under the coffee table.

Louie was back. Matt was coming back from the wrong road a harsh childhood had set him upon. Temple's work was rip-roaring on two fronts, what with her expanded ideas for the Jersey Joe Jackson attraction at the Crystal Phoenix and Spuds Lonnigan's place on Lake Mead.

Temple slumped against the big, soft sofa pillows and almost purred audibly to keep Midnight Louie company. He leaned against her hip and flipped his big tail over one leg, where it twitched now and then.

And, Temple thought with a lamentable lack of charity given her recent church attendance, Crawford Buchanan had been utterly, publicly, deliciously foiled in his scheme to hog the Gridiron and humiliate her. Talk about turning the tables on someone! Little did he know it . . . yet, but Crawford had suffered his defeat under the spot-lit glare of an entire closing number. Even the showgirls were snickering at his cowardice in not showing up, the deepest cut of all for a self-proclaimed ladies' man like Buchanan.

Life is good, Temple thought, studying Louie's expression of utter satisfaction, and sharing the feeling.

Life is simple. Life is . . . open to anything.

The baddies who were sabotaging the Phoenix in hopes of pulling off a spectacular heist had been spectacularly exposed and corralled. The crowd's applause had voted Danny Dove's first Gridiron the best ever. Everyone obviously loooooved Temple's put-upon skit, even with inadvertent last-minute additions, and Louie had merited another mug shot for the newspapers.

Temple yawned, then rose, giving Louie a farewell pat.

She picked up her shoes and skated into the bedroom on slick, stocking feet. Matt wanted to catch up on her martial art lessons, and she supposed turnabout was fair play. *She* had been doing all the tutoring lately.

She frowned as she changed into the shapeless set of sheeting called a gi. He was also nagging her about not giving up on group therapy, rightfully deducing—what a Sherlock he was becoming!—that she had missed several sessions.

Group therapy! Temple padded barefoot into the living room to dig her doorkey out of what had instantly become her Sunday, going-to-church handbag, a pale straw clutch purse buried in her closet for months until today.

She didn't need group therapy (although she had no objection to one-on-one sessions of the proper kind), not with everything in her life falling so neatly into place. Even Lieutenant Molina had treated her with an air of resigned collaboration last night instead of the usual official exasperation.

Let's see, Temple thought, eyeing Louie's impressive suburban sprawl on her couch, particularly in the southern region, i.e., the stomach. She had her key, gi and what else did she need . . . ?

She blinked at the white-hot daylight filling the open French doors to the patio. Better shut them, just in case. And . . .

Sunglasses.

They weren't in the uselessly tiny purse. She tossed it on the sofa and removed her watch. Oh, no—only a minute to meet Matt down by the pool.

Where had she left her sunglasses? Imagine, heading off the biggest heist planned in Las Vegas for years only the night before, then misplacing her sunglasses in her own place the morning after. Not that a lot of intervening byplay hadn't happened to addle her brain. Still . . .

Temple put her hands on her hips. "All right, come out, come out, wherever you are, with your earpieces up."

Nowhere in the white serenity of her living room did she spot a telltale blob of red-and-gray. The bedroom? No, she never would have taken them in there.

"Okay, Louie, 'fess up. Where did you hide my sunglasses? Did you knock them under the sofa?"

She bent to lift the sofa skirt. Three dust bunnies, a lipstick and a TV schedule from . . . four months ago. Uh-oh, hadn't been cleaning like a whirling dervish lately.

Temple huffed back to her feet. "Where are they?"

"Try the patio," a deep voice suggested in a silky purr.

Temple glanced suspiciously at Louie. He could talk now? Boy, was she in trouble!

No, Louie could *not* talk now, or ever.

Temple realized that the sun had passed behind a cloud; the bright day beating at her open French doors had suddenly dimmed.

She looked up.

A silhouette filled the door frame, from bottom almost to the top.

"Do you mean these?" the same voice asked, not Louie's at all, but not unfamiliar at all either, now that it was at close range.

Midnight Louie wasn't the only one who had deigned to come back.

Into the living room, wearing aviator-style mirror shades and a Hawaiian shirt, walked Max Kinsella, holding out Temple's misplaced sunglasses.

Midnight Louie Washes His Paws

Ordinarily, I have the last word. (Or the next-to-last word. My overeager "editor" insists on exerting her "topping" privileges.)

For the first time, however, I have virtually nothing to communicate.

I am naturally, dear readers, as shocked and startled as you by the terminal turn of events to this latest adventure of mine.

I have no idea why this Max character has chosen to reappear, or why he should be allowed to do it when I am the Hero of the Hour and having a nice private pet with my devoted roommate, Miss Temple Barr.

As for Mr. Max Kinsella's chosen attire, I can only say that I am shocked to my soul by the tackiness of his ensemble. I had hoped that Miss Temple had better taste than that. Hawaiian shirts belong on Hawaiians, and that is all, unless they suit for cleaning rags.

I have always found an elegant, understated look sufficient in my own attire, to the point where I am accused of wearing a "uniform." You will not catch me bounding about in day-glo collars (an odious invention to begin with).

As for the impact on this sudden return on the lives and times of those around me, I cannot bear to speculate.

It has been brought home to me (excuse the expression) during my ramblings recently that relationships are less easy to sever than one might think. I find myself now caught in the common Yuppie trap. In my middle years, when I should be enjoying the fruits of my labor by resting as much as I can, I am pincered between the needs and wants of two generations—that of my forebear father and my apparent sprightly offspring. As for my vaunted sire, I do not consider Three O'Clock Louie too obnoxious a parent, as long as he keeps his distance and his nose and mitts out of my territory, which is Greater Las Vegas. I will cede him the environs of Temple Bar. But Temple Barr (note the double "r") and surroundings are my exclusive territory and that goes for trespassing dudes of the human species as well.

Then there is the matter of the personage now going by the moniker of "Midnight Louise." I am not amused.

I cannot single-handedly stop the deluded and doting individuals at the Crystal Phoenix from abasing themselves at the paws of this more than somewhat pushy pussycat. Nor can I prevent her from claiming, and others from conferring, the too-close-for-comfort name of Midnight Louise.

But I do not have to like this blatant upstart's greedy ways with my former territory and even my identity.

Now a trespasser of another sort is offending the atmosphere of my own home with a shirt that looks like it was cut from one of Electra Lark's muumuus. I had intended to enlighten my many fans on the fine points of the preceding adventure, to impart the inside tidbit and share the intricate deductions of my convoluted mind that led to another Midnight rescue.

However, I am too distraught at the present time to dissect the deductive process.

The deduction I am mulling at the moment is that Miss Temple Barr is about to get a good taste of what it is like to have voices, faces and inquiring minds from the past sticking their long-gone noses into her current affairs and associations.

I doubt that she will be any happier at the prospect than I am, but it is only fitting that roommates share even this cross to bear.

Carole Nelson Douglas
Wipes Her Hands
of the Whole Affair

As annoyed as Midnight Louie is by certain last-minute develop-ments, I suppose it could be worse. I could, for instance, be re-sponding to his usual end-of-the-tail venom. I am confident that he will recover from his shock in due time and will have much more to say about the Mystifying Max *et al.* in a later volume.

I also refuse to be drawn again into a pointless exchange of rhetoric with Louie. Sometimes in their careers writers find them-selves collaborating with colorful but unlettered individuals who try to run away with most of the credit.

All too often my brief opportunity to share professional con-cerns and techniques with readers has been short-circuited by Louie's caustic comments. So I'd like to take this opportunity to answer a common question: "How much in your books is real?"

Aside from the inescapable contributions of Midnight Louie, I too draw upon my own history. For many years, for instance, I contributed satirical skits to the Gridiron shows in my former state.

When I first wrote for the local Gridiron, I was fresh out of college and a lowly merchandiser at the daily newspaper. I accepted a company-wide invitation to submit Gridiron skits, not realizing that non-reporters (and women) weren't expected to respond. My innocent temerity in crashing what amounted to a closed shop in those dear, dead days beyond recall so astounded the Gridiron committee that I was invited to attend the post-show dinner for all contributors, even though they hadn't used my skit. They wanted to look me over.

I was the only woman present, aside from a spouse or two, and happened to sit next to my newspaper's managing editor. When I told him I wanted to become a reporter, he suggested I take the "reporter's test" in Personnel.

I duly did, finding it to consist solely of hard science sections and the rules of every sport known to man, including such everyday amusements as lacrosse. Even the "arts" section focused on what I considered masculine bailiwicks: architecture and music, to the exclusion of literature and the visual arts. Naturally, I did not get a dazzling score. However, I had gone off the chart on the "persuasion" rating. Within months, thanks to the editor's support, I was a full-fledged reporter despite lacking a journalism degree.

I still was ineligible to attend a Gridiron show. Women simply weren't allowed in then. Women were not allowed into many places and events in the ancient sixties (even women politicians who were rudely satirized in Gridiron skits weren't allowed to attend). Since I had written satirical skits throughout high school and college, I wasn't about to stop simply because I wasn't allowed to *see* the shows I was writing for. So I continued to lampoon local and national events, and continued to get my Gridiron skits returned with the editorial injunction: "dirtier."

Just what kind of show were they running here? Within two years, I became the first woman to officially attend a Gridiron show along with hundreds of male political, business and media leaders, and I found out.

Women were admitted at last because ticket sales were slumping and the shows were costly. When the bottom line sags, iron-clad exclusions tend to snap like rotten rubber bands.

A sign that I had successfully integrated myself into the Gridiron show I had never seen came when a neighboring executive in the audience, quite drunk, leaned toward me during one skit and suggested that "It's a shame a nice young lady like you has to listen to this."

"Listen to it?" I replied with some amazement. "I *wrote* it!" In another two years I became the first woman show chairman of my local Gridiron. That show achieved several firsts—participation by 40 people instead of the same eight insiders, the first multimedia satirical slide show, and the first mobile set piece (a baby-blue outhouse on wheels).

It, like Midnight Louise, did not impress the old hands.

At the post-Gridiron party, a fellow writer lurched up to tell my husband and myself that "the really classic Gridiron show" was one he had chaired, which he wrote all by himself in two weeks flat. The Gridiron died, appropriately, when this paragon of modesty again became show chairman a couple of years later. Any communal project twisted to oblige the egos of a self-serving few does not survive.

I no longer write topical satire. I don't need to since I became a fiction writer, which allows me to make up (almost) everything. Fiction really *is* stranger than Truth.

Trust me.